Ellie Darkins spent her formative years devouring romance novels and, after completing her English degree, decided to make a living from her love of books. As a writer and editor, she finds her work now entails dreaming up romantic proposals, hot dates with alpha males and trips to the past with dashing heroes. When she's not working she can usually be found running around after her toddler, volunteering at her local library, or escaping all of the above with a good book and a vanilla latte.

Melissa Senate has written many novels for Mills & Boon and other publishers, including her debut, *See Jane Date*, which was made into a TV movie. She also wrote seven books for Mills & Boon Special Edition under the pen name Meg Maxwell. Her novels have been published in over twenty-five countries. Melissa lives on the coast of Maine with her teenage son; their rescue shepherd mix, Flash; and a lap cat named Cleo. For more information, please visit her website, melissasenate.com

D0988495

Also by Ellie Darkins

Frozen Heart, Melting Kiss
Bound by a Baby Bump
Newborn on Her Doorstep
Holiday with the Mystery Italian
Falling for the Rebel Princess
Conveniently Engaged to the Boss
Surprise Baby for the Heir
Falling Again for Her Island Fling
Reunited by the Tycoon's Twins

Also by Melissa Senate

For the Twins' Sake
Wyoming Special Delivery
A Family for a Week
The Baby Switch!
Detective Barelli's Legendary Triplets
Wyoming Christmas Surprise
To Keep Her Baby
A Promise for the Twins
A Wyoming Christmas to Remember
The Maverick's Baby-in-Waiting

Discover more at millsandboon.co.uk

SNOWBOUND AT THE MANOR

ELLIE DARKINS

THE LONG-AWAITED CHRISTMAS WISH

MELISSA SENATE

MILLS & BOON

First Published in Great Britain 2020
by Mills & Boon, an imprint of HarperCollinsPublishers,
1 London Bridge Street, London, SE1 9GF

Snowbound at the Manor © 2020 Ellie Darkins
The Long-Awaited Christmas Wish © 2020 Melissa Senate

ISBN: 978-0-263-27904-7

1120

MIX
Paper from
responsible sources
FSC® C007454

FSC
www.fsc.org

This book is produced from independently certified FSC™
paper to ensure responsible forest management.

For more information visit: www.harpercollins.co.uk/green

Printed and bound in Spain
by CPI, Barcelona

SNOWBOUND AT THE MANOR

ELLIE DARKINS

For all the people working tirelessly
to keep us safe and healthy.

CHAPTER ONE

Jess pulled up in front of the grand old manor house and shut off the engine of her rental four-by-four, suddenly wondering whether she had just made an enormous mistake. But what choice had she had? The hotel she'd booked for the conference near by would be occupied by someone else now that the research symposium was over, and she was meant to be meeting her best friend, Lara, here. If she managed to fly in from skiing in the Alps as planned, that was. She didn't have many options for finding somewhere to stay in York three days before Christmas. And driving home wasn't an option: the news was full of stories about the gridlock in the south of the country, and the impassability of even the motorways.

At least she'd had enough foresight to reserve a car well suited to Yorkshire in the winter, and so she'd driven it to their destination, deep in the moors, and now could only hope that her best friend's plane was going to be able to land, and that she'd get here before the blizzard that had suddenly taken meteorologists by surprise reached the north of the country.

She checked her phone to see if she had a message from Lara, but there was nothing. No signal. She was going to have to log on to the Wi-Fi in the house and check her messages to find out whether her friend had managed to get on a plane before the flights were all cancelled. Otherwise this was going to be a lonely weekend. And if the travel reports were to be believed, a lonely Christmas as well. Her parents' town in the south of England was already a couple of feet deep in snow, and the news was full of warnings not to try to travel.

A pre-Christmas getaway in a country manor, courtesy of her BFF's social media queen career, had seemed like the perfect way to prepare herself for the trauma of a family Christmas. And if she had fantasised about a series of events—adverse weather conditions, perhaps, a freak blizzard—making it impossible for her to return to the stultifying atmosphere at her parents' house, it had been just that—fantasy.

She hadn't really believed when she'd booked her mid-December conference and her weekend with Lara that she would end up missing Christmas with her parents for the first time.

Any time she'd contemplated not going home before, she'd imagined the heartbreak on her mum's face when she'd have to tell her, and it had been enough to kill the fantasy. At least this way she could tell her mum that there had been nothing that she could do about it. And she would go home as soon as the roads were clear.

She wasn't a monster. She was just...relieved.

The annual torture of a 'family' Christmas had been cursed ever since her sister died when Jess had been fourteen, and her sister only eleven. And then her parents' marriage had died along with her. Not that they were willing to declare it dead. The prospect of Christmas overshadowed everything, from the moment she pulled on her first black tights of the autumn, until she escaped back to her own home the day after Boxing Day. New Year had always been the beacon at the end of the holiday season, the light at the end of the tunnel that had got her through the trying week before. And Lara had always been her partner in crime, always known the most exclusive parties or hot new restaurants. Something to break her out of the sadness imposed by her parents.

She cracked open the car door and shivered. Good thing that she was kitted out for a Yorkshire winter. Her conference packing had included full thermals underneath and a long down coat on top, and she regretted nothing about her decisions. She grabbed the coat now and searched on her phone for the access instructions she'd screenshot back when she'd had phone signal.

Someone should be at the house to welcome you. However, if there's no one available to greet you, use the key safe...

Blah-blah-blah...

Well, there were no other cars or tyre tracks in the snow, so unless someone had walked here through the woods she was all alone. She shifted the leather holdall from the passenger seat of the four-by-four and ventured out of the safe warmth of the car.

The door to the house was grand and imposing, a huge arch of dark wood towering above her head. The key safe was tucked discreetly into a corner of the church-like porch, and she keyed in the code with rapidly numbing fingers.

The door opened into the hallway of all her Hogwarts dreams—dark wood panelling and exposed stone everywhere she looked. A staircase eight feet wide and gloriously uneven rose along one wall, leading to a gallery that traversed the other two sides of the hall. Decked out for Christmas, the house shone. Fairy lights wove through boughs of greenery draped along balustrades and bannisters, LED candles covered the huge sideboard. A fire was laid in an inglenook fireplace so large she could comfortably sleep in it, and at the centre a tree that must have topped twenty feet, rising through two storeys of ancient house to the rafters above. Lara had seriously undersold this place. But then, with her life of luxury goods arriving unsolicited on her doorstep in the hope of a mention on her social media channels, perhaps Lara had grown accustomed to this sort of grandeur.

Good job she was here to keep her friend down to earth, Jess reflected. She hunted down the welcome pack from the owner of the house and found a folder on a sideboard with the all-important Wi-Fi code.

She tapped it into her phone and synced her messaging app, but there was nothing from Lara yet. There was still a chance she could get here tomorrow, she supposed, though as she checked her weather app she felt a sinking sensation. The roads were bad. And getting worse by the hour. In all the excitement of missing her nightmare family Christmas, she hadn't really considered that if Lara didn't get here she would be in this huge old house—looking a little spookier, now that she thought of it—completely alone, in the middle of the Yorkshire moors.

She traipsed through to the kitchen and cracked the

door of the industrial walk-in fridge. A full Christmas dinner was ready for the oven—a turkey the size of a light aircraft, with all the trimmings. The owners of the house clearly had no interest in skimping on Lara's stay. Either they had more money than they knew what to do with, or they were blowing the last of their marketing budget on the hopes of a business-changing endorsement from Lara.

Who wasn't here yet.

Given the fact that they were paying to let someone stay here over Christmas, rather than charging through the nose for it, she was going to go ahead and assume it was the latter option. Which meant if Lara didn't make it, their big gamble was a bust. She felt a twinge of sadness if that meant someone losing their livelihood.

She knew what it was like to have only a tenuous hold on your income. It wasn't as if she hadn't known going in that academia was a notoriously insecure profession. But her research into the cancer that had taken her sister from her was important enough to make it worth it.

She and every other academic in their twenties and thirties were scrambling to secure a handful of permanent, secure research positions. And then out of the blue, at the York conference, she'd landed a job offer. But one that would mean uprooting her life, and moving hundreds of miles away from her parents—which would devastate them. They had already lost one daughter, and they liked to keep her close.

But, of course, she could be massively overthinking this and the house and the decadent contents of its fridge might be owned by some faceless venture capitalist who didn't give a damn about anything other than it turning a reasonable profit.

Eventually, as she explored the house, peeking round doorways and opening cupboards, a message from Lara pinged.

Sorry, battery died. Still at airport in Geneva. They're telling us no flights landing in UK until Boxing Day. Don't hate me? Merry Xmas?!

So, it was official. She was stranded, alone, for Christmas, in a house that had probably accumulated centuries' worth of ghosts. She looked around the place and suddenly the flickering faux candlelight, with it shadows and dark corners, was more sinister than charming.

A glance at the window confirmed that it had been snowing heavily in the time that she'd been exploring, and the light was fading fast. Even if she had been having second thoughts, and her parents' awkwardly silent Christmas had started to seem more appealing, it was too late to change her mind. She had no doubt that the roads that had seemed a little dicey a couple of hours ago would be completely impassable by now.

The overhead lights in the kitchen flickered, and she narrowed her eyes. If those ghosts were even thinking of coming out to play, she was going to have to…sit here and let them? Oh, she was an idiot, she told herself. She had walked straight into horror movie territory—willingly. And all for the sake of pretty content for Lara's social media feeds. She was every terrible millennial cliché.

A deafening peal of bells sounded at the same time

as the lights cut, and she was left in darkness, the only light from the flickering candles on the sideboard. Before she had a chance to decide just how terrified she was, the bells pealed again, and she realised the sound was coming from the direction of the front door.

She turned the huge iron handle reluctantly, knowing that this was the point in the movie at which she would be yelling at the heroine not to be so stupid. As the hulking great door cracked open, a gust of snow and ice rushed at her, pricking goose bumps all over her skin. Just as she had decided that this was a terrible idea, and she should bolt the door and find the nearest duvet to hide under, a heavy weight crashed against her and took the matter out of her hands. She staggered backwards as a tall, stubbled man with reddish-brown curls sprawled on the floor at her feet and started melting snow all over the mat.

Jess stepped away from him in alarm, but really, sprawled out on the floor he didn't look all that frightening. He looked pretty vulnerable, actually. And cold. Really, really cold. He was shivering violently, huge, racking shakes coursing through his body. His jeans were soaked through above his boots, and his face was pale above the beard.

'Need…to…warm…up,' he said through chattering teeth. It was snowing hard, the temperature well below freezing. Leaving him on the doorstep would be effectively leaving him to die. She'd no choice but to let him in, but she would keep the fire irons handy, just in case. Except, he didn't seem to be moving. At least, not very effectively.

'You need a hand there?'

She took the grunt and subsequent lack of movement

as a *Yes, please, I'd be ever so grateful*, slipped a hand under each armpit and heaved.

Between them, they somehow got him far enough inside that she could slam the door shut and forestall the snowdrift accumulating on the doormat. He lay on the ground, still racked by those shivers, but not otherwise moving, and she realised she was going to have to do something more proactive than just watch him die from hypothermia in front of her.

She gave him the look-over from head to toe again and realised that the wet clothes would have to go first. And the wettest part of him was his jeans. She grabbed a couple of candles from the sideboard and ran quickly to the kitchen to stick the kettle on the mercifully hot plate of the Aga. Then stopped again on her way back to light the fire in the great hall and collect the fur throws from the backs of the chairs. She had no idea if it would make a difference in a room this size, but she also had no idea whether the heating would be working with the power outage, and it would surely be better than doing nothing. When she got back to him, he was reaching for his boots with little success. She grabbed the first and pulled, nearly falling on her butt when it slid from his foot without the satisfying pop that she'd been expecting. The second went just as quickly, which left the prospect of wrestling this man—at least a foot taller and quite possibly a hundred per cent heavier than her—out of wet jeans. There was no place in this situation for either of them to fully maintain their dignity, but she didn't fancy sharing this old house with a corpse, so what choice did she have?

She closed her eyes and reached under his jacket for the button for his fly. He batted her hands away immediately, then tried to do the job himself with clumsy fingers.

'I'm sorry, but we need to get your wet clothes off you and warm you up. I'm not exactly thrilled about this either.' She pinned his arm under one knee as she tried again—eyes open this time. The button slid reluctantly through the hole and she breathed a sigh of relief as the zip slid all the way down without catching on anything. It was only when she had the jeans undone that she realised she had no idea how she was going to achieve this next part of the operation. She reached for the fabric on either side of his hips and tugged, but the trousers went nowhere, weighed down by the considerable bulk of his body.

'A little help here?' she suggested, shoving him none too gently in the side. He lifted his hips, just enough for her to be able to pull the wet denim down to his ankles and then off completely.

CHAPTER TWO

Warm.

That was all he needed. To feel warm again. And to sleep. He was so tired. Stupid heading out into the snow rather than coming straight here. Stupid. Should have known better. Did know better.

He just needed warmth. And sleep.

The woman who'd opened the door was tucking blankets around him and muttering something about finding a phone. He tried to speak. To tell her he just needed to sleep. But the sounds that emerged didn't resemble words. Lara. Was that her name? She was gone anyway. His legs were starting to feel like they belonged to him again. If he cracked an eyelid he could see his jeans in a puddle of snow melt so he closed his eyes. Tried not to think, to remember how they got there.

The fire was burning in the grate, but it was too far to feel the lick of the heat from its flames. He tried to sit, but found his body simply wouldn't obey. Closing his eyes again, he was blissfully heavy, sinking into the floor. He wanted so badly to give in to it. To sleep for days. But the warmth of the room was starting to clear the ice from his brain, and he remembered that sleep was bad in these situations. He tried to snap himself back to consciousness but settled on woozy.

The woman was talking in the other room but he could only hear one side of the conversation and guessed that she had called 999. No chance. The roads would be blocked for hours. No way a chopper could land. Didn't need an ambulance anyway, just needed to be closer to the fire.

She walked back into the great hall and stood looking at him. He tried to rouse the energy to sit up and tell her he was fine, but his body still didn't seem to be cooperating. He just needed to move. Even with the heavy damask curtains drawn, it was draughty by the door. But it was a good twenty feet to the hearth; he'd never make it.

She approached cautiously, like she would the grizzly bear he was sure that he resembled after his hour in the woods.

'Hey,' she said, giving him a shake, which made him wonder how good a job he'd done of waking himself up just now. 'I just spoke to 999 and they said we're completely inaccessible.'

'Don't need an ambulance.' The effort of speaking sapped him of what little energy he'd been summoning, and the urge to sleep was becoming harder to resist.

'Well, frankly, I disagree,' she said. The corner of his lips raised involuntarily. 'But that's a bit of a moot point because they're not sending one. But she said to get you as warm as I can. We need to get you closer to the fire, and you need to stick these in your armpits, apparently'—she brandished a couple of tea towels folded into heat packs.

He started to struggle against the blankets and she

helped to free him; he tried not to notice when her hands brushed against his bare skin, but against the ice of his limbs they felt like fire. When he stumbled, trying to stand, she wedged herself under his arm to stop him falling, and they shuffled towards the fire. Eventually, he collapsed against a large sofa, pulling the blankets around himself.

She poked at the fire for a minute while he struggled with the blankets, but then took pity on him and pulled them up to his chin. She even found a woolly hat in the pocket of her coat and pulled that on him too. Even if he'd had the energy to put up a fight, he would have stood no chance with his arms pinned by his sides.

She dropped into the chair opposite, still not taking her eyes off him. *She thinks I'm a murderer*, he considered. And no wonder, he thought, the reality of their situation starting to hit him.

Shouldn't someone else be here? Wasn't she meant to be bringing someone with her? His brain still felt hazy on the details. But it didn't seem as if there was anyone else in the house.

'What's your name?' she asked.

'Rufus,' he said, trying to control the shivering to bite out that one word. It would feel so good now to just close his eyes and drift off. How much harm would it do, now that he was indoors and warming up?

'Rufus,' she said, and he realised he liked the sound of his name on her lips. That woke him up a bit. 'Any particular reason you were freezing to death on my doorstep?'

'My doorstep,' he said, groaning at the thought that she was keeping him talking. Keeping him awake.

Bloody people on the end of the bloody phone didn't realise he was fine now. Just tired. Needed to sleep.

'Pardon me?'

He opened an eye at the surprise in her voice. She didn't know this was his house?

'My house. My door, my doorstep.' He got the feeling he was really doing a terrible job of explaining, but the cold was like cotton wool in his brain, making it impossible to think or speak clearly. If she'd just let him sleep, he was sure he would feel better.

'You're the owner of the house? Oh, good. I'm glad in a crisis we've established that it is, in fact, your doorstep. You're right—the "freezing to death" part barely needs acknowledging at all.' She looked at him for a moment, narrowing her eyes. Maybe she was wishing she'd left him out in the snow after all.

'Not planning on dying,' he tried to clarify.

She shrugged. 'And I wasn't planning on dragging a stranger into the house by his armpits and taking his trousers off.' He groaned. He didn't need reminding of that. 'What a shame that I'm the one who had to change her plans.'

He frowned again, and despite her obvious frustration he saw another hint of a smile playing around the corner of her mouth, turning up a bottom lip that was just a little fuller than the top. Her mouth bracketed by smile lines.

'Shouldn't have had to do that,' he said, hoping he sounded sincere through the shivers. 'Sorry.'

'Well, I figured a corpse on my doorstep—'

'My doorstep'

'—wouldn't be very festive. There's no way I would

be out in that weather without my thermals and I felt sorry for you.'

That thought caught in his brain, clearing out some of the fog. He looked at her properly, his eyelids finally cooperating, so that his gaze could sweep her up and then down.

'You're wearing thermals?' he asked.

'I'm in Yorkshire in the middle of a blizzard.' Her hands had come to rest on her hips, and he wondered if she was angry. Mainly she seemed faintly amused by him and his frozen brain functions. 'What else would I be wearing?'

'I'm here too,' he couldn't help but point out. 'Not wearing thermals.'

She held her hand up to stop him—held his gaze too, and he couldn't look away. Seemed like moving nearer the fire must be doing the trick, because gradually the frost had been leaching from his limbs, and, with that look that had just passed between them, he was starting to feel positively warm.

'You're not even wearing trousers,' she pointed out, scuppering his argument. 'And you nearly died, which is what we're discussing here, so I get to win that one, I think.'

'Let you have it,' he said, leaning back and letting his eyes close, starting to loosen the blankets and try to locate his arms. She was going to be desperate to get rid of him, he considered. Whatever plans she'd had for the house this weekend, he was sure that he didn't feature in them. But with the snow still coming down outside, and no thaw predicted for days, she couldn't see how she was going to manage that. He wondered if she'd realised yet that they were stuck with one another until the storm had passed.

'So are you going to tell me what happened?' she asked, addressing the elephant in the room.

'Was in the woods. Got cold,' Rufus said, attempting to shrug but hampered by the many layers of blankets. 'The snow.'

'Wow, you really are so forthcoming. If it's some sort of state secret...'

'I was coming to unlock the house,' he told her, his tongue and his brain moving more easily now that the warmth of the fire was reaching deep into his chest, spreading through his body and thawing his brain. 'Hit a deer. It ran off and I tried to find it—didn't want it dying slowly. Snow came in fast. By the time I realised I was in trouble, I was closer to the house than the car.'

She looked at him for a moment, and he wondered whether she was revising her opinion of the man who had forced his way into her house. His house.

'What were you going to do with the deer?' she asked, her voice full of trepidation.

Or maybe she was thinking that he'd tracked an injured deer into the woods to get a kick out of putting it out of its misery. He dreaded to think what must be showing on his face to have given her that impression.

'You the RSPCA?'

'I'm the woman who found a random bloke on her doorstep and haven't called the police. Yet. What were you going to do with the deer?'

'My doorstep. I was going to ring the vet. Can't say I had much more of a plan than that. What were you going to do with me?'

The corner of her lip lifted in a smile again. He felt

another shot of warmth at that, the thought that he could make her smile, even when he was barely making sense. Her brown eyes shone beneath a heavy dark fringe.

She looked deliberately nonchalant. 'Put you out of your misery with a handy rock and then use you to stock the freezer.'

He closed his eyes with just the barest hint of a smile on his lips. 'Seems fair.'

CHAPTER THREE

GOD, BUT THAT SMILE. Not that she could even really call it that. It was hardly dimples and sunshine. It was the deepening of the lines that bracketed his mouth from the corner of his nose into that dense beard on his chin. It was an extra crow's foot by his eye, in that split second before the lid fell shut. It was…it was a hint of something soft hiding somewhere inside this big bloke. She was intrigued.

She prodded him gently in the ribs. 'I'm meant to keep you awake.'

'I am awake,' he protested, unconvincingly.

'The eyes-open kind. You need to warm up.'

He looked over at the fire.

'I'm warm,' he said.

She shook her head. 'You're sleepy at five in the afternoon. You're staying awake until I say you can sleep.'

'You always so bossy?' he asked, and she prickled.

'I'm not bossy. I should have left you out in the snow. Now, are you waking up or am I going to have to take drastic measures?' This time, both eyes opened, just wide enough to assess her, like an unfriendly cat deciding whether she was worthy of its attention.

'Be. More. Specific.'

His tone stopped her short, and all of a sudden the central heating must have kicked in, or the fire suddenly heated up—did they do that? Because her cheeks were aflame and she absolutely refused to believe it had anything to do with old grizzly here, and the way that his whole body seemed to hum with tension as he ground out those three little words through a clenched jaw.

'I was thinking *EastEnders*,' she said, scrambling to say anything other than what she was thinking. 'Really loud. All those lovely cockney accents I'm sure you love.' He forced both eyes properly open. 'Or I could sing. I mean, I'm terrible, but I can probably manage some Christmas carols. Make it all festive in here.'

He dragged himself a little more upright, looking decidedly more scary than he had a moment ago.

'No carols. No soaps. Nothing bloody festive. I beg you.'

'Welcome back, Ebenezer,' she said with a smile. This was too, too easy. But begging? There was something about the idea of this man begging her that she definitely liked. Deep down in her stomach where warmth was developing pretty rapidly into a heat she couldn't ignore.

'If this is your house,' she asked, trying to change the subject, 'and you look like a scared kid at their first nativity at the mention of Christmas, how did it get so pretty?'

Another grunt, another shrug. 'It's what you people want. For your feeds.' Oh, so he *did* think she was Lara. She'd wondered. But she liked having this little piece of knowledge that he didn't, and she squirrelled away her secret until it wasn't useful to her any more.

'And you like to give people what they want?' she

asked, and then shook her head at herself. Why did everything she said suddenly sound so *dirty* all of a sudden? 'I mean, you're clearly Mr Customer Service here... And what do you mean by *people like me*?'

He gave a disdainful roll of his eyes. '*Influencers*. Southerners. City types. You want boughs of holly and pretty candles. Picture-perfect. Substance optional.'

'Right...' she replied, taking in the look of disdain and deciding not to correct his mistake, not when it was so much fun to bait him instead.

'And of course you let these city-type southern influencers stay in your home out of the goodness of your heart. Because you're such a giver.'

A cloud crossed his face and, although pleased that her cutting remark had hit its mark, she couldn't ignore the accompanying twinge of regret that she was responsible for it.

'Need the exposure,' he said simply. 'Estate's in trouble and I'm trying to launch a business. Can't do it without social media.'

She nodded, taking in his dour expression, and decided not to prod further.

'I don't know if you care, but you totally nailed it,' she said, keeping her voice casual. 'It's beautiful in here.'

He looked around, his gaze resting on the tree in the window, the holly on the mantel and wrapped around the balcony of the gallery. The candles burning on the hearth and the fire blazing in the grate.

'Can't take credit really. Just copied what my mam used to do.'

'Used to...' Jess panicked and it must have shown in her eyes.

'It's okay. She's not dead,' he said with a bark that might have been a laugh. 'I just meant when we used to live here. Done it at the new place this year. Proper Mrs Claus.'

'Something tells me you're not exactly a grateful recipient of all her Christmas cheer.'

'What gave me away?' he asked with a long blink, his eyes sliding shut.

She aimed her foot at the centre of his ribcage and shoved.

'Eyes open. Sleep's for the weak, remember.'

He groaned. 'Was working till two this morning. Just need a quick—'

'No.' Though maybe—*maybe*—his admission of why he was so tired had her looking at him in just a slightly different light.

'How long do I have to stay awake?' he asked, pulling himself a little more upright against the sofa.

'Yeah,' she said, realising that no one had actually given her the answer to that one, 'the operator wasn't exactly clear.'

'You didn't ask?' Rufus shot her a look of pure condescension that in other circumstances she would have given him hell for. But, given his currently defrosting state, she was going to cut him a little slack. A very little.

'I was quite busy not letting you die. Maybe I shouldn't have been so diligent. I guess you need to stay awake until you don't feel too sleepy any more.'

He groaned again. 'Oh, good. Sane *and* rational.'

'Well, it's the best I've got,' she told him, finally losing her temper. 'So if you want to call 999 and ask them, feel free. But I'm not tying up their phone lines because you want a nap.'

'We should sort out the lights,' he said after they had sat in silence for a few long minutes.

'Well, you can't blame me for the electricity being out. Pretty sure that's your department. But leave it for now. At least until you've had a chance to warm up properly. It might not even be something that can be fixed at this end. I'm guessing the snow is causing some problems out there.'

She poked at the fire for a minute while he struggled with the blankets, but then took pity on him and pulled them up to his chin. Despite the murderous look on his face, his arms were pinned by the blankets, so there wasn't much he could do about it.

She dropped onto the sofa, still not taking her eyes off him.

'What are you going to do?' he asked. 'Shouldn't you be taking pictures of something?'

Oh, he definitely thought she was Lara. And shallow and thoughtless as well, it seemed. Well, if he wanted to think the worst of her, and of Lara, then who was she to disappoint him? She whipped out her phone without thinking and snapped a shot of him, wrapped up like a cocoon, woolly hat and all.

'My followers really love authentic content. It's normally me showing my vulnerable side, but it's great that you want to get in on the act.'

'Post that and I'm turfing you out in the snow.'

'Ha, I'd like to see you try. You could barely stand up half an hour ago. I reckon I could still take you.'

His eyes narrowed and he suddenly looked serious, as if realising for the first time that the two of them seemed to be very much stranded out here, and it would be perfectly reasonable for her to be freaking out about being trapped with a strange man.

'You know I was joking, right? You're completely safe. I give you my word.'

She examined his face as he stopped speaking. The lines around his eyes that showed genuine concern, the sudden tension she could see in his body, even through the layers of blankets and furs. He was genuinely concerned for her, and she melted, just a fraction, even against her better judgement.

'That's a pretty crappy old phone.'

She glanced down at the screen, and the grainy shot that she had managed of him wrapped in front of the fire. It had coped terribly with the low light, and the battery was looking dangerously low even though she'd plugged it in in the car on the way over here. And now of course the power was out and she had no way of charging it.

But more to the point, if she was going to reveal to Rufus that she wasn't in fact her social media starlet friend, there was going to be no better time to do it than now. His mistake had been genuine, and understandable. And her failure to correct him so far equally understandable, given that she had had a life-threatening emergency to attend to. But if she kept it up any longer she would be moving from smudging the truth to outright lying.

If she hadn't already guessed that his business was probably riding pretty heavily on the investment that he'd made in hiring Lara, she might have been a little less forgiving of his terrible manners, but, all things considered, she knew that she had to fess up.

'Ha, so, about that…' she started, and saw a new line form between Rufus's eyebrows as he watched her. She fidgeted with her hair, tucking some longer strands behind her ear then smoothing her fringe forwards.

'Did Lara happen to mention that she was bringing a friend with her this weekend?'

The line turned into a full-on frown, and she pulled one of the sofa cushions onto her lap, crossing her legs and letting the couch cocoon her a little deeper.

'Meaning you're not Lara?'

She gave a half-smile and shrugged.

'I assumed the friend was male. Not…'

'Me?'

'Right. Of course, it was stupid of me to assume.'

'I'm not her girlfriend,' she said quickly, and then wondered why she had been so keen to clarify that particular point. 'We're friends, and we haven't hung out in a while, and we wanted…' She trailed off, not quite sure why she was explaining all this to Rufus. 'Only, I know how much Lara charges for this sort of thing, and now she's not here, and you're stuck with me and my crappy phone. And I'm sorry about that.'

It hit him in waves, she saw. She wasn't here. Lara wasn't coming. His business wasn't going to get the boost it so urgently needed. And then… She didn't know him or his business well enough to know what the end point of that chain reaction was, but, judging from his expression, it wasn't anywhere good. She shuffled to the end of the couch and let her feet drop, untucking one of the blankets that he was struggling against until his arms were free.

'You okay?'

'Yeah,' he barked, and then looked apologetic. 'I'm fine. I'll be fine. I just need to think.'

'I'll message Lara,' Jess said, trying to think the whole thing through. 'I'm sure that there must be something we can do. Even with this piece of junk.'

'I have a decent camera on my phone,' Rufus said. 'It's not bad. I use it for the marketing shots for the website.'

'Then I'm sure we can manage something. But Lara's the expert. She's been stuck in an airport for getting on for twenty-four hours and I can guarantee she's spent every single one of them coming up with a plan. All we need is some power so we can get the Wi-Fi router working.'

'I told you I should be looking at that.'

'And there is plenty of time. It's not like we have a whole lot of options other than hanging out here. You've stopped shivering,' she commented, noticing that his face was no longer deathly pale, his nose and cheeks even looking a little pink.

'The fire's good,' he said, and she wondered whether she was ever going to get anything other than monosyllables from him. She could see that he was distracted by her revelation that she wasn't Lara, and left him to his thoughts, not wanting to interrupt some pretty fierce-looking arguments he seemed to be having with himself.

'We should light more of the fires,' he said eventually. 'The heating is mainly electric storage radiators. They'll be warm from heating up overnight, but if the power doesn't come back then tomorrow we'll be freezing. Even if the power comes back, it's hard to keep it warm with the central heating alone. You'll want a fire in the bedroom tonight.'

At that, she realised she hadn't thought about sleeping arrangements. Surely in a house this size she didn't have to worry that there wasn't room for them both. But if he had been expecting Lara and her guest to share...

'I have a sofa bed in my study,' he told her, obviously guessing the direction of her thoughts. 'I won't intrude on your use of the rest of the house. I know you're not Lara, but we had an agreement and you shouldn't worry that I won't honour it.'

Her forehead creased. Was that what he thought of her, that she was worried that she wouldn't get the sole use of this incredible place? If it hadn't been for Lara, she would never stay anywhere other than the budget hotels she put on the university's expenses for conferences. It would hardly be a hardship if he slept in one of the guest bedrooms.

'Thanks,' she said. 'But if we're both staying here, you shouldn't feel as if you have to keep to your study. It's a huge house. There's plenty of room for us both.'

He stood, emerging from the blankets like a giant moth from a chrysalis. 'It's fine. We'll work out how to deal with each other as we go along, I s'pose.'

Deal with each other. Charming.

She followed him up the staircase as he wrapped the blankets tight around his shoulders again, the heat of the fire dying away with every step.

He stopped when he reached a huge oak door halfway along the gallery, and paused, his hand reaching for the handle.

'I should probably explain...' he started, before he opened the door. 'When Lara said that she was bringing someone, I'd assumed it was a partner, and…well. Never mind. You'll see for yourself.'

He pushed open the door and Jess gasped.

More candles. More fairy lights. This time wound around the four-poster bed, right the way up to the panelled ceiling. Enormous bunches of flowers graced each bedside table and rose petals had been scattered generously across the top of the quilt. The result was overwhelmingly romantic and rendered her quite speechless.

Which was awkward, given that Rufus's social skills didn't seem to be quite up to this level of misunderstanding either.

'Did your mum do this too?' Jess asked, and then felt blood rushing to her cheeks. She looked at a bedroom decorated like this, and her reaction was to talk about his *mother*? There was something seriously wrong with her.

Like the fact that she'd spent so much of the last ten years studying and working that she hadn't spent nearly enough of it dating. She wasn't even sure if Rufus was her type. If she even had a type. But from the pink in his cheeks, he'd found her comments as wildly embarrassing as she had.

'No, this was all me.'

She knew her cheeks were glowing red and hoped that the lack of overhead lighting was hiding it. But she turned towards the fire just in case to hide her face. Pulling the matches that she'd picked up downstairs out of her pocket, she crossed to the hearth. The newspaper knots in the bottom of the grate caught light quickly, and Jess watched as the flames licked up the kindling and started creeping up the logs balanced on top.

The overhead lights came back on with a flicker and

Jess was torn between relief that the atmosphere had just become that little bit *less* atmospheric, and worry that Rufus could now see just how red her face was.

'It would be a shame to waste all this,' Jess said, and then quickly stumbled over her words when she realised how that must sound. A quick glance at Rufus's face proved that he had taken that the really wrong way and she backtracked frantically. 'I mean, you've made it look beautiful, and if Lara were here she'd be photographing the heck out of it. Just…don't touch anything, okay? You said you had a camera? Now would be a good time to go and find it. Was it in your jeans? And—' she glanced down, felt her cheeks colour again '—maybe put on some trousers. Do you have anything you can wear until they dry?'

He looked down at his legs, seeming to remember only at that moment that she had stripped him half-naked, and then back up to meet her eyes. 'I'll find something.' He pulled the blankets a little tighter around himself. 'And I'll get the camera.'

'Good. I'm going to call Lara now the power's back on.'

Jess breathed a deep sigh of relief as he left the room. She pulled her phone from her pocket and called Lara, thinking that she really needed to get this phone plugged in before they lost power again. The snow outside was showing no sign of slowing down: she needed to plan ahead if they were going to be stuck here for the foreseeable future with the power in and out.

'Jess!' Lara shouted as she picked up the phone. 'Does this mean you don't hate me? Are you okay? You didn't message me back!'

Jess laughed. Let it never be said that Lara under-reacted to anything.

'I'm fine. And I don't hate you—I know you'd be here if you could be.'

'You know I would. Instead I'm in a crappy hotel without even a minibar to my name and I'm going to be stuck here until Boxing Day. Did you make it to Upton Manor? Are you okay there on your own?'

'Mmm,' Jess said, wondering where she should even start explaining what had happened since she'd arrived. 'About that. I'm not actually—speaking in the most literal sense—alone.'

'What's that supposed to mean?'

'It means…well, I guess you must have talked to Rufus, to set all this up. Right? The owner? Well, he kind of got stuck in the snow and showed up here dying of hypothermia, and now…well, we're both pretty much stranded here.'

'Right.' The shocked silence at Lara's end of the phone was so out of character that Jess felt compelled to rush and fill it.

'And he's not wearing any trousers.'

Of course, that was the moment that Rufus chose to return. He had abandoned his coat and blankets wherever he had gone off to search for his camera, and had returned wearing jogging pants and a thick woolly jumper. More than one, in fact, by the looks of it.

'Actually, that data point appears to be incorrect,' she said into the phone, face in flames again. Was Lara going to speak again? 'Um…anyway, given that this whole arrangement was between you and Rufus, I guess you need to speak to one another to sort it out.'

She looked up at Rufus as she handed over the phone

and he simply raised one eyebrow at her before saying 'Hi, Lara' as if the woman currently standing in front of him in the achingly sensual bedroom hadn't just commented on his state of undress.

Aside from the occasional *hmm* and grunt, the conversation with Lara seemed to be entirely one-sided.

'I think we can manage that,' Rufus said at last, before handing the phone back to Jess. She looked at the screen to see that Jess had already hung up.

'Are you going to tell me what that was all about?' Jess asked.

'Lara said we need to take photos. She's refunding me her fee but said she'd be happy to share anything we can send her, and I really need this exposure. She suggested we make the most of you being here—apparently her followers like you making a cameo on her feed. It's not as good for the business as if she were here, of course, but it's better than doing nothing. Are you okay with that? The photos, I mean.'

When your best friend is an Instagram celebrity, you learned pretty early on not to mind too much having your photo taken. But surely the point here was to promote Upton Manor. Not her.

'I guess it's okay, if that's what Lara thinks will work. Are you happy? I guess you have a lot riding on Lara's promotion.'

Rufus rubbed a hand over his forehead. 'To be honest, I'm not sure. There's nothing we can do about the snow, so we just have to make the best of it.'

But he looked decidedly troubled at the thought. When he'd said earlier that the estate was in trouble, she guessed he'd really meant it.

'Got my phone,' he said, changing the subject. 'It was

in my jacket pocket all along. I can sync it to Lara's account so we can upload stuff to her cloud. Lara said to get plenty of the room before you unpack. Apparently you'll make a mess.'

'Oh, that is so…' *True, actually.* Though entirely unfair for Lara to tell a stranger that. She took a few shots of the bed on his phone, knowing that they wouldn't come out well, with the light in front of them, but sometimes Lara like to use some imperfect shots in her stories—all the better for appearing hashtag-authentic, she knew.

'I found trousers,' Rufus said behind her, so out of the blue that she found herself genuinely blinking in surprise.

'Um… I noticed,' she replied, not sure what the least inappropriate response was to that statement.

'You told Lara I hadn't, and I know this is awkward. I wanted you to know I found some. We left some stuff in storage up in the attic.'

'Well, great.' What, suddenly he was the chatty one and she was all monosyllabic?

It was just… It was hard to talk. Or think. Or breathe, now that he had drawn her attention to the trousers he had found. She wasn't sure if he was aware, but the soft jersey fabric was leaving absolutely nothing to the imagination. She could see…well. *Everything.* She turned away, knowing that rational thought wasn't going to return until she did. Except everywhere she looked, she saw sex and romance. This entire room had been designed to do that. She shut her eyes and took a couple of deep breaths. She needed to think of something that would make it impossible for her to be turned on at the fact that she was snowed in at a secluded romantic break with a stranger wearing trousers that perfectly outlined his…everything.

She squeezed her eyes tight shut.

'My mother!' she said suddenly, striking gold. 'I have to call my mother and tell her I'm not going to be home for Christmas. She'll be devastated.'

'Which is a good thing?'

'Congratulations, you correctly interpreted a human facial expression.'

Good, she had her snark back. She knew what she was doing with snark. And Rufus had turned slightly, angling his body away from hers into lighting that was far less distracting.

'You don't like to go home for Christmas,' he stated, and she had to give him credit. Though it was hardly a huge leap from what she'd already told him.

'It's complicated,' she said, the adrenaline leaving her body as she started to really think how upset her mum was going to be. How sad and quiet the next few days would be for her parents without her there for them to focus on. To remind them of why they were still in a relationship that had stopped making either of them happy a long time ago. She had tried to tell them, as gently as she could, over the years that she would rather they were happy apart than miserable together, but they seemed to be determined to hold themselves to their wedding vows long after anything resembling love had left the building.

'I should leave you to it,' he said, walking towards the door. 'Call me if you need anything.'

Would she call him after she had finished talking to her parents? From the troubled look on her face, he was betting that it was going to be a painful conversation, one that would have been made a million or so times better if she were stuck here with Lara, rather than a man who didn't know how to look after his own family, never mind a stranger. But the thought of her sitting up there—upset and alone—hit him in a way he hadn't been expecting.

If the weather reports were anything to go by, it would be days until they would be able to get out of there. Even his parents' house, just a few miles away, was beyond their reach. He'd proved that by walking through the woods like the idiot that he was and nearly getting himself killed. If he'd ever needed a reminder that he wasn't sufficiently responsible to take care of anyone other than himself, then that was pretty timely. Still, he hated the thought of Jess sitting alone upstairs if she was upset. Perhaps when she was finished talking with her mum he would just knock on the door and check she was okay.

It seemed like the least he could do, all things considered. And, speaking of mothers, if he was going to be leaving an empty place setting at his parents' dinner table on Christmas Day, he supposed he was going to have to let them know. His phone started ringing, and it seemed as if his mother was psychic, on top of everything else. He accepted the video call and forced a smile.

'Rufus, love, what are you wearing on your head?' It was only as the call connected that he realised he was still wearing Jess's hat, complete with adorable furry bobble.

'All right, Mam?' he said, pulling the offending item off his head.

'Are you at Upton? I rang earlier but you didn't answer and I was starting to get worried!'

'Yeah, I'm here. It's a long story but the car didn't make it. I hit a deer.'

'Oh, my—'

'I'm fine. I'm fine. Don't mither. But I had to walk the rest of the way.' He carefully edited out the getting lost, cold and nearly dying part. 'But I made it up to the house.'

'Have you got power up there?'

'On and off. But it's on just now.'

'That's good. But I can't believe you're going to be stuck there all…'

'Mam?' he asked as her voice trailed off.

'I was going to say *alone*, until your friend joined us.'

He glanced over his shoulder and saw Jess standing in the doorway, her mouth a little O of surprise. And his mam, on the screen, eyebrows practically disappearing into her hairline.

'Oh. Yeah. Mam, this is Jess, she's one of the guests who was booked into the house for the weekend.'

The smile on his mam's face was knowing. And irritating.

'You're lucky you didn't get stuck in the snow, love. And you came on your own, did you?'

On the screen he watched as Jess approached, and pretty much wished he could disappear. Or make his mam disappear. Of course she was going to make this thing with Jess even more awkward than it already was. She lived for this kind of thing.

'Oh, my friend Lara was meant to be here too but her flight was cancelled.'

'So the two of you are stuck there together. How… unfortunate.'

If it wasn't for the enormous grin on her face he might have been able to believe her.

'I've got to go. I'll call you later. Let's see what the weather does before we panic too much about Christmas.'

'Ah, no. You're stuck there until the New Year I'd have thought. I won't expect you until next year. Now, you two look after one another, won't you?'

His mam hung up and he pocketed his phone slowly, delaying the moment when he would have to turn and face Jess.

'That seemed to go well,' she said, and he had no choice but to turn to answer her. The fire he'd lit was sending flashes of colour into her hair, picking out hints of gold and chestnut in the deep brown. She was slight, even with the many layers she claimed to be wearing, and he had the suspicion that he could just tuck her under his arm, into his body, and surround her completely. Which he absolutely would not be doing. If the last year had taught him anything it was that he shouldn't be making himself responsible for other people, because he was in no way up to the job.

He had failed in the role so badly. He had ignored his responsibilities here for too long, off chasing his own career, a Michelin star, while his dad had been trying to keep the estate afloat—nearly killing himself in the process. And then when he finally came back—taken a look at the estate that he'd always assumed would be waiting for him when he was ready—he found that there was barely anything of it left. Most of the property and land had been sold to finance their debts, and there was only the manor and the cottage left.

He had had the chance to be a provider, a protector, and had failed at both. The fact that he was even here with Jess was complete proof of that.

'Yeah, Mam takes these things in her stride,' he said. In fact, if it hadn't been for her relentless optimism, he wasn't sure how they would have got through the last year. 'How did your call home go?'

'Not well.'

Her grimace said it all really, and he resisted the urge to wrap an arm around her shoulders.

'They'll miss you?'

'They'll miss... My sister died. Charlotte. Just before Christmas, when I was a teenager,' she said, and looked surprised at herself. 'It's a difficult time of year, and this makes it worse.'

'I'm so sorry, about your sister.'

'Thanks. It was a long time ago. But Christmas has never really got any easier.'

'I can imagine.'

He could, actually. More realistically than was comfortable. When they'd all sat vigil around his father's bedside last year, waiting to see if he would recover from his heart attack, from the massive surgery that had followed, he'd tried to picture a Christmas without his father there. Had tried to imagine how his family would work around the huge void that he would leave.

But his dad had pulled through against the odds, and the loss hadn't been him, but their home. When Rufus had taken the reins on the family finances while his dad was sick, he'd found debt after debt. The family was in financial crisis, and their biggest asset was Upton

Manor. Which was far too big and too grand to be a family home when that family was in debt up to their eyeballs. So he'd convinced his mam and dad to move to the one small cottage they still owned on the estate, and he'd put the big house to work as a luxury rental, a filming location, a corporate getaway. Anything he could think of to get some money coming in. And it still wasn't enough. The bookings had been steady, but he needed them to be spectacular. And he hadn't managed to fill the key Christmas booking slot, with all the extra revenue that should have brought. So he'd gambled his whole marketing budget on Lara—and had been scuppered by the snow. Now the only option he had to get the social media exposure he needed was to make the best of Lara's suggestion that he take some photos of Jess that he could use.

He looked at her more closely now, trying to draw on what little photographic knowledge he had. The light in here was pretty, if he could find the right setting on his phone to capture it. But the composition was all wrong.

'You mind?' he asked, picking up the camera from his desk and pointing it towards the wing-backed chair by the fire.

'Me?'

'Well, no one's going to want to look at me.'

She frowned, but sat in the chair, pulling the blanket he'd abandoned off the back of it and wrapping it around her shoulders.

He looked at her objectively, tried to imagine the image popping up on someone's social media feed. The picture still needed something. He plucked a leather-bound book from the shelves behind his desk and handed it to her. Nearly there.

'Wait there,' he told her, then disappeared down to the kitchen.

He pulled together some ingredients—cream, chocolate, sugar—and picked out an old Denby cup and saucer that he thought was similar to one he'd seen on Lara's Instagram feed.

Once he'd added whipped cream, chocolate shavings and an amaretto biscuit to the hot chocolate, he snapped a couple of shots of the drink and then carried it upstairs.

He stopped in the doorway, watching Jess for a moment. She turned a page of the book and settled deeper into the chair.

Then he must have given himself away because she looked up. And maybe she was flushed from the fire, but it looked quite a lot like she was blushing.

'Good read?' he asked. He'd pulled it from the shelf without really looking but wondered now what she had been sitting here reading while he was downstairs.

'That looks amazing,' she said, obviously spotting the hot chocolate. It wasn't the only thing that did, he thought, watching her for a moment longer than was comfortable.

'Here.' He handed her the drink, and as her face lit up he snapped a quick picture with his phone.

'Don't drink it yet,' he warned, concentrating on the settings menu. He took another couple of shots, playing with the different levels to try and make the most of the light from the candles, the fire and the wall sconces.

'Okay,' he said when he was happy. And then fired off a couple more as she took her first sip, her eyes closing sensuously as she cupped the drink in her hands. There was a smudge of cream on her top lip, and he couldn't stop looking at it, until her tongue flickered out and caught it.

He was staring. Any second now she was going to look up and catch him. And he couldn't drag his gaze away.

'What?' she asked, when she finally glanced up and saw him watching her.

'Nothing.' He shook his head. 'These should sync with Lara's account. Let me know if she messages you about them.'

'This hot chocolate is seriously good,' she said, after another long sip. 'Did you make one for yourself? You should. You still need to warm up.'

'I'm okay,' he said, realising that he was. The sleepy feeling had gone, and his limbs no longer felt heavy. Between the electric storage heating, the fires they had lit, and the heat packs Jess had shoved into his armpits, he was finally feeling warm. He owed her his life, he realised. And instead of thanking her, he had snapped and been generally unfriendly.

'I… Erm… Thank you,' he said, not sure how else to say it other than just coming out and saying it.

She startled, sloshing hot chocolate into her saucer. 'What for?'

'For dragging me in here and warming me up. Y'know…saving my life.'

'Oh, well. Having you die on me would have been really inconvenient.'

'It's a bit fuzzy, to be honest, but I have the feeling I wasn't an easy patient.'

She laughed aloud at that, and he felt it in his gut as the smile reached her eyes.

'You were an absolute pain in the butt. You were

one grunt away from being dragged back out onto the doorstep.'

'Like I said…thank you.'

'Well, I guess I should thank you too,' Jess said, 'given that I was only ever Lara's plus-one, and now she's not here and you're stuck with me. I'm not sure what I would have done if I'd been here on my own.'

'You've decided I'm not a serial killer, then?'

'I think you'd be too scared of what your mum would say.'

'That's fair, actually. She liked you.'

Jess frowned. 'She hardly spoke to me.'

He shrugged. 'She did. I could tell.'

'I'm sorry you're missing Christmas at home. Who else will be there?'

'Mam. Dad. My brother and sister. Probably an elderly neighbour or some waif or stray. They tend to find someone.'

'Sounds amazing,' Jess said, looking sad.

It sounded like something she'd only seen in sentimental Christmas movies and supermarket adverts since Charlotte had died. But, from the unguardedly sappy look that Rufus was wearing, she knew that his family Christmas must be all that and more.

'And you? Do you have other siblings?'

She shook her head. 'It was just me and Charlotte. Now it's just me. And Mum and Dad.'

'That sounds…peaceful.'

'It's quiet. Not peaceful.'

'I'm sorry. I didn't mean—'

'No, it's fine. There's just an atmosphere,' she said, wondering why she was spilling this to a virtual stranger. 'They're not very happy. But they pretend to be. At Christmas. For me. It's worse.' It was also the first time she had ever said that out loud. Lara knew, of course, that she was always miserable at Christmas, but she didn't think she'd ever spelt out exactly why— she had always just assumed that she was sad about Charlotte. And she was, of course, but there was more to it than that. And she had no idea why she was telling Rufus all this now, other than the fact that she was here, with him, at what had always been the hardest part of the year.

Maybe it was the fact that he was part of the reason she wouldn't be home this year. Maybe it was seeing his mum on the phone. So happy and relaxed that it had thrown her situation into such stark contrast.

'That sounds hard,' Rufus said, his face serious. 'A lot of pressure on you.'

'It is what it is.' She shrugged. 'Though it's fair to say being stuck here instead isn't exactly the worst result I could have hoped for.'

'Did you plan it like this?' He sounded more amused than shocked.

'Hand on heart, I absolutely did not plan it. I had to be in York for a conference. When Lara asked me if I wanted to come here afterwards I told her that I had to be home for Christmas. I was meant to be driving back down on Christmas Eve.'

'You couldn't have driven down before the snow hit?'

'Not without missing my presentation at the conference. And I'd worked too hard to do that. By the time the presentation was over, the roads in the south were chaos. Coming here and hoping that Lara would make it was the only option I had.'

'And now you're stuck here with me.'

'And now I'm stuck here with you,' she confirmed, trying to remind herself that that was a bad thing. But right now she was wrapped in a blanket, in a wing-backed chair before an open fire, sipping a hot chocolate that had to have been sent straight from the gods. And on top of all that there was this tall, bearded, actually quite decent-seeming guy stuck here with her. And all that added up to—well, a pretty okay weekend, if she wanted to think about it that way.

Not that she was going to get up to anything with Rufus. No—she had been sworn off men for a long time. Her mum and dad had given her every reason to devote herself to becoming an old spinster. Because if the alternative was marriage? No, thank you.

What made it worse was that they had been happy, once. She remembered a childhood home filled with noise and parties and, well, fun. And then Charlotte had got sick, and all the joy had been drained out of them. All of them. And instead of supporting one another, her parents had started to resent each other.

Jess had thought that they would break up when it first went bad. Had hoped for it, in fact, when it became apparent years later that they had long stopped making one another happy. She had even hinted to her mother that if she was staying in the marriage for Jess's sake, that she would understand if she didn't want to do that any more. But no. They had carried on, slowly making one another more and more miserable. So if that was what became of a good marriage under stress, Jess was going to opt out before it even began, thanks for asking. Because even when you thought that you were one of the lucky ones, it could all fall apart.

So she'd kept herself busy with her studies and her work, with the occasional fling to scratch an itch when she felt lonely.

Which was why this attraction to Rufus was so... inconvenient. Because her tried and trusted instinct of steering well clear whenever she worried that she was a little too interested wasn't going to work with them stuck here alone like this.

And now that he had thawed out and was behaving like a reasonably normal human being, she had to admit to herself that she was interested. Oh, he was good looking. But there was more to it than that. It was the way that he had spoken to his mum on the phone. The concern that he had showed her when she had explained about her sister, and her lonely family Christmases. It was the fact that he had blushed, when she'd reminded him that she had taken off his jeans. There was something about the sight of a man who could dominate her in every way—taller, heavier, more solid than she was—being unable to hide that sign of vulnerability that was making her feel a little hot and bothered.

Her phone pinged, saving her from whatever dodgy direction that thought had been heading in.

Photos look good! Can't believe I'm missing out

Jess checked Lara's Instagram and there she was, curled up in the armchair. Rufus had captured her in the moment before she'd sipped the hot chocolate, with food lust in her eyes and her lips pursed into a slight pout. Not exactly subtle. She rolled her eyes and showed it to Rufus.

'Lara likes your photos,' she said. And it seemed

her followers did too, because the likes were racking up quickly.

She scrolled down to read the caption:

Can't believe my best friend @Jess is curled up with this hot chocolate while I'm snowbound at the airport. So jealous, and wishing I was on our perfect Christmas getaway @UptonManor. Keep checking back for updates from Jess and Rufus. I promise it's much more interesting than where I am right now! Do you all have holiday travel disasters to share? Love and sympathy in the comments, please, friends!

Jess smiled. Lara had pitched it perfectly, of course, and she had no doubt that she would have new followers flocking to the Upton Manor page. She clicked through Lara's stories and found in-progress shots of the hot chocolate along with another shot of her by the fire, from behind this time, her profile silhouetted by the warm light from the fire.

Turned out Rufus had a pretty good eye. Between his skills with the camera, and Lara's ability to sell the setting to her readers, they might still make a success of this.

'I can't believe it,' Rufus said, staring at his phone. 'I've just got two hundred more followers. From one post alone.'

'Repost it into your stories and cross-post onto your feed,' Jess said, reading Lara's latest message. 'Respond to all the comments and use plenty of emojis. Lara's fielding as many of them as she can but apparently it's good to have your authentic voice in there too.'

Her phone chimed again. 'Good. She's happy. Says to keep the content coming. So should this have been your first Christmas away from Upton?' she asked, thinking back to something he had said earlier.

'Yeah, Dad was unwell last year so we didn't really celebrate.' She couldn't help but notice how he automatically included his family in his answer.

'I'm sorry to hear that,' Jess said, sensing pain behind Rufus's neutral expression. 'I hope he's doing better now.'

'Aye, he is, thanks. Nothing like a massive heart attack to make you embrace a healthy lifestyle.'

'Sounds like that must have been traumatic for all of you.'

'Well, for him most of all. Of course, it didn't help that... I'm sorry. Don't know why I'm telling you this.'

She frowned, looked around and pulled a footstool between her and the fire, then shot Rufus a determined look.

'Sit. Talk. We're going to be stuck here for a while. Might as well get to know each other.'

Which, from the expression on his face, seemed to be a terrifying concept. But he sat, glancing between her and the fire, and dropped his elbows to rest on his thighs.

'So your dad getting sick and leaving this place must have happened pretty close together. Were they connected?'

He nodded. 'When Dad was taken into hospital I offered to look after some admin stuff. Finances. Turned out—we didn't really have any finances. Dad hadn't let on how bad things were—thought he could fix it all himself. Which nearly killed him.'

'And you had to try and piece it all together while he was sick. Sounds like it must have been tough. And things were bad enough that they had to move out?'

'I just couldn't see any other way. There was one small cottage that they hadn't sold off yet. The tenant had just moved out and it made sense to move them over there and rent this place out instead.'

She nodded. 'Seems sensible.'

'It was the only solution that I could think of. I called the bank, explained that we had a plan and negotiated some grace on the mortgage. Same with all the other bills that we owed. I was lucky that people were generous when they heard what had happened to Dad. And then when he was well enough, we told him what I'd done.'

'And he wasn't happy?'

'He was devastated. He'd practically put himself into an early grave trying to avoid leaving the house, and then I'd come along and done it anyway.'

'Sounds like you didn't have much of a choice,' Jess countered.

'That's not the way he saw it,' Rufus said, shaking his head. 'He didn't tell me he was angry, but I knew anyway.'

'How do the others feel about it?'

'The same, I think. Gutted.'

Jess frowned, her forehead creasing. 'It wasn't your fault that you all had to move out, though. Not if there weren't any other options. You just did what you could in a difficult situation.'

Rufus shrugged. 'Dad says that he always managed to find another way. Something always came up at the last minute. He was still convinced that if he hadn't been ill then he would have worked something out.'

'Except the something that came up at the last minute this time was him getting ill from the stress. I'm sure you did the right thing,' Jess said with certainty.

'Well, I'm glad you are, because no one else is.' He shrugged. 'Apparently leaving the house has been *almost* inevitable for about three hundred years. And then I was the one to blink and give in.'

Jess scoffed. 'Doesn't sound much like giving in to me. Sounds like you were pretty bold.'

'Yes, well. I'll let you argue that one out with my dad.'

'So your dad's…okay?' she asked.

'Well, he's alive. I'm not sure that he's okay, to be honest.'

'I imagine he must feel pretty guilty.'

He frowned, causing parallel lines to appear between his eyebrows.

'What would he have to feel guilty about?'

'Well, it sounds like he worked himself into a hospital bed trying to keep you all in your home, and it wasn't enough.'

'That was my fault.'

'I don't imagine it was anyone's fault,' Jess said. 'This house is…ridiculous. I mean, it's beautiful. And amazing, and everything. But it's *enormous*. I can't imagine what it must cost to keep a place like this just watertight and warm. There's a reason the National Trust exists, and it's the fact that it's all but impossible for a private family to maintain something like this.'

Rufus shook his head, still not ready to be convinced. 'Other people manage.'

She shrugged. 'And where's the sense in comparing? Every situation is different, and from what I've heard you did well to prevent this place being sold. At least it still belongs to your family, right?'

'For now.'

'Is your dad mad at you? Because I hear you blaming yourself a lot. And not a single thing that you've said makes me think that it's your dad that thinks you're to blame.'

'He doesn't have to say anything. I just *know*.'

Jess threw her hands up. There was clearly no point arguing with him. 'Well, you're right. That seems like empirical proof. I'll use that in my next paper.'

Suddenly Rufus looked curious, and he jumped on the change of subject. 'Your next paper? You know, you never told me what you actually do.'

'You know, I know what you're doing. Nice try.'

He shrugged. 'You mean well, but I'm not sure this one can be fixed. Let's talk about you.'

She waited a beat, considering. 'Fine. But I'm warning you, you might have said all you want to, but I don't think I'm done.'

He smiled weakly. 'I'll pencil in a haranguing at a later date. Now I want to know about your work.'

He shifted on the stool, and she realised that they had been sitting in his study long enough for a couple of logs to burn down, and the dregs of her hot chocolate to go dry and grainy in the bottom of the cup.

'We can talk about me later. But we should really get the shots that Lara wanted of the house before I properly unpack and make a mess of all your hard work.'

'Right,' Rufus said, standing and brushing down his

trousers self-consciously. 'Should I go and do them, or do you want to…?'

'Lara likes faces. She says they get better engagement.'

He stared at her so long she felt a strong urge to rub at her face, as if she had a smudge on her cheek or something.

'You have a nice face,' Jess said.

She wanted to die the minute that the words left her mouth. Perhaps if she went outside and just lay in the snow, her face would stop burning and she could pretend that that had never happened. Maybe. It would be worth the hypothermia. Except, Rufus's cheeks were pink again too, right there on the cheekbones, and that was such a good look on him that it was hard to regret her words. Still, she needed to backpedal.

'I just mean, we should take some shots of you too. It'll be good for the brand.'

'Fine, if you think that's what Lara wants. For the record, though, your face is nice too.'

She had just got those cheeks of hers under control, and now they were burning worse than ever. He was only thinking about the Instagram feed, she told herself. This was all just business to him, no matter how intimate it might feel being holed up together here in the snow. She uncurled herself from the chair and walked self-consciously from the study, aware that Rufus's eyes were on her as they made their way along the gallery and round to her bedroom.

'Was this your room?' she asked, trying to imagine the house as a family home, with Rufus and his brother and sister running around the empty halls, heaps of wrapping paper and abandoned packaging everywhere on Christmas morning. She'd seen enough of his mum to know it must have been full of energy and joy. And noise. A far cry from the awkward silence currently filling the great hall, where she could hear the crackle from the logs in the fireplace on the floor below.

No wonder the family were all missing this place. That Rufus was mourning what he had lost. She knew as well as anyone how hard it was when big changes hit your family. When you suddenly had to adjust to a new normal, when you had been perfectly happy with the old one.

She opened the door to her room and was hit by warmth from the fire, which had been burning away behind the closed door while they were in the study. The décor, unsurprisingly, seemed no less over-the-top after an hour away from it, and she tried to imagine what she and Lara would have made of it had she got her flight before the snow had set in. They would have been doubled up with laughter, she imagined, at the thought of their plans for a pyjama- and Scrabble-heavy weekend being mistaken for a debauched couple of nights involving rose petals and champagne. There was no doubt it would make for some pretty content for the Instagram feed, though. She'd picked up Rufus's phone in the study and fired off a couple of shots now, capturing the heart of petals on the bed and the champagne glasses on the side table. A tall cheval mirror was reflecting the fire from the other side of the room and she crossed to stand in front of it, wondering what Lara would make of her very hashtag-authentic outfit of thermal leggings, worn-in boots and layers of knitwear that no one would mistake for cashmere.

'I really don't know what to do with all this,' Jess

said, contemplating the mass of rose petals that she'd gathered into a pile.

'Here.' Rufus snatched up a crystal bowl from the dark wood sideboard on the other side of the room and crossed to the bed. They scooped handfuls of petals into the bowl, until there were just a few strays on the pillows that Jess stretched to pick up.

'These smell beautiful,' Jess said, picking up the bowl and giving it a long sniff. 'Mind if I keep them up here?'

'If you want,' Rufus replied, dropping down to sit on the edge of the bed, but then standing up, looking uncomfortable.

'Sorry,' he said. 'Sometimes it's hard to remember I don't live here any more.'

'Was this your room?'

He shook his head. 'No, my parents had this one. Mine was far less grand—they stuck us up in the attic once we were old enough to be out of earshot.'

Jess smiled. 'Sounds very *Boy's Own*.'

'I don't know about that. My sister was up there with us. They're still bedrooms—you can take a look if you want.'

'I'd like that, maybe once the house warms up a bit. I'm not sure that I want to leave the fire. And you should sit, Rufus, if you want. You have more right to be here than I do. It's not fair that you should feel uncomfortable.'

'You're a guest,' he said.

'Well, and so are you, sort of, if it makes you feel better. I dragged you in from the cold and saved your life, which means I get to decide what to do with it. And right now I really think you should relax.'

'Is that what you and Lara were planning on doing?'

She nodded. 'Yep. Our plan for the weekend was pyjamas, movies, Scrabble.'

'Scrabble?'

'Lara's a fiend.'

'How about you? Maybe I'll let you beat me later.'

'Let me?' She raised an eyebrow. 'Wow. You don't know who you're messing with.'

The buzz of her phone in her pocket stopped that intense look from becoming uncomfortably long, and she tapped on Lara's message. She'd cropped one of the mirror shots, and Jess realised for the first time that she had captured Rufus in the glass behind her, and he was looking at her with an expression she could only describe as heated. She zoomed in on his face a little further, and then nearly dropped her phone in panic as he came to stand beside her.

'More from Lara?'

'Uh, yeah. She's happy with the shots from in here.'

'Can I see?'

If she could have thought of a single good reason to say no, she would have done. But these photos were the key to saving his family home and his business. They were the whole reason that she was here, and she couldn't think how to avoid him seeing them. She handed the phone over, surreptitiously tapping the back key so that he couldn't see how close a close-up she'd made it.

'Oh,' he said, his eyebrows furrowing together. 'I didn't realise you'd taken that.'

'I didn't realise you were in it,' she told him honestly.

And then, just as they were both staring at the phone, a message popped up from Lara. Three flame emojis.

Which everyone knew translated as *Oh, my goodness, check out the scorching sexual chemistry.* Jess rolled her eyes. Lara's timing was impossibly, perfectly terrible.

She wrote back.

You're right. The log fires are our only source of heat. Well spotted.

And then she pocketed her phone before her friend could heap any more embarrassment on her.

'Does she want us to take any more tonight?' Rufus asked.

Jess made an executive decision.

'Probably best to wait for natural light. These are good for now for her stories, but she'll want them better lit for the main grid. So I'm going to say we're off duty.'

'In that case…are you hungry?'

She tried to think back to the last time that she had eaten and could only think of the nondescript beige food that she'd found at the hotel's continental breakfast buffet. And suddenly she was ravenous.

'I'm starving. Shall we raid the fridge?'

'Did Lara mention that catering is…kind of my thing? I'm a chef, and the food's included in the weekend. In fact, we should probably get some pictures of that too.'

Rufus pulled a giant tray of lasagne from the fridge and stuck it in the Aga, then dug around in the fridge for salad and olives and other things to pick at while they waited for it to warm up.

'What would you be doing, if you weren't here?' she asked on a whim, thinking about her parents, wondering whether they were home alone together on a Satur-

day night, sitting silently in front of the television and
wishing they were anywhere else.

'Saturday night before Christmas? In my old life, I'd
be at work. No chance of being out of the kitchen before
midnight. And then back here for booze, board games,
snacks with whoever was still awake. An argument with
my brother, probably. The traditional Taylor night in.'

'I can't decide whether that sounds terrible or wonderful.'

Rufus lifted his shoulders, then let them drop. 'If it
helps, it's usually both. What about you? What would
you be doing if you were with your family?'

She had to suppress a shudder. 'Forced conversation. Awkward silences. Trying to subtly convince my
parents to separate.'

He watched her for a long moment as she realised
she'd been far more honest than she'd intended.

'I'm sorry,' Rufus said, his voice so full of empathy
that she felt the warmth of it in her bones.

'They never recovered,' she said, wondering where
this need to talk was coming from. 'They were both
so…devastated when my sister died. And they could—
they *should*—have turned to each other. To support one
another. To get through it. But it was like…' She hesitated. Realised there was a tear in the corner of her eye
and swiped it away before it could betray her. 'They
both just stopped talking. As if that would somehow
change something.' She shook her head. 'I'm sorry. I
really don't know why I'm telling you this.'

'Because you're stranded in my house at Christmas
instead of being with them?'

She shrugged. 'Maybe. Did your family rally round
when your dad was sick?'

'We all had to pitch in. Between that and me moving back here and packing up the house it's been a full-on year.' And it had brought them all together, that much was clear from the way that he spoke about them.

And that was the thing: some families, some couples, survived these traumas. Others didn't. And until you were in the middle of it—in a brightly lit hospital corridor in the middle of the night, hearing terrible news and wondering what your life was going to be now—you didn't know which way it was going to fall.

There were plenty of people—her parents included—who thought they were in a happy, stable marriage. And then when the worst happened, they discovered that that wasn't enough.

Which was precisely why Jess had steered clear of anything remotely resembling a serious relationship her entire adult life. What was the point if even something you thought was perfect could disintegrate in the space of a heartbeat? Or the space where a heartbeat should have been.

'Right. Enough wallowing—'

'It's okay to wallow if you feel sad,' Rufus said gently.

'Enough wallowing,' she repeated. 'Now you've made me realise how hungry I am, we have to eat.'

He pulled the lasagne out of the Aga and reached for a serving spoon without looking up. All muscle memory, she realised. He'd grown up in this kitchen. Was a part of it.

They took their steaming plates of food to the huge table in the centre of the kitchen and she plonked herself onto a bench opposite Rufus, and Jess was struck by how intimate this was. She couldn't remember the last time she'd had dinner alone with a man.

These days her social life was mainly messaging Lara and the occasional departmental social. And she'd never really minded that before. But, sitting here with Rufus, trying to remember how to hold a conversation that didn't revolve around work, she realised that this was an adult life skill she really should have mastered by now.

'You asked earlier what I do. I'm a researcher, looking at genetic links in childhood cancers. It's such a cliché, but after we lost Charlotte I was just drawn to it.'

Rufus looked surprised. 'You want to help other families. It's not a cliché. It's—I don't know. Remarkable. Isn't it painful? The constant reminder?'

She thought about his question. 'It's always painful. At least this way it's doing some good.'

He narrowed his eyes, as if trying to slot these pieces into the puzzle picture he had of her. One that had somehow got stuck on his mistaken assumption that she was Lara.

'How did you and Lara meet?' Rufus asked, sparing her the trauma of trying to remember how to converse like a normal human being.

'Oh, university. We were flatmates and she's never really got rid of me.'

'And the pre-Christmas thing is a one-off?'

'Nope. Annual event. We used to try and get so drunk that it would numb me right through the big day. Last couple of years have been more just a massive inoculation of moral support.'

He smiled. 'She sounds like a good friend.'

'She's the best.'

'I'm sorry I was… I don't know…rude about her earlier. When I thought you were her.'

'Well, you were rude, but I accept your apology. I do wonder though why you invited her here at all if you think so little of what she does.'

'No, I don't.' He clocked her doubtful expression and doubled down. 'I can understand why you think that after what I said. But I respect the work she does. I know she's very good at it. I just don't want to see my home reduced to *content*. I don't like having to stage "real life", so that people can come here and make-believe my old life for the weekend.'

She nodded. 'You're mourning this place too,' she observed. 'And I don't blame you. It's beautiful. I would have been heartbroken to leave too.'

'It's not that it's beautiful,' he said, an edge to his voice. 'That's the problem. That's all social media is going to show, and it's only a fraction of what this place is. What it means to me.'

'Then tell me. Help me understand.'

'It's…it's where I belong. It's where my brother belongs. And my sister. And my parents. It's the place where I feel most like me in the whole world—I thought that it would always be here. Instagram doesn't care about that.'

'Then make it care.'

'And how do I do that?'

'I don't know. That's Lara's department. But you have an opportunity here. Lara has a huge following. Millions of people view her posts, and you're the one with the camera. So don't show them the gloss. Show them what this house means to you. Show them things that no one else would never see because they didn't know to look for them. Show them what makes this a home, not just another luxury rental.'

He stared at her, and she started to shift uncomfortably. If she'd gone too far, she'd just created an atmosphere in a house that neither of them could escape from. She might as well have gone home for Christmas and put up with an atmosphere she at least knew and understood.

He nodded slowly, and she could see that hint of a smile turn up the corner of his mouth. 'I think I can do that. I know I can. But I'm going to need your help.'

CHAPTER FOUR

RUFUS LOOKED AT the clock on the kitchen wall again. Five minutes past nine. When he'd said goodnight to Jess last night she'd asked him to give her a shout if she slept past nine—her phone had died, and she couldn't be sure it would charge overnight, so she couldn't set an alarm.

He poured two cups of coffee and glanced at the clock again. Why was he hesitating? She'd specifically asked him to wake her, but somehow the thought of taking coffee to her in bed of a morning felt so…intimate. And the thought of sharing something like that with Jess was intimidating. Because he knew there was something between them. It had been obvious from the moment his head had cleared yesterday and he'd found himself sharing the house with a woman who'd dragged him in from the snow, saved his life, and then kept up a steady stream of snark in the hours afterwards. And he'd found it pretty irresistible. Seeing her curled up in the chair by the fire in the study, he had found it hard to hide just how irresistible. But, regardless of what he was feeling, he knew that he wouldn't act on it.

Some time in the year that his father had been recuperating, he'd decided that he wasn't going to be responsible for another family. He'd had a go at acting as provider, and he'd messed up, so badly that it had uprooted his entire family from the home that they'd loved for generations. and for what? His ambition? A job that he'd had to leave anyway?

He was at least smart enough to know that he should never be in the position of being responsible for other people's happiness.

So he was going to knock on her door, deliver strong coffee, and retreat, ideally without making eye contact.

And after that his focus was going to be on his camera, and on showing the world Upton Manor as it was truly meant to be seen.

He carried the coffee up the stairs and across the gallery, listening out for any sound that would indicate that Jess was awake and he was off the hook. But the house was silent, in a way that he never remembered it being before the moving trucks had turned up. He knocked on the door gently and then more loudly, waiting for a shout of 'I'm up' from the other side of the door. Which never came.

He opened the door a crack and peered in, but the heavy curtains were pulled across and he could barely see anything in the darkened room. 'Jess,' he said, but her name came out as a croak. He called her again, his voice louder this time, pushing open the door to allow more light to spill in.

Jess sat bolt upright in bed with a scream, and Rufus jumped, splashing hot coffee on his chest in the process. He had no choice but to set the cups down on the sideboard just inside the door.

'Hey, it's me. It's Rufus,' he said as he stepped

through the door, holding up his now empty hands. 'You asked me to wake you up.'

'I… I did. I'm sorry for screaming; didn't know where I was for a second. Is that coffee?'

'Yeah.' For want of anything better to do, he picked up both the cups, carried them over to the bed and handed one to Jess. She took a long sip, and he winced, knowing just how hot it was.

'Is it working?' he asked as she ventured another, more cautious, sip.

'I do not want to be awake right now.'

'You know, I'm not sure I would have agreed to this whole wake-up call thing if I'd known you were so aggro in the morning.'

'Sorry. And thanks. It would only have been worse if I'd slept any later. I owe you one.'

She shifted on the bed and he hesitated, not sure if it was an invitation, but then her head dropped back on the pillows and her eyes drifted closed and he knew he needed to stick around for a bit if she was going to stay awake.

He sat on the edge of the bed, and the movement of the mattress woke her again.

'I wasn't asleep.'

'Glad we cleared that up.'

Her hair was smooshed into some sort of asymmetrical beehive, and her face still had creases from the pillow, and the whole look was so utterly adorable that he had to look away because it was absolutely not part of his plan to adore her in any way.

As if she'd sensed the direction of his thoughts, she lifted a hand to her hair, patted it a few times from different angles and rolled her eyes.

She sat up properly, resting her arms on bent knees as she blew on her coffee.

'Do we have exciting plans for today?' Jess asked.

'I'm going to take more photos for Lara. I was going to wrap up and head out into the snow. Make the most of the sun being out for a bit.'

'Back on the horse?'

'Something like that. You should come with me—if you see me wandering into the woods after a deer you can yell at me not to be such an idiot.'

'Noted. Seriously, though.' She lowered her coffee and gave him a stern look. 'Are you feeling okay? Because you could just sit by the fire today and carry on warming up.'

'I'm fine. I mean it.' He hated people fussing over him. It was bad enough that he had let his family down, but he was at least capable of taking care of himself. Most of the time.

He glanced back at Jess—the creases were fading from her cheeks, her hair had settled around her shoulders and her eyes fell shut every time she took a sip from the cup.

'Right,' she said at last, draining the last of the coffee and straightening her spine with resolve. 'I'm awake. I'm alive. Thanks so much for the coffee. Shall I meet you downstairs in five and we can head out?'

He dragged his eyes away from her and headed for the door, pulling it closed behind him when he heard her feet hit the floor and he knew she wasn't going back to sleep.

Jess scrambled out of bed and rummaged in her bag for her thick woollen socks and a couple of jumpers.

After she'd asked Rufus last night to wake her if she accidentally slept in—post-conference fatigue had a habit of messing up her body clock—she'd pulled on tartan flannel PJs, making sure there was nothing on show if he came in to wake her this morning. And that she didn't freeze half to death in the night.

After a chilly—and necessarily quick—stint in the bathroom, she pulled on thermals, trousers, layers of knitwear, and dug her snow boots from the bottom of her bag. If they were going out in the snow then she was going prepared. She could see from the window that a few more inches had fallen overnight, and Rufus had been the proof yesterday of how important it was to be careful out there.

She bounded down the staircase into the great hall, where Rufus had swept out the remains of yesterday's fire and laid a new one with logs from the basket by the hearth. The power had stayed on overnight, which meant the electric heaters were warm, but they were going to need more wood to get them through the next few days if the supply couldn't be relied upon. The wall sconces flickered, a timely reminder that they couldn't depend on modern technology to see them through the crisis when the weather was so extreme.

Rufus appeared in the doorway that led down to the kitchen, piece of toast in hand.

'Did the lights just flicker in here?'

'Yeah, I think so,' she said, glancing up. 'Do you think we'll lose power again?'

'Not if I can help it,' he said, a collection of frown lines gathering on his forehead. If a power line came down somewhere, or something else happened on the grid, she wasn't sure what he was going to do about it.

But from the sternness of his expression this wasn't the moment to mention it.

'Do you want toast?' he asked, gesturing with his own slice, and Jess's stomach rumbled an enthusiastic yes. She followed him through to the kitchen and found a rack full of toast and sticky jars of jam and honey. She slathered a slice with butter and honey while Rufus filled a couple of Thermos mugs with freshly brewed coffee.

'Are you planning a major expedition?' she asked with eyebrows raised.

'You've got your thermals, I have coffee. Let's try no one getting hypothermia today.'

'I'm fine with that part. I'm mainly planning half-hour stints in the outdoors broken up by long stretches on the sofa with a book. We're just taking a few photos, right?'

'Right. And I should probably get some more logs out of the woodstore. But you're welcome to stay inside if you want.'

'No! I want to come out and play. But I will not be staying out so long that hypothermia measures will have to be taken. Just to be clear.'

'Crystal clear. The coffee is an added bonus, not a life-saving measure.'

'Then hand it over,' she said with a smile.

As she took the cup from him, her fingers brushed against his wrist, and she felt him freeze at the exact same moment she did. He looked up and found his gaze on her face, and she was reminded of that spark she'd felt yesterday, when they'd been cocooned in a candlelit house, cut off from the world. But it seemed that spark hadn't died when the fires had burned down to embers last night. She'd half wondered if it had been summoned by the sheer quantity of fairy lights, but here they were in bright daylight and it was definitely still there.

She drew her hand back, because as delicious as sparks could be, they had to be handled with care. Sparks, all too often, led to feelings. Feelings led to relationships, and relationships led to heartache. She'd experienced and witnessed it enough in her life, and had precisely zero interest in exposing herself to any more.

She'd acted on sparks before. In controlled circumstances, when she'd been absolutely certain that she knew how she was getting in and when she was going to be getting out. Right now, these circumstances were anything but controlled. They'd been thrown together, entirely unexpectedly, with lashings of Christmas and adverse weather conditions thrown in for extra pressure. So she was going to back the heck away, and pretend that she hadn't noticed anything concerning in the first place.

'I need to get my coat and my hat—' Which she'd last seen on his head yesterday. Fortunately he produced it from the pocket of his jacket without comment and she pulled it straight onto her head. 'Right, then. I'm ready.'

She pulled aside the heavy brocade curtain that covered the front door and felt an immediate blast of cold air from the draughts finding their way around the ancient oak panels. When she opened it, snow had accumulated in the porch, and she was glad of her snow boots as she crunched slowly out, testing her footing to see if she was going to suddenly slip.

But the snow was deliciously soft and powdery underfoot, and she felt a huge smile spread across her face as she took in the great expanse of white all around her.

All across the landscape, as far as she could see, was virgin, untouched snow. The trees were heavy with it, icicles hung from the entrance to the porch, and a spider's web glistened with tiny crystals. She grabbed her phone from her pocket and snapped a couple of pictures, the natural light meaning that even her junky old phone could capture something quite beautiful.

'Pretty,' Rufus said, coming up behind her and looking at her phone screen. 'But Lara wants faces, remember.' He lifted his phone and fired off a shot before she had a chance to disagree.

'Pretty,' he said again, looking at the photo, where he had captured her in profile, the light glinting from the cobweb making a bokeh effect behind her. He was probably just complimenting himself on the composition, Jess told herself, feeling colour rising on her cheeks. It would be so much more convenient if he was.

'Uh, nice one,' she said, before stomping off through the snow, glorying in each crunch of the snow underfoot as she crossed the drive and turned back to look at the house. 'It's like something out of a fairy tale,' Jess said as Rufus came to stand beside her and followed her gaze to the big old house.

'That's the problem, though,' he said. 'It looks like a fairy tale, and people don't believe that it's real. That's it's warm and has a personality of its own. That's what I want to show people.'

She took a picture of him looking up at the house, the yearning in his face for his home. Lara was going to eat this up, she thought, uploading her last few photos to her friend's cloud account.

'Come on,' Rufus said. 'I just want to check there's nothing I can do about the power out here, check the place is secure. Then I'll get some more logs from the outhouse and we can get you back in by the fire. That sound okay?'

'That sounds…efficient,' she answered. 'Um, any chance of, say, some fun?'

He frowned. 'You were all *I'm only staying out for half an hour…*'

'Precisely. I want to have half an hour of fun. Taking photos. I heard no snowmen, snowballs or snow angels in your plan. This is a shocking oversight.'

'You think I want to lie in the snow after yesterday?'

'Good point. You are exempt from snow angels. You are not exempt from the rest of it. I thought you wanted to show that this place has personality. That might involve, you know, *you* having a personality.'

'I'm trying really hard to see how that can be anything but an insult. I'm coming up with nothing.'

'I'm just saying that this house doesn't have a personality all on its own. You love it because you grew up here with the people that you love. You're going to have to show some of that if you want other people to see it.'

'Fine. I get it. There will be fun in the snow. Just as soon as I've checked the fuse box.'

'I'm very glad to hear it. Now—snowman. I'm going to warn you—I have a problem with half-arsed. I'm expecting great things of myself, and of you.'

He raised an eyebrow. 'Are you this competitive about everything?'

'Generally, yes.'

'Then I'm glad we never got to Scrabble last night. I suspect you would have been vicious.'

She shrugged. 'I guess you'll never know if you're

too chicken to try. If your masculinity is too fragile to lose to a girl, there's not much hope for you.'

'Fragile…wow.'

Jess shrugged, trying to hide a smile. 'I guess you'll just have to prove it.'

'You're on. Scrabble later, snowman competition now.'

She grinned, unable to resist a challenge. Or that look on his face, apparently. 'Competitive snowman-making. You do know how to make a girl happy.'

She started gathering snow in a pile around her, pushing it together to form a ball. Her gloves were soaked through within seconds, and her fingers started to sting as the cold set in. But she glanced over at Rufus and smiled at the fierce concentration on his face as he piled snow on top of snow until he had a pile nearly to his hips. She took a couple of photos while he was looking the other way, getting bright blue skies and clear winter sun in the background. On a summer's day she'd look at that sky and expect to bake beneath it. But apparently all it meant for them for the next few days were temperatures that never crept above zero.

The main roads would be gritted and cleared pretty soon, she guessed. But out here in the wilds of the moors at the end of a winding lane, they just had to wait for the thaw.

And try not to get into trouble in the meantime, she reminded herself, realising she had been staring at Rufus's arse for way longer than could be considered appropriate. Especially for someone who had sworn to herself, at least once already this morning, that she was steering well clear of the chemistry she had to acknowledge existed between them.

Rufus glanced over his shoulder, and she was glad she'd already shifted her gaze upwards and hadn't been caught perving on him. That would have been awkward.

'You've slowed down,' Rufus commented. 'You ready to go in and warm up?'

Jess rolled her eyes. 'Nice try.' With that she started to roll the snowman's body around, gathering more snow as she went, until it was as high as her waist. She made a smaller ball for the head, added her hat and scarf, and glanced over to check out how the competition was getting on.

Rufus had built a rather austere-looking snowman and was currently carving out arm shapes. Jess came to stand beside him and grinned at the concentration on Rufus's face.

'Okay, you make a good snowman,' she acknowledged. 'I'll give you that.'

He turned and smiled at her, and it was so unexpected that it caught her off guard, disarming her with its easy openness. Woah. She clearly needed much better defences. She picked up her phone and took a couple more pictures of the snowman. Everything seemed that little bit safer through the lens of a camera.

Rufus slung an arm around the snowman's really-quite-impressive shoulder and took a selfie. Jess leaned into the shot from the other side and grinned at the lens as Rufus took another couple. He came round to show her, and she grinned at the result.

'Nice work. He's very handsome,' she told him. 'But your nose is red. You look cold.'

'Yours is red too. And don't think I didn't notice that your hands are freezing.'

'I wasn't hypothermic yesterday. We should go inside.'

Rufus shook his head. 'I haven't checked the fuses. Or fetched in the wood.'

'They'll still be there in an hour,' she told him. 'Anyway, I finished my coffee ages ago and my caffeine levels are slipping dangerously low. It's my turn to put the kettle on.'

Rufus hesitated, so she pulled out the big guns. 'I'm not going inside until you do. So if you want me to warm up, you're going to have to go in too.'

'Fine. You're stubborn. I'll go in, we'll make coffee and I'll head back out soon.'

Jess nodded. 'Acceptable.' She retrieved her hat and scarf from the snowman, and winced when the snow inside the hat settled on her head. Rufus laughed and brushed snowflakes off the length of her hair. As it had earlier, the touch of his hand stopped her dead, and the smile fell from her face as she realised that she'd let herself get too close. Again. And maybe Rufus was feeling it too, because he hadn't moved either. His hand had come to rest on the side of her face, where she could feel a single snowflake melting on her cheekbone. She waited for Rufus to brush it away, thinking that would break the spell. But his hand didn't move. His fingers were cold, but her skin beneath them was aflame. And either he had taken a step towards her or she had moved towards him, because somehow his chest was brushing against the front of her coat, and his mouth was the only thing that she could see.

And his hand was cupping her cheek—and how was hers on his waist?—and their frozen breath was mixing between them.

The touch of his cold lips on hers shocked her out of her paralysis and she took a decisive step back.

'I'm sorry,' Rufus said immediately.

'No need to apologise,' Jess said, trying to school her features into something neutral. 'It was as much me as it was you. But I don't think it's a good idea.'

'No, of course not. I feel the same. Can we just forget this?'

Ouch. Surely him agreeing with what she had already said shouldn't hurt quite so much?

It was just her ego, she told herself. And her ego had no business sticking its nose into this. All her decisions when it came to Rufus were to be made entirely by her head. No other body parts got a say in the matter at all. She had to be sensible about this because if the electricity in that kiss was anything to go by, this would get very dangerous very quickly if she wasn't on guard against it.

'It's already forgotten,' she said, and hoped he couldn't sense the size of her lie, because she was sure that she'd never told a bigger one.

They walked slowly back to the house, trying to ignore the atmosphere, but once they were enclosed in the porch it seemed to swell and fill the space.

Jess breathed a sigh of relief as the old iron latch on the door gave way, and they walked through to the space of the great hall. The fire was roaring now, the heating on full blast too, and Jess shed layers as she crossed over to the kitchen to put the kettle on, warming her hands on the Aga and waiting for the feeling to come back to her fingers. While the coffee was brewing she went digging around in the pantry, looking for mince pies. Lara knew that Christmas wasn't Christmas without them. They were the only saving grace of this time of year as far as she was concerned, and her best friend wouldn't have forgotten them.

'Looking for something?' Rufus asked, making her jump, and nearly topple off the crate she was using as a makeshift step stool.

'Mince pies,' she said, still making a mental inventory of what was on the shelves, sure that she must just be missing them somewhere. 'I know Lara wouldn't have forgotten.'

'Ah. She didn't.' He stepped into the pantry and squeezed behind her. She pressed herself against the shelf, trying to stop his body brushing against hers, but the sudden movement set her off balance again, and she fell back against him, just for long enough for his hands to rest on her hips to steady her.

'Sorry,' he said, snatching back his hands as soon as she had regained her balance. 'I should have realised there wasn't enough room.'

'Easily done.'

Jess tried to brush off the feel of his body against hers, but found that she couldn't do it quite so easily. She stepped back into the doorway of the pantry while Rufus scanned the shelves, until he pulled down a jar with a triumphant hurrah.

'Mincemeat,' Jess said, eyeing it dubiously. 'Don't tell me I'm expected to DIY them.'

Rufus scoffed. 'Oh, come on. Everyone can make a mince pie.'

'Not me.' She shook her head, but Rufus looked at her with patent disbelief.

'But you're a scientist!'

She laughed. 'You seem to have a very poor understanding of what a scientist does. I can confirm that at no point in my academic career have I been called on to bake.'

'Then I guess I'm going to have to teach you.'

'I'm unteachable. Many have tried.'

He smirked. Smug. 'Did they have a Michelin star?'

Jess rolled her eyes. 'Always with the trump card. Come on, then, do your worst. It'll make good content, if nothing else,' she added, trying to remember that when it came down to it, theirs was a business relationship. But Rufus stiffened at the word 'content' and she knew she'd said the wrong thing.

'I just meant…'

'It's fine. I know what you meant.'

There was no point trying to backtrack, not when she could see how tense his shoulders were. How set his expression. She'd have to show him, not tell him, that she understood that his childhood home was more than just a pretty backdrop.

'Okay, what else do we need?' she asked. If they were going to bake she was at least going to pretend to be enthusiastic. 'Even I can guess that flour is on the list.'

They grabbed ingredients as he reeled off a pastry recipe and carried them all to the marble section of the worktop. To keep the pastry cool—she had the theory of baking down. It was the practical that she'd always failed.

She concentrated on rubbing butter into flour, aware of Rufus vaguely watching her from the side. When she had the breadcrumb texture she knew she was meant to be looking for, she turned to ask Rufus if it was done, but he opened his mouth to speak at the same time.

'I'm sorry for snapping.'

'It's fine. I understand why you did. I know how you feel about this place.'

'But I shouldn't have taken it out on you. That looks good,' he added, nodding at her mixing bowl. 'You can add the egg, and it might need some cold water but go steady. You don't want it sticky.'

Jess followed his instructions with a hefty dose of scepticism. She'd lost count of the number of times that Lara had tried to override her genetic inability to bake and had been left aghast at their joint failure. But Rufus was turning out perfect circles of pastry lids to cover the neat spoonfuls of mincemeat filling, and then cutting delicate holly leaves to decorate the tops. Really, he was too much.

She stood back for a moment and watched him work, absorbed in placing tiny holly leaves on the top of each pie, positioning them with an exactitude she saved for her lab work, before looking over the whole batch and tweaking a leaf here and there.

'I think…' she started, not sure how she was going to square this skill with what she knew of Rufus. All this…and he could bake. 'I think they're remarkable.'

Rufus laughed and Jess felt the tension leach from her shoulders as the last of the atmosphere dissolved.

'I think you're easily impressed.'

She looked at her own batch of pies—which were, despite her best efforts, rather raggedy-looking—and shook her head.

'Baking is magic, not science. And I definitely don't have the touch.'

'Yours are very…charming.'

She laughed at the obvious exaggeration. 'That's generous.'

Still, Rufus slid both trays into the hot oven of the

Aga and set a timer. Jess sipped at her forgotten cup of coffee and leaned back against the countertop.

'Do you need to go back outside?'

'That depends. Can I trust you with the pies?'

'Well, you set the timer. So if they burn I'm placing the blame firmly at your door. But I'll take them out when the buzzer goes off if that's what you're asking.'

'Okay, well, I'll just be out the back door. Shout if you need me.'

'I promise not to burn the kitchen down in the next ten minutes.'

He smiled and paused in the doorway, holding her gaze for a beat, and then another. And the whole time she was aware that the longer they were trapped here, the stronger this connection between them seemed to be.

'Go,' she said, her voice not much more than a whisper. She needed him to walk away. From her. From whatever this was between them. Because she wasn't sure that she was capable of doing it all on her own. And she needed to, because the alternative was risking pain, and she'd had enough of that.

The timer pinged on the Aga and she grabbed a tea towel to pull the trays from the oven. She marvelled anew at the precision and beauty of Rufus's mince pies, and tried not to think about the fact that he'd just spent the last hour making them for her, just because she'd told him that she couldn't bear the idea of Christmas without them.

And that was a level of thoughtfulness and generosity that she could do without. Especially coming from someone she was already finding inconveniently attractive. She was just trying to remember whether she was meant to turn them out onto the cooling racks when Rufus clattered through the door with a flurry of snowflakes and a huge basket of logs. She rushed to help him, and they lowered the basket between them.

'I had it,' Rufus said, a slight frown creasing his forehead.

'It was nothing.' Jess replied, wondering what she'd done to annoy him now. Well, at least when he was scowling he was considerably less attractive. And she would take any help that she could get on that score.

'I'm going to grab another basket,' Rufus announced. 'Do you need any—?'

'I've got it under control.'

Okay, so he was clearly peeved about something. With any luck, he'd hold that thought for the next few days, until she could get away from him. Safely away from temptation.

Rufus leaned his forehead against the door of the woodshed. He shouldn't have snapped at her. It wasn't fair to take it out on Jess. It wasn't her fault that he was feeling this way. This desperate desire that was becoming harder and harder to ignore was entirely on him. Of course, she might be feeling it too. He wasn't completely oblivious. But he was the one who had to keep his feelings in check. He was the one who had sworn that he wasn't going to have a relationship, because relationships led to family—and he knew he couldn't be trusted with one of those.

But it wouldn't have to be a relationship, said a rebellious part of his brain. It wouldn't have to lead to anything. It was just the two of them. In the place he loved most in the world, with huge amounts of decadent food, opulent decorations and luxury booze. They could just walk away. They could have this time here and then forget about one another afterwards.

Except Jess didn't want a fling. Oh, he was pretty sure that she wanted *him*. But their aborted kiss and the way that she had jumped away from him in the pantry told him all he needed to know. She was fighting this too, and he was sure that she had her reasons. Who was he to disagree with her? He'd overstepped once by kissing her—what had he been thinking?

He wouldn't do it again. She was his guest, however strange the circumstances, and he couldn't have her uncomfortable here. He wanted her safe and warm, and happy. And that meant denying these impulses. And all he had to do was take himself out into the sub-zero temperatures every hour or so to counteract the fire that she had been stoking in him for the past twenty-four hours.

He concentrated on filling the basket full of logs. If the power went then they'd lose the storage heating and they really needed to keep at least a couple of rooms warm. He needed to make sure there were candles and a torch in every room too, before night fell. There wasn't much he could do about the weather, but he would make them as safe as he could if the worst happened.

He pushed the door to the kitchen with his shoulder and deposited the basket of logs next to the fire, and caught Jess draping a tea towel over something. When she looked across at him, his heart stopped for a moment. She was trying hard to hide it, but she was upset. As he stood back up, her lower lip slid between her teeth and she bit down, and then he knew something was badly wrong.

'What is it?' he asked, crossing over to her in three long strides and brushing her hair back from her face to see it better. 'Jess, did something happen? Is it your parents? Or Lara?'

'No, no.' She tried to fake a laugh, but it came out as a strangled gulp. 'It's nothing like that. I was just trying to turn out the mince pies and...well...'

She removed the tea towel to reveal a pile of sorry-looking pastry and mincemeat. 'I knocked the corner of the cooking rack, and... Gravity took care of the rest.'

He let out his first full breath since he'd walked into the kitchen and pulled her into his chest, his heart pounding with relief. He let his eyes close for a second while he regained control of his heart rate. And realised he had her head still pressed to his chest. He released her with a start and took a step backwards for both of their sakes.

'I'm so sorry,' Jess said, looking over at the demolished mince pies.

'It's just pastry,' he said. 'I saw your face and thought something dreadful had happened.'

'But they were so perfect.'

'It doesn't matter. Honestly. Did any survive the fall?'

She pushed forward a plate with two of her mince pies on it. Raggedy pastry and leaky filling and all.

'One each,' Rufus declared with a rush of positivity. 'I'll make us another pot of tea and we can eat these by the fire. What's the matter?' he asked as she stood locked by the countertop, her face still a picture of distress.

'I don't know. It's just... Christmas. And being here. And thinking about Mum and Dad at home without me. It's such an unhappy time for them. And I've just left them to it.'

'You said yourself you would be there if you could be,' Rufus said gently. 'You can't blame yourself for the weather.'

'But they're so unhappy,' Jess went on. 'Mum's so miserable, and so is Dad, and I don't know why they are torturing themselves. No, that's not true. I do know why. It's because of me. They stay together for my sake, and it's made things unbearable for all of us.'

Rufus cupped a hand around her elbow, pulling her gently over to a chair. 'Jess, did something else happen while I was outside?'

'Yes. No. Just a call from my mum asking if there was any change in the weather. The roads down there are clearing. She thought I might get back at the last minute. And the sound of her voice when I said it didn't look likely… I just don't know why they would want to live like that. It's hard enough seeing it from the outside. I can't imagine what it must feel like from the inside.'

Rufus resisted the urge to pull her close again.

'I'm sorry that she upset you,' he murmured. 'I wish there was something I could do.'

She let out a long breath, her body relaxing a fraction.

'There's nothing you can do. Nothing I can do either. Believe me, I've tried. They've made their decision. They're both old enough to know they could make a different one.'

Rufus sighed. 'It doesn't make it any easier for you. To see them so unhappy.'

She shook her head.

'No. No, it doesn't.'

'Is this why…?' he started, but then stopped himself. He was massively overreaching. Whatever her reason for walking away from the kiss that they had barely started earlier, for jumping when his body had brushed hers by accident, he was sure that they were good ones. And none of his business.

'Why what?' she asked, looking up at him and meeting his gaze. And, with her eyes locked on his, caution was impossible.

'Why you're wary of this. Us. This…spark.'

She stiffened, leaned away from him. But it wasn't anger on her face. It was something closer to fear.

'I never said that.'

'I know. I'm reading between the lines. Woman who grows up seeing her parents in an unhappy marriage is wary of relationships.'

'We're not having a relationship.'

'I know that. And I have my own reasons for being wary too. But if you're steering clear because you think all marriages end like your parents', I just want you to know that you're wrong.'

'Well, thanks for mansplaining that to me. I'm aware that not every marriage is unhappy. My point, Rufus, is that any marriage can *become* unhappy. In the space of a day. A moment. Relationships are tested all the time, and some of them fail. Misery can blindside you. Just like that.'

He crossed his arms. Stared at her.

'I just think that's sad. That you'll deny yourself because you're scared of the worst.'

'I walk away from one kiss. Tell you one snippet about my life and you think you know me. You don't know the first thing about me.'

Well, that was a challenge if ever he heard one.

'I know something,' he said, maintaining their eye contact. He held it—another challenge—but she dropped her eyes and looked away.

'Look, I'm sorry about the mince pies,' she said, getting up and making a pot of tea, bustling and never meeting his gaze. She poured them both a cup, grabbed the plate of mince pies and headed for the door to the great hall.

He walked through a few moments later, finding Jess on the sofa closest to the fire, her legs curled under her and her hands clasped around her mug. He came and sat opposite her, and took the mince pie from the plate that she nudged towards him.

'I'm sorry,' they both said at once, and he smiled, saw the expression reflected on Jess's face.

'Can we start again?' he asked. 'Your mince pies are delicious.'

She laughed. 'That sounds like a very dodgy euphemism.'

'I'm offended. I never joke about mince pies.'

She snorted, contemplating the thick, uneven pastry. 'It was really kind of you to help me bake.'

'I enjoyed it,' he said honestly.

'Oh, my goodness,' Jess exclaimed suddenly, 'the pictures! We didn't get a single one before I dropped them.' She rolled her eyes and groaned.

'It's fine. We can make more tomorrow. What did you want to do with the rest of the day? I'll find something for lunch soon.'

'How about I beat you at a couple of games of Scrabble in between reading and Christmas movies?'

'That sounds like a challenge.'

'Oh, it absolutely is.'

She was scrupulously well-behaved while they played, even passing up the chance of a triple word score on an absolutely filthy word that she knew would make Rufus blush. Because they were being scrupulously well-behaved. They were resisting the temptation that had led them to nearly kissing earlier, because it was the sensible thing to do.

And that was why she was packing herself off to bed at little after nine in the evening when she didn't have work, or anything at all, to do the next day. Because her self-control could only stretch so far, and Rufus was testing the limits with every passing minute.

CHAPTER FIVE

WAS JESS AVOIDING him or had she slept in? This house was big, but not *that* big, and he'd know if she'd left her room. But it was nearly ten and there had been no sign of her since she had retreated to her room ridiculously early last night. That had to be on purpose.

Thank goodness she was being responsible and showing a level of self-control that he wasn't sure that he would be able to match if the tables were turned. Because everything in him was telling him to go and seek her out. Not to *do* anything, but just to hang out. He was probably just lonely. The electricity was out again, which meant no Wi-Fi and no connection to the outside world. She was literally the only person he could talk to.

And he knew that that fact had absolutely nothing to do with why he wanted to see her. He just *wanted* to.

Eventually, just when he thought he might actually lose his mind, she wandered into the kitchen as he was making a coffee, pulling a tray of mince pies from the Aga.

'Hey,' he said, trying to keep his voice neutral. 'Remind me not to leave you alone with these.'

'Oh, hi,' Jess said, faltering in the doorway, a trace of a smile on her face. 'You made more mince pies.'

'You said it wasn't Christmas without them.'

They stood without saying another word while the kettle boiled to a whistle.

'Coffee?' Rufus managed to say. And then, 'What are your plans for today?' As if he were a regular person who could string a sentence together in front of the woman that he fancied, rather than a tongue-tied teenager.

Jess faked a weak laugh, and he stopped what he was doing to narrow his eyes at her. 'What?' he asked.

'So… I just spoke to Lara and she had this idea. I think it's ridiculous, but she's pretty adamant.'

Rufus crossed his arms and leaned back against the worktop. 'Why do I feel like I should be worried? Very worried.'

'She said that you had a licence to use this place as a wedding venue.'

He felt blood rushing to his cheeks, and tried to hide the flush with a cough. 'Yeah, it's a big money-maker for venues like this.'

'She wants some pictures to appeal to that market. She wants me to make a veil out of a lace tablecloth or fashion a flower crown out of mistletoe or something. She just told me to make sure it looked romantic. Tell me you think she's being ridiculous.'

'She's being ridiculous,' he said, but there was a catch in his voice.

'But?'

'But…' He hesitated. Was he really going to say this? 'It is an important revenue stream. And when I was in the attic, I *may* have noticed that my mother's wedding dress is boxed-up up there.'

'You're kidding me.'

'I sort of wish I was.' He groaned. As if his feelings for Jess right now weren't complicated and inconvenient enough, they had to start talking weddings? But Lara was right. The wedding industry was a big market. He couldn't afford to ignore it—or to ignore Lara's advice. However much he might suspect that she might be meddling.

'Your parents must have got married in the eighties, right?' Jess said, and he guessed she was looking for an out. 'I bet your mum had big poufy lace dress. It's not going to work for Instagram.'

He shook his head. 'Actually she wore a replica of my great-grandmother's dress. Edwardian. Kind of beautiful.'

Her eyes lit up. 'Then she's not going to want me to play dress-up in it.'

'Why not? Pretty sure it was in the fancy dress box when we were kids. She's not precious about that sort of thing.'

'You're really going to make me do this?' she asked, her eyes wide.

'I'm not going to make you do anything, Jess. I hope you know that.'

'You're as ridiculous as she is,' she retorted.

He shrugged. 'Lara's your best friend. You must like ridiculous sometimes.'

Jess rolled her eyes. 'I can't believe I'm agreeing to this.'

Rufus smiled, just a little. 'You're agreeing?'

'Ugh.'

Jess contorted her spine, but it was no use. The dress had two dozen buttons up the back and there was no way she could reach even half of them. She looked in the mirror and tried to decide whether she was decent enough to call Rufus in for his help. She'd done the buttons at the base of her spine—the dress fitted perfectly—but there was still a swathe of bare skin up her back. And she wasn't going to get any more covered up without help.

The dress was cut high at the front, with lace sleeves. Once these bloody buttons were fastened she would barely have an inch of skin on show. But for that to happen…she was going to have to invite Rufus in here. And then she was going to have to stand while he slipped button after silk-covered button through the tiny loops that traced a path up her spine. Would have to stand there and pretend that the thought of his fingers so close to her skin wasn't making her burn up with wanting him. Making her second-guess all the very good reasons why she had pulled away from that kiss the day before, and told him—and herself—that it wasn't going to happen.

'Rufus,' she called, crossing to the bedroom door and opening it a crack. 'I think I'm going to need some help here.'

She turned back from the mirror when she heard the creak of the door and Rufus stopped dead on the threshold, his lips slightly parted, his mess of red-brown curls falling over his forehead.

'You look…'

She blushed as she waited for him to finish that sentence, but, wherever it had been going, he seemed to have fallen permanently off track.

'I can't get the buttons,' she explained, turning so that he could see the back of the dress. 'Do you think you could…?'

He cleared his throat and she looked away. It was too much, trying to maintain eye contact when he was looking at her with such naked appreciation. Desire. Need. Her eyes clashed with his again in the pitted reflection of the cheval mirror and she let her lids close, avoiding what was impossible to ignore.

His fingers brushed against her skin as he slipped each button through a loop, and she finally let out a breath when he reached the nape of her neck, tumbling her hair over her shoulder to keep it out of the way.

She stared at her reflection. Was this…real? She'd told herself for so long that she would never want this. That marriage was a trap—that at some point, when you least expected it, it would become a source of misery. And yet, looking at herself wearing this dress, with Rufus standing just behind her, watching her, she could imagine wanting it. She wanted him. She understood for the first time how people could take that risk. Because some things couldn't be ignored or avoided. Not for ever. Sometimes you had to take a risk, because walking away was impossible.

She heard the click of a shutter and knew that Rufus had taken a photo of her, still looking wide-eyed in the mirror. He moved to change the angle, and she turned to look at him over her shoulder, wishing she could know what he was thinking. Whether the sight of her in a wedding dress had freaked him out as much as it had her. He looked intent, focused on the screen of his phone, and she wasn't sure whether the twin lines between his brows were concentration or something else. One of them was going to have to do something to break this tension before it broke her.

'Where should we do this?' she asked, and Rufus glanced up at her with surprise.

'What did Lara suggest?'

'The only thing she said was to stay away from cliché.'

'So let's do something different.'

'Like what?'

He smiled, and she melted a little, before pulling herself together. 'Let's go to the kitchen.'

Rufus walked ahead of her—the narrow skirt of the dress hampered her slightly on the stairs—and when she reached the kitchen Rufus was shaking icing sugar over the cooled mince pies and arranging holly leaves on a plate.

'I thought we were taking pictures?'

'We are. Come. Sit.'

He pulled out a chair at the table, and she noticed that he'd moved some decorations around, so that there would be boughs of greenery behind her in the shot.

He placed the plate of mince pies in front of her and she raised an eyebrow in question.

'You're meant to look like it's your wedding day. Which means you have to look like you're in love.'

'Which means mince pies?'

'I saw the look on your face when you ate the last one. It was something to behold.'

'You're laughing at me.'

'Trust me, I'm not. I'm very happy to have put that look on your face, by any means. Now, are you going to eat the pies?'

'It feels...exhibitionist, doing it with you watching. Knowing you're taking pictures.'

He held her gaze for a beat.

'In a good way?'

Heat rushed to her cheeks and she decided there was nothing that she could possibly say that wouldn't inflame the situation further, so she closed her eyes, resigned, and bit into a mince pie. She could feel the powdered sugar on her top lip, and the filling was still warm. There was a hint of something spiced in the pastry and as her eyes closed she heard the click of the shutter again. She flicked a glance up to Rufus, and caught him grinning, looking down at the phone screen.

'Perfect,' he said, and she felt a little strange, knowing that he was looking at her face on the screen as he spoke. 'Next stop, the great hall.' She narrowed her eyes at the amusement on his face but followed him anyway. He pulled a stool out in front of the Christmas tree and she watched as he grabbed an umbrella from the stand by the door and climbed up on the stool to remove the star from the top of the tree.

'How do you feel about climbing up here?' he asked, pulling a bench further away from the tree, and then looking down at the screen, kneeling down and playing with different angles.

'What did you have in mind?'

'I thought if you stand up here, and jump, and we get the angle right, it'll look like you've got the star on the top of the tree.'

She grinned. 'What could go wrong?'

'Want to try?'

She nodded, reaching to take the star from him, and taking his outstretched hand as she struggled to climb onto the bench with her lace skirt.

She frowned at Rufus, down on one knee with the phone. 'Am I close?' she asked, holding the star in what she thought was about the right place. Rufus dipped lower, until the phone was resting on the floor.

'I just can't get it. Can you jump?'

'Jump? In this?'

'I can't get the angle right. If you can't jump, I could lift you?'

'Someone needs to take the picture.'

'We can prop it up on something. Use the timer.'

'You've completely lost the plot.'

'Possibly. Do you trust me enough to give it a shot?'

She rolled her eyes. This was going to end in tears. She was sure of it. But she threw her hands up. 'Okay, if you think it will work. My life in your hands and all that.'

He set the timer on the phone and ran the three paces over to the bench. His hands were on her waist before the red light started flashing and she barely had a chance to catch her breath before he had lifted her straight in the air. She reached out to clutch his shoulders, squealing with the surprise of it, and as the flash popped she realised she hadn't even tried to get the star in the right place.

Rufus showed her the result on the phone and she couldn't help but laugh—her arms were flailing, her eyes were wide and her mouth wide open in a shocked grimace.

'I think we may need another attempt,' she said, looking up and meeting Rufus's eyes.

The second and third attempts weren't much better, and on the fourth Rufus's arms began to shake as he held her as high as he could. She managed to remember to reach the star into the spot that made the angles work, and the results were definitely improving.

'One more?' Rufus asked, scrolling through the results.

She nodded. 'One more. Might as well turn on burst mode so that we've got the best chance.'

Rufus fiddled with the settings and propped the phone back on the floor. She waited on the stool while Rufus ran over to her, climbing up beside her and then hoisting her in the air with a very unflattering grunt. She reached the star as best she could, and tried to remember to do something balletic with her legs so she didn't look as if she was launching herself at Rufus in a rage. The burst of shutter sounds stopped, and she dropped her hands to Rufus's shoulders to steady herself as he lowered her.

She was pressed flush against Rufus as he let her down beside him, his hands burning through the lace at the waist of her dress. 'Do you think we got it?' she asked, her hands still resting on his shoulders.

He blinked, and she wondered whether he had heard her. The way he was staring at her right now, he definitely looked as if he had other things on his mind. Her gaze dropped to his mouth just as his tongue darted out and flicked over his lower lip. She pulled herself away, remembering the talk she'd given them both yesterday. The one where she'd reminded herself of why she didn't want to do this. Rufus's arms tightened around her waist for just a fraction of a second before he let her go.

They filled another couple of hours with laughter and slightly dubious photography—Rufus found her sheepskin boots and a huge checked blanket, and dared her to take some pictures outside. She posed in the wedding dress with their snowmen, threw snowballs at the camera, and felt her cheeks and her nose redden with the cold, until she had to admit defeat and retreat to the fire.

* * *

'This afternoon I was thinking fire, blanket, book,' she said carefully. 'Want to join me?'

Under a blanket? Any day. Except he couldn't say that out loud. He shouldn't even be saying it in his head. He needed to be more careful than that. Couldn't slip into the flirting that seemed to come so easily to them when they weren't fighting it hard enough.

'I agree that sounds like the best kind of Christmas Eve plan. But there are some things I need to do first. How about we watch a movie in a bit?'

'Sure.' Jess shrugged. 'But what's so pressing on Christmas Eve? It's not like we can even leave the house.'

'I know. But the weather forecast is predicting more snow tonight. A lot of snow. I just want to make sure we're prepared.'

She narrowed her eyes. 'If you say so. Though I doubt much has changed since the last time you checked.'

That wasn't the point. At this moment, they were both dependent on him to ensure that they were safe and secure, and he couldn't just sit back and hope that nothing would go wrong.

'There are just a few more things I need to deal with. I'll be back soon. Promise.'

Jess's phone buzzed in her pocket as she watched Rufus walk away.

Oh, my God. Oh. My. God. What is going on with you guys?

Jess sighed. If only she knew she might be able to tell Lara.

Don't know what you're talking about. It's just for the Gram.

Then she took a few atmospheric shots of her cosy set-up in front of the fire and hoped that would satisfy her friend.

Cosy. But the followers want more of Rufus!

Followed by a whole line of aubergine emojis. Subtle.

Well, Jess knew how the followers felt. There were parts of her anatomy that wanted a whole lot more of Rufus too. It was a shame that following those desires would be such a terrible idea. Not least because their recent conversation had made it perfectly clear that he wanted her too.

Not only that, but he'd also seen exactly why she was holding back and made her question herself.

She knew that her reasons for not having a serious relationship held up to scrutiny. There was no way that she was opening herself up to the chronic misery that had been eating away at the family for a decade.

But they weren't necessarily talking marriage here. In fact, it was hard to imagine a scenario less likely to lead to a serious relationship than two strangers with nothing in common being holed up in a remote location before one of them returned to their home hundreds of miles away. Well, if her home was hundreds of miles away. In all the drama of Rufus's arrival, she'd half forgotten the job offer she'd received at the conference. But she'd promised to let them know her decision in the new year. She should be at least thinking about what she wanted to do for the next few years.

But even if she was living in the same county, she was hardly committing to him. No, what they had here were the perfect ingredients for a no-strings-attached fling.

She couldn't understand what was making her hold back. Rufus had told her already that he had his own reasons for not wanting to get involved—but did they extend to something casual? Something they could walk away from before the new year, and pretend had never happened? That was a very tempting thought. She snuggled deeper into the cushions on the sofa and let her eyes close as a series of very tempting scenarios for how they could spend the afternoon crossed her mind.

Rufus could find her here, in front of the fire, pull the blankets around them as they slipped down onto the rug in front of the hearth.

Or he could lift her in his arms, carry her up the stairs and across the gallery to deposit her on the giant bed that dominated her bedroom. He'd pick her up as if she weighed nothing and throw her on the bed, holding nothing back.

Her eyes flew open at the creak of a floorboard behind her, and she felt her cheeks flame because there was only one person it could be.

'Sorry, did I wake you?'

She answered *no* automatically, without thinking, and now she had to come up with a reason she was lying here with her eyes closed and her face burning red.

'Resting,' she told him lamely. Like an elderly aunt or a pre-schooler.

'Resting,' Rufus said with a smirk that made her wonder whether he had guessed the real answer—*I was just lying here fantasising about you carrying me up to bed with your big, manly arms.*

It was bad enough that she was thinking things like *big, manly arms* without him being able to guess how lame she was.

But from the look on his face, he didn't exactly seem to mind that.

'Did you sort out…whatever it was you needed to sort?' she asked, cursing the way that words deserted her when too much space in her brain was being occupied by inappropriate fantasies.

'Nearly done. I want to double-check the batteries in the torches in the upstairs rooms.'

'Do you really think that we'll lose power again?'

He shrugged. 'I don't like how the lights keep flickering. If the storm tonight is worse than yesterday then I wouldn't be surprised. Either way, I want us to be ready.

'Ready for action,' Jess said, and wanted to facepalm herself. Why did her mouth do this around him? Why couldn't she put sensible words in the right order, just because she was preoccupied with how much she liked his arms, and his beard, and his thighs? And the fact that he heard more than she said out loud.

'I just want to protect you,' Rufus said with a catch in his throat that Jess wasn't expecting. She leaned forward, resting her elbows on her knees. Well, this conversation just took a swerve, she thought.

'Why does that sound like we're talking about more than the blizzard?'

'We're not,' Rufus said, shaking his head. 'You're a guest here. I'm responsible for you.'

Right, and that was all there was to it…

'You've been responsible for a lot of people the past couple of years,' she said.

'What's that meant to mean?'

'It's not meant to mean anything. I just find it interesting that after a time taking on big family responsibilities now you're all anxious about protecting me when I never asked you to, never expected you to, and really don't need you to.'

He frowned. 'Fine. Then I'm doing it for myself, if you don't need my help.'

'It wasn't a personal insult, Rufus.'

'This has nothing to do with my family's circumstances,' he barked, angry.

'Fine. Forget I said anything.'

She wasn't sure how the conversation had descended into this. She'd obviously hit a nerve, but that didn't excuse Rufus turning into a bear about it.

'I'm sorry,' he said, dropping onto the other sofa. So much for her fantasies about blankets and fires and... well. She'd try not to think about too many of the details.

'The thought of the weather and how the house is going to stand up to it is putting me on edge. I shouldn't take it out on you. And I never wanted to imply that you need taking care of. Or that it should be my responsibility to do it.'

'Apology accepted,' Jess said, deciding not to prod any harder at the sore spot she'd identified. It was none of her business if he had hang-ups over what had happened with his family over the last couple of years. If he felt guilt about moving them out of Upton Manor. After the snow melted and Christmas was over, she'd never see him again. He could nurse his wounds—or ignore them—however he wanted, and she'd never think about it. Or him.

'Did you get much reading done?' he asked, and she seized gratefully the change of subject and atmosphere.

'About three sleepy pages,' she replied, sitting back on the sofa. Reading at a snail's pace with no footnotes. No pressure. Bliss.

'Are you still up for a movie? Now that the power is back?'

'Sure. If it means I don't have to leave this spot for the rest of the afternoon. Except maybe to get snacks.'

'Or dinner,' Rufus suggested.

'Right. Dinner. My body clock is so far off when I'm not working. Do you know what Lara had planned? She's the real foodie. I don't in any way pull my weight in the kitchen.'

'Come explore with me,' he said, standing and holding out his hand.

She raised hers, trying not to advertise the fact that she was having to brace herself for the idea of his skin on hers. It would be so much easier if she were immune to this. If she could just be indifferent. But if there was a key somewhere for turning these feelings off, she didn't have a damn clue where to start looking for it.

Her fingers met his and her hand slid into his palm as she tried to hide a wince of pleasure at the contact. Surely it shouldn't be so sudden, so immediate, so automatic—her response to him. He'd only touched her in a way he might help an elderly relative, and it had made her dizzy for him.

She wondered whether he felt it too. Whether the way he flexed his hand when he let go of hers was just easing some ache or pain, or if he had felt the same pulse of energy that she had.

She followed Rufus through to the kitchen and lingered by the door of the pantry while he scanned the shelves, aware of the heat that she had felt when they had shared that tight space the day before. But she had jumped away from him then out of instinct, because she hadn't wanted to find herself on a slippery slope that would inevitably lead to feelings and heartbreak. But she'd had time to think since then. To think, specifically, about what she wanted. Because the *who* was clear. She wanted Rufus. And she was starting to think that if she wanted, if they both wanted, they could lay down some hard boundaries about keeping this temporary and just take what they were both clearly craving.

Now all she had to do was find out if that was what Rufus wanted too. She wouldn't normally be hesitant in asking for what she wanted—but she wasn't normally in the position of having to live alongside the person who turned her down if that was the way this was going to go. She wasn't going to force a conversation that would make this situation more difficult. If it happened, it happened.

She realised her eyes had dropped to Rufus's arse just at the moment that he turned around and caught her. The corner of his mouth quirked up and she wondered if he was going to call her out on it.

'You thirsty?' he asked, brandishing a bottle of prosecco. She raised an eyebrow. Boy, was she.

'In the fridge for later?' she suggested, and she wondered whether Rufus was being deliberately provocative, because she was well and truly provoked. But she wasn't going to bite, or drink, yet. Not until she could be sure that they both knew what they wanted and were going to be able to extract themselves afterwards pain-free.

They gathered crackers, cheese, chutney and antipasti and created a luxury picnic spread on the coffee table by the fire. Jess tucked her legs under her and piled her plate high while Rufus looked through the Christmas movies on the streaming service.

'What do you reckon,' he asked as she spooned chutney onto her plate. 'Rom com? Action? Sentimental?'

'Action. Definitely action,' Jess replied. They were stirring up plenty of atmosphere without adding fictional romance to the mix. They settled on an eighties classic and Jess crossed the room to pull the heavy curtains, where the low winter sun was flooding the room with light and reflecting off the tv screen.

'It's really coming down out there now.'

Rufus came to stand behind her, reaching past her shoulder to pull the curtain back a little. The sky was heavy and dark, and the footprints they had made earlier were rapidly disappearing under a layer of fresh snow.

There was a draught coming from around the old leaded windowpanes, but Rufus's body was throwing out heat behind her. He smelled faintly of the fire and spices. All her Christmas fantasies rolled into one man.

She breathed in a big lungful of him, and couldn't help the smile on her face, just from knowing he was close. She could lean back, just a fraction, and she would be touching him. She could soak in that heat, feel her body relax into him. All as long as she could promise herself that she was going to be able to walk away afterwards.

She'd never had that problem before. But then, she'd never felt so drawn to someone either. The practicalities were going to take care of that. There were hundreds of miles between their lives. For now, at least. They had no reason to see one another again. It was two or three days. Four at most, surely. How hard could she fall for him in four days?

It had been forty-eight hours, and she'd managed to resist touching him, mostly. If things carried on moving at that pace... She wouldn't have done half the things she wanted to by the time she left. No, if she was going to act out even a quarter of the fantasies she'd been nursing since she'd clapped eyes on him, she was going to have to start asking for the things she wanted. Rufus had told her that he had his own reasons for not wanting to get too close. But if he wanted a fling, they could make this work.

One way to find out.

She turned her head to tell him exactly what she was thinking, and there was his mouth. She didn't want to talk any more. She glanced up and found his eyes on her, and then her eyes were on his mouth again, watching it move closer, until her eyelids fell closed and she gasped as she finally felt the brush of his lips against hers, just for a fraction of a second before he pulled away. She leaned in this time, reaching up on tiptoe to reach him, brushing their lips together a second time, feeling the curve of his mouth as he smiled. His fingers brushed against her jaw on their way to her hair, and she let his palm take the weight of her head. His other hand came up to thread into her hair, and she abandoned all control to him, feeling her face relax into a smile as his fingers wound through her hair and tilted her head. Taking his time to give her exactly what she wanted. When his mouth found hers again, it was hungrier, more demanding, and she opened her mouth to him, tasting him and taking what she wanted. Her neck and her toes were burning from trying to compensate for the difference in their height, and, just as she was starting to think that something was going to have to give, Rufus's hands left her hair and wrapped around her waist, lifting and turning her and pinning her to him so the whole of the front of her body was plastered against him. And he was every bit as hard and as soft and as hot as she had been imagining.

The cool draught from the window behind her raised hairs on the back of her neck, and all the time she was burning to be closer to him.

Her fingers eased between their bodies, seeking out the buttons in the soft flannel of his shirt, and she let out a growl of disappointment when she eventually found her way underneath and discovered more cotton rather than the bare skin she was desperate for.

Rufus broke the kiss, resting his forehead against hers, and all she could hear was the rapid gasps of their breath and the pounding of her blood in her ears.

'I've been wanting to do that since the minute you dragged me in here the other day.'

She laughed quietly. 'You were barely conscious.'

'And I still wanted to kiss you. I must have it bad,' he murmured.

She stiffened slightly. She'd got distracted and forgotten that she was meant to be doing this with boundaries in place. She probably should have got that out of the way before anyone started talking about having anything.

She tried to step away, before remembering that her toes had left the ground some time ago. She looked behind her, reaching for the windowsill, and Rufus let go as she hitched herself onto the cold tile.

'We should maybe talk about what that was,' she said, hoping that this wasn't going to throw too much cold water over the situation. 'And what it wasn't.'

Rufus ran a hand through his hair. 'Yeah. Well. I suppose we should.'

'You already know I don't do relationships. But if you wanted to do this, whatever this is, while we're here, then I'd like that. But nothing more.'

'I said I had it bad. Not that I was going to propose. You don't need to freak out.'

'I'm not freaking out. I just don't think it's fair to do this without us both having our cards on the table.'

'Good. I've seen your cards. Can we get back to doing what we were doing before we started talking about them?'

She grinned. If this was 'the talk' over and done with and they could get back to 'the kissing', then she was very okay with that.

She wrapped her legs around his hips in response and let out a squeak as he lifted her from the windowsill and carried her over to the sofa. He dropped back onto the seat so she fell in his lap, knees straddling his hips. She could just lean in and take everything that she had been fantasising about for the last two days. But she wasn't going to. Not yet. Not now she was allowed to just *look*. She'd been sneaking glances and trying not to let him see how she felt for too long, and the freedom to look at him without hiding how thirsty she was for him was almost as good as kissing him. At the very least, it was a delicious appetiser.

'You're not kissing me,' Rufus said, raising his eyebrows a fraction as his hands moved lazily from her butt along her thighs, leaving a path of heat in their wake. 'Why?'

She shrugged. 'I like looking at you.'

'I like you looking at me.' She lifted a hand to his chest, undid another button or two, and slipped her hands inside. 'I like you touching me.'

'Good. I was planning on doing it some more.'

Her hands explored lower, reaching for the hem of his T-shirt and pulling until she encountered warm skin.

'Don't stop,' Rufus gasped and she leaned in and dropped a kiss on his lips, and Jess moaned as his hands found her arse again. She'd meant to give him a playful peck before getting back to the looking. But she was drawn in by the heat of it, and couldn't drag herself away.

Rufus's hands went higher, to her waist, his fingers tightening and pulling her closer, until she wanted to climb inside his skin.

'God, it's amazing kissing you,' Rufus said, pausing to draw breath. 'You taste of mince pies. Like Christmas. I want to unwrap you.'

She laughed at the cheesy line, but she was with him on the sentiment. She lifted her arms above her head and welcomed the touch of cooler air on the band of skin exposed around her midriff. He grabbed the three layers of sweaters and lifted them over her head, leaving her in the silky slip that she had put closest to her skin that morning. Under the thermal layer that Rufus had found so funny yesterday.

Not so funny now that it was the only thing between her and the slight chill in the air that the fire hadn't banished.

Rufus's fingertips trailed down her arms, skimming the goose bumps, and then left her breathless as he flipped her back on the sofa, covering her with his body and pulling a blanket over the pair of them, creating a cocoon of warmth around them, a bubble of heat inside the old, isolated house.

She froze for a second at the sudden change of pace, and Rufus drew back, looking at her carefully.

'Is this okay?' Rufus asked.

'I...uh...' It was a struggle to form a coherent thought, never mind string words together, and the truth was, she wasn't sure what she wanted right now. Rufus sat up though, putting a little space between them. 'Maybe we need a breather,' he said. 'Christmas Eve is meant to be all about anticipation, and if we're not careful we're going to have torn through all our gifts before we even make it to Christmas Day.'

'Anticipation,' Jess said, pleased that Rufus had read the situation, read *her* so well. 'Got it. Good idea.'

Rufus felt as though he'd barely breathed for the past day, anticipating these moments when he was close enough to breathe Jess in, and now he was tearing himself away for the promise of more anticipation.

But really he needed to get his head together. They'd talked about what this was—or what it wasn't, as Jess had been so keen to specify. But she obviously still had her reservations, and there was no way that he was steamrolling them into something that she might regret. He didn't want to rush this. He wanted to savour it. Savour her.

'Where are you going?' Jess asked, propping herself up on her elbows to watch him as he drew the curtains and chucked a couple of logs on the fire before he sat down and pulled Jess into his lap.

'We said a breather; I didn't know you meant you were going to leave,' Jess murmured, turning her head and pressing a kiss to his throat.

CHAPTER SIX

'YOU CAN'T SEND THAT,' Rufus said with a grunt, looking at the photo on his phone screen.

'Why not?'

'Because you can see what I'm thinking.'

'Really? What were you thinking?' But she was only asking to tease him. He looked hot. Heated. He was looking at her as if he was counting the minutes until he could peel away her layers of soft, cosy knitwear to get to what was underneath.

It was undoubtedly a very good look on him.

And one that she wanted to keep for herself.

Just for the next few days.

After that she would give him back to the universe and have no claim on that particular expression. Jess pinged the photo to her own phone, and then deleted it, trying not to think too hard about the stab of regret she felt at the thought that soon—way too soon—she would be giving up the right to make him feel that way.

But she didn't have to do it yet.

She put the phone down, curled her hands into the front of Rufus's sweater and pulled him down for a kiss. And before she closed her eyes, she got another glimpse of it. That look that said he was going to burn her alive and make her thank him for it. She would. She would thank him and repay the favour and then he'd look at her like that again, and the house would become a black hole, pulling the emotion out of her. Making her spill more and more of herself.

She couldn't allow that to happen.

This was just a kiss. It might—she hoped, desperately—lead to *just* sex.

That was just bodies and skin and mouths. It was good and then it was over, and she wouldn't have to think. She never regretted what she walked away from because she knew the alternative to walking. The alternative was staying, the way her mum stayed. The way her dad stayed. And then you held those positions until you were empty. Until you'd given up on and forgotten the idea that life could be anything but that.

And she wouldn't do that to herself.

Walking had always been easy before. But she'd never had to walk away from Rufus. If she'd met him out in the real world—the one with passable roads and mobile phone coverage, she would have seen the danger right off. She would never have allowed herself the luxury of kissing him. But this wasn't the real world. This was a snowbound winter fairy tale that she'd be driving away from just as soon as the tyres on her rental car could handle the Yorkshire snow, and their paths would never cross again.

She would kiss him goodbye, and delete his number, and block him on Instagram and forget everything that happened here. She glanced at the photo again. But she wasn't sure how she was ever meant to forget that someone had once looked at her like that.

But that was the only plan she had, so she was going to have to go with it.

Her phone rang as she was looking at the screen, and she broke away from Rufus with a start.

'I… We… It's Lara,' she said, looking at the screen. 'She's video calling.'

She answered the call, too flustered to think about what else she should do, as Rufus ducked away from her so she wasn't left with trying to explain to Lara why they were sitting far closer than was reasonable for two people who hadn't just had their tongues in each other's mouths.

'Hey, Jess. What're you up to?' Lara asked. 'I loved the snowy pictures. Why did you stop? Did something happen to distract you there in your isolated manor with no outside interference? I can't imagine what that might be.'

Jess felt colour rising to her cheeks and wished she had the ability to hide her feelings from Lara. But her best friend had known her too long and too well to risk it.

'I knew it!' Lara cried, and Jess glanced behind her to make sure that Rufus was out of earshot.

'I don't know what you think you know, Lara, but you're wrong. There's nothing going on here.'

'Right. I don't believe you for a second. Just try and fit some more photography in around your extracurriculars, will you? I'm sending you a list of shots that I need. Get them to me as soon as possible. We are building some momentum here and it's killing me that I'm not there to do this myself. Whatever it is that you're not telling me, you can get back to it when I've got my content.'

Jess tried to hide a smile, not wanting to give away any more than she already had.

'One,' she said, rolling her eyes at the phone, 'I'm not up to anything. Two, we sent you photos this morning. Photos I froze my fingers off and got snow in my hair for. Three, stop being a drama queen. Send me the list and we'll get to work. Because there's nothing else I'd rather be doing right now.'

'Good. Send them over as soon as you can. And if you get into anything really extracurricular then be sure to keep those to yourselves. I'm not sure that either I or my followers could cope with that.'

'Get your mind out of the gutter, Lara,' she said with an affectionate smile. 'I'm hanging up now. Goodbye.'

'I take it we've got more work to do,' Rufus said, coming up behind her, wrapping his arms around her waist as soon as the coast was clear.

'Apparently we've been slacking. She wants more content. Lots more.'

'Sounded as though she might have wanted to know what we've been up to instead.'

'I wouldn't know what to tell her. We kissed. We agreed to walk away when we leave here. It's hardly the fairy-tale stuff her imagination is probably cooking up. Look, this is private, and I want to keep it that way. I don't want this thing to become something that generates clicks, you know. I want to keep it just between us.'

He turned her round in his arms, brushed his lips against hers.

'Which is why I'm so glad we're the only people here right now.' She let herself sink into the kiss, drowning in the heat and the size of him as he wrapped his arms around her shoulders, until his warmth and weight and bulk were all around her. Until her phone buzzed in her pocket, a message from Lara, no doubt, reminding her that she was on to her, expecting her to drop her extra-curriculars—as she put it—and concentrate on content. She dragged herself away from Rufus, immediately missing the warmth of him.

'Me too. Really. But Lara is not going to leave this alone, so we had better get it over with.'

She pulled her phone out of her pocket and scanned down the list. There were requests for various flatlays. Fine, she knew what she was doing with those: they were an Instagram staple. She just needed some props, a pretty surface to lay them on, good lighting and a steady hand to take a shot directly from above. But the full Christmas dinner would have to wait until tomorrow.

'Looks like we're going to be busy,' Rufus said, reading over her shoulder.

'This isn't exactly what I had planned for the rest of the day,' she said, in a snit. That eyebrow rose higher.

'You had plans? I want to hear them.'

She smiled as she raised her eyes to meet his. 'Who said they involved you?'

He let out a sound that could only be described as a growl as he dragged her back close, knocking her phone to the ground.

'They better had. Otherwise I'll start making plans of my own.'

She smiled as his lips met hers. 'Fine. I'm sure I can make room for you, if you insist.'

'Oh, I absolutely insist.'

It was only as she felt her body relax into his that she remembered that last time she'd been this close to him they had been interrupted and if they didn't get on with taking these bloody pictures then Lara would be interrupting them again. If there was one thing that she was sure about her plans it was that there was no space for Lara in them anywhere.

'We need to get through this list. I know Lara, and she will start cracking the whip if we don't get on with it.'

'Fine, I'm sure you're right,' he said, releasing her and reaching for where his phone had dropped to the floor.

'Well, we can't do the food today,' he said. 'The turkey will take four or five hours in the oven. But we can crack through the flat-lays.'

Jess scrolled through the list again, which had grown since the last time she looked. She was sure that Lara was trolling her, because since they'd last spoken there seemed to be a lot more call for pictures that involved her on a bed, with rumpled-up blankets, cable-knit socks and a tray of props beside her. And she knew that Lara knew it was impossible to get these kinds of shots without help. Lara had once drowned an iPhone in a full cup of coffee trying to get the perfect bird's-eye shot by sticking her phone to the ceiling. No, Lara knew that this would mean recruiting Rufus to photograph her lounging in bed, and if that wasn't such a deliciously enticing thought then she would definitely have been mad at Lara for meddling.

'Pictures in bed?' Rufus asked, raising an eyebrow. Her cheeks heated again, wondering if she and Rufus were having matching fantasies.

'Not like that,' Jess said, tapping the Instagram icon and pulling up a few pics from Lara's feed to show him what she meant. Rufus scrolled through, looking thoughtful.

'This is what she wants?'

'As close as we can get it.'

'Do I hang from the ceiling to get that angle?'

She thought of the afternoon she had spent in Lara's flat clambering on the bed frame, grabbing hold of ceiling lights, trying to get the perfect angle and lighting while keeping her feet and her shadow out of the frame.

That first time they'd ended up collapsing in a giggling heap in the middle of the bed once the iPhone-meets-coffee-cup disaster had been cleared up.

'There is generally climbing, yes.'

'And you're okay with this? Pictures of you in bed?'

She shrugged. 'There's nothing sexy about it. The more layers of knitwear the better, as far as Lara's Instagram is concerned. She's usually up to her ears in cables and cashmere.'

'Then I guess we should make a start. What do we need?'

Jess reeled off a list of things they would need from the kitchen, from a tray of tea and snacks to a roll of foil for a reflector. Thankfully the snow outside was bouncing around plenty of natural light, so they shouldn't need too much editing. She was gathering blankets and cushions, considering colours and textures, when she heard footsteps behind her and Rufus shouldered open the door.

'This looks intense,' he said, taking in the piles of textiles she had gathered up as she walked through the house. He left the tray on the sideboard and came to stand beside her. 'This one lived on my bed,' he said, pulling a soft quilt from the pile.

'You didn't want to take it with you when you moved out?'

'It wouldn't look right in my flat. It's always been here. It would be weird to see it in a new place.'

She realised she hadn't actually considered where Rufus lived now. He was so much a part of the house, the house was so much a part of him, that she couldn't imagine him anywhere else.

'Where do you live?' she asked, and the surprise on his face made her wonder whether he'd forgotten too. Whether he was as caught up in this fantasy as she was.

'Oh, I share a flat in Upton with my brother. The village. I need to be close to the manor house for maintenance stuff.'

'I can't imagine you living anywhere but here.'

He shrugged. 'I moved out years before Mum and Dad had to leave. I was so focused on my career. I'd set myself a goal, and sacrificed everything trying to achieve it. I never expected to spend my whole life here but…'

'But you expected to come back. One day.'

'One day. Yes. I thought I'd spend my dotage here. And so did my dad. I guess we're both coming to terms with that.'

'Does it help if I tell you again that none of this is your fault?'

'I'm not sure how that can be true, when I was the one who abandoned this place. Abandoned my dad to deal with it all himself. But I appreciate the sentiment. How about you distract me instead?'

She felt her lips curve into a wry smile, aware that Rufus was quite deliberately changing the subject. But there was no point pushing him to talk if he wasn't ready.

'And how would you like me to distract you?' she asked.

He looked her up and down. 'First, by masterminding these photos so your phone goes quiet.'

Right on cue, it buzzed with another message notification and she knew Lara was still sending through her instructions.

'And then I'm going to trust your imagination.'

Good. Because her imagination was proving to be exceptionally vivid today, and she was looking forward to putting some of her ideas into action. All the more so now that she knew Rufus was along for the ride and wasn't going to ask more of her than she had to give.

She layered up blankets on the bed, and then dug through her bag looking for the knee-high socks she knew that she'd packed. She snagged them from the bottom of the holdall and pulled them on over her leggings.

She knew what this really needed was a plaid shirt, which she didn't have with her. But Rufus did. But it was a little early in this…whatever this was…to start wearing his clothes. Or undressing in front of him, come to that. She looked down at the soft fake cashmere she'd pulled on that morning. The colours and textures worked with what she had on the bed. It'd do for now. But if she found herself wearing Rufus's shirt at some point over the next few days… It wouldn't be the worst thing that could happen.

'Where do you need me?' Rufus asked as she pulled her socks up to her knees. Well, wasn't that the question…

'Um, on the bedside table? Are you okay to stand on it?'

'On the four-hundred-year-old antique? Sure.'

'Oh, God.'

'It's fine,' Rufus said, chuckling. 'It's survived four centuries. I think it can handle Instagram.'

'Right.' This had better be worth it. 'On that side of the bed though,' she said, gesturing over to the side near the window. 'We want the natural light behind you.'

'You're good at this.'

She lifted her shoulders and let them drop. 'When Lara started out it was mainly the two of us messing around, making things up as we went along.'

'And you weren't tempted to follow her into being an influencer?'

She shook her head. 'I like my research. My job. I help Lara out because she's my friend and I love her, but I wouldn't want to do it all the time.'

She climbed into the middle of the bed, poured tea into the cup that Rufus had put on the tray with its saucer, and tried to arrange her limbs in a way that would get maximum knitwear into the shot and hide as much of her face as possible, all without spilling the tea. She'd seen Lara do this dozens of times, but had never tried contorting herself into these positions before.

'How's it looking?' she asked Rufus, who had one foot on the corner of the bed, and one on the bedside table.

'You look beautiful,' he said, checking his phone. She felt the blood rise in her cheeks at his compliment.

'This is meant to be about the house,' she reminded him.

'Yeah, that's holding its own too,' he said, snapping a couple more pictures.

Jess smiled to herself, deciding not to push any further. The sexual chemistry was crackling as tangibly as the logs in the fire on the other side of the room, providing a hum of tension in her belly. A warm glow full of promise for later.

Rufus leaned a little closer, bringing the camera right overhead, and she turned slightly, letting her hair fall in a curtain to block her from view. She'd been on Lara's feed before, but wasn't wild about becoming the face of Upton Manor. That was totally Rufus's job. So if she could duck behind her hair, she absolutely would. Except Rufus seemed determined to capture her features. He leaned in closer still, causing the tray to wobble, and she looked up in alarm.

The click of the phone sounded just as her eyes reached the lens of the camera, and Rufus hastily backed up onto the bedside table and then dropped to the floor.

'Wow,' he said, looking at the screen. And Jess had to admit, she could see why he'd said it. He'd captured her as her eyes had widened when the tray wobbled. The doe-eyed result was pretty arresting, even if she said so herself. Rufus scrolled back so she could see some of the other shots and they had done Lara proud. The room looked beautiful, and she was happy that she'd managed to get all her limbs in the right place to set it off.

Rufus pulled up Lara's social media feeds and swiped through some of the shots that Jess had highlighted for him earlier.

'You know…' he said, looking closely at the photos '…if I were playing spot the difference here…' he pointed the phone in Jess's direction '… Lara seems to have socks on bare legs. Whereas you're layered up. If we were going for total @*lara* authenticity here, we need to match.'

'Are you offering to strip off for the camera?' Jess asked.

'I was offering to help you out of those leggings,' he said with a smirk. 'Just for artistic purposes, of course.'

Jess laughed, a little nervously. 'You're an absolute scoundrel. We're meant to be working.'

'A scoundrel?' Rufus's crow's feet crinkled as he smiled. 'Has anyone been a scoundrel in the last century? I've never been accused of being a bad 'un before.'

'Maybe Upton Manor is getting to me,' Jess said, leaning back on her elbows. She had no intention of sending Lara pictures of her wearing long socks with bare thighs. But that didn't mean that they couldn't have a little fun with the set-up they had here. It would be a shame to waste the opportunity to lose some clothes for a perfectly unimpeachable reason.

'Okay,' she said, letting just one corner of her mouth rise in a hint of a smile. 'Chuck a couple more logs on the fire, though. It's starting to feel cool in here.'

Rufus's eyes widened in surprise before his face broke into a grin as he walked to the fire and built it up. Good, Jess thought. He was planning on settling in for a while. She had an enormous bed, the most picturesque, romantic setting she could imagine, a gorgeous man doing her bidding, and she had every intention of pretending that this was real life for as long as she could get away with it.

She moved the props off the bed, and then crawled back among the nest of blankets, leaning back on her elbows as Rufus tended the fire.

He turned to her with a wolfish grin, before climbing up onto the foot of the bed, and pulling her towards him by the ankle. She laughed as he crawled towards her with intent, until his hands were planted either side of her head, his knees astride her hips. She turned her head and nipped at his wrist, smiling at his gasp of surprise and then squeaking when he pressed a kiss to her lips. And just as she was about to pull him down and deepen the kiss, he was gone, sitting astride her hips and smiling down at her.

'You bite,' he said.

She propped herself back on her elbows, closing her eyes for a second in pleasure at the weight of him on top of her.

'Sometimes. When I'm pinned...'

'I should let you go, then,' he said, but she grabbed the front of his sweater before he could move.

'Don't you dare.' She pulled him down for another kiss, firm but still sweet. And didn't object in the slightest when his hands smoothed down her thighs, across the sensitive spot behind her knees, towards the tops of her socks.

He pulled away, rolled on his side and propped his head on his hand, as he pulled her knee up. His fingers dipped into the top of her sock, teasing again at the back of her knee. Jess lifted herself up on her elbows again, watching. Her eyes locked on Rufus's fingers as they continued their exploration, slowly easing down her sock, until the skin of her ankle was exposed. She gasped as his fingers brushed against bare flesh for the first time. He looked up and met her eyes, his face consumed by a smug, masculine smile. She rolled her eyes, leaned forward and kissed him, before nudging him with her knee. The other sock came off considerably more quickly, and then she was lying beside him, his face intimately close as his fingers trailed along the waistband of her leggings. She bit down on her bottom lip, and watched his expression as he looked up. 'Okay?'

he asked, nudging her sweater up, and she nodded enthusiastically as he hooked a finger under the elastic and started to inch them slowly down.

'Still okay?' he asked, and she pulled lightly at his sweater again, until she could reach to plant another kiss on his lips.

'Don't you dare stop.'

She sank back on the bed as the fabric passed her hips, and she had a brief moment to thank her morning self that she'd pulled on lace this morning. Had she known? Thought? Hoped? That this was where the day was headed? Of course she had. This was everything that she'd wanted when she'd woken that morning.

'So pretty under all these layers,' Rufus breathed, pressing a kiss between her belly button and the top of the lace. The soft hair of his beard tickled her, and she squirmed with pleasure. But then his mouth was gone.

Rufus watched, entranced, as inch after inch of soft, creamy thigh was revealed. He was certain he hadn't breathed in minutes. Maybe hours. And he couldn't now. Not when he was so close to Jess and fighting to keep his self-control.

He let out his breath as he finally slipped the fabric over her feet, and then skimmed his hands up smooth shins, past the point he'd found behind her knees and up to her waist.

It was only when he was sure that he had a handle on his self-control that he kissed her. And he only allowed himself a second before he pulled away. Getting naked hadn't been the plan here, and he had to remember that.

He reached for the socks, where they lay abandoned on the bed, and Jess looked up at him languorously as he knelt and pulled the sock over her toes, and then slid it up, letting his fingers lead the way, and drinking in Jess's gasps, the way that she let her eyes fall closed as she caught her bottom lip between her teeth and bit down.

'You're putting clothes back *on* me?' she asked between breaths as he reached for her other foot.

'Of course,' he said, letting his face break into a smile. 'We need these photos, right? Otherwise we'd be downstairs drinking tea and watching a movie.'

'Right,' she said, her voice breathy and distant. 'Tea. Movie.'

Except when he pulled the sock up, and his fingers brushed higher, she arched her back off the bed, and he nearly lost his resolve.

She pulled him down to her by his sweater again, and it really was bloody brilliant when she did that. As far as he was concerned, she could grab him and kiss him every moment that they had here together. If it wasn't for one thing. He'd told her he was taking her clothes off for the sake of these photographs and he wasn't having her on. If she wanted to seduce him on her own time, on her own terms, he would let her do that. Once he'd done exactly what he'd promised to do, and not a thing more.

'Where are you going?' Jess demanded as he pulled himself away from her.

'This wasn't for me,' he said, gesturing to the milky white skin showing between her socks and her sweater. He picked up his phone and climbed back onto the bedside table.

'Are you...?' Jess turned to look at him. 'What are you doing up there? Get back here. I wasn't done with you.'

He smirked, took a photograph and showed her the

screen. She looked divine in the warm afternoon light. Her lips pouted with dismay. Climbing back down, he regarded her all stretched out on the bed. She turned onto her side and regarded him carefully.

He smiled. 'It's Christmas Eve. It's all about anticipation. And,' he added softly, 'it's about making sure we both know what we want. And what we don't want. I was invited into your bedroom to act as photographer. If you want me for anything else, you're going to have to ask me for it. Specifically. Very specifically.'

'I hate you,' Jess breathed, dropping back on the bed and breaking their gaze, looking up at the canopy of the bed.

CHAPTER SEVEN

'No, YOU DON'T,' he told her confidently, leaning in to press the briefest of kisses to her lips. 'Now, let's get the rest of these pictures done for Lara. I want the whole evening with no chance of interruptions.'

'You do realise I'm going to have to put my clothes back on for that to happen.'

He groaned as she pulled on her leggings and layered up thermal socks. Anticipation might have made Christmas Eve magical when he was a kid, but it was downright killing him now. He watched Jess as she worked, taking a couple of pictures from different angles, dipping down until her eyes were level with the mattress. From there she got the twinkling lights and the crystal bowl from the sideboard in the background. And from a different angle, the window and the fire, the bright light darkening the foreground into moody silhouettes.

'I like that one,' Rufus said. 'The house looks lived-in. Cosy.'

He leant against the side of the bed as they scrolled through. Then she turned abruptly.

'Don't move,' she instructed. He rested his forearms on his knees while she adjusted something on the touch screen and then leaned back, pointing the camera in his direction.

'I like this one,' she said, showing him the result. 'It was missing heart. It needed you. You belong here.'

'Yes. Well. I used to.' He pushed himself to his feet. 'Let's get this finished.'

Two hours later, Jess scrolled through the pictures on the phone screen, trying to decide which to send to Lara. Not the ones of her on the bed, bare-thighed, her eyes full of lust. No, those were for her and Rufus only. But the others she could share. And her favourite: Rufus leaning back against the bed, arms propped up on his elbows. Lost in thought. Deliciously shaggable. Looking every inch as if he was as much a part of the house as the walls and the floorboards. No wonder he was mourning the loss of his family home. If only she could make him see that it wasn't his fault. But she knew it wasn't her job to do that. He just had to decide whether he wanted to hold on to that guilt or not.

She wondered whether that guilt had anything to do with those reasons he'd mentioned for not wanting a relationship. Not that it affected her either way. She'd been as clear with herself as she had been with Rufus that this was a strictly time-limited offer. Whether or not he was going to make something work with someone else once she was just a fond memory was none of her business. She had to make sure that she remembered that, otherwise she was going to find herself in trouble.

Rufus dropped beside her on the sofa and she leant into him without taking her eyes from the screen. It was just so…perfect…that he was there and she could do everything that she'd been wanting to do since he'd fallen so dramatically into this house and into her life.

Well, almost everything that she wanted to, until they'd put the brakes on things earlier. As if she wasn't at breaking point already. They'd studiously avoided touching each other while they'd taken the rest of the photos that Lara had requested.

She'd got Rufus in front of the camera as often as she could. He was the one who had wanted to show this house with personality, and heart, and he'd done just that. Had shown just how much he was a part of the structure of this house, and how it was a part of him. And the results were stunning, and bittersweet, because this wasn't Rufus's home any more, and might never be again.

But they'd done exactly what Lara had asked of them, and they had to hope that it would turn the business around, and that Upton Manor would at least stay in the family rather than having to be sold off. She highlighted the pictures that she wanted to send and synced them with Lara's cloud account.

'Are we done?' Rufus asked, pulling up the list and scrolling through.

'Everything but Christmas dinner. I've already told her that will have to wait until tomorrow, so I think we're officially off duty.'

'That is very good news,' Rufus said, his arm dropping to wind around her waist, and then dragging her onto his lap until she was as close to him as she'd been desperate to be for the past few hours. 'I've wanted this. You. All afternoon.'

'I thought Christmas Eve was all about anticipation,' Jess murmured.

Rufus groaned and glanced at the clock above the mantel. 'It's hours until midnight. Well, at least let me feed you, because I'm pretty sure that you've completely missed the fact that it's dinner time. And then we could actually watch the movie that we said we were going to several hours ago.'

'And when you say we're going to watch the movie...'

'I'm open to distractions. When you're ready, if you're ready.'

His hands came up to cup her behind, pulling her down more firmly on top of him, tipping her forward until her forehead rested against his.

'But first, let's eat,' he said, pulling the blanket over her legs. And dropping a last kiss on her lips before he left through the door to the kitchen.

Thank God Jess's hesitation earlier had forced him to slow down. Because if they hadn't agreed to this breather, this chance to let the anticipation grow, he was pretty sure he would have lost his mind by now. But it was only a stay of execution; he didn't think for a minute that they were both going to keep a lid on their self-control for much longer.

And he didn't need to examine his feelings. They had both agreed that they weren't letting feelings into whatever it was they were going to share while they were here.

He boiled some water for pasta. He'd stocked the freezer with a rich ragu sauce that would be perfect with tagliatelle and a grating of fresh parmesan.

Was he carb-loading them before a long night? All right, well, that wasn't the worst idea he'd ever had.

He'd had a *lot* of ideas, and had no intention of getting any sleep.

Jess wandered through to the kitchen and leaned against the doorframe. 'That smells delicious. You were right. I absolutely need you to feed me.'

'See. You should trust me.'

'I do,' she said, her voice losing its playful tone. 'I trust you.'

He crossed the kitchen, throwing the tea towel he'd been using over his shoulder. Cupping both of her cheeks in his hands, he kissed her slowly, sinking them both against the doorframe.

'Good. I'd never hurt you.'

'I know.' She hesitated though, and he knew there was more to that sentence.

'But…' he prompted.

'No buts,' Jess said. 'These few days are what they are. It's what we agreed. What we both want.'

'If you've changed your mind—' he started, before Jess interrupted.

'I haven't. Not about what I want. Not what about what I don't want. I'm not sure what's making me feel melancholy.'

'Christmas blues? Are you missing your family? I know you said Christmas is hard with your parents. But sometimes the hard thing is still better than the… alternative thing.'

She rested her forehead against his chest and he threaded one hand into her hair, pulling the other tight around her waist.

'I do miss them. It doesn't make sense to be sad about it.'

'What's sense got to do with anything?' he said into

Jess's hair. 'If you're sad, you're sad. There's nothing wrong with that.'

She looked up at him from under her fringe.

'Thank you,' she said. 'You're sweet.'

'Hmm. Don't tell anyone.'

She grinned.

'Who would I tell?'

A timer went off behind them and Jess turned towards the noise. 'Tell me I can eat whatever it is that smells so amazing.'

He smiled. 'Why don't you pour some wine?' He gestured to where he'd left two glasses and a bottle on the table 'And I'll serve up.'

When he found her at the table, bringing two steaming bowls, Jess let out a moan of pleasure. Rufus was right. Being away from work and out of her usual routine was messing with her body—she was absolutely starving. Thank goodness Rufus was here to remind her to eat, because left to her own devices she wasn't sure that she would be able to think beyond her need to be close to him.

She only had a moment to thank fate that she had met him here. Now. Where they had strict boundaries in place, imposed by geography and the weather. Because if she'd met him at home, at a party, in a bar, she would have run a mile. She would have recognised their chemistry, how potent it was, and she would have known that she wouldn't be able to handle it. But here, she knew she didn't have to rely on her self-control to keep things simple. Circumstances would mean that she couldn't fall deeper into this than she could pull herself out. Circumstances made this safe. Made Rufus safe. Though when she thought about it, it wasn't Rufus she had to worry about. It was her own mind, her own heart, that she had to be careful of. But here they had a built-in escape route. She didn't have to keep her defence guarded, because this wasn't going to last more than a few days, whatever happened. Which meant that she could sink into tonight—whatever adventures it brought—with no reservations.

And she was going to positively *dive* into this pasta. Was Rufus so intent on feeding her up because he had big plans for her tonight? If so, she was totally on board with that. He should start mainlining carbs himself, because all this thinking time they were giving themselves was helping her come up with a long, detailed list of everything she wanted to do with him.

'This is incredible,' she said, taking her first mouthful of pasta. 'How did you knock this up so quickly?'

'It was in the freezer. I cheated. I told you that food's part of the deal. Sometimes I come in and do a supper club thing, sometimes I just stock the fridge and freezer, depending on what the guests want.'

'Well, I don't know which one of you I love more right this minute. Lara for asking you or you for cooking it.'

'I am fully prepared to take the credit,' Rufus said with a smile that seemed slightly strained. Was it because she'd said the L word? Surely he couldn't read too much into it when she'd dumped him into the same category as her best friend. It was the same sort of simple, platonic love that she'd feel for anyone who cooked her a meal this delicious. She decided to take a large sip of wine, and hope that the atmosphere eased without her having to address the issue head on.

They gradually eased back into small talk as the

pasta in her bowl rapidly receded, and by the time she eventually laid down her spoon and fork he was back to giving her long, heated looks that made her want to start tearing off items of clothing. His. Hers. She didn't really care, as long as some garments started hitting the floor fast. He met her gaze and smiled.

'I know exactly what you're thinking,' Rufus said. She thought for a second of telling him he couldn't possibly read her mind. If it wasn't for the fact she knew that what she was thinking was written all over her face.

'And…so?' she prompted, hoping that his mind-reading abilities extended to giving her exactly what she wanted.

'Pudding first,' Rufus said, and, although she had been hoping to skip straight past it, if the dessert was anything like as decadent and rich and delicious as the main course, it would be worth putting their evening on hold for, just for a few more minutes. No longer, though. She was still hungry. And not a saint.

'Shall we take these through with us?' Rufus asked, pulling a couple of chocolate puddings from the Aga and turning them out into bowls. Thick chocolate sauce oozed from their centres and ran down the sides, settling in a pool of rich, melty goodness, so delicious-smelling that it was enough to wipe any disrobing plans she'd had clear from her brain. Well, for as long as it would take to devour that pudding.

She snagged the glasses and wine bottle from the table while Rufus brought the pudding, and then she burrowed into the blanket nest that they'd abandoned earlier. Rufus handed her the pudding and a spoon, and she couldn't even wait until he was sitting beside her before she took that first delicious mouthful.

She moaned with pleasure, and by the time she opened her eyes Rufus was sitting next to her with his eyes full of intent.

'I think I'm just going to eat this until midnight.'

'I'm not sure I'm that chuffed about being replaced by a pudding.'

'Well, you made the pudding. So it's not like you're *not* entertaining me.'

'And yet I can think of ways I'd rather be doing that.'

'*And yet…* Christmas Eve, anticipation, et cetera.'

He lifted his spoon to his mouth, and she watched, enraptured.

'You're right, though. If we're going to resist temptation, this is as good an alternative as I can think of.'

'Amen to that,' Jess said, loading up her spoon again.

She sank deeper into the sofa cushions as Rufus reached for the remote. 'Shall we hit play?'

'Mmm,' Jess agreed, her mouth still full of chocolate. Rufus laughed as he pressed play and the first notes of the opening credits rang out of the sound bar under the screen.

Jess's spoonfuls of pudding grew smaller and smaller, eking out the sensual pleasure contained in the bowl for as long as possible. And—she shot a sideways look at Rufus—perhaps delaying the moment when they would both have their hands free.

The great hall was lit with just the sparkling lights from the tree and a few candles on the sideboard, one of which must be responsible for the delicious spiced winter berry scent that was currently diffusing around the room.

When her bowl was scraped clean, and her spoon

licked of any trace of chocolate, she looked up and found Rufus watching her again. Amused.

'I was worried for the pattern on the bowl.'

'If it had tasted as good as the chocolate did, it wouldn't have survived.'

Rufus laughed. 'Great commitment,' he said. She decided to completely ignore the C word, as he had with the L word earlier. There was no reason it should freak her out, all out of context as it was.

Rufus pulled the bowl from her hands and put it on the coffee table along with his own.

'Come here,' he said, pulling her close and wrapping his arms around her waist from behind.

He wondered how long he would last before he broke and kissed her. He hadn't been exaggerating earlier when he'd told her how much he loved kissing her. It had hit him like a punch to the gut, that moment when her lips had met his and confirmed this attraction was entirely mutual and entirely explosive.

It had taken all his self-control to keep that kiss light. To invite rather than demand. And then when Jess had told him what she wanted, and it fitted entirely with what *he* wanted—walk away, no strings—he'd wondered if he'd dreamed her up.

His wrist brushed against bare skin as he wrapped his arms around her waist, and Rufus gritted his teeth as he demurely pulled down Jess's top and tucked the blanket around her shoulders. It was a good job pulling the curtains had left them almost in darkness, because he was sure that if he could see what he was feeling right now, the ping of his self-control snapping would be audible three counties over.

* * *

Glass shattered in a hail of bullets and Rufus reached for the TV remote to turn the volume down. He shifted round to get a better look at Jess's face, and nearly came undone at the sight of her teeth closing on her bottom lip.

His hand threaded into her hair, and he soaked in the glorious tangle of it. His thumb reached to brush against her cheek and she smiled, shifting so that he was above her on the sofa, her body angled beneath him.

He held his breath as he leaned in to kiss her. 'You taste of chocolate and red wine. You are every delicious treat today.'

She smiled at him. 'Because you haven't let up feeding me.'

He leaned into another kiss. 'I like looking after you.'

'I wasn't complaining,' Jess said, reaching for him and pulling him back down.

The fire of bullets sounding on the TV made Jess jump and they both laughed as Rufus reached for the remote and turned the volume down even lower.

'So much for watching the movie,' Jess said, her hands coming to rest on Rufus's shoulders. He pushed her hair back from her face, dropping kisses where her forehead was exposed.

'I'd rather watch you,' he said, smiling.

'What happened to anticipation?'

'It's lost its shine. Is this okay? Midnight feels like it's days away. Weeks.'

Her hand reached round to the back of his neck, pulled him down for a deep kiss.

Rufus groaned at that, because no amount of waiting could make this feel more right. He couldn't imagine any way that it could feel more perfect than it did right now.

Until Jess shifted under him, revealing that band of bare skin at her waist again, and this time he couldn't—didn't have to—stop himself from dropping his hands there and exploring. 'Is this okay?' he asked as his fingers stroked the soft skin of her belly, and one of her legs coiled around his, locking their bodies together. He pulled away to get a better look at her, and her eyes were undone and her cheeks flushed, her lips parted as she tried to catch her breath. It was without doubt the sexiest thing he had ever seen.

But he could only look for a second before he needed to kiss her again. How had she done this to him? She had only been in his life for a handful of days, no doubt would be gone from it again soon—it was what they'd agreed. It was the only future that this had, but he felt a pang of regret, going into this knowing that it couldn't last. That was his choice, he reminded himself. More than a choice. It was an obligation. He'd decided not to have a relationship, a family, because he knew that he couldn't be trusted to put their needs above his own. Jess hadn't believed him when he'd told her it was his fault his parents had had to leave Upton. That it was the backdrop to luxury mini-breaks and Instagram photoshoots rather than the family home it had always been meant to be.

She'd been insistent that there was nothing else he could have done—that he wasn't to blame for going off and chasing his own ambitions rather than staying here and supporting his father. All of which was easy to say when she hadn't been there. Hadn't seen the disappointment in his dad's face when he'd learnt that even when he was released from hospital, he wouldn't really be going *home*.

'Rufus?' Jess pulled back, looking at him. 'Are you okay? Where did you go? You were all in your head.'

'I'm here,' he said. 'I'm here, with you.' He punctuated each word with a kiss. 'For however long we have.'

For however long we have.

Why had those words given her shivers? Maybe it was the words, or maybe it was the fact that Rufus's hands had resumed exploring under her sweater, inching higher as he pressed kisses to her lips, her jaw, her neck. She reached down for the hem of her sweater and Rufus pulled his body away from hers, giving her room to work, though his lips didn't break from hers until she dragged the fabric in between them, revealing the silky vest she'd put on that morning, wondering—hoping— that this was where the past few days had been leading.

Rufus's breathing was heavy as she dropped her sweater on the floor, and his eyes were kind of dazed.

'Bed?' he asked, and the broken gravel of his voice would have been enough to get her there with him even if she hadn't spent the last three days going out of her mind with wanting him.

'Bed.'

CHAPTER EIGHT

'REMIND ME AGAIN why we waited three days to do that?'
Rufus said, his eyelids as heavy as his limbs. Beside
him, Jess was still trying to catch her breath, and he
pulled her closer with an arm around her waist.

'Because we're idiots,' she said, turning towards him
and pressing a kiss to his chest before settling her head
on his shoulder. 'Just so you know, I'm not waiting three
days for round two.'

She yawned; Rufus tensed. No, because in three days
the snow would probably be gone, and so would she.
But now was not the time to be thinking like that. Not
when Jess was warm in his bed and there was still a foot
of snow down the lane. There would be plenty of time
to lament how little time they'd had once this was over.

Jess reached for the phone in her jeans pocket, where
they'd landed on the floor, and he turned to spoon her,
pulling the blankets close against the cold air of the
bedroom. 'It's past midnight,' she said, dropping the
phone on the bedside table and turning in his arms.
'Merry Christmas.'

'Merry Christmas,' he murmured, kissing her again.
'This is absolutely the best start to a Christmas Day
I've ever had.'

'I should hope so.'

Rufus woke in the morning to goose bumps on his shoulders where the blankets had been tugged down, and the tip of Jess's nose cold against his chest. He grabbed a couple of blankets from the floor and tucked one around Jess as he eased himself from under her arm, and then wrapped the other around himself while he went to tend to the fire. They had been too distracted to remember to build it up last night and were paying the price for it now.

He poked the last few embers and added some kindling, waiting for the flames to lick up the knots of newspaper before adding a few logs.

He looked towards the bed where Jess was still sleeping soundly, and smiled. He wished that he had known to wish for her before now.

He shivered in the chill of the room and pulled on more layers, knowing that the great hall would be positively arctic with the fires burned down low. He opened the door just a crack, not wanting to wake Jess, then decided to wrap the blanket back around himself as he went out into the cold.

'Nice cape,' Jess said, and Rufus turned towards her. She'd startled him, she realised, and wondered what had him so distracted that he hadn't heard her coming. She slipped her arms around his waist under the blanket and pressed her cheek into his chest, hoping that this wasn't about to get weird. With morning afters, there was generally at least the option of a hasty exit if one of the parties decided that they were having second thoughts. But neither she nor Rufus had an escape route—even if one were needed.

He turned to rest back against the Aga and opened the blanket far enough to wrap her up with him as he leaned down and brushed his lips against hers.

'Good morning,' he murmured against her mouth. 'I was going to bring you coffee.'

'Then I should have stayed in bed. I was cold, though. Thought I'd see if I could find someone to warm me up.'

'How's that going?' he asked, his hand cupping her cheek as he turned her head to one side and trailed kisses along her jaw.

'I found this great big guy with a cape...' she said, eyes rolling as Rufus's lips found the spot on the side of her neck that made her utterly melt. 'I'm wondering if he's up for it.'

'He was planning on making you breakfast first, so you're going to have to decide what your priorities are.'

'Sex, food or coffee? You really want me to choose?'

'You've got about three more seconds of that,' he said, his voice cracking as her hand slipped into the waistband of his trousers, 'before coffee and breakfast are off the menu.'

She held up her hands, all innocent, as she took a step away.

'Feed me. Caffeinate me. Take me to bed. In that order,' she said, laughing. He shoved a plate of toast at her.

'Eat quickly.'

'Efficient. I like it,' she said, sliding onto the bench on one side of the big oak kitchen table, staying close to the heat of the Aga. 'Are we meant to be cooking already?' she asked, glancing at the big clock on the wall and trying to remember how long Rufus had said that the turkey would take to cook.

'It's already in the oven,' he said. 'It'll need hours, so we don't have to do anything yet.'

'Good,' Jess said, finishing her toast. 'Because I was planning a few more hours in bed. Are you coming?'

When Jess woke later that morning, the house smelled of Christmas. She wasn't sure whether it was the pine branches on the fire, the smell of roast turkey, or Rufus beside her that smelled the most delicious. Or maybe it was this exact combination. Perhaps if Rufus could bottle it and sell it, it would solve all his financial troubles.

She propped herself up on an elbow and looked down at Rufus, still fast asleep on the pillow next to her. How had she ended up here? Well, she knew how. And why. Because Rufus was officially scorching hot, and she had a lot less self-control than she'd thought she had. But how had she found herself with a guy that she really genuinely liked, and—it turned out—was incredibly compatible with, and really, really, didn't want to leave. This was the sort of situation she had spent her whole adult life avoiding. She could tell herself that she was just going to walk away when the snow cleared, but sooner or later she was going to have to face the fact that she felt…more…just *more* than she had for anyone else for a long time. And when they finally got out of here, maybe walking away wouldn't be as easy or as painless as she had convinced herself it would be before they'd slept together. Not that she had any regrets on that front. Some things were worth a little pain, and sex with Rufus definitely fell into that category.

'You know it's creepy to wake up and find someone watching you.'

She smiled as Rufus rubbed sleep from his eyes and then leaned in for a kiss. She had meant to keep it light, teasing, until Rufus's fingertips brushed the nape of her neck, holding her close to him, and her whole body sank into him, hot against his side from her shoulder to her toes.

'I have to go and baste the turkey,' Rufus said at last, breaking their kiss.

'That had better not be a euphemism,' Jess said, falling back on the pillow and watching as Rufus pulled trousers and what looked like half a dozen sweatshirts on. He laughed and leaned in for a last kiss.

'Nothing weird. Just your actual, literal, Christmas dinner to cook.'

'I must have been really, *really* good in a past life,' she mused, noting the smug smile that turned up the corner of Rufus's mouth.

Really, it was a good job that they weren't going to get a chance to get used to this, because he would be seriously hard to walk away from in the real world.

'I'll jump in the shower then come and help,' Jess said, dragging herself upright and wrapping one of the blankets around her shoulders.

'Thanks, but I think I'll have enough to do without you randomly throwing things on the floor.'

She threw a cushion at his head. 'One time! I dropped the mince pies one time.' She laughed as the cushion landed back on the bed beside her and Rufus blew her a kiss.

Half an hour later, she followed him into the kitchen—it had been nearly impossible to drag herself out of the scalding hot shower. The fire wasn't kicking out much heat yet, and when she checked the dial on the electric heaters they were already turned up as high as they would go.

She pulled on enough layers to keep the chill out, and then added a scarf for good measure.

'You look toasty,' Rufus said, grabbing her for a quick kiss before turning back to the pots steaming away on the stove.

'It's nice and warm in here,' she said, unwinding the scarf and pulling up a stool. 'Are you sure there's nothing I can do?'

'I'm sure,' he said, checking the potatoes quickly, and then coming to the table with a cup of coffee for them both.

'Merry Christmas,' he murmured, tucking her hair behind her ear and brushing a lingering kiss to her lips. She moaned, wondering if they couldn't just skip Christmas and spend the day in bed instead.

Except she had felt her phone buzz in her pocket twice already, and she guessed it would be Lara hassling her about the pictures they had promised her.

'I'll take the action shots, then,' she said as Rufus pulled out a knife and started chopping carrots. As she pressed the button on the camera, the lights flickered and for a second she wasn't sure if she had blinked and imagined it until she saw the expression on Rufus's face. It wasn't just her who'd seen it—he had too, and he was worried.

She slid her arms around him from behind and rested her face against his back. 'Don't worry,' she said. Not that she understood why he was so tense about the power going out. This house was more than four hundred years old. She was sure that they'd manage if they lost power for a while.

'It could be fun,' she said. 'A blackout, I mean. Candles. Fires. Just each other for entertainment…'

'No phones. No heating. No way of contacting the outside world in an emergency…'

'Presupposing an emergency happens, when we have no reason to.'

'Yes, well, emergencies don't tend to announce themselves in advance. They just sneak up on you and your life is suddenly changed and you don't know how it happened.'

She thought for a moment. 'Like your dad's heart attack.'

He directed a scowl in her direction. 'My dad's heart attack has nothing to do with this.'

She crossed her arms, not prepared to let him off the hook. 'If you say so. That traumatic event must have barely affected you at all. I don't know what I was thinking.'

Reaching past him, she stole a carrot stick, crunching as she watched him rearrange his features into something neutral.

'How about we don't worry about it until it actually happens? I know you've already prepared everything you could. I trust you.'

She saw the muscle of his jaw tick and pressed a kiss there, reaching as she did so for more of the carrots.

He tapped the back of her hand playfully, the atmosphere between them easing a little. 'If you keep eating them at this rate, there'll be none left for dinner.'

She huffed, taking just one more. 'What can I say? You wore me out. I need to refuel.' He smiled at that, and she let herself breathe a little easier. Things had threatened to get heavy there for a minute and that had never been what this was about. They had agreed that this was just a bit of fun. And there was nothing fun about digging into one another's hang-ups. She certainly wouldn't have wanted him digging into hers. It was just hard, seeing him so obviously hurting over something that had been so completely out of his control.

But it was Christmas, and she would avoid arguing if only for the sake of that.

'I'm not sure Lara's followers are interested in me peeling carrots,' he said, his features warming to her.

'You look hot with a speed-peeler,' she said, taking another couple of pictures.

'What, like this?' he asked, holding a particularly large carrot in a way that bordered on obscene, reducing Jess to a fit of laughter.

'I am definitely not sending these to Lara,' she said, showing him the photo reel. He laughed too, and suddenly she could breathe again. Until her phone started ringing, and her mum's name showed on the screen.

'I have to take this,' she said, moving a step away from him. She knew this was going to be hard, and having Rufus listen in would only make it harder.

She walked through the door to the great hall as she swiped 'Answer' on the screen.

'Hi, Mum,' she said. 'Happy Christmas.'

'Happy Christmas,' her mum said, obviously trying to inject some jollity into her voice, but Jess could hear how fake it was.

'Are you and Dad having a nice morning?'

'Oh, you know...'

And she did—she did know. And it broke her heart.

'Mum, do you think...?' She took a deep breath. Thought of all the hints that she'd dropped all those years, and all the times that she'd stopped short of coming out and saying what she'd been thinking. 'Are you happy?'

Her mum's silence said it all.

'Because I worry about you,' Jess went on. 'I really want you to be happy. Dad too. And I don't think you make each other happy any more. Not since we lost Charlotte. I'm sorry, but it's Christmas, and I just can't bear the thought that you two have been miserable all this time, and if what you think I'll feel if you split up is any part of why you haven't, just…don't. Please.'

'Jess, your dad and I love you very much.'

'I know! I know you do. But you don't seem to love each other any more. You don't seem to make each other happy. And maybe we should all go to lots of therapy together. I don't know. I just know that something should change. Because the way things feel isn't right.'

It had taken this—being here, away from her family—for her to realise that she couldn't just carry on. She couldn't get through another Christmas with all this unsaid. Something had to change.

She spoke to her mum for a few more minutes, assured her that everything was fine at Upton, and the local weather reports were expecting a thaw in a couple of days. She even managed a couple of words with her dad before the lump in her throat got too big to ignore and she made her excuses and hung up, with promises that they would all talk some more when she got home. She sat on the sheepskin in front of the fire, winding her scarf round her neck while she looked into the flames, wondering how her family had been reduced to this. Wondering whether she'd invented those childhood memories of laughing, happy parents, noisy Christmas mornings, ripping through paper with Charlotte.

No, she reminded herself. Those memories were real, and she owed it to Charlotte to remember that. To fight back against the pit of despair her parents threatened to pull her into. That they had pulled each other into. She just wished that she could make them happier. That she could undo the years that they had spent not talking about how they really felt and being miserable instead. The years that she had spent without her sister. With a part of herself missing.

It was the reminder that she needed, at just the right time, of why she didn't do this. Why she didn't get involved. Why she had agreed to walk away from Rufus when the snow was gone. She was never going to live how her parents did. And if that meant walking away from a man like Rufus then that was what she would have to do.

'Hey,' said a voice behind her, and she looked up to find Rufus leaning against the staircase, watching her. 'Are you okay?' he asked, crossing over to where she was sitting on the floor. He sat behind her, his strong thighs bracketing her hips as he pulled her back against him and wrapped his arms tight around her.

Jess nodded, not trusting herself to speak just yet, and Rufus pressed his lips to her hair.

'I'm sorry you're sad,' he said gently. 'Today especially. Is there anything I can do to help?'

'This,' Jess said softly. 'This is good. This is helping.'

She rested her head back on his shoulder and let her eyes fall closed. She *would* walk away from this when the snow was gone.

It was the only way to protect herself from repeating

her parents' mistakes. But she was here now. And so was Rufus and they both knew what this was. So, she was going to soak this up, and absorb enough comfort from his body as he would give her.

'Mmm,' she murmured. 'Is that roast potatoes I can smell?'

'And here I thought it was my body making you feel better. You're only in this for the food.'

'In my defence,' she said, opening her eyes and turning her head so that she could see his face, 'the food is spectacularly good.'

He grinned. 'And the rest?'

'Satisfactory, so far,' she said with a smirk.

And then before she knew what was happening, she was on her back, the sheepskin rug tickling the back of her neck as Rufus loomed over her. She hooked her ankle around his as a shiver of anticipation shot through her body.

'Satisfactory,' he repeated, his face deadpan as he lowered to his elbows, pressing the breath from her chest—as if she even cared about breathing just now.

'Sounds like I need more practice,' he said, his lips brushing her temple, her ear, her jaw.

'You're going to burn the potatoes,' she said, biting her lip to stifle a moan. The only thing that felt better than what Rufus was doing right now was winding him up while he did it. But then his mouth was on hers and there were much better things to do with her tongue than talk.

'They're crunchy.'

'You say crunchy, I say burnt.'

'They're crunchy, and I don't regret a minute that they were in the oven.'

She smiled. 'Good. I should hope not.' She tipped the potatoes out into a serving dish, and snapped a few shots for Lara.

'Do you think we made enough?' she asked with an ironically raised eyebrow at the banquet laid out before them.

'So I don't know how to cook for two. It's fine. There's lots of space in the freezer. Are you done with that? Do you think we're going to get to eat any of it while it's still hot?'

'I'm nearly done,' she said, pouring gravy on the two full plates she'd staged with silverware and glasses on a table in front of the kitchen window, where they could take advantage of the natural light. And once the photo shoot was done, Rufus whipped a couple of hot plates from the Aga and carried them through to the dining room, which had been too dark for the camera, but was the perfect backdrop to an intimate dinner that they had barely wanted to dress for. Rufus had laid one place at the head of the table, and the other just to one side. The centrepiece had been pulled over between them, so that their little corner of the grand dining room was every bit as cosy as any table for two.

She slid into the seat beside Rufus and reached for the wine bottle, pouring them both a generous measure of the rich, delicious burgundy that they had opened the night before.

'Are you feeling better?' he asked as she tucked into the roast turkey.

'Yes, much better, thank you. I didn't expect to feel

sad today. I thought I felt like that because I was forced to spend it with my parents.'

'But it turns out you were sad anyway.' He reached for her hand and squeezed. 'And that's okay. You miss your sister. The way your family used to be. The way your life used to be.'

'Yes. I think you're right. Just like you do,' she answered and waited for his automatic denial. But instead he frowned, a crease appearing between his brows.

'Yes. Like me, I suppose,' he said. 'We have that in common. Lives that could be simplified by the existence of a time machine.'

'I'm not sure that a time machine ever simplified anything. But I wish I could have Charlotte back. Failing that, I need to find a way to be happy without her. I can't go on hiding from the problems in my family for ever.' He squeezed her hand, and her heart swelled a little at the unspoken support, and had to remind herself that its presence was only temporary. She couldn't rely on him to make her Christmases bearable, because this time next year he would be long gone. No, she was going to have to figure that one out by herself.

She pulled her hand from him, shaking herself into the present. 'Come on,' she said, picking up her cutlery. It would be criminal to let this food go cold. They chatted as they ate, and she felt the sadness fade. The warmth and cheer that she and Rufus had found here gradually pushing out the darker parts of her heart, making room for something else. Someone else. He wasn't going to stay there. She knew that. They both knew that. But it made her wonder. When this was all over, was she going to let those parts of her creep back to how they had been before? Or was she going to keep pushing against those thoughts and feelings that made her unhappy and see if she could replace them with something new? It didn't have to be Rufus. She didn't want it to be a man. She'd seen what had happened to her parents when they had given too much of their hearts to another person for safe keeping and found them inadequate to the task. But she could fill it with *her*. She could look at the hurts that she had absorbed from her parents and decide whether she wanted those parts of her past making decisions for her.

Or she could embrace Christmas the way that she and Charlotte had when they were children and decide unequivocally for herself that joy in the Christmas season was going to be her gift to herself this year.

She smiled as she reached for one of the crackers on the table and held it out to Rufus.

'We're missing something,' she said, and Rufus narrowed his eyes at her.

'What's going on?'

'I want to see you in a stupid Christmas hat,' she said, shaking the cracker at him now.

'Give over. I wore your bobble hat for hours. Wasn't that enough?'

'Nope. You wore the hat because I was saving your life. This is to entertain me, and I find that I'm full of Christmas spirit. And that means you have to wear the paper hat.' He scowled at her and she pouted shamelessly. 'Unless you want to ruin Christmas completely.'

He groaned as he pulled the cracker, and the contents spilled onto the table between them. Jess picked out the hat from among the detritus and stood up, leaning to pull it onto Rufus's head. But then a pair of muscled arms was wrapping around her waist, pulling her into his lap.

She shrugged, trying to suppress a smile. 'Fair trade,' she said, pulling the hat further down onto his head, linking her hands behind his neck and leaning back to get a better look at him.

'Very festive.' She laughed at his frown and pulled her phone out of her pocket for a selfie. 'Are you pouting for the camera?' she asked.

'No. Just for you,' he said, finally breaking and cracking a smile. 'What's brought about this sudden burst of festive cheer?'

She shrugged, and couldn't help but notice that Rufus's eyes dipped to her cleavage as she did so. Good. Having his mind there fitted perfectly with her plans for the rest of the day.

'Oh, nothing,' she said, shrugging again, and very much enjoying the expression on Rufus's face when she did so.

'Just been thinking about a few things. Deciding a few things.'

His brows drew together for a moment.

'Good things?'

'Very good things,' she confirmed, pulling herself close again, until her nose bumped against his, and his eyes closed as a smile spread over his face. 'I've decided not to be sad at Christmas any more.'

'That sounds like a good decision,' Rufus said, his hands curving round her bottom and pulling her in tight. 'Let me know if there's anything in particular I can do to make you happy.'

She smiled, and brought her mouth to his.

'Oh, I've got an idea or two,' she said, between kisses.

'Well, Merry Christmas to me,' Rufus gasped.

CHAPTER NINE

JESS LISTENED TO the *drip-drip-drip*, wondering whether rain indoors was something that she should be sufficiently concerned about to pull Rufus's arm from around her waist, open the hangings on the four-poster bed and extract herself from the warmth of the quilts and of the man sleeping soundly beside her. But the constant sound of water was causing another problem—one less easy to ignore—and that cast the deciding vote. She would set all sort of speed records diving into the bathroom and be back in the bed before the sheets had cooled.

She inched out from beside Rufus, untangling their legs and pulling gently on her hair where it was caught beneath his head.

He moaned softly as she slipped from the sheets, but she pulled the bedclothes higher and watched as he drifted back into sleep. Without her. She stood and looked at him for a moment, not able to put her finger on why that should cause such a sharp pang of regret. This wasn't the first bed that she'd slipped from before dawn. Not the first time she'd left someone sleeping, not even realising that she wasn't beside them any more. Rufus was dead to the world. It absolutely was not rational to be annoyed at him for something he had done—or not done—while he was sleeping. She grabbed a blanket from the foot of the bed and wrapped it around herself as she went through to the bathroom.

When she returned, Rufus still slept soundly. And there was still that drip-drip-drip that had made it so impossible for her to fall back to sleep.

Drip.

She spun, looking for the source of the sound.

Drip.

She spun again. That was it. There was no point getting back into bed until she'd found where it was coming from and reassured herself that the ceiling wasn't about to cave in on them both.

Drip.

It was coming from near the window. She crossed to that side of the room, checking the floor for puddles and the ceiling for suspicious-looking damp patches, but couldn't see anything out of place.

Drip.

She drew back the curtains and watched as a single teardrop of water slid down an icicle hanging from the lintel outside, and hit the sill below.

Drip.

That was it. That was the sound that had woken her, that had made it so impossible to get back to sleep. It was the thaw. It was the snow and ice receding. It was her and Rufus…leaving. She settled on the windowsill, pulling the blanket tight around her, tucking herself in, right up to her neck as she leant against the side wall of the window seat and followed the slow but inevitable progress of each drop of ice melt from the icicle to the ledge below. She looked out over the driveway and the lane. It looked no different than it had yesterday, but she knew that was deceiving. The temperature had risen, probably by just a degree or two, and that tiny, barely perceptible change would be all it took to melt the intimacy that had grown between her and Rufus in the four days that they had been here.

She jumped as the curtain jerked back behind her, and she found Rufus, rubbing at his hair with the heel of one hand, the other finding the nape of her neck, absentmindedly winding into a curl there as he leaned towards the window pane, his breath misting the glass.

'It's thawing,' he said, his hand stilling on the back of her neck. 'The ice is melting. The snow soon too.'

She leant into his hand, rested the side of her head against him as he stood even closer. They watched the window, the icicle beyond it as the sky lightened. The sun crept over the horizon, sending streaks of pink and red and purple across the sky. Jess wasn't sure when Rufus had slipped onto the seat beside her, when his arms had sneaked around her waist and pulled her back against his chest. All she knew was that by the time the sun was fully up, her fingers and toes were ice, the dripping had stopped, and she never wanted to move.

'How long, do you think?' she asked at last.

'Until the road is clear?'

She nodded, suddenly finding it hard to speak.

'Tomorrow. The day after at the latest.'

'We should make the most of being here, then. To-gether…'

She tried to make her voice light. Playful. Tried to make it sound as if this was just what they'd said it would be all along. Just something fun. Something they would both walk away from without a backward glance when they left this place. Rufus kissed the top of her head. And now she was watching the snow melt, making no effort to move, and wondering what she had done. Why her heart hurt at the thought of this beautiful landscape looking lush and green in the spring.

'What do you want to do today?' Rufus asked, his voice a rough murmur in her ear. Involuntarily, her arms tightened around his, locking them together.

'This,' she said. 'Or drawing the curtains and pretending the sun isn't up yet.' She held her breath, not sure how Rufus would react to that. The first time she had so much as hinted that she wasn't going to be just walking away from this as if nothing had happened. He found her hand under the blanket and brought it to his lips.

'You're cold,' he said, his voice gruff as he stood, holding out a hand to pull her up. 'Let's eat,' he said, his face inscrutable. 'We'll make a plan when you're warm.'

Jess wrapped her hands around her mug and grinned as Rufus served her avocado and poached eggs on toast.

She could get used to this.

Or…not. She reined in her imagination, her smile faltering. There were a million places she could get avocado on toast. She didn't need Rufus for that. She didn't *need* him for anything. He was a nice added bonus to this delicious breakfast, that was all. She had to keep reminding herself of that.

'What does your Boxing Day usually like?' she asked.

'Mum and Dad used to force us outdoors and the habit's stuck. The last few years we've gone ice skating at the rink by the church.'

'That sounds amazing. I'd love to go skating. I don't suppose you have a convenient frozen lake kicking around the place somewhere?'

He frowned, and then grinned mischievously. 'No frozen lake. But leave it with me. I have an idea.'

She grinned, finding his enthusiasm infectious. If this was to be her last day here, then she wasn't going to spend it brooding. She was going to spend it counting the times she could bring a smile to his mouth and he to hers.

'I will actually explode if you keep feeding me like this,' she said, leaning back, leaving half a slice of toast on her plate.

'Well, I have an idea if you want to work it off,' he said, and she hit his arm affectionately.

'Get your mind out of the gutter.'

'Get *your* mind out of the gutter, lass,' he countered, smiling. 'That's not what I meant. Wait here. Don't leave the kitchen.'

'Oh. You in charge. I like it.'

He leaned down and kissed her on the lips. 'If you want me to keep my mind out of the gutter, you've got to stop saying things like that.'

But he dragged himself away, and she reached for the teapot in the middle of the table, topping up her mug and wondering what he was planning.

He returned with a grin on his face and his hands behind his back. 'Close your eyes.'

'No way. God knows what you'll do to me.'

'Close your eyes or you won't get your surprise.'

She narrowed her eyes. 'I'd better like this.' Then she let them fall closed, waiting with her breath held.

She started when she felt his fingers touch her foot, but he stilled her.

'Trust me.'

And how could she not, after everything that they had shared here? And then her foot was being pushed into a stiff, unyielding boot. She snapped her eyes open and was faced with the sight of Rufus trying to wrestle her foot into a neon pink rollerblade. 'Oh…my…were these *yours*?'

'My sister's,' Rufus replied. 'Mine are right here.' He pointed behind him to where a pair of black skates with fluorescent green laces sat on the tiled floor.

'Please tell me you know how to use them,' she gasped, excited at the thought.

'I know what I'm doing,' he said, tightening the ratchet at her ankle and making her gasp. 'Do you?'

'Nope. Not in the slightest.'

Rufus groaned slightly as she leaned down and helped him with the second skate.

'Then this is going to be interesting.'

Rufus left his skates off and pushed Jess by the hips through to the great hall. He'd rolled up the rugs and pushed the furniture to the walls, leaving them with a decent-sized rink in the middle of the room, with the Christmas tree towering at the centre.

'Oh, my God,' Jess said when she saw it. 'Rufus, this is amazing. I can't believe you made me an ice rink.'

He couldn't ignore the warmth that grew in his chest at the pure delight in her voice. Really, if he could just spend the rest of his life making her happy… No, there was no place for thoughts like that. This had nothing to do with his life. This *wasn't* his life any more. He wouldn't have been able to offer this even if he'd wanted to. This wasn't his home any more. He was an interloper here now, just like her. He shook his head. This was fun. He was meant to be remembering that. Fun.

He spun Jess around, and caught her when she wobbled, her knees turning inwards as she fought for stability.

He grinned. 'Ready to try on your own?' he asked. Jess fixed an expression of determination on her face.

'Depends. Are you ready for me to skate rings around you?'

He laughed out loud.

'Come on, then. Show me what you've got.'

She pushed away from him, wobbling across the floor towards the fire, finding her balance and gliding with more and more confidence as she turned to face him. Of course she was a natural. He pushed his hands in the pockets of his jeans and leaned back against a table, not taking his eyes off her as she skated towards him, and then pinned him against the table with her hands beside his hips.

'This. Is. Amazing,' she said, punctuating each of her words with a kiss. He curled a hand to the nape of her neck, trapping her against him while he leisurely explored her mouth, only breaking off when he felt her start to slip away from him. She laughed as he caught her by the hips and pulled her back in.

'Maybe skates *weren't* such a great idea.'

'Skates were an amazing idea. Now come and race me.'

'Okay. You asked for it.' He pulled on his own skates, watching as Jess glided round the room, wobbling less and less as she found her feet.

With his boots firmly laced, he skated up beside her and reached for her hand.

'You want to race?'

Her eyes gleamed. 'I am absolutely ready to beat you. Bring it on.'

'Loser does the washing up,' he shouted as he sprinted around the tree, laughing at how much he sounded like his teenaged self. He hadn't been so… daft…for ages. Not since his dad was ill at the very least. Part of him wanted to tell himself that it was being back here, at Upton. But with a glance backwards at Jess, he wasn't sure how much he believed that now.

He stumbled as his skate caught on an uneven floorboard, but he righted himself and glided across to Jess. No wonder Jess was wobbling. Perhaps they would have been better off on the smooth kitchen tiles. But this was all worth it for the squeal of pleasure he heard from Jess as she crashed into him, narrowly avoiding a much harder meeting with the floor. Any excuse to hold her by the waist, pulling her closer until he could feel her body flush against him, her hips close, her sweet-smelling hair under his chin. He tipped her face up to his, and loved the smile that he found on her lips as he kissed into her mouth.

'I think I like how uncoordinated you are in these things,' he said, and laughed when she kicked his shin with the stopper on the front of her skate.

'I'm not uncoordinated. The floor is uneven,' she murmured, not bothering to take her mouth off his to talk. Whatever the reason, he was happy for it if it meant having her in his arms. Not that he needed an excuse. They had dispensed with those days ago. Now he could lean in and kiss her. Just like…that. For no reason other than they both wanted him to. Too soon, she was pulling away from him, skating shakily backwards as they made a circuit of the room.

'Do you know any tricks?' she asked. 'I bet you do. I want to learn.'

'Um, doing tricks your first time on rollerblades on an uneven floor is maybe not our best move,' he replied, raising his eyebrows.

'I've done so many things this week that were not the best idea that I've lost count. Now, show me or I'm just going to make it up myself.'

He heaved out a sigh and skated out backwards around the room, his feet crossing over one another as he spun around.

'I can definitely do that,' Jess declared as he came to a stop in front of her.

She pushed away on strong legs, picking up speed as she circled the room. Until she picked up one foot, tried to spin on the other and her front brake caught in a knot hole in the floorboard.

He dived to try and reach her, but he knew even before he started moving that he wasn't going to make it in time. He winced but didn't look away as she reached out to break her fall with one hand. Her yelp of pain masked the snap of bone that he was bracing himself for. He dropped to the floor beside her as she cradled her wrist against her chest. Her lower lip had disappeared between her teeth as she bit down on it. Hard.

'Oh, God, do you think it's broken?' she asked, looking up at him, her eyes wide with shock, her face pinched with pain.

He had no idea. But regardless of whether the bone was actually fractured, all he could be sure of right now was that she was in pain, and they were stranded, with no way of getting her to a hospital. All because he'd thought it would be fun to surprise her with a skating rink without properly thinking through the consequences.

'I don't know,' he said gently, putting an arm around her back, breathing out as she let her head rest on his shoulder. 'I think we should get some ice on it. Try and keep it still until we can get you to a doctor.'

He helped her up onto one of the sofas pushed back against the wall, flinching when she gasped as he helped her to stand. He pulled a blanket around her, and then knelt to unlace her boots, pulling them off and throwing them to one side, then doing the same with his own. 'I'll be back in a minute,' he said, walking quickly to the kitchen and digging round in the chest freezer for the ice pack he knew was in there somewhere.

This was all his fault. There was no way to sugarcoat it. He had been so keen to impress her that he had created a death trap of a skating rink, all the while knowing that they were trapped here without any reasonable hope of medical care.

He had been kidding himself that he could just walk away from her. He'd known, for longer than he'd admitted to himself, that he wanted more. More of what they'd shared here these past few days. Just more of *her*. And here was the cosmic payback—the reminder that he couldn't, shouldn't, be responsible for anyone but himself. When he was close to people, trying to take care of them, they got hurt. He had been on the brink of asking Jess if they could see one another after they had got out of here. But here was the reminder he needed that he shouldn't. He had needed to remember that. Remember that the thing he could do for Jess was to put some emotional distance between them. More than anything else, that was what was going to keep her safe.

He found the ice pack at last, and as he pulled it from the freezer the kitchen light flickered and went out.

'Rufus?' Jess called from the hall. 'Did you do that?'

'Another power cut,' he called, taking a torch from the pantry before he walked back through. The fire in the grate was casting light and shadow onto Jess's face, and he sat lightly beside her, careful not to jar her arm.

'Here,' he said, pressing the ice pack to her wrist, which was looking worryingly swollen. 'This will help. And these.' He handed her a couple of painkillers and a glass of water. 'How does it feel?'

'Pretty sore,' Jess said, her face still tight.

'I'm going to call 111. See if there's any chance of getting an ambulance out here.'

'You said yourself that the lane won't be passable until tomorrow.'

'But if it's broken…'

She gritted her teeth. 'Then it will still be broken tomorrow. It's okay; I can wait.'

'You were happy to call an ambulance for me,' Rufus reminded her.

'That was different and you know it. You were barely conscious and I thought you might die. This is just a sprained wrist.'

The tension in every part of her body told him that this wasn't 'just' anything.

'A broken wrist.'

'Fine, Doctor. Whatever you say,' Jess said, her voice shaky. 'But don't call. Please? It can wait until the lane is clear.'

He couldn't fight her. It wasn't fair when she was hurt. 'Okay. Tell me what you need.'

'A hug?'

Rufus exhaled. That he could do. He knew that they had to end this properly. When they left. But she needed him, and they were here now. He just had to remember that this was his fault. That this was the reason he was going to walk away. Because Jess deserved someone who could be trusted with her. Who made good decisions. Not someone who would let her get injured when they were stranded.

He eased his arms around her gently, pulling her against him, and flinching at her sharply indrawn breath. He'd hurt her—again. Then she relaxed into him and she pressed a kiss to the top of her head. 'I'm sorry,' he said into her hair. Jess looked up at him, frowning.

'What have you got to be sorry for?'

'This was my idea. If I hadn't—'

'This was the *best*. I mean, injuries notwithstanding, I absolutely loved it. Seriously. Best Christmas present ever.'

He sighed. 'Yeah, well, all things considered, I'm not sure it was worth it.'

'Yeah, well, as literally the injured party here,' Jess said, frowning 'I'm pretty sure that this is my call, and I say it was absolutely worth it. And I'm hurting, so you're not allowed to argue with me.'

She turned her face up for a kiss, and he pressed his lips to hers, all the while knowing that deep down he couldn't agree with her. This was absolutely his fault.

CHAPTER TEN

BLOODY HELL, IT HURT. For a minute she wished she hadn't been so adamant about Rufus not calling an ambulance. But she had seen that there was no way that the lane would be passable. And now that the latest painkillers were kicking in—and her second glass of red wine—it was bearable. Just. What was less bearable was the sudden distance that she felt from Rufus.

It wasn't as if in her state she was up for any sort of high jinks. And it wasn't as if he'd been anything other than perfectly attentive. He'd carried her up the stairs—despite her protestations that it was her arm that was hurt, not her legs, and she was perfectly capable of walking. He'd helped her into her pyjamas, guiding her sleeve over her swollen, bruised wrist, and wincing as if he could feel her pain himself. And then he'd leaned against the headboard, pulled her between his legs, propped her arm up on a pillow, and fallen asleep with his arms wrapped around her waist.

She'd leant into him, soaking in his warmth against the cool of the house as she watched time slip away on her phone as she waited for morning. This was their last night together. And she was spending it in his arms, with him feeling further away from her than he ever had in the time she'd known him. She shifted a little, uncomfortable, and felt Rufus's arms tighten around her. He didn't want to let her go, but he would. He had already started to. And that was what they had agreed all along. It was what they both wanted. She had known that this was how it would end. She just hadn't expected to feel it like this, with him slipping away even as he clung on to her in his sleep.

She couldn't believe that she had started to think that maybe these feeling they had for each other had a chance outside of this snowbound fairy tale. But he was the kicker. The proof that she wasn't ready. For any of this. And the proof of what she already knew, that even something that felt perfect could unravel in your hands, quicker than you were able to gather it up. At least she'd found out now. A relationship that couldn't survive a skating accident was never going to make it in the real world. It was better to know that now.

The sun gradually rose, a shard of pale light around the edges of the curtains. The alarm on her phone chimed—time for more painkillers. Thank goodness, because her wrist was throbbing. She reached for the packet on the bedside table, somehow elbowing Rufus in the stomach as she did so. He sat bolt upright, startled, jarring her wrist, until his eyes focused and then creased with concern.

'Jess, I'm so sorry. Are you okay?'

'Fine, fine,' she said as he took the packet from her, and popped the pills out of the blister pack that she'd been struggling with.

'So...do you think the roads are clear?' she asked. If this thing was over, there was no point in dragging it out. It was clear that Rufus wanted it done, and if he

was out already, there was no point in sticking around.
She knew where that led. Suddenly she was grateful for
the lesson her parents had taught her. Sticking around
once the light had gone out only made things worse.

She scooted out of bed, swallowed her painkillers
with a gulp of water and crossed over to the window,
hugging her arm to her chest. Pulling back the curtains, she started at the unfamiliar view. Great swathes
of snow had melted, leaving their snowmen stranded
in a sea of grass, a reminder of a time when things between them had been full of promise. Well, there was
no point thinking about that now. The sun was up. Yesterday was over. Christmas was over. It was time to get
back to real life. And the sooner the better. She flashed
back to yesterday morning, watching the ice melt, safe
in Rufus's arms. Well, not today.

'Snow's gone,' she said, turning to look back at him.

'That's great,' he said, standing up.

No need to sound quite *so enthusiastic.*

'I meant because we can get your arm seen to...' So
something of what she had been thinking must have
shown on her face.

'Of course.' She pulled on a jumper, wincing as she
pushed her arm through the sleeve, but brushing off Rufus's offer of help. It took less than an hour for them to
pack her things, and then the door was locked, Rufus
threw her bag in the boot of her rental four-by-four
and they were crunching across the driveway, Upton
Manor growing ever smaller in the wing mirror, until
they rounded a corner of the lane and it disappeared
completely.

CHAPTER ELEVEN

'YOU DON'T HAVE to stay.'

The emergency department in the hospital Rufus had driven to was overflowing with patients sitting on piles of coats in the waiting room, and trolleys lined up against any available wall space. The nurse who'd triaged her had warned them that they were in for a long wait.

'I'm not leaving you here alone,' Rufus argued, frowning.

But she couldn't do this. Couldn't pretend things between them were still normal now that they had left Upton. 'I won't be alone. I messaged Lara, let her know what was going on. They finally scheduled a flight and she'll be here by this afternoon.'

He watched her for several long moments, the harsh fluorescent lighting throwing deep shadows beneath his eyes. 'So that's it? I'm dismissed?'

She creased her brow. She thought he'd be pleased to be let off the hook—now he was angry with her?

'It's not like that. We both said that this would be over once we were away from Upton Manor. I know you want it to be. So there's no need to stick around out of some sense of... I don't know. Duty, I guess.'

The lines between his eyebrows deepened. 'You think that's why I'm here? Duty?'

'Isn't it?' she asked, not sure she wanted to know what his answer would be.

'I'm here because I want to see that you're okay. Just because things aren't going to carry on between us doesn't mean that I don't care.'

Jess huffed: she didn't understand why he was making this so hard. She thought that she was giving him what he wanted. What he'd said he wanted. 'Actually,' she said, 'I'm pretty sure that is what it means. Or at least that you don't want to care.'

'Are you saying you don't care for me? That you would go, if the situation was reversed?'

She shook her head. 'Of course not, but—'

'So do me a favour and give me a little credit.'

Ouch. She'd forgotten just how grouchy Rufus could be. He'd softened, so slowly she hadn't noticed it in the days that they'd been together. And now he was back, the block of ice that had fallen through the front door of Upton Manor two days before Christmas. Well, she needed him even less than she needed the Rufus she'd gone to bed and woken up with, and she had no qualms about kicking him out on his ear.

'Seriously, Rufus. I've got a long wait ahead of me. I'm in pain, and I just want to put my headphones in and zone out until they can see me. This is me letting you off the hook. Honestly, you should go. I want you to go. Please?' She didn't have the energy for this. Her body didn't have the capacity to deal with her heart breaking as well as her wrist. She needed to pretend that she didn't feel any of this, and she couldn't do that with him sitting beside her, being more…just *more* than she'd ever thought he would be.

'We're breaking up in a hospital emergency department?' he asked.

That caught her attention. 'Breaking up? We were never together. We never wanted that. This is what we agreed all along.' This was why she needed him to go. She could barely think straight right now, never mind explain how she was feeling. This was all too much.

'I know, but… I just didn't see it ending here. Like this.'

And there he went, proving her point entirely, and reminding her of why she'd told herself all along that she didn't want to make this work. 'Well, what have I been saying all this time? That's how it happens. You think everything is fine and then something happens and it's not any more.'

Rufus leaned forward, his elbows resting on spread knees, and his eyes fixed on the floor as he took several deep breaths. Eventually he looked up, fixed her with an intense stare. 'Can I at least call you? Check that you're okay?' He held her gaze, refused to break eye contact with her, so that she was the one who had to look away. Those painkillers were doing nothing for the tearing pain in her chest. She needed him to walk away before she changed her mind, begged him to stay and made a huge mistake.

'Yes, okay. You can call. But, Rufus, please just… just go.'

Lara burst through the doors three hours later and swept Jess into a huge hug, only loosening her grip when Jess squealed and reminded her about the probably broken wrist currently trapped between them.

'You silly thing—how did this happen?' Lara asked. 'I wasn't worried when the photos stopped because I assumed you were making the most of being bunked up with Rufus. Where is he, anyway?' She looked around the waiting room, as if she expected him to pop up from behind a row of chairs or something.

'Oh. I asked him to go.'

Lara gaped at her, her mouth and eyes wide. 'And he actually went?'

'Yes! I wanted him to. I didn't give him a choice.'

'Um, *why*?' Lara asked, still looking at her as if she was missing several important cognitive functions. 'Seriously. Am I missing something here? Was I deluding myself thinking that you guys got it together?'

Jess sighed, slouching into the back-breaking chair. How long had she been here now? How long since Rufus had walked away? Since she'd pushed him away?

'It was nothing,' she lied. 'Just passing the time until the snow cleared.'

Lara crossed her arms and fixed her with a look. 'You know lying to me doesn't work. Not even when you're at your best. And you're seriously not at your best just now. How's the arm?'

'Really bloody painful, now that you ask,' Jess said, trying to force a laugh.

'I'm sorry. We don't have to talk about Rufus if you're not ready. But we can whenever you are.'

Jess nodded. 'Great, let's pencil that in for *never*, shall we?'

'It worked, you know. Upton Manor's engagement is through the roof. It's going to be fully booked all year, and I have this friend who does location-scouting for a movie production company... Never mind. I'll tell you

about that later. My followers loved you, as always.
And Rufus. You looked really good together. It was…
fairy tale.'

'Precisely. Fairy tale, as in "not real". And possibly
cursed,' Jess said, letting her black mood show. 'It was
fun, but it's over, and I'm not ready to talk about it.'

'Okay,' Lara said at last, drawing Jess close with an
arm around her shoulders and planting a big kiss on the
side of her head. 'So what's going on with the doctors?
Did they give you the good drugs yet?'

CHAPTER TWELVE

RUFUS GLANCED AT his phone for the thousandth time that morning. He'd muted his Instagram notifications because he just couldn't keep up with them. Jess had been right. Lara had worked her magic—even from a different country. But his feed was so full of Jess that he couldn't bear to look at it—never mind like, comment and share. He knew he needed to do it, but he couldn't. Not yet. Not when so many of those comments were asking what the deal was with the two of them, and he didn't know how to answer.

No, that wasn't true. He knew what was going on. They were over. It had all melted away with the snow. Just how they'd agreed. The problem was that he didn't like it. He wanted…he wanted *her*. It was as simple as that. He needed her. But nothing had changed. None of the reasons he knew she'd be better off without him.

And so he was here, in his parents' house, mainlining Twiglets and avoiding mince pies, and trying to answer his family's questions about how he'd spent his Christmas without touching on anything X-rated. Or showing the gaping hole that seemed to be growing in his chest since Jess had kicked him out of the hospital. He should just pick up the phone and call her. Just to make sure she was okay. To make sure that Lara had turned up and she wasn't still stuck alone in a corridor somewhere.

But Jess didn't need him.

So why couldn't he stop thinking about her?

'A watched phone never rings, love.'

He rolled his eyes at his mam. She'd been dropping hints, getting less and less subtle since the minute she'd arrived at the hospital to pick him up, eyes equal parts concern and curiosity. Once he'd assured her that he was okay—the call to the same hospital they'd been summoned to when his dad had suffered his heart attack wasn't an ideal Christmas present—he'd known that she could see that something had happened.

'You know you can tell me about it, don't you?' she said, pressing gently on what she must have known was a sore spot.

'About what?' Playing dumb was the only weapon he had, and he knew that it was nothing against his mother's arsenal.

'About whatever it is that happened that's got you looking so sad. About why you're stuck here all glum, instead of being wherever Jess is right now, trying to work out whatever's happened.'

'Nothing's happened, Mam. I keep telling you. She lives down there. I'm here. We enjoyed getting to know each other for a few days, and now we've gone back to our own lives. It's what we both wanted. Want.'

'Well, call me interfering—'

'You're interf—'

'But, love, you don't look like someone who's got what they want. You look like someone trying to come to terms with losing someone.'

He crossed his arms. There was no point having this conversation. It wasn't going to change anything. 'Even if I wanted—'

'Which you clearly do.'

'Even if I wanted things to be different, we don't always get what we want. What would be the point of saying that I want Jess? That I want to see her again because I think I'm falling for her? That I see myself building a life with her? Some people just aren't meant for that. Shouldn't have other people relying on them.'

His mam creased her eyebrows together thoughtfully. 'Why do I get the feeling we're not just talking about Jess here?'

'We are.' He huffed. 'And we're not, I suppose. It was my fault that you and Dad had to leave Upton. My fault that he's heartbroken about it.'

She scoffed. 'His heart was already broken. I've got the cardiologist's report to prove it. But you're right—it was Upton Manor that did it. It was trying to take responsibility for the family without accepting help. Without talking to me. Without being willing to compromise. Because I would have gladly gone years before we did if I'd known how bad things had got. If I'd been able to spare us your dad's heart attack. Don't repeat his mistakes, please, Rufus. Why don't you try sharing the problem? What's stopping you?'

Jess flicked through the TV guide, trying to find something in there that would make the hinterland between Christmas and New Year feel slightly less like the *Twilight Zone*. But it was either a Disney movie or sixties sitcom reruns, neither of which were going to work for her current melancholic state of mind. The initial flurry of excitement when she'd arrived home had fizzled in the twenty-four hours since she'd been back.

Lara had offered to take her straight back to her flat in Oxford, but she wanted to finish the conversation she'd started with her mum on Christmas Day. And it had gone better than she had thought. She'd offered to go to family therapy with her mum and dad. Or grief counselling. Or *anything* that would crack through the icy silence of her childhood home.

She'd made the error of checking her email. To find the job offer that had been made at the conference waiting for her in writing. If she took it, she'd be working a half-hour drive from Upton Manor. If she wanted to give this thing with Rufus a shot, there was nothing practical stopping her. Nothing at all in her way other than the fear that one day, without warning, her life would descend to the same level of sadness that she was currently soaking in at her parents' house. She looked up as her mum cleared her throat, standing in the doorframe, coat on and handbag over her shoulder.

'Will you be all right if we nip out for an hour?'

'It's just a broken wrist, Mum. Where are you off to?'

Her dad appeared behind her mum, and Jess didn't recognise the look that passed between them.

'We thought about what you said, on the phone, about talking to someone, and we managed to get an appointment. I don't know if it will…'

Jess launched herself off the sofa and wrapped her mum in a hug. 'Thank you,' she mumbled, the words almost lost in her mum's scarf.

She pulled herself upright and took a deep breath. 'I'm so happy that you're doing this,' she told her parents. 'And I really, really hope it helps you to be happy.'

Her mum gave an awkward smile. 'Well,' she said, 'that's all we want for you, too.'

After all these years, they had decided that what they had was still worth fighting for.

She could do that. She could fight. Even if it didn't work, even if it was too late, she could choose to fight, rather than hide out of fear of failure.

She was left with only one question on her mind—what was the fastest way to get to Yorkshire with only one functional arm? Would Lara drive her three hundred miles north just two days after she'd done the exact same journey in reverse? And then helpfully make herself scarce so that she could have this thing out with Rufus? Was that even what he wanted?

Sure, he had seemed hurt when she'd asked him to leave—but she'd done it because she'd felt him pulling away. So...what? She'd torched the thing to the ground rather than have a grown-up conversation about her feelings. Maybe she was more her parents' daughter than she thought. But she wasn't going to accept that she couldn't change her behaviour. She had a choice about whether she wanted to make her future, or just have it happen to her. And she was going to choose the option that at least had the possibility of Rufus in there.

She was digging in the sofa cushions, looking for her phone to call Lara and ask for the mother of all favours, when she heard her mum talking to someone in the driveway. Probably something that she'd ordered online in the sales, hoping that some retail therapy would fill the new Rufus-shaped hole in her life. She carried on looking for her phone.

'Jess...'

She spun on the spot, to find that the doorway was filled with Rufus, and she clutched the sofa cushion to her stomach. 'What are you doing here?' she asked. Was this real? Was he here because he wanted her? Because he wanted to try and make this thing work? Or was it something else?

He did something with his face, and she couldn't decide whether it was more smile or grimace.

'Talk to me, Rufus. I'm losing my mind here, imagining things. Did I leave something behind at Upton Manor? Is this a lost property thing?'

'I… I don't know what kind of thing this is. Other than a *I couldn't bear waiting another minute to see you* thing. Is it okay? That I'm here?'

She was slightly breathless, but she couldn't quite believe that this was real. She nodded, hesitantly.

'I'm not sure I should be doing this' he said. 'I told myself I shouldn't be doing this. I don't know if I can make you happy. If I can keep you that way.'

'No one can see into the future.'

'And you're suddenly okay about that?'

'No. But my mum and dad just left for marriage counselling. They decided they still want to work at what they have. It's hard not to be impressed by their example.'

'And if I mess up? I want to look after you.'

'I don't need looking after. And what if I mess up? We work at it, if we think it's worth it. Do you? Think it's worth it? Are you willing to try?'

'You know I am. I'm here.'

He smiled—definitely a smile—and she felt her heart physically swell with anticipation. 'I think this is an *I'm falling in love with you* thing,' he said. And she thought her heart might actually burst. 'An *I can't be-lieve we've been so stupid* thing.'

She dropped the cushion, and he frowned as his eyes followed it to the floor.

'What the heck are you doing to the sofa?'

'Looking for my phone,' Jess said, as if it was the most normal thing in the world. 'I needed to call Lara. It was urgent.' He was by her side in a second, his hand disappearing down the back of the sofa and re-emerging a moment later with her phone.

He held it out to her, but she didn't take it from him. Instead, she just smiled. 'I don't think I need it now.'

'You said it was urgent.'

'It was. I needed Lara to drive me. To you. But you're here.'

He took a step closer, and his hands dropped to her hips. Bending his head, he caught her eye. 'And what were you going to say when you got there?'

'Well, I was thinking about telling you that I was an idiot to make you leave. And I'm sorry. And can we talk about what we want and what we're both scared of? And maybe being grown-ups about this relation-ship that we seem to be having?'

She was madly in love with every single one of the lines that appeared around his eyes as he smiled at her. 'Okay. Well, I think I would have liked it if you'd turned up on my doorstep and told me all that. Maybe you could tell me all of it here instead.'

'Instead you turned up on mine. And told me you're falling for me.' She looped her good arm around his neck, reached up on tiptoe, and pulled herself a little higher.

'So what does this "being an adult" thing entail?' he asked, his voice a murmur.

'I think telling me you're falling in love with me was a good start.'

'Yeah?'

'Yeah. I'm thinking of trying it out.'

His lips curled into a smile. 'I think I might like that. When you're ready. And if you're not, we'll talk. There's nothing that we can't deal with if we talk. And if I'm going to spend half my life on the motorway so that we can do that face to face I don't care. I'm still in. It broke me to walk away from you thinking I wasn't going to see you again. I never want to feel like that again.'

She brushed a kiss against the corner of his mouth. 'So if I told you that I had a job offer from the university, and I was thinking of taking it, you wouldn't think I was jumping the gun?'

'I think that would be just about the best thing that I'd heard all year. I'd beg you to take it. To give me a chance. To give *us* a chance.'

'Okay,' she said on an out-breath. 'Okay, then. I'll take it. I'll take you. I'll take everything.'

EPILOGUE

THERE REALLY WERE an ungodly number of buttons on this dress.

She fidgeted as Lara fastened them up her spine, and she twitched at her lace sleeve.

'Stand still,' Lara said, flicking her spine with a finger, 'or this is never going to end.'

'Ow, that hurt.'

'Good. Now stand still.'

Jess looked down at her wedding dress, the same one she had tried on her first Christmas at Upton, and smiled. As if she could even think about wearing anything else to marry Rufus.

The past year had seen changes at Upton—film crews, back-to-back bookings, a subtle but steady climb in the bank balance. And it had never looked more beautiful than it did this morning, decorated in holly and mistletoe, fires burning, candles everywhere. Just as it had the first time that she'd seen it.

And then the dress was finally fastened and her hair was perfect and Lara was handing her a bouquet, and she couldn't believe that she was really doing this.

Marriage had looked like a trap her entire life, until she'd met Rufus and he'd made it feel like an adventure. And her parents, who had seemed so entombed by matrimony, had decided that it was worth fighting after all, and her whole worldview had been tipped upside down and thoroughly shaken.

The constant, throughout, had been Rufus.

And there he was, waiting for her at the bottom of the staircase as she stepped carefully down, his reddish-brown curls temporarily tamed, a sprig of holly in the buttonhole of his suit jacket. A far cry from the half-dead man she'd dragged over the threshold a year ago.

'You look beautiful,' he said as she reached him, leaning in for a kiss before they'd even started on their vows.

She glanced over at her parents, still working. Still fighting for one another, even after everything had seemed so bleak. And Rufus's parents, who had never faltered in their love for one another, even when they had faced the worst.

It turned out getting married was shockingly easy. *Repeat after me. Sign here. Smile there.* And then it was for ever—her and Rufus. Looking after one another. Looking after Upton. Bringing their families together. Fighting for each other.

For ever.

* * * * *

THE LONG-AWAITED
CHRISTMAS WISH

MELISSA SENATE

Prologue

One month ago, November

US marshal Rex Dawson thought he was alone on the footbridge across the Bear Ridge River in a rural Wyoming nature preserve, but a cute dog had come out of nowhere. The medium-size mutt was sniffing at the water's edge on the side of the bridge, just a few feet from where Rex stood. He glanced around the wilderness on all sides for the dog's owner, but he didn't see or hear anyone. Rex would know if there was anyone nearby; it was his job to be attuned to his surroundings. And because he'd been waiting over an hour for a rogue witness who hadn't shown up, Rex had been on red alert.

"Hey, buddy, you alone out here?" Rex asked, walking over to where the stray was pawing at something in the water against the wooden post of the bridge.

The dog looked up at him, head tilted. Some kind of shepherd mix, Rex figured, taking in the cinnamon and black markings and the tall, pointy ears that had to be four inches high. Rex glanced at what had caught the dog's interest. A bottle—with what looked like a rolled-up piece of paper inside. It was one of those old-fashioned glass milk jugs, the kind with a wide neck and body and a metal cap.

"Message in a bottle?" Rex asked the dog, giving him a pat behind his ears.

He picked up the dirty bottle. He knew this type well. Rex had grown up on a dude ranch that his grandparents had started, and the family's milk had come from their cow, Lizzie. His grandmother had liked old-fashioned milk bottles, but with the hinged tops. When his grandparents had passed on fourteen years ago and his dad had inherited the Dawson Family Guest Ranch, Bo Dawson had soon sold off the animals to pay for his drinking and gambling addictions and there was rarely milk in the fridge, despite his six kids. "Water is free and comes right out of the tap," Bo would say, pointing at the sink. Rex still couldn't think of the ranch without his dad coming to mind.

"Some things never change, buddy," he told the dog. The sweet-faced mutt stared at Rex with those old-soul amber eyes. No collar. Too skinny. Dirty. A little on the timid side. He looked cold and lonely and hungry. Definitely a stray. "C'mon," Rex said. "Let's go warm up in my truck and we'll see what the note in the bottle says."

The dog tilted his head again and seemed to be saying, *You talking to me?* Rex headed for the small gravel parking lot, his new friend following. He got a blanket from the cargo area of his SUV and made a bed of sorts on the passenger seat. "Up you go," Rex said, and the dog hopped in. Rex turned on the ignition, heat filling the vehicle, and the dog sighed and stretched out his long, narrow snout, resting his chin on Rex's knee.

Aww. He petted his new buddy behind the ears, then looked at the bottle. "So let's see what this message says." He uncapped the bottle and fished out the rolled-up yellowed paper. It was a letter to Santa, dated fifteen years ago.

Dear Santa,
All I want for Christmas is a family. Just
a mom OR a dad would be fine. I'm not

picky. I would also really love to have a brother or a sister. But if that's asking for too much, I'll just take a mom or dad. I've been really good this year. You can ask Miss Meredith—she runs the foster home.
Maisey Clark, eight years old
Prairie City, Wyoming

One-two punch straight to the heart. Damn. He could just picture little Maisey Clark, sitting in her foster home in Prairie City and writing out this note in her best handwriting. He imagined her swiping an empty milk bottle, sliding in the rolled-up letter to Santa and tossing it out into the river, hoping it carried all the way to the north pole.

The bottle certainly hadn't gotten very far. "But I hope her Christmas wish came true," he said to the dog. "Think it did, River?"

River. Guess he'd named the stray. For where he'd found him, where he'd found the bottle, containing a fifteen-year-old letter to Santa.

He had to know. Actually, it was more than that—he *needed* to know that Maisey Clark had gotten her family. Between the cold, skinny stray dog and the fervent wish for a parent, Rex knew he should be counting his blessings. Yeah, his job was stressful and he'd been through some stuff he'd like to forget. But he had family. Despite losing his dad last December when the two of them had unfinished business, the six Dawson siblings were always there for one another. Sometimes he didn't appreciate that enough.

"What do you think happened to Maisey, River?" he asked. "She'd be twenty-three now." He really hoped her wish had come true. That she'd been adopted by a wonderful family. "Maybe they even had a cute pooch like you."

River licked his hand and looked at him with those sweet eyes.

"I sure would like to take you home," he said, petting River's side. "But I don't really have one. I have a condo in Cheyenne I rarely use because I'm always on the road."

Right now, he was hours from that condo but just outside Bear Ridge, where he'd grown up and spent as little time as possible. He couldn't rescue a dog when he was home maybe once every three months and otherwise lived in hotels across the country.

"I do know where to take you, though," he said, scratching River under the chin. "The Dawson Family Guest Ranch. My sister and two of my brothers live on the property, and if one of them can't take you in, they'll find you a good home." He had no doubt about that.

Rex pulled out of the parking lot, his head a jumble of Christmas wishes, stray dogs, rogue witnesses and tomorrow's three meetings, including escorting a witness to court. Day after tomorrow he'd be accompanying a seventy-two-year-old widower to his new life in the Florida Keys, going over protocol of the witness protection program and sticking around for a while to get him acclimated to life under a new identity. Rex knew that wasn't easy. But being on the run, scared and alone, wasn't easy, either. Rex hoped to find his missing witness—the one who'd agreed to meet him at the river today but hadn't—by Christmas.

Finding Maisey Clark should be a lot easier. If not a simple Google search, then through his access to databases. He had to know what happened, that Maisey *had* gotten a family. He wasn't one to believe in Christmas wishes—or any kind—coming true. But for Maisey he'd make an exception.

Chapter One

Two weeks before Christmas

Rex was one for three on his must-do list. Finding Maisey Clark not only *hadn't* been easy, but impossible. He'd tried everything, but her name never came up in any of his searches. He took it to mean she'd been adopted and therefore had a different last name. He wanted to believe that, anyway. He had managed to get in touch with the "Miss Meredith" who Maisey had mentioned in her letter, but the foster mother had told him Maisey had moved to a different group foster home the following year, and given her age, Meredith doubted she'd been adopted, though she'd been unable to say for sure. Not knowing made him itchy.

And his rogue witness never responded to any of Rex's calls or texts. Not that Rex was giving up on him. The past few days Rex had been chasing down leads in Montana, determined to find the guy. Rex believed in justice—for the victim and family, for the witness's future, for the criminal to rot in prison. Rex was running on fumes, but he hadn't agreed with his boss that he needed two weeks off leading to Christmas. The boss had insisted. And so here Rex was, with two weeks R & R on the Dawson Family Guest Ranch. He'd still work during his time off. He had to.

The one thing Rex had accomplished? Getting that sweet stray dog a new home—right here at the ranch with his sister, Daisy, who'd fallen for River on sight. Despite being a busy new mother of a five-month-old baby and the guest relations manager of the ranch, she'd adored River so much that she'd hoped no one would claim him. River hadn't had a microchip, and after checking with local shelters and posting ads, no one had come for the dog. River was hers.

Now Rex sat in Daisy's big country kitchen in the farmhouse he grew up in. River was asleep in his plush blue dog bed by the stone fireplace.

When he'd arrived at Daisy's this morning, officially on vacation, he'd gotten a serious welcome from the pooch he'd rescued from that cold riverside, the dog so excited to see him that Rex vowed to come visit more often. His family and River. He'd only been at the ranch for a few hours, catching up with his siblings who lived and worked on the ranch, but coming home early for Christmas might have been a good idea after all. He did need this break. He had some things to figure out—and he wasn't even sure what those things were. That he felt unsettled was an understatement.

All he knew was that ever since his brother Noah had rebuilt the guest ranch last spring, the place *didn't* remind him of home—a word that had always come with baggage. He liked the ranch now, could breathe here, think here.

"I have a very attractive, interesting woman in mind for you," Daisy said, setting out ham, cheese, a delicious-looking baguette and mayo and mustard on the kitchen table.

River opened an eye, smelling lunch.

Rex cut the bread. Daisy was a notorious matchmaker. "Let me stop you right there. I'm here for two weeks, then back on the road."

Daisy narrowed her eyes at him. "Are you ever going to tell us what you do? Noah thinks you're a spy. I say FBI."

Rex smiled. He'd never told his family what his job was because of the nature of the work; it had to remain secret and so he chose not to discuss it. "I'll tell you this—you're on the right track. But trust me, my job is the main reason you shouldn't fix me up, Daisy. How can I have a relationship when I'm never home? I don't even have a home, not really."

"This *is* home, Rex. Forget that sterile one-bedroom condo in Cheyenne. Build a luxe cabin like Axel did on the property. We have thousands of acres in the Wyoming wilderness. You can still do whatever it is you do with the ranch as your base."

She wasn't wrong about that. But he'd spent so much time thinking of this ranch as *not* home that building a cabin on the property hadn't really entered his mind, no matter how much he liked the place now. He was planning to stay with Axel the first week of his vacation and Daisy the second. Their brother Noah and his wife, Sara, lived in the foreman's cabin just a quarter mile down the road with their twins and there wasn't room for Rex, though they'd invited him anyway, because they were nice that way. "Our sofa is your sofa," Noah had said.

With Daisy's baby, Noah's eight-month-old twins and Axel's toddler, there were already quite a few members of the next generation of Dawsons. And they were far removed from the not-so-great last fifteen years. Those little ones would grow up entirely differently than their parents had, with a real appreciation of the Dawson Family Guest Ranch and its history.

"Wait," Daisy said. "Did I just hear Tony?" She cocked an ear toward the stairs and the nursery on the second floor. Pure silence. "Nope. Or maybe he fussed and soothed himself back to sleep. Harrison and I have been working on that."

Rex had gotten to see his cute nephew for about ten minutes this morning before the tyke had yawned so hard Daisy had had to put him down for a nap.

Daisy sat, and they made their sandwiches. "Hey, guess what," she said. "We're restarting an old Dawson Family Guest Ranch annual tradition—a daylong Christmas fair like Gram and Gramps used to put on for the guests. Remember?"

He remembered. He'd loved those fairs, which always included reindeer and a Santa hut, multi-colored lights everywhere. His grandparents had always seemed magical to him, despite how homespun and rooted and practical they were.

"We always have a lot of kids, but with the Christmas fair advertising, bookings with children skyrocketed, so I hired a full-time nanny for our babysitting program." Daisy told him all about the Kid Zone, a huge room in the lodge staffed by a few energetic employees so that guests could drop off their children to partake in ranch activities the kids might be too young for or not interested in. "The nanny oversees the Kid Zone and the three sitters. I'm telling ya, Maisey Clark is a godsend. She's been here only a couple days and—"

Rex almost dropped his ham-and-cheese sandwich. "Wait, Daisy. Did you say *Maisey Clark*?"

"Yes. Why? You know her?"

He stared at Daisy, barely able to believe this. "Is she in her early twenties?"

"She's twenty-three, but has a lot of childcare experience and great references. Why?"

Eight plus fifteen. Bingo. He'd been trying to track down this woman for a month and here she was? Mind-boggling. "I think I do know her. Sort of. I'll tell you about it after I confirm it's the same Maisey Clark."

"The Kid Zone closes at six. First floor in the lodge. Big colorful sign at the end of the hall."

River came padding over and put his furry black chin on Rex's thigh. *We found her, River,* he silently told his buddy while petting his head. *Now we'll learn if her Christmas wish came true.*

He sure hoped it had. Because he felt like something deep inside would settle, that wrongs would be righted, that foster kids writing to Santa for a mom or a dad would be heard.

He wanted to rush over to the lodge right now, but he figured he'd wait till closing time, when she wasn't busy and surrounded by children. Maisey Clark was a half mile away from where he sat. The coincidence *had* to mean something. *What* he didn't know, but it was Christmastime and it seemed like close to a miracle.

Maisey Clark added a stuffed reindeer, two small balls and three action figures to the big basket she carried around the various sections of the Kid Zone. She looked around the colorful space, each area marked for different age groups. Spotless. Her second workday at the Dawson Family Guest Ranch's childcare center was over, all the kids—and the huge room in the lodge—picked up.

She closed her eyes for a second, barely able to believe she'd gotten this perfect-for-her job just when she'd hit rock bottom last week. Her previous full-time job at a day care barely paid enough for Maisey, a single mother without support from anywhere, to make rent and utilities, let alone keep her six-month-old daughter in diapers. But there'd been cutbacks and Maisey had been let go and she'd been frantic.

The posting she'd noticed for this job—nanny at the Dawson Family Guest Ranch—was so perfect she hadn't dared hope to get it, but she had. Room, board and a salary—plus Maisey could bring her baby to work. "Room" was a small but cute and clean cabin nestled in the woods just a quarter mile from the lodge. "Board" was free meals and snacks in the ranch's amazing cafeteria. Omelets for breakfast. All the soup and salad and sandwiches she could eat at lunch. And entrées for dinner she hadn't been able to afford in the grocery store, like fish and steak. The salary wouldn't come for another week when she received her first paycheck, but she had enough diapers and baby food to get her through. She was used to buying secondhand for her baby girl when it came to pajamas and her snowsuit and just about everything in her tiny nursery in the cabin, but it was Christmastime, and Maisey would love to buy Chloe something special. She'd see.

If there was one thing Maisey understood, it was that the rug could be yanked when you least expected it. Oh, she thought her husband loved her? Nope. Would care that he had a child coming into the world? Nope. Long gone. Never met Chloe and wasn't interested. Nor was his family,

since he'd told them Chloe wasn't even *his*—liar. A job that seemed secure? Ha. No such thing. Maisey Clark was a realist. The most important thing was building a nest egg, an emergency stash of cash in the bank for when the rug did get pulled. A friend and coworker from the day care had told Maisey to find herself a sugar daddy to marry, but first of all: *ew*, and second of all: no. Maisey would stand on her own two feet. She could only rely on herself, something she was well used to.

She took the basket over to the check-in desk; housekeeping would pick up all the toys for disinfecting from sticky little fingers coated with animal cracker crumbs and juice box drippings. She loved those sticky fingers. Maisey adored the children, from infants to teenagers, who'd come through the Kid Zone the past two days. Not that she hadn't gotten peed on by a baby—once (a rookie mistake)—and broken up two bad arguments and had to call one boy's parents to pick him up because he wouldn't follow the rules. She took the bad with the good. Working with children, listening to them, being there for them, had been all she'd ever wanted to do. Her heart had been set on being a teacher, but affording college was still a pipe dream. One day, she'd get there.

For now, all she wanted was to go home to

her sweet little cabin, heat up last night's left-over pasta carbonara from the ranch cafeteria and watch a funny movie. Maybe some mindless re-ality TV.

She heard the door to the Kid Zone open with its loud jangle and she turned around. A man came in, glancing around, his eyes stopping on her. His entire body stopped, too. He just stood there staring at her with a look on his face she couldn't read.

"Maisey Clark?"

Uh-oh, she thought, taking in the tall, dark-haired guy with the assessing blue eyes and won-dering what he could possibly want with her. It wasn't so much that he looked like a cop that he seemed like one. He worked in some official capacity—that much she was sure of. The way he'd said her name. The way he was staring at her as if sizing her up. She walked over to him hold-ing the basket against her stomach like a shield. "Yes, I'm Maisey Clark. What can I do for you?"

"I have something that I think belongs to you," he said, reaching into the backpack on his shoul-der and pulling out something covered in Bub-ble Wrap.

What could it be? Did she even own anything breakable? With a six-month-old baby and a job taking care of many kids big and small all day, she wasn't the Bubble Wrap type.

As he unwrapped it, she gasped, her hand covering her mouth. "Omigosh," she whispered.

It was a bottle. A dirty, scratched-up old milk bottle with a metal cap. And there was a rolled-up piece of paper inside. She knew what that note said. She knew because she wrote it. Fifteen years ago.

"You found this?" She shook her head. "I can't believe it."

"What I can't believe is that you're right here, working at my family's ranch, when I've been looking for you for a month. I'm Rex Dawson," he added, shifting the bottle to his left hand and extending his right one.

She shook his hand, warm and strong. "Mais—" she began, then smiled. "Well, you know who I am. "*And* what I wanted for Christmas when I was eight years old." Suddenly that seemed a little too personal, like he knew too much about her. "Where'd you find it?"

"About ten minutes from here by a footbridge across the Bear Ridge River." He held it out to her.

"Well, that's no surprise," she said, taking the bottle and sighing. Part of her wanted to pull out the note and read it, but another part couldn't bear to. "That it didn't get very far. On its route to the north pole," she added with a smile.

"That must mean what you wrote, what you wished for, never came true." He looked kind of crestfallen, which touched her.

"Nope. Never did." As she was hit with a few memories she didn't want to think about, she changed the subject. "You're a cop, right? Or work for the state in some capacity?"

His eyes widened. He seemed both surprised and impressed. "Federal law enforcement. But how could you know that? My own family doesn't know what I do for a living."

"When you're a foster kid, you get used to officials—how they sound, how they stand, the way they look you over, assessing. So you're FBI?"

"US marshal," he said.

"I was close."

He laughed, but then sobered. "Alarmingly so. I'm not sure why I was so forthcoming. My family doesn't even know what my job is exactly."

"Well, you know my biggest secret—what I used to want for Christmas more than anything, and now I know yours."

He gave her something of a smile and seemed to be assessing again.

"When you first said my name, I thought maybe

you were a dad here to pick up your child and didn't realize your wife beat you to it. No kids left," she added, waving an arm at the empty room.

He glanced around the huge space, which had several well-marked sections—for babies and toddlers, for preschoolers, for big kids and for teens. There were play structures, a rock wall, basketball hoops, a library, chairs and tables, countless beanbags, games, lots of balls and foam blocks and the Kid Zone sitters besides herself to watch the kids like a hawk. Maisey always took care of the babies and toddlers. Because the six cabins at the Dawson Family Guest Ranch were booked from two-day packages to weeks at a time, the guests were always changing.

He raised an eyebrow. "Well, that would be impossible since I'm not married and don't have kids and don't plan to."

She felt her smile fade. Something in the way he'd said that told her he meant it, that something had happened. Bad experience, maybe. She knew all about that.

"And there *is* one left," he said. "That quiet little baby over there." He pointed behind her.

She turned and smiled at the sleeping baby girl. "That's actually my daughter, Chloe. She's six months old. Perk of the job is getting to bring her to work."

He looked at the baby, then back at her. "At first I thought the reason I couldn't find you in the system was because you'd been adopted and your last name changed. Then just a minute ago, I figured you'd gotten married. But if you did, you clearly kept your maiden name, so now I'm confused why I couldn't find you."

"I got married at eighteen and was so excited to join my husband's family, take his name. But turns out he wasn't very family-oriented. Or vows-oriented. I tried to make things work, and when I finally got pregnant, he told me we were through. I haven't seen him since that night."

Oh, Lordy. Why had she said all that? She could feel her cheeks burning and turned slightly away from him.

"So you took back your maiden name," he said gently.

She nodded. "Very recently. I missed the connection to my parents, anyway. They didn't leave me on purpose. I'm glad to be Maisey Clark again. And I do have a family now—with Chloe and our cat, Snowbell. So really, I did get a family—just took fifteen years from the time I wrote that letter."

The look on Rex Dawson's face, pure compassion, had her off balance. *Thanks but no thanks.* Anytime she got personal, talked about her past, which was rare for her, she felt so vulnerable, so exposed. She hated the "oh, you poor thing" pity she got whenever she was put in a position to mention how she'd grown up.

Chloe's eyes fluttered open, and Maisey walked over to the baby swing and lifted her up.

"Guess I'd better get this little one home," she said, kneeling in front of her open tote bag for Chloe's fleece snowsuit. "I live in the cabin between here and the cafeteria." She pulled out the snowsuit, the bag still overstuffed with everything she and a baby could need for an eight-hour day in the Kid Zone, from extra onesies to two changes of clothes for Maisey in case she was thrown up on—it had happened twice her first day—to bottles and diapers. She tried to get the milk bottle inside, but there wasn't room, so she started taking things out to reconfigure.

"I'll walk you home and carry the bottle for you," he said. "It's my fault you have an extra thing to lug."

"I've got it," Maisey said, but now a burp cloth had gotten stuck in the zipper in her haste to get going. "Or not," she added with a sigh.

Accept help when you need it. Rule of getting by in life, she reminded herself.

He extended his hand for the bottle. She smiled and gave it to him, extricating the burp cloth and managing to shove everything back in and get the bag zipped up this time.

"You know, I'm glad you found it and brought it to me," she said, standing up. "I have closure on it now. One of my foster sisters and I wrote letters to Santa that same day and we both threw our bottles in the creek that ran behind the home. She was a year older than I was and said she didn't believe in Santa, but since I did, I would get what I wanted and she surely wouldn't. Two days later, an estranged aunt came to take her home and formally adopted her by that Christmas. She called to tell me she'd believe in Santa even when she was ninety-nine."

Maisey smiled at the memory of her sweet friend with the long auburn hair and freckles.

"Are you two still in touch?" he asked, putting the bottle in his backpack and slinging it over his shoulder. Broad, she couldn't help but notice.

"We lost touch when I got moved out of Miss Meredith's group home. But I'm glad she got all my Christmas spirit. I never was able to get it back," she said, then rolled her eyes at herself for saying too much again.

Even though she wasn't looking at him—she was looking anywhere but at him—she could tell he was studying her.

"Well, I have a quarter of Christmas spirit,

maybe an eighth, so I get it," he said. "I'm hoping I get to half by the big day."

She stared at him. "Why? You have a burning Christmas wish?"

"More like there are some things I want to accomplish—work related. And some things I need to figure out."

"Well, the ranch is definitely the place for that," she said. "I'm from Prairie City, which is still plenty quiet despite it being a bigger town, but out here in the wilderness, you can really think."

"That's what I'm hoping for." He unexpectedly picked up her big pink tote and put it on his other shoulder.

Good-looking *and* kind.

She got Chloe bundled in her fleece snowsuit with the bear ears, the much-appreciated gift from her former coworkers at the day care. Once Chloe was settled into her stroller, they went into the hallway of the grand lodge. She locked up and turned the sign on the door over, indicating the Kid Zone was closed till 9:00 a.m. tomorrow.

"Christmas is everywhere on the ranch," she said, eyeing the huge tree, trimmed to the nines, by the curving staircase at the end of the hall. "Honestly, sometimes it's hard to look at, and sometimes a piece of red tinsel will remind me of my parents and I want to wrap myself in it, you know?"

Ugh. There was that compassion on his face again. Why was she being so talkative, so open with this guy? She didn't know him at all.

The bottle, the memory—of everything it invoked—had done a number on her, most likely. Maisey always like to think she was immune to nostalgia and sentiment. And then whammo. Her mother's voice. Her dad's hugs. She'd have to close her eyes, wanting to keep them close and push them away at the same time.

Story of her life.

"Honestly, it's hard for me to just be on this property," he said, his gaze on the tree. "Unfinished business. Christmas always makes me feel pressured to come here, to count my blessings, to slow down. I want to be here *and* on a plane flying away right now."

"So you get it," she said, goose bumps on the nape of her neck. He *really* got it. "But I *am* counting my blessings. I have my Chloe. And I have this job. I was getting really worried about my bank account when I saw the ad posted for the nanny job at the ranch."

"I'm glad it worked out," he said on almost a whisper, and she glanced at him, wondering what he was thinking. She didn't see pity in his expression. Then again, it was his job to have a poker face.

His gaze moved to Chloe. "Your baby looks very content. My three siblings who live on the ranch all have kids—babies and a toddler, so I'm learning to read faces and cries for when I need to babysit."

She smiled. "Uncle Rex."

"Another thing I never thought I'd be. Now I have three nephews and a niece. Proving that old adage right—life is full of surprises."

"Good and bad," she said, then immediately wished she could take it back. *Stop telling him your every thought*, she silently yelled at herself.

"I'd clink to that if I were holding a glass of eggnog."

She laughed. "I *love* eggnog. I might not have any Christmas spirit, but I never pass up eggnog."

Once outside in the cold, biting air, she stared at the two evergreens flanking the lodge, both festooned with white lights. Beautiful—but she tried to avoid looking at them.

"When Chloe's a little older—two, I guess—I'll get more into Christmas, I'm sure," she said. "The last thing she needs is Mom saying *bah humbug*. Christmas is everything to kids."

He glanced at her, and she could tell he was thinking about the eight-year-old whose Christmas wish hadn't come true. *Darn it. Shut up, Maisey. Stop. Talking.*

They headed down the gravel path that led to her cabin. It was nestled in the woods, and she loved it. Her boss, Daisy, Rex's sister, had hung a beautiful wreath on the door as a welcome gift, and Maisey had been so touched. It was the perfect amount of Christmas. Enough to serve as a reminder but not enough to make her go into the bathroom and sob.

At the cabin, she unlocked the door and wheeled in the stroller, Rex right behind her with the tote bag. He put it down, then unzipped his backpack and pulled out the bottle, which he set on the console table. Right beside a photo of her and her parents, a Christmas tree behind them. Maisey had been five. But by Christmas Eve she'd been in the foster home that Miss Meredith ran.

He picked up the photo. "I can understand why Christmas is hard for you." He put the frame down.

She felt tears stinging. "This is Chloe's first Christmas, though. I hate being a Scrooge. It's not fair to her. I should at least get a tree for the cabin."

"I can picture one right by the window," he said, looking in that direction, then all around the sparsely decorated open-concept first floor. She only had the basics for furniture since she and her ex had lived in a trailer with a lot of built-ins.

Once she got her first paycheck, she'd see what she truly needed.

"There's a great Christmas tree farm in Bear Ridge about five minutes from here," he said. "It's open till ten and well lit. I'd be happy to take you tomorrow night. My treat. As a welcome gift."

She looked down at Chloe in the stroller, her hazel eyes so alert. *New traditions*, she told herself. *For Chloe. Do it for her.* "You Dawsons sure are nice," she said. "Your sister gave me the wreath on the door." She wouldn't be able to afford a tree otherwise, not for a week, anyway, so although she didn't love taking what felt like charity, she nodded. "Thank you."

And just like that, he was picking her up from the lodge at six tomorrow. With a peekaboo to Chloe and a smile to her, he left. The minute the door closed behind him, she felt his absence.

"What's up with that, Snowbell?" she asked as her white cat padded over to slink between her ankles. She knelt down to scratch Snowbell by her tail, her favorite spot. "Good-looking. Kind. Knows too much about me."

Maisey Clark had been stomped on by the giant boot of heartache, and picking herself up from that—from her parents' deaths, to the constant disappointment of never getting adopted, to her husband's betrayal—had been tough. That last one she'd gotten through because of Chloe. Her daughter needed her.

She took Chloe out of her stroller, peeling her from the bear fleece snowsuit, relishing the soft weight of her baby in her arms. She snuggled Chloe against her chest. She had everything she needed now. And tomorrow night she'd have a tree, too—for her daughter.

What she didn't need? A hot, generous man distracting her from what was important. She'd thank Rex Dawson for his thoughtfulness when they lugged the tree here, and that would be that. No talking, no sharing, no gut-spilling. No imagining herself in that gorgeous man's arms. Fantasies like that were all too easy to make come true. But cold hard reality always came around— the next morning or a few weeks or even a few years later.

If she was actually going to have a little Christmas for her daughter, the last thing Maisey wanted was to ruin it.

Chapter Two

The next afternoon, as Rex helped his two-year-old nephew, Danny, build a tower of blocks in his brother Axel's mansion-like log cabin, he couldn't stop thinking about Maisey. That she was *real*—the person behind the letter to Santa. That she was so pretty with big pale brown eyes, long silky blond hair in a ponytail down her back. His reaction to her had caught him by surprise. Of course, he knew there would be a connection because of the bottle, the letter inside, but everything about her—particularly her honesty or maybe her vulnerability—drew him hard. She was so young, just twenty-three. She deserved the anticipation of a bright, shiny future. Instead, she could barely stomach Christmas.

Not that Rex should talk. At thirty-one, he was as world-weary and cynical as they came, having seen the worst of people and what the worst could do to law-abiding citizens. Rex had been a marshal for so long that distancing himself from people was ingrained.

That he wanted to kiss Maisey goodbye last night, even on the cheek, though he'd been thinking about her lips, wasn't a good sign. It meant he was both emotionally and physically attracted. He was leaving in less than two weeks, the day after Christmas, and he had no doubt in his mind that Maisey Clark needed a forever kind of man, someone ready to settle down and be the great husband she deserved, the great father to her baby daughter. He wasn't that guy. So he'd better forget about her lips and face and hair and how powerfully drawn to her he was. Maybe it was a protective thing.

Yes. That was it. That made sense. She was young with so much responsibility, and she'd had no one behind her since she was a very young child. He felt protective; of course he did.

Though if Maisey barely wanted a Christmas tree, he had no doubt she didn't want a relationship mucking up the works, either. Which also made him feel oddly protective of her. He *wanted* her to want, to hope, to dream.

"Unck Rex, higher!" Danny said, pointing at the top of their tower, which was about three feet and just a little taller than his nephew.

"Higher? I'd better put you on my shoulders so you can get the blocks up there," Rex said, and the little blond imp climbed on, a block in each hand. Rex was on his knees and Danny added the blocks, cheering and pumping his little fist in the air.

"You are so meant to be a dad."

Startled by the voice and the comment, Rex turned—carefully since he had a toddler on his shoulders—to find his sister-in-law Sadie smiling at him, his brother Axel behind her as they came in the front door. And behind them were the dogs—Axel's yellow Lab, Dude, and River. Last night, when Rex had been leaving Daisy's to go to the lodge with the bottle, River had followed him out and lain down in front of his path, putting his chin on Rex's shoe. Daisy had said River was clearly trying to tell them something—that he knew he was meant to be with Rex. He reminded his sister that he lived on the road and in crummy hotels and couldn't take on a dog, and Daisy had said she'd consider herself River's foster mother until Rex figured out that he belonged on the ranch.

You had to hand it to Daisy for trying.

So now River would be staying with him at Axel and Sadie's, which they were more than fine with. River had such a sweet temperament and was gentle with Danny, who was well used to dogs since he lived with Dude. And the two pooches had become best buds.

And if Rex were honest, he'd admit how much he liked having River with him. The dog had felt like his from the moment he'd rescued him. That feeling, though, the *belonging*, grated on him, and he wasn't sure why.

But that discomfort was always with him, and it was why he *wasn't* meant to be a dad. Luckily, there was so much noise and activity right now that Rex didn't have to comment on what Sadie had said.

Axel and Sadie took off their zillion layers— hats, gloves, scarves, boots—then came into the living room. Rex set his nephew down and he went leaping into his dad's arms, who hoisted him high and turned him upside down and sideways to his son's complete joy.

"Oh, God, Axel, don't make him throw up lunch—and all over my favorite rug," Sadie said, laughing.

Axel grinned and gave Danny a big kiss on the cheek and set his son down.

"Can I knock over the blocks, Unck Rex?" Danny asked.

"That is what they're for!" Rex said with a grin. "On three. One. Two—"

Danny charged ahead, gleefully knocking the foam blocks all over his play area. He tossed two handfuls up in the air and let them rain down on him and the dogs. Dude and River gave the blocks a sniff, then went into their beds by the fireplace, River with his favorite toy in his mouth, a squeaky stuffed squirrel that Rex had bought him the day he'd brought him over to the ranch.

Okay, so he did love that dog. Fine. But when it came to relationships with *two*-legged creatures, he was better off just avoiding them altogether. He met terrific women on the road all the time, often at hotel bars across the country where he'd go to unwind after a rough day, and those times when he really needed the company in every way, he was completely honest. Those encounters always left him feeling empty, though. The last time he'd actually tried a relationship—with a fellow marshal, a woman he'd really fallen for—she'd blasted him when he couldn't propose after six months of dating, of long-distance phone calls and hard-to-arrange rendezvous. *This is the real point*, she'd said, wagging a finger between them. *Love.*

He had loved her—he was pretty sure, anyway—

but he hadn't been able to bring himself to propose. So maybe he hadn't loved her? Maybe he just wasn't ready for a lifetime commitment? *Or maybe I'm just not the right woman*, she'd thrown at him before storming out of his life. That was six months ago.

Rex sighed and stared at the beautifully decorated Christmas tree by the floor-to-ceiling windows across the room. There were countless brightly wrapped gifts around the tree, a few with his name on them, which he saw when Danny had led him over to ask him to point out the ones with *his* name.

Rex thought about what his sister said earlier, before Rex had left for the lodge to meet Maisey. *Oh, you should know—about dating? Axel said the same thing. Not interested. Look at him now. Married with a baby on the way and a very doting daddy.*

Rex could hardly believe it. Fatherhood sure did suit Axel, though. But Rex? No. Being a doting uncle was easy.

Fatherhood was something else. All the Dawson siblings knew that. Even if half of them were now—quite happily—parents.

He thought about the difference between this cabin and Maisey's—the complete lack of holiday decorations in her place, despite her wanting to give her baby girl a special first Christmas.

From what Maisey had said about her finances and from the lack of furniture in her cabin, she didn't have much.

He'd stop by the general store in town, which had lots of garland and lights and tree-topper stars and ornaments. Then after they brought home her tree tonight, he could help her trim it. Over the next week and a half he'd add lots of gifts for Maisey and her baby and even a catnip mouse or two for Snowbell. Yes. He'd give Maisey the Christmas she'd been long owed and the one her baby girl deserved, and he could drive off back to his life on the road, belonging nowhere and to no one. The way he liked it.

But his gaze landed on River, his cinnamon-and-black body curled up in the plush red plaid bed, the old-soul amber eyes soft on Rex. *We belong to each other*, the dog seemed to be saying.

Luckily, his nephew chose that moment to catapult into his lap for a giant hug and Rex stopped thinking too far ahead.

"Would you like to make an ornament with your name on it for the tree?" Maisey asked the girl sitting by herself on a mat and looking glum. "We have a whole 'make your own' station over there," Maisey said, pointing. The table, overseen by one of Maisey's very energetic staffers, had been a huge hit today.

It was five thirty and only two kids remained in the Kid Zone, nine-year-old Zara and thirteen-year-old Tyler, who had been shooting hoops for almost an hour straight and showed no signs of tiring. The dribbling and ball landing with a hard bounce had become kind of soothing ambient noise. Tyler's parents and younger sister were at the petting zoo presentation on the animals. Earlier this afternoon, the sister had been in the Kid Zone while the parents and Tyler went fly-fishing. Zara and her parents had arrived at the ranch today and were staying through Christmas.

The girl's hazel eyes were a combination of pissed off and hurt. Maisey only got to notice when Zara pushed her long dark hair away from her face.

"Nope" was the response as Zara crossed her arms over her chest and stared straight ahead.

Tough customer, Maisey thought. "Maybe a game of jacks or cards? Crazy Eights?"

"No and no." Zara wouldn't even look at Maisey.

"I think your mom said she'd be back to pick you up at 5:45. That's fifteen minutes to fill. What are you in the mood to do?"

"First of all, I know how to tell time. Second of all, nothing!" With that, Zara got up and stalked over to a purple beanbag and flopped herself down.

Yikes. Angry and disrespectful, which Maisey would let pass because it was her job to know when to discipline and when to give a kid some space. She also knew that when a kid was hurting, they usually didn't want to be left alone. But in this case, she got the sense she should give Zara a little time to cool down.

Still, that didn't mean Maisey couldn't say one more thing. She made a show of picking up errant balls and blocks and dumping them into a basket she held. There was a stuffed tiger by Zara's beanbag. She headed over and picked it up.

"Zara, I didn't mean to crowd you. Just let me know if you need or want anything."

That seemed to enrage the girl even more. She snapped her head fast in the opposite direction. What mattered right now was that Zara knew Maisey was here for her.

The door opened, and Tyler's dad came in. "Hey, buddy. Time to wash up for dinner. I hear it's burrito night at the caf."

Tyler nodded, dribbling the ball up to the hoop. "He shoots, he scores, the crowd goes—" he said as he shot the final basket. And missed.

"Mild!" Zara finished, rolling her eyes.

Tyler laughed good-naturedly and chased down the ball and shot a three-pointer. "You mean wild!

Whoooo. Whooosh," he said, making a mega-phone around his mouth.

Zara rolled her eyes again and turned away.

Maisey waved a hello at Tyler's dad and the two left. Half a minute later, Zara's parents came in. You could hear the girl's sigh clear across the room. Interesting. The bad mood extended to her folks.

"Hi, Zara!" her mom said with what looked like a cautious smile to Maisey. "I hear it's bur-rito night in the caf tonight. You get to choose your fillings."

"At least I like burritos," Zara muttered, get-ting up from the beanbag.

Maisey noticed the mom and dad give each other a look. Had Zara meant she didn't like her mom with that "at least"? The tension from the girl definitely carried over as she headed out, re-fusing her dad's hand.

Family angst. Whatever was going on, the parents seemed loving and caring. Maisey knew everything was relative and she couldn't com-pare her lack of parents to Zara's, but she couldn't help thinking, *You have no idea how lucky you are*. What she would have given for someone to care that she loved burritos. Or that when she was young and then a teenager, she missed hav-ing parents, people who loved her, cared about her, *so* badly that she'd have to go very still until she could get ahold of herself, accept the unacceptable.

Rex Dawson was going to be here soon to take her tree shopping, so Maisey got busy giving each station a last look over. One of her sitters had gone through each section to make sure everything was tidy for tomorrow and the place looked great. No one would ever know that many kids of various ages had come and gone through these sections today.

Six p.m. Ready. She got Chloe in her stroller and was heading to the door when Rex came through. Was he that good-looking yesterday? He wore jeans and a black leather jacket, a red plaid scarf around his neck.

He smiled a hello and played a round of peekaboo with Chloe, who gave a gummy smile. "I borrowed an extra car seat from my sister and she helped me install it properly, so we're all set to go."

That was unexpected. Maisey was so used to not only doing everything for herself and Chloe, but thinking of everything. She liked that he'd not only thought of the car seat issue but that he'd installed it. Properly, no less. Now, *that* was an aphrodisiac. As was how he'd folded up Chloe's stroller and put it in the cargo area, then held her car door open for her. Little things that were actually big things when you wished you had more than two hands on a daily basis.

With Chloe settled in her rear-facing car seat, they headed off to the Christmas tree farm, driving past the ranch gates onto the long gravel road.

"So how'd you find the bottle with my letter to Santa, anyway?" she asked. Maisey had always wondered if someone had found it. Right after she'd tossed it in the creek and watched it get carried away by the fast-moving current, she'd been sure someone wonderful would find it and come get her, a family with children and pets. As the years wore on, she figured the bottle was still in the river. Turned out she was right about that.

"I was supposed to meet someone, a witness to a crime, on a park footbridge over the Bear Ridge River, but he didn't show."

"Yikes. Maybe he got scared? I don't really know how any of that works."

"Witnesses are definitely scared. They testify and get whisked off somewhere they've never been with a new identity. It's hard stuff. But the trial starts soon after the New Year. I need to find the witness before then."

"Sounds so stressful—for you, too."

He nodded. "Everything about it is stressful.

I like being a marshal and don't. Suited to it and not. Sounds nuts, right?"

"I kind of get it. A catch-22. You'd be crazy if you *did* like it."

He smiled. "Exactly. Anyway, because I was on that bridge at that exact time, I met River. My dog. My sort-of dog. He's the one that found your bottle. I saw a cute stray sniffing something and went to check it out. I got your bottle and my sister, Daisy, got the dog. That was a month ago."

"Why didn't you take him in?" she asked. She'd met River when she interviewed with Daisy Dawson at her farmhouse. He'd been curled in his dog bed and looked so sweet and content. She'd had no idea he'd found her bottle. Next time she saw him, she'd give him a good petting.

"I don't have anywhere to call home, not really. I keep a condo in Cheyenne but I'm rarely there. I live in hotels."

"So you're just here on vacation till Christmas?" she asked. That would make it easier not to fall for his gorgeous face and long, lean body. She loved his intense blue eyes and strong nose and jawline. His black leather jacket. Not to mention all the inside stuff. Like how kind he was. Generous. Thoughtful. He asked questions and listened, though granted, that came with the territory of his job. Still, he wasn't working now and he still asked and listened. She barely knew Rex Dawson but he made her feel...*seen.*

He'd be leaving town in less than two weeks. Knowing that, she couldn't possibly fall madly in love with him and get her heart handed to her. Unless she was stupid. *So don't be stupid,* she told herself. *Say thank you and move along, away from those blue eyes and how strong and sexy he looks.*

"Yup. Boss-ordered. Then I'm gone again."

"Good to know," she blurted out before she could stop herself.

He turned to look at her for a second. Oops—again. Why had she said that? She shouldn't have even thought it. Rex Dawson's comings and goings had nothing to do with her. *Because you didn't know he existed before 5:59 p.m. yesterday and now you're in his SUV, your baby in the back seat, on the way to choose a Christmas tree, his treat. Thanks to Rex, Chloe will have a Christmas tree tonight.*

But pulsating deep inside her was the fact that he'd found the bottle. In that one letter she'd so carefully rolled up and slid inside, he knew everything about her. That sounded crazy, but it was the way she felt. Her essence, summed up in Dear Santa. The yearning for a parent to take care of her, care *about* her, love her, want her. The *come get me, please. I don't belong here. I need a family.*

Saying she wasn't picky. That she didn't want to be greedy in the hope for a sibling in addition to a parent.

Maisey bit her lip and turned to look out the window. The man sitting beside her missed nothing. Not what was in that letter. And not now with her sudden obsession with the passing trees. She could feel him glancing at her.

"You okay?" he asked. "One thing you should know about me is that I'm an asker. In my job, you can't take anything for granted or think you know someone. You have to ask. And most times, when I do, the person cracks."

She felt something inside her shutter. And her eyes narrowed on him. "I certainly don't want to crack, Marshal."

He glanced at her. "Bad choice of words. In my profession, it means I got to the witness in a *good* way, got underneath the fear and earned their trust."

"I just want a tree for Chloe. I'm not interested in trusting a man who's leaving town the day after Christmas."

That got her another quick glance. "You're a straight shooter like me."

"Might as well be," she said. Suddenly she wanted to jump out of the car, grab Chloe and run.

Because dammit, he *had* cracked her. He'd gotten under her skin, where she let few people. He had her with that assessing gaze and understanding and kindness. The been-there-done-that aspect of his job that had him experience his share of awful, even if not directly. Then again, he'd said his father died. He knew about pain and loss firsthand.

"Are you close with your mom?" she asked, needing to change the subject.

His shoulders relaxed a bit, so he was clearly glad she had. "We speak once a week, but I don't get to see her often. She's living her dream down in Florida on a small farm with an orange orchard. She has a new husband she loves and who adores her, three dogs, four cats and a parrot she taught to say nice things to her. 'Squawk—you look so pretty today, Diana. Squawk—beautiful dress, Diana.'"

Maisey laughed. "We could all use that parrot."

He nodded. "We sure could."

"So you mentioned your dad died. I'm sorry. I certainly know how that feels."

"Last December, a few weeks before Christmas. We weren't close. He made that impossible for all six of his children." The shoulders tensed up again. "He basically drank himself to death."

"I'm so sorry," she said, noting the hard set of his jaw, the way he stared out the windshield.

"I'm sorry about your parents, Maisey. And you were so young. Clearly eight or under. Was it an accident?"

"Fire," she said, staring down at her lap, clasping and unclasping her now sweaty hands. "We had a small farm, just a couple of cows and goats. My mom liked to make her own dairy products and sell them at the farmers' market in town. She made her own labels, too. Baby Maisey was the name of her little business."

The gentle smile he sent was so full of sympathy that she almost lost it. *Do. Not. Cry*, she told herself.

"I was five years old and in the house with my mom," she went on. "My dad was in the barn. It was a few weeks before Christmas and a candle set the living room curtains on fire. My dad got me out and went back in for my mom but—" She stopped, tears stinging.

He slowed the car and pulled over onto the side of the road, took off his seat belt and angled to face her. "I'm so sorry." He took her hands and held them.

She closed her eyes for a second, needing the comfort and wishing she could reject it, but his hands felt good around hers. "I was so confused afterward. That they were gone. I didn't understand. There was no family to take me in, so I went into the foster care system and ended up in a home run by Meredith, who was very kind. I got lucky."

"I met her. She seemed very nice and caring."

"You met her?"

"In my quest to find you," he said. "I hope that doesn't seem intrusive. You mentioned her in the letter to Santa. So when I couldn't track you down by your name, I looked her up."

Huh. She didn't know he'd gone that far. "That's nice—that you went to the trouble to find me."

"I had to know what happened. I needed to know that everything worked out all right."

Except it didn't. Then or now. "Well, I do have my own little family with Chloe," she said, sucking in a breath. She didn't love talking about this. At all. "That first year I was at Miss Meredith's," she heard herself saying, "some of the young foster kids in the house, three and under, would be picked up by a social worker to meet with a prospective family, and they'd be adopted. I never even got that far." Sometimes, when she talked to Rex, it was like the words came from somewhere deep inside her and not of her own volition. Trick of the marshal trade? He could make people talk? He certainly wasn't pushy.

"I wonder why," he said. "You must have been remarkably cute as a kid."

She laughed. "Why do you say that?"

"Because you're so beautiful now," he said, and she saw his entire body go stiff as if that had come out of him not of *his* own volition. "Um, plus, based on the letter," he added very quickly, biting his lip, "you were a really nice, thoughtful kid."

Oh, Marshal, she thought. *You like me. That way.* She smiled, then tried to hide it. She couldn't get into a flirtatious situation with this man. *Playing. With. Red. Hot. Fire. Leaving town, remember?*

"We'd better get driving," she suggested. "Don't want all the good trees taken."

He smiled and signaled and pulled back onto the road.

There. Good. He wasn't so focused on her. Facing her. Seeing her expression. "And thank you for saying that. Both things," she added. When was the last time anyone said she was beautiful? "I was always very tall for my age, so at five I looked like I was eight, and by the time I was eleven, I was five foot nine. It's harder to get adopted as an older child. I used to wish I was petite, but I like my height now."

Her mom was five-nine, too, and Maisey had eventually learned to stand up straight and tall the way her mother had. *This is me.*

"My whole family is tall. Daisy's five-nine or

five-ten. And when River stands up on his back legs? Six feet at least."

She smiled. "He's such a pretty dog. I met him during my interview at Daisy's house. There are pictures of your family all over her refrigerator. You're so lucky you have five siblings."

"I do feel lucky about that," he said. "They're good people. Every last one. And the babies are cute, too."

"I met them all my first day," she said. "That adorable Danny came over to meet Chloe in the Kid Zone and said he wanted to babysit her."

"He's hilarious. I'm staying with Axel and his wife, Sadie—Danny's parents."

"Oh, there's the sign for the Christmas tree farm," she said, pointing.

He turned onto the gravel road, where several of the evergreens were lit up with white lights. "One rule about picking a tree," he said as he pulled into a spot. "It has to be spectacular. It has to make you think, This *is my tree. This is* Chloe's *first Christmas tree.*"

Two more weeks of this and she wasn't supposed to fall insanely in love?

Right.

Chapter Three

The tree *was* spectacular. And six-month-old Chloe, from her spot in the baby carrier attached to the front of her mom's wool coat, had chosen it. Rex and Maisey had walked up and down the rows at the Reed Family Christmas Tree Farm, Maisey stopping in front of a gorgeous Fraser fir, and Chloe had waved her hand at it and gurgled something unintelligible.

"Chloe has spoken!" Maisey said, laughing.

One of the employees came over and said they'd made a great choice and got out his camera, a new Polaroid. "Picture comes with every tree purchase. Nice to get a photo of your family at the farm."

Rex froze, aware that Maisey had the same strange look on her face that he must have had on his.

"I'd love a photo," Maisey said, breaking the tension.

"Gather close," the man said.

Rex stood at Maisey's side as close as he could without actually physically touching her, the tree behind him. The man snapped the photo, which slid out of the camera, and he waved it around to develop.

"There you go," he said, handing Rex the photo. "Beautiful family. That's one cute baby you two have."

"Aww, thanks," Maisey said with a big smile, not glancing at Rex even once.

The man made a few funny faces at Chloe, who stared at him with her big hazel eyes. "All rightie, then. Let's get this beauty on top of your vehicle."

Phew. Rex was glad to escape to that task.

We're not together, he wanted to tell the guy, a total stranger. *That's not my baby.*

Interesting how Maisey had said *thanks* with a smile.

Because she liked the idea of them being mistaken for being a family? Because there was little point in making a thing over correcting the guy, who'd been just making pleasantries?

She thanked him as he paid, and once the tree was secure on the roof of Rex's car, they headed back to Maisey's cabin, the photo in a cup holder in the console between their seats.

"So that was awkward," she said. "The man mistaking us for a family." She kind of snorted. Maybe he'd been wrong about thinking she'd liked it. She was just being nice back. She picked up the photo and looked at it quickly, then put it back.

"Well, I can see how he thought we were," he said. "Even if I can't imagine myself with a wife and child. Nice for others to think I'm—" He stopped talking. He was saying way too much as it was.

"You're what?" she asked, and he could feel her curiosity about what he'd been going to say.

"Like a regular person," he found himself telling her. "Your typical guy who plans to get married, buy a house, start a family. That I come off as that man always surprises me because inside I feel so removed from that."

He glanced over to find her tilting her head with an expression that said she was thinking, *Very interesting. I'm going to analyze you later.*

"So I have two big boxes of Christmas decorations in the trunk. We can have that tree decked out in a half hour."

Her face brightened. "Wow. I wasn't expecting that. Thank you again."

He smiled, a warmth hitting his chest. He liked doing things for her, helping her.

When they arrived at her cabin, she headed in to put Chloe to bed. He eyed the photo and put it in the glove compartment, then texted Axel to come give him a hand getting the tree in and set up. Just as Maisey came back out, Axel was driving up in one of the golf carts they used to get around the ranch. Axel's cabin was a good five miles from the main hub of the guest ranch.

"Hi again," she said to Axel. "How's that adorable Danny?"

Axel grinned. "Last I saw him, he was flying his stuffed superhero lion around the living room and over the tower of blocks he built. He's excited about going to the Kid Zone for a bit tomorrow."

"Can't wait to see him again," she said. "I'll go make sure the spot where I want the tree is all clear."

As Maisey went back in, Axel narrowed his eyes at Rex. "Um, what? How did this happen?"

"We kind of knew each other. Long story."

"I've got time," Axel said, undoing one of the bungee cords securing the tree.

"Well, since she didn't have a tree, I thought I'd take her to get one."

His brother stared at him, a grin forming. "I see."

"No, you do not," Rex whispered. "It's not like that. I'm leaving after Christmas. It's not like anything can happen between me and Maisey."

"Famous last words, brother," Axel said. "I said that and then I met a single mom with a toddler, and now I'm a dad with a baby on the way."

Rex swallowed, which Axel must have caught because he laughed.

Dammit. "Can we just get the tree inside?" Rex said with a scowl. "I've got two boxes of decorations in the back, too."

"Oh, do you," Axel said, the grin back.

His annoying brother helped him get the tree in the cabin in front of the living room windows where Maisey indicated.

"That's some tree," Axel said, staring up at it, then him, the glee still in his eyes. "I'll go bring in the boxes." He was quickly back with them and set them by the tree. "I'll leave you two to do the trimming. See you tomorrow at the Kid Zone, Maisey."

"Thanks for your help," Maisey said. Then Axel and his grin were gone.

"You look so much like your brother. Noah, too. Daisy's hair is lighter than both of yours, but you all look alike."

He nodded. "Dead ringers for our dad. Sometimes that gets us into trouble."

"How so?"

There he was again, telling her stuff he didn't mean to say. Why did he keep doing that?

"Let's put it this way—Bo Dawson didn't have much respect for wedding rings. He pissed off a lot of people, both men and women whose hearts and trusts and money he took. He was also an alcoholic and remembered very little of the crud he pulled. He inherited this ranch from his parents and within a year ran it into the ground. If I showed you pictures of what it looked like when we inherited it, you wouldn't believe it."

"So Christmastime must be very complicated for you, too," she said. "Since he died last December. He might not have been an easy person to care about, but I have no doubt you cared deeply. You and all your siblings."

For a second he could only nod. Bo Dawson had had his good points, though toward the last few years they were fewer and farther between. He'd always lived in the moment, which was sometimes a good quality and oftentimes his worst. He could be fun to be around, could charm a smile out of anyone. Even when he was disappointing someone, which was a constant, it was hard to walk away, to tell him it was the last straw. A couple of his siblings had reached that breaking point. So yeah, complicated.

"Exactly right" was all he could say about that to Maisey, who seemed to understand him a bit too well. "When he died, he left us the ranch, what was left of it, and wrote us all letters. Actually, some weren't quite letters. He left my oldest brother, Ford, a map of where he'd buried his mother's diary, which to this day Ford hasn't found. And he left Axel a list of addresses."

"What was yours?"

"A key, plain silver, no writing on it. I have no idea what it opens and there wasn't a letter with it. At first I thought the key must have opened the old front door to the farmhouse or the old gate, but it didn't work. I've tried it on just about every old lock that Noah kept around after the rebuilding."

"Maybe it's just symbolic? A metaphorical key à la welcoming you back home?"

Rex shook his head. "My dad was more literal. It opens something on this property, something he wanted me to find." He threw up his hands. "No idea what, though. Frustrating like he was."

She nodded. "How about some eggnog as we decorate the tree?"

"Feel free to spike it," he said.

She grinned. "I happen to have some Baileys Irish Cream." She disappeared into the kitchen, and just as she came back with two glass mugs, her cell phone rang. He took the glasses from her. "Ooh, it's the boss. Hi, Daisy… Nope, this is a great time to talk."

Rex couldn't help but notice Maisey's expression change from happy curiosity to something a lot like dread.

"Me? Well, um, hmm," she said. Then listened some more. "Well, of course you can count on me… Rex? He happens to be here right now helping me with my Christmas tree. I'll ask him… Okay. Thanks, Daisy. Bye."

"Should I even ask what that was about and how I came into the conversation?" He smiled, but she still seemed kind of shaken.

"Daisy said she realized today that all the kids presently at the ranch will be here through the day of the Christmas fair, which is in five days. She loves the idea of doing a kids' show of some sort, and I can have set rehearsal times during Kid Zone hours for any children, staff and guests who'd like to participate." She bit her lip. "I'm not sure… As you know, I'm not very Christmassy. And to be honest, this kind of thing—a big fair, kids—really might pull a lot of heavy sadness out of me, you know?"

"Pulling sadness out of you might be a good

thing, though, Maisey. If you can look at it that way, I mean."

She turned away a bit and shrugged. "I don't want to let your sister down. She's the reason I have this great job in the first place. And apparently a lot of kids are looking forward to being part of the fair. We can put on a short concert of kids' holiday songs that even your nephew can participate in at just two years old. The whole idea sounds adorable. I can handle that, right?"

"It depends. What was the 'I'll ask Rex' about?"

She smiled. "Daisy suggested I recruit you to help me with the kids' concert, since you're on vacation and all."

"Oh, did she?" Rex asked, good-naturedly rolling his eyes. "Of course I'll help. Sign me right up."

"Really? Just like that?"

"Just like that," he said.

She stared at him for a moment. "We have the same amount of Christmas spirit. I have none and you have a quarter to an eighth, so that's barely any. We're putting on the children's Christmas show?"

"Yes. Yes, we are. Because I have a plan for you, Maisey."

Say what? "A plan?"

"You're going to get back your Christmas

spirit. One hundred percent. That's my job till I leave."

Her face fell, not what he was expecting. Which was dopey of him. Christmas was hard on them both. Had been for years, much, much longer and more painfully for Maisey. Sometimes Rex could be as dense as his sister was always accusing him of being.

"Sorry," he said. "I'm overstepping." It was so…complicated, and not, at the same time.

"I can't get back my Christmas spirit, Rex. Pleasant thought as it is. Christmas to me means losing my parents. It means waiting year after year for Santa to come through with a family for me to join. It means a ragged hole so deep inside my chest that even seeing Chloe in a Santa hat can't fill it. She helps—don't get me wrong. But Christmas and I just aren't a pair. I love the idea of the show but…"

"I hear you. And if anything gets to be too much with the show, I'll be there to help take over."

Now her face really did fall. "Why are you so damned nice?" she asked, her eyes glistening. "Ugh, now I'm all emotional."

He smiled. "Multicolored lights or white?" he asked. "How's that for a subject change?"

"Perfect. Why don't we each take a long sip

of our spiked eggnog and then everything will be better."

He raised his glass and so did she. They clinked, held each other's gazes, and it took a lot to move his eyes off her pretty face, her eyes holding many different emotions.

I do want to give you back your Christmas spirit, Maisey. And I'm going to.

An hour later, Maisey sat on the sofa, Rex beside her, her attention split between the beautiful tree and the man. They'd wrapped red tinsel and white lights and hung multicolored balls, and had long finished their spiked eggnogs. Snowbell sat on the arm of the sofa, grooming her face.

"The tree is missing something," he said.

She looked over at it, the lights bright and the garland and tinsel so festive. The tree made all the difference in the formerly dull living room. "Looks great to me."

He shook his head. "Ornaments. All the decorations are the standard stuff. There are no personal ornaments."

Maisey picked up her eggnog and took a long sip. She was about to go down the ole memory lane and wasn't sure she wanted to. "When I first got married, I bought a ton of ornaments for our tree. Nothing pricey since we didn't have much money. And a few days later someone actually stole the tree right out of our trailer. Believe that?"

He grimaced. "I don't want to believe it."

"Want to know the worst part?" she asked.

"No," he said. He reached for her hand and gave it a squeeze. "But tell me."

"Before the fire, I was playing with two of the ornaments in the living room, making them have a conversation on the coffee table. There was a princess figure and a cat. The cat was Siamese and had the greenest eyes. The ornament was on the long side and slender, and I loved it so much."

"You lost it in the fire," he said, his expression so full of compassion.

She shook her head. "Nope. The cat ornament was in my hand when my dad came rushing in for me. I got out of the house with it. I lost it when that idiot thief stole the tree from the trailer."

"What the hell is wrong with people? Who does that? Who steals someone's Christmas tree?"

"There weren't any presents under it at least. But I lost the one thing I had left of my parents. My favorite ornament. Snowbell here isn't a Siamese, but she reminds me of the ornament with her green eyes and skinny face." She gave Snowbell a scratch behind her ears. When she'd found the cat as a stray during her pregnancy, she'd been so struck by a similarity in their faces. Or maybe it was just wishful thinking.

"Have you tried to find a replica of the ornament online?" he asked. "Not that it would be the same."

"Oh, I want it. Bad. There are cat ornaments, but I've never found that exact one. If there was one thing I would ever ask Santa for in a letter again, it would be that."

Snowbell moved from the arm of the sofa onto Maisey's lap. She petted the cat's back, earning a purr. Maisey was grateful for the distraction, something to take her thoughts off loss—and off Rex, sitting way too close despite being a good foot away. He reached over to pet Snowbell and their fingers collided. She felt it in her *toes*.

She wanted him to stay *and* go. Stay so she could be around him, look at him, talk to him. Go so she could get back her equilibrium and stop saying too much. Did she have to tell him about the ornament? The stuff that poured out of her mouth was nuts. Half of what she told Rex Dawson she'd never even told her husband when they were first married and she'd thought he'd cared.

"What do *you* want for Christmas?" she asked. There. She'd gotten the topic of conversation off herself and on to him. Not that she wanted to know too much about him. Every time he opened up to her, she found herself drawn closer and closer.

"To be assured I'll find my witness when I leave."

What, you were expecting him to say "To kiss you, Maisey Clark. Just one unforgettable kiss to remember you by that in fact will knock me off my feet so hard I don't leave"?

Right. She might not have much Christmas spirit, but the Christmas wishes ran deep.

"Speaking of leaving," he said. "I'd better get going." He stood up and gave Snowbell a final scratch by her tail.

Hmm. Suddenly he was dashing out the door. Maybe he didn't like talking about himself. Or maybe the whole evening had just been a lot. "Thanks for everything," she said. "The tree, the trimming…and listening."

"Anytime. So what time should I come by tomorrow for the kids' concert planning meeting?"

"Wow. You *are* an official," she said. This was a man who clearly took his responsibilities seriously, from finding his rogue witness to a children's holiday show. "How about my lunch break? It's just a half hour, but that should be enough to get the ball rolling. One p.m. in the cafeteria?"

"I'll see you then." He headed toward the door, giving the tree a glance. She also noticed that while he put on his leather jacket and wrapped the red plaid scarf around his neck, his gaze stopped on the photo of herself and her parents. Or maybe she'd imagined it, because he was suddenly saying goodbye and "Tell Chloe good-night for me if she wakes up during the night," which of course the 3:00 a.m. waker would, and then he was gone.

Maisey wanted him to come back immediately.

As Snowbell wound around her legs, she took in a breath. "I'm in trouble with this one," she told the cat.

She looked at the tree, marveling at what a difference it made in the cabin with its twinkling lights and red and silver balls hanging on the fragrant branches. When Maisey had been married, when she'd thought she'd finally have the family she always dreamed of, she'd tried to make their trailer as festive as possible at holiday time, but she realized she was overcompensating for everything wrong in her marriage, trying to wrap it in lights and bows and ornaments.

Everything that mattered, truly mattered, was sleeping in the nursery. She had to remember that and stop thinking about the guy who'd made this tree happen—the guy who'd be gone right after Christmas. And he was *not* taking her heart with him.

Chapter Four

If he were honest, Rex thought the next morning as he poured a cup of coffee in the quiet of his brother's kitchen, he would have told Maisey that what he wanted for Christmas was to restore her Christmas spirit. Granted, finding his witness was paramount and the need was always humming under the surface. If he could just reach the man, talk to him, Rex was sure he could convince him to come under protection, testify and then live a safe life in the witness protection program.

But his wish, his fervent wish, was to give Maisey back Christmas. For the girl she'd been, the woman she was.

And dammit, he was going to find that Siamese cat ornament. After all she'd been through, some-one stole the last thing she had left of her parents? Attached to a Christmas tree? He shook his head for the zillionth time, disgusted by the creeps and criminals out there. Injustice, from the pettiest of crimes to the whoppers, always reinforced his dedication to his job and the US Marshals' motto: Justice. Integrity. Service.

Finding the ornament online was turning out to be as difficult as searching for Maisey and the witness had been. Nothing. There were plenty of Siamese cat ornaments, but none with green eyes or that were long and skinny. Luckily, he had a good idea of what it looked like. He'd been able to see it pretty clearly on the tree behind her and her parents in the photo on the console table in her hallway, which he'd noticed again as he'd been putting on his jacket last night.

And leaving, which he'd been loath to do.

What was it about this woman that pulled him in so hard? The letter to Santa? That she was all alone in the world with a baby? She was young, just twenty-three, but Maisey Clark was doing just fine. She was focused and independent, took care of business. Something about the combination of everything she was, including undeniably sexy, drew him like never before.

Except he wasn't open to a relationship. Or becoming a father. *So watch your step, Rex.* Even if Maisey would be open to dating short-term while he was here—which he doubted—he knew he could never think of her as a fling. She was already underneath his skin. She'd gotten there before he'd even *met* her.

He took a long gulp of coffee and a bite of the bagel he'd toasted and slathered with vegetable cream cheese, then opened up his laptop, planning to put in an hour checking into his witness's possible whereabouts, looking into credit card usage. When he logged in to his work site, a message greeted him from his boss. Vacation means vacation. See you on the twenty-sixth and not before—that goes for online, too. This is an order.

Rex shut his laptop, shaking his head. How was he going to put work out of his thoughts for the next week and a half without going nuts?

By focusing on what else you want: bringing back Maisey's Christmas spirit. And a perfect part of that plan would be taken care of by helping her with the concert. For the next bunch of days she'd be immersed in Christmas, which wouldn't be easy, and he'd be right there when it got rough, with a shoulder or an ear. Whatever she needed.

He had four hours until he'd meet Maisey at the caf, so he figured he'd do what he did in downtime at the ranch. Try a bunch of locks with the key his father had left him. Axel and Sadie, who'd joined the ranch staff when she'd married Axel and now served as the nutritionist, planning meals for guests with all kinds of restrictions, were both at work, and Danny was at the Kid Zone.

He called his brother Noah. As the one who'd rebuilt the ranch last winter and spring with a crew and now served as the general manager— his wife, Sara, was forewoman—Noah might be able to solve the key mystery. "Okay, there have to be a few other locks we haven't tried to open with my key. What are we missing?"

Noah had saved a lot of the old doors to the cabins and barns in case he wanted to repurpose them, but they'd tried all those. No dice. Last Christmas, when all the siblings had been home, they'd tried the attic, looking for anything with a lock among their dad's possessions, but except for a toolbox with an old lock on it that took a tiny key and a locked trunk they'd all been sure was the jackpot but wasn't, Rex hadn't found the key's purpose.

"Maybe the key doesn't open something on the ranch," Noah said. "Maybe you've been looking in the wrong place."

He'd been thinking about that lately. But where, then? And what? "So a safety-deposit box. A locker. But where? I don't even know where to start."

"Somewhere Dad must have frequented," Noah suggested.

Rex had no clue, though. He hadn't spent much time with his father the past few years before his death. His job had kept him away, but so had his memories. Maybe more so. His mother would drop off him and Axel and Zeke as kids after the divorce, and his dad would disappear, no food in the fridge. They'd call their eldest brother, Ford, who had a different mother, and Ford's mother would drop off takeout for them, shaking her head. If they called their own mother, they knew she'd be furious at how negligent Bo Dawson was, and they wouldn't be allowed back. Back then, they'd wanted to spend time with their dad any way they could, the good with the bad.

Once his dad married Daisy and Noah's mother and they'd come to visit, there were always delicious home-cooked meals. But she'd died when Rex was thirteen, and Bo had gotten worse. Noah and Daisy had truly been on their own as tweens and then teens. Rex knew that Noah's relationship with his father had been nothing short of turbulent. But he'd made peace with that this past year—which had helped Rex believe that anything was possible.

"Besides bars?" Rex asked.

"Maybe you *are* looking for a bar, Rex. Though I don't know why a bar would have lockers. Employee room, maybe? Oh—gotta go. Runaway goat with a group of kids cheering her on."

Hermione was the resident escape artist. No matter how strong Noah and Sara fortified her corral and her outdoor fence, she got out and ran for the hills. The only good news was that the guests loved it. The escape and the chase. Hermione could always be coaxed over with a bowl of hay with peaches in it.

"Good luck," Rex said.

"You, too. Start with Hot Rods, then try Wacky Dan's. Those were his two favorites. Who knows?"

Words to live by. Rex put his phone away and made a plan to stop by both bars tonight. He'd drag one of his siblings with him. In the meantime, he'd go help his brother corral the runaway goat.

The moment Maisey walked into the cafeteria, the O'Leary kids raced up to her, seven-year-old Lara throwing her arms around Maisey's waist, five-year-old Sam holding out his brownie and asking if Maisey wanted a piece, but only a little piece, which made her laugh, and three-year-old

Tommy simply clapping at her side as though she were a movie star.

She could get used to this. The children were the one part of the Christmas show that made it all seem doable instead of potentially painful. These kids were joyful, bursting with life, and would make even having a spare moment to think about her own losses and sad times just about impossible. She hoped, anyway.

"Hi, Maisey," called adorable Jack Lopez from his table with his parents, ten years old and a budding scientist. His younger sister, Kyra, sat reading a Harry Potter book that probably weighed more than she did. Kyra looked up and grinned at Maisey.

Huh. This was a lot different from the reception she was used to at the day care. The kids there had liked her a lot, sure, but here, she was the "special grown-up" in the Kid Zone who was all about fun. The kids adored the two staffers, too, high-energy young adults whom Maisey adored herself.

How did I get so lucky? she asked herself as she sat at a back table, accepting a big hug from the eight-year-old Caletti twins, Amelia and Ava, on their way out. Tyler, the teenage basketball player, gave her a high five as he left, but Zara, glum as always, walked right past her. The girl gave her a glance but not a smile or a hello. Her parents smiled tightly at Maisey, and she was too curious what the deal was with the dynamic. Something must have happened in the family. But unless one of the Harwoods opened up to her, she couldn't exactly just ask.

Rex came in, filling the doorway with his six-foot-two, long, lean but muscular hot physique as he glanced around for her. As his gaze stopped on her, tingles zapped along her spine.

She sprang up because of butterflies zapping around her stomach. "Shall we hit the line?" she asked, gesturing at the front of the cafeteria, where a few guests and several staff members were making their choices. "I hear the loaded potato soup is amazing. I think I might go for that and the half sandwich combo. Maybe a BLT. Or turkey. Or a turkey BLT."

Oh, Lord. Shut up, Motormouth Maisey. Were there women who were effortlessly sophisticated and alluring and full of mystery when she was talking about turkey sandwiches? Then again, the less "hot" she was in his eyes, the better. She didn't want him to be interested in her that way. Knowing he was attracted might give her a little ego boost, but she certainly wasn't looking to get involved with anyone, let alone a man who was leaving in less than two weeks. *We've been through this, Maisey,* she told herself with a firm mental conk on the head.

"Potato soup might be just what the doc ordered—wind is whipping out there today."

Yup. And the reason why the Kid Zone had been packed this morning. Almost all the guests and staff kids had been in, whether for an hour or all morning. When it got truly cold but there wasn't enough snow for cross-country skiing or snowshoeing, the indoor petting zoo and lodge activities were the best bets. When kids got their fill of petting the goats and marveling over the llamas and the rehabilitating reindeer, they headed into the Kid Zone.

They were standing very close in the cafeteria line, burgers and fries ready to go, sandwiches made to order, a soup and salad bar, and then the day's specials. She and Rex both got the soup-and-sandwich combo, a BLT for her and a turkey club for Rex. Back at the table, they dug in to their lunch, but since she only had a half hour, they had to get down to business.

Maisey pulled out her handy small notebook and a pen. "Okay. Children's holiday concert— which is four days from now. I have a little experience with this from the day care where I worked. Because we have mostly young kids, I'm thinking we put on a concert for the parents with, say, five songs, kids in adorable costumes with fun holiday props. All the kids involved who want to be. Parents can sign them up and drop them off at a set time for rehearsals every day."

He lifted the second half of his sandwich. "Sounds great, Maisey. I'll be your right-hand man, builder, set designer. Anything you need."

A kiss. Right now.

Oh, man. Where had that come from? She knew where. From how close they were sitting, working together...

"You two are under the mistletoe, so you have to kiss," a voice said.

Maisey whirled around. Fourteen-year-old Annalise Vega stood on a chair behind them, holding up a sprig of mistletoe tied with a red-and-green plaid ribbon over their heads.

"Kiss, kiss, kiss, kiss!" she called out.

The entire cafeteria, not that there were so many people left, began chanting and clapping.

"I don't think they'll stop until we kiss," Rex said.

"A quick peck, then. On three."

He kissed her on two. Warm, fast and leaving her wanting more. How could she have possibly felt that kiss along her spine, across the nape of her neck? But she had. Tingles.

"Just where did you get that, anyway?" Maisey asked Annalise.

"Found it in our welcome basket when we arrived. My mom told me it was mistletoe, the kissing plant. Whoever stands under it has to kiss." Annalise giggled and blew them a kiss, then ran off.

"So we have my sister, the guest relations manager, to blame for this," Rex said.

A big part of Maisey wanted to thank her boss. She liked that kiss.

"You'll text me about what you need for the show?" he asked. "I'm all yours, seriously, so load me up with tasks."

All hers. When he said stuff like that, she immediately found herself fantasizing about a different Maisey living an alternate life, one in which she trusted people, trusted romance. One where the man she found so sexy and alluring and kind and generous would be sticking around.

"I will," she said. "And thank you." She glanced at the clock on the wall. "Time for me to get back to the lodge."

"I'll walk you," he said with an easy smile.

Sigh. Of course he would.

Because he was fast seeming like everything she'd ever wanted in a man, a husband, a life partner.

Chapter Five

By late afternoon, Maisey had spoken to just about all the parents who'd either dropped off or picked up their children in the Kid Zone. All were on board for having their kids in the holiday show. Rehearsals would be every morning at nine thirty so that the children could have a half hour of unstructured playtime first and then get into singing mode. So far, this was coming together without a hitch. They'd only have four days to create magic, but kid magic was its own special kind. Even with flubs and forgotten lyrics, the show would be special and fun for everyone—most important, the young participants.

"I knew you'd pull this off in no time," Daisy Dawson said, coming over to where Maisey stood in the baby-and-toddler section. Tony, Daisy's five-month-old son, and her brother Noah's eight-month-old twins were all napping in bassinets a few feet away, a lullaby player on low. Somehow, the ambient noises of the Kid Zone helped put all the littlest ones down when it was time for their naps, and the loudest ball dribblings and happy screams didn't awaken them. Axel's son, Danny, was jumping in the small ball pit with another toddler. Hannah, one of the Kid Zone sitters, was supervising them while Maisey spoke to her boss. They could clearly hear the toddlers singing the one line they'd learned from a song, "Frosty the Snowman." Which was more like "Frotty Noman" over and over between giggles.

Between lunch with Rex and coming back to work, she'd created a song list, starting with "Frosty" and ending with "All I Want for Christmas Is My Two Front Teeth." All the kids thought that was funny.

"The show will be adorable," Maisey said. "And I can really focus on rehearsals and getting the kids ready for the big day because your brother Rex has agreed to be my set builder, costume designer and all-around right-hand guy."

Daisy beamed, twirling the end of her long

brown ponytail around her finger. "Oh, has he?" She leaned a bit closer to whisper, "You do realize that's unusual for Rex. Or maybe you don't since you're new around here. It's *very* unusual."

Hmm, a little matchmaking going on here? Rex's sister definitely wanted her to know that Rex didn't go around offering to help with kiddie holiday shows.

The happy goose bumps that had run up her spine started fading. "Even if I were in the market for a relationship, which I'm not for a million reasons," Maisey said, "he's made it very clear he's leaving town the day after Christmas."

"Ha—I've heard that one before. Noah, Axel and I are all proof that definitive statements about ourselves and our plans are poppycock."

Maisey laughed. "That's sort of good to know. Maybe I'm not totally cynical about love at twenty-three even though I feel like I should be. I've already got a failed marriage."

Daisy glanced around to make sure no little ears were in hearing distance. "You're talking to someone whose first fiancé, Tony's biological father, left her at the altar. Literally. He sent me a Dear Jane text five minutes before the wedding. A half hour later I went into labor on the side of a service road out in the middle of nowhere. A guest at the ranch, a man I hadn't yet met, came along and helped bring my baby, Tony, into the world. We're married now."

Maisey's eyes popped. "Wow."

"My trust level those early days and weeks of knowing Harrison McCord? Zero. But when love conks you over the head, there's no running from it."

Maisey grinned. "I suppose not. Probably wouldn't get very far with a serious conk."

"That's it exactly. Rex can try leaving, but it'll be futile."

Hmm. Maisey came from the school of *when someone tells you something about them, believe them*. Could she loosen up a little and see where things with Rex Dawson might lead? She'd just have to take it day by day. Moment by moment, actually.

A text pinged on Daisy's phone. "Guest emergency," she said. "Emergency meaning Cabin Four is out of paper towels and one of the kids spilled his lemonade all over the floor. Let me go give my little guy one last peek before I skedaddle." She walked over to Tony's bassinet and gently kissed his head. "See you later, love," she said to her son. On her way out, she added, "And who knows, Maisey—we just might be family by New Year's."

Maisey smiled but her stomach was churning.

Family. Family. Family. What she would give to be part of a family like the Dawsons. But the last time she got hopeful about joining a family, she'd been sorely disappointed. Besides, she and Rex weren't even a thing. They were just…friends, really, who happened to share one electric kiss under the mistletoe in a cafeteria. Was it even a kiss? A peck. It was a peck. She'd better stop daydreaming that there was anything going on with her and Rex, because there wasn't. Daisy's hopeful words aside, Rex seemed very sure of his plans—to leave. To go back to his world as a US marshal.

"Emily signed me up to be in the show, but I'm not doing it," a voice muttered.

Maisey had been so wrapped up in her thoughts that she hadn't even seen nine-year-old Zara Harwood walk up beside her. The girl's arms were crossed over her chest, her chin lifted and her expression half sad, half defiant.

Then her mind caught on the name Emily. Maisey distinctly recalled the Harwoods, Emily and Ethan, referred to Zara as their daughter. But Zara referred to her mother as Emily? If Zara were fourteen or fifteen, Maisey would chalk it up to teenage rebellion. But Zara was only nine.

"Well, if you don't want to sing in the show," Maisey said, "you don't have to, but I would love it if you did. I was hoping you'd be one of my special apprentices, too."

Zara tilted her head, the grim expression softening. "What's an apprentice?"

"A very important helper. An assistant. It's a special job. We have ten kids in the show, including you if you decide to be in it. Several are really young and I need extra-special assistance with helping them learn the songs. I've seen you carrying your iPod with your earbuds in, so I figured, *Now, there's a girl who really likes music.* You'd be a big help to me."

"Really? I could do that." Zara bit her lip, the hands coming out of her pockets.

Thank you, universe. Maisey had only been half-sure the girl wasn't going to tell her she didn't want to help with "her dumb show" and go storming off.

"Can you tell me what songs we're doing?" Zara asked. "I want to download them."

Maisey could jump up and down in joy. Yes! She told the girl the songs and Zara scampered off to a beanbag.

A few minutes later, Emily Harwood came in, and this time, Zara ran over to her.

"Guess what? I'm going to be a special app—" She turned to Maisey. "What is it called again? The special assistant?"

"Apprentice," Maisey said.

"I'm going to be a special apprentice for the kids' holiday show," Zara told Emily. "I might be in the show, too. I haven't decided yet."

"That's so great!" Emily said. "I hope you'll be in the show, too. You have such a beautiful voice."

Zara's face fell. Why, given the compliment, Maisey had no idea. "I said I don't know yet."

"Well, it's great that you're going to be an apprentice." Emily glanced at her watch. "It's time for your horseback riding lesson. All ready?"

Zara nodded and went to her cubby to put on her boots and jacket.

"Oh my gosh, thank you," Emily whispered to Maisey. "You have no idea how helpful this is for her and us as a family."

Maisey was dying to ask why exactly, but she couldn't pry. If Zara or Emily wanted to share, they would. Maisey had always hated being asked about her situation when she was a kid. Even when someone asked something as simple as "Where did you grow up?" Maisey would get a stomachache. Yes, she'd grown up in Prairie City—before and after her parents' deaths. But the real answer seemed less like a place and more like, *I grew up in a few different Prairie City group foster homes*. Once, she'd said that and the person, who'd just been making small talk, had practically run away in discomfort.

Maisey watched the pair leave, buoyed by how differently Zara was carrying herself. No slumped shoulders or trailing behind. She was talking to Emily for once, too. As they disappeared through the double doors, in walked Rex Dawson. Maisey wasn't one to exaggerate, but the world seemed to move in slow motion and he sauntered over to her in his black leather jacket and sexy jeans and brown cowboy boots.

"I hear all my nieces and nephews are in one place, so I thought I'd come visit them," he said.

She had a feeling his sister would say that also wasn't something he usually did. Maybe Rex Dawson had a crush on her, too. Now she sounded like the twenty-three-year-old she was. Did thirty-one-year-old men have crushes? Maybe.

"Well, your baby niece and nephews are all sleeping over there," she said. "But Danny appears to be building a skyscraper out of big blocks." She pointed to where the toddler sat, tongue out in fierce concentration as he added another foam block to the top of his tall tower. Hannah gave him a high five.

"Nice building!" Rex said, walking over. "It's taller than you!"

Maisey noted how Danny's adorable face lit

up at the sight of his uncle. He came racing over, flinging himself into Rex's arms. Rex lifted him high, then dangled him upside down and sideways before giving him a big hug. Danny was full of giggles.

"Knock down tower?" Danny asked Hannah.

"Go for it!" the sitter said.

Danny took a running leap and crashed through the tower. Then he and Rex scooped up the blocks into their basket. The boy let out a giant yawn. Then another.

"Someone's ready for his nap," Maisey said, holding out her hand. "Your mat and favorite blankie and lovey are all ready." She held out his stuffed lion wearing a red cape.

"Want to hear a story before nap time, Dan the man?" Rex asked.

Danny grinned. "Yes! Zul souphero lion!"

"You got it," Rex said, carrying Danny over to the nap area and the navy blue mats behind a curtain.

Danny let out a giant yawn and then the two disappeared from view. Maisey stood just to the side of the curtain, taking a peek in. Rex was taking off Danny's sneakers. Then he settled the boy under the superhero blanket, a little pillow under his head, and sat beside him as he started a story about his stuffed superhero lion.

Maisey heard a big yawn. Then Rex continued the story. Then silence. A few seconds later, Rex emerged. "Asleep in three seconds," he whispered.

"A record for sure." Maisey felt so tongue-tied as she just stared at Rex like a fool, unable to look away from his gorgeous face and blue eyes and that incredible body. The guy had her completely hooked now. Kind and generous with his time? Check. Trying to give her back the Christmas spirit she'd lost a long, long time ago? Double check. Sweet and gentle with little kids? Be still, her heart.

She was now in official trouble, her head and heart in serious jeopardy. No matter what Daisy said, Rex had said quite a few times he was leaving after Christmas. The next time someone dangled mistletoe over their heads, she'd have to go running.

"So this was Dad's favorite bar?" Rex asked Axel as they walked into Hot Rods, located at the end of Main Street in Bear Ridge. Some people were at tables, drinking beer. A waitress was delivering two plates of fried something to a couple who were lip-locked even as she set down the food. A couple of guys were playing pool.

"Apparently," Axel said. "Meets all the requirements. Pool table, dartboard, long bar, jukebox, free peanuts, even a dance floor for his hookups."

There were two couples slow dancing to an old Eric Clapton song. He could well imagine his dad, hanging heavily on the woman he'd met, sloshed out of his mind.

Axel ordered them two draft beers, and Rex cracked open a peanut from the bowl full of them and popped it in his mouth. As the bartender set down the beers, Rex said to him, "Our dad used to come here a lot and we think maybe this key—" he fished it out of his pocket and held it up "—might open something here. Locker?"

The bartender eyed the small key. "There are some lockers in the employee lounge, but they have combination locks. And that key wouldn't fit either the front or back door." He shrugged.

"Well, this was a long shot," Rex said. "But thanks."

As the bartender helped another set of customers, Axel took a sip of his beer. "We can check out Wacky Dan's. After I beat you at darts."

"You mean after I wipe the sticky, peanut-shell-covered floor with you," Rex said with a grin. They ordered a platter of mozzarella sticks to share, then headed over to the dartboard just as a Bon Jovi song came blaring on the juke-box, bringing up more dancing couples. A trio of middle-aged women came in, and several eyes turned toward them, beer guts getting sucked in, hair getting smoothed back. This place was definitely more couples-oriented and pickup-ish than Rex had expected. He'd pictured lonely, drunk men half slumped on the bar, getting into fights and passing out on the floor. Bo Dawson had been a ladies' man till the end, so Rex supposed this being his favorite bar wasn't all that surprising. He probably met most of his girlfriends here.

"What do you think Dad might have left you?" Axel asked, taking aim at the board and hitting very close to the bull's-eye.

Rex shrugged. "I've spent the past year trying to figure it out and I can't even imagine. I seriously can't come up with anything. I think of all of us, I was maybe the least close to him."

"Yeah? Why do you say that? I'd think Zeke would say that about himself. And definitely Ford."

Zeke, a successful businessman in Cheyenne, had left town when he graduated from high school and barely looked back. Growing up, Zeke had kept his head down and focused on his school-work, determined to find a way out of the future Bo Dawson seemed to lay in front of them. Ford, their eldest brother, definitely had his share of problems with Bo Dawson.

"Yeah, good point," Rex said. "And the main reason Ford would say that is because he's a cop and Dad liked to skirt the law. Dad would see him coming for a visit and make himself scarce. Ford told me outright about those times and how it made him feel. But they were close once, when Ford was a kid. Dad and I never were. Never talked."

"Why do you think that was?" Axel asked, pausing with the dart in his hand.

"Once, when I was fifteen, he said, 'You're the kid who's gonna move far, far away and we'll never see you again.' Which shocked the hell out of me because I realized how well he did know me. All I could think about back then was leaving and going far, far away."

"Huh, interesting. So maybe the key you've been searching for is metaphorical, like Daisy suggested. Maybe it's not to anything but just refers to you having a key back to the Dawson Family Guest Ranch."

"Yeah, maybe. I just don't think so, though. That wasn't really Dad's style. He was more in your face with what he wanted us to know."

Axel shot his dart. Close again but no cigar. "Agreed. The list of five addresses he left me was plenty in my face."

Rex had joined Axel on the last address he had

left to visit back in the summer. Each of the addresses had shed light on Bo Dawson—from his childhood, to a family he'd been generous with, to an old girlfriend who'd helped Axel understand Bo better, make peace with his complicated feelings. Rex had always thought his brother was a real lone wolf, a former search-and-rescue operative who'd come home to take charge of guest safety and lead wilderness tours for the ranch. Suddenly the guy was married to his perfect match and they shared a two-year-old Rex adored and were expecting a baby.

As the waitress plunked down the platter of mozzarella sticks on the table holding their beers, Rex thought about how if Daisy had her way, the key and what it unlocked would lead him back home for good, too—to settle down and get married. *Married, married, married.* The word echoed in his head, sounding foreign or made up, something that couldn't possibly apply to him.

But then Maisey, with her long blond hair and pale brown eyes, and baby Chloe, with her big hazel-ish eyes and bear-ears hooded fleece snowsuit, came to mind. As did the old bottle he'd found and the letter to Santa. The tree they'd trimmed.

The two-second kiss under that sprig of mistletoe in a well-lit cafeteria at midday.

He'd felt that kiss *everywhere.*

Not a surprise, given how attracted he was to Maisey on so many levels.

Axel flew a dart, this time landing right in the bull's-eye. "Ah, success." He took a slug of his beer and made quick work of a mozzarella stick slathered in hot sauce, then another. Rex grabbed one before his brother ate the whole plate. "So what's going on with you and Maisey?"

Oh, crud. "I'm helping her with the kids' holiday show. That's what's going on."

Axel's smile was slow and wide. "Sure, Rex. Because you do that kind of thing."

"Maisey and I have history."

Axel downed another mozzarella stick. "How? She's been at the ranch, like, three days."

"A month ago, when I found River poking around the water's edge at the nature preserve, he'd been sniffing an old bottle. Turns out there was a message inside. A letter to Santa dated fifteen years ago."

"And?" Axel said, taking a sip of his beer.

"And it was signed Maisey Clark. I tried everything to find her because I had to know if she got what she'd asked Santa for. But I couldn't track her down. Then Daisy tells me she's the new Kid Zone nanny."

Axel shook his head. "Wow. That's some crazy coincidence. Like you were meant to know her."

"Or to find out what happened—if she got her wish."

"Did she?" Axel asked.

"Nope. I'm here till the day after Christmas and I want to give her back her Christmas spirit. Give her and her baby daughter a good holiday. That's all this is about."

The slow, wide smile was back. "And you like her."

That kiss came to mind. The feel of Maisey's soft lips. The slight scent of a floral perfume. And all the other…stuff the kiss had engendered. "So I like her. I'm still leaving. Day after Christmas. I've got a complicated case to deal with. And a marshal's life is on the road, hotel after hotel. I live out of a suitcase."

"I'd think that would have gotten old by now."

Rex sighed inwardly. It had. But he still felt deeply committed to his job. He believed in what he did. He rarely thought about what had driven him to become a marshal—a very old case involving a frenemy of his dad's who'd turned to armed robbery and escaped custody. Bo Dawson had swindled the guy in a blackjack game right before he'd been arrested, and they'd all been sure—as kids and teenagers—that the criminal would come after them for revenge. The US Marshals Service had caught the man a day later, but the fear, the worry, the instinct to protect those he loved, had stuck with Rex. He'd had to become a cop first, but then he'd set his sights on the US Marshals to chase down fugitives.

"You'll be back, bro. I'll put money on it."

Not an option, he thought, but Axel had hit another bull's-eye, then another and was busy gloating, so Rex didn't have to argue. He didn't really have the argument in him; the feeling was just *there*, deep inside.

"Wanna hit up Wacky Dan's and see if they have lockers that take keys? It was Dad's other home away from home."

"Another time," Rex said, grabbing a dart and needing to hit the center. If he did, he'd feel less off-kilter, and all his wayward thoughts—about Maisey mostly—would fall into line. He aimed, he shot… The dart barely stuck and landed on the floor.

"That means I get the last mozzarella stick," Axel said, snatching it up.

Rex laughed, glad to know some things never changed, like brothers. Everything else in his life seemed so unsettled, even though nothing really was. He'd leave soon, find his witness, take his next case.

It's the soft stuff inside your chest that's got you out of whack, he realized. And a woman and a baby he couldn't stop thinking about, wanted to help, protect, care for.

The sound of a spoon hitting a glass over and over many times snapped Rex from his thoughts. Half the place was clinking their glasses, grinning and chanting toward a couple on the dance floor.

"Mistle-toe, mistle-toe," they were chanting.

Rex glanced up, and sure enough, a sprig tied with red ribbon dangled from a hook in the ceiling right above the couple's heads. The couple gave the bar quite a show, to claps and cheers.

He had to admit he'd heard something of a parade in his head after that short, sweet kiss with Maisey in the cafeteria. Over in two seconds, but the clangs of cymbals nonetheless.

Serious physical attraction and caring about someone equaled danger, as far as he was concerned. But he had no idea how to possibly step back.

Chapter Six

In the morning, Maisey was over on the far side of the Kid Zone, which had been turned into the Dawson Family Guest Ranch Children's Holiday Show central. The kids had worked hard on lining up and taping together six big poster boards to create a huge backdrop that would hang from two hooks on the ceiling above the stage. Thanks to two artistic teens, Tyler and Annalise, who'd penciled in the name of the show surrounded by little Santas, Mrs. Clauses, elves, reindeer and candy canes, the festive banner was being painted by kids of all ages. Maisey had carefully taped it onto the mat flooring so that the kids could easily work from all sides without shifting the banner around.

"Oops," said five-year-old Sam O'Leary. "I got red paint out of the lines on my *H*."

Maisey glanced over at where Sam was lying on his belly, propped up on his elbows in front of the *H* in *Holiday*, a paintbrush in his hand and a frown on his adorably freckled face. She was about to tell him that was absolutely fine when Zara Harwood, Maisey's song apprentice, scooted over and looked at Sam's handiwork.

"I know!" Zara said, pushing her brown ponytail over her shoulder. "If you make that part of the *H* a little wider, no one will know you painted out of the line."

Sam brightened as he looked at Zara, then dipped his paintbrush into the red paint, widening his *H*. "It worked!"

"Awesome," Zara said, looking quite pleased with herself and rightly so.

Maisey wanted to scream with happiness. Since she'd started working here four days ago, Zara had barely said five words. Now she was engaged, working collaboratively and being a real sweetheart to the younger kids.

"High five!" Maisey whispered to Zara, holding up her hand with an appreciative smile.

Zara grinned and gave her five, her hazel eyes so happy, then went back to painting in an elf.

Huh. Maybe working on the kids' show would be an unexpected blessing instead of the potentially painful experience Maisey had feared. So far, she was so busy rehearsing songs and teaching lyrics and coming up with set ideas, plus taking care of Chloe, that she hadn't had much time to think about her own complicated feelings about Christmas. So far, so good.

"So what are you asking Santa for?" thirteen-year-old Tyler, who'd finally stopped dribbling and shooting to help paint, asked Annalise, whom he seemed to have a huge crush on. His moony-eyed staring was a clear giveaway.

Annalise looked up from where she was painting a reindeer. She shot Tyler a grin. "World peace and AirPods Pro."

His mouth dropped open. "Hey, me, too! And the two pairs of new sneakers I want. And basketball camp this summer."

"I'm asking for a kitten," eight-year-old Ava Caletti announced.

"Me, too!" her sister, Amelia, added. "They're gonna be twins like us!"

Maisey adored the Caletti twins. They both had flame-red long hair in braids and green eyes and liked wearing brightly colored leggings with long T-shirts.

Ava nodded. "But not identical probably. I want mine to be orange."

"I want a black kitten with white paws."

"What are you asking for, Zara?" Annalise asked, moving to the other side of the banner to start painting a Mrs. Claus.

"Nothing, okay?" Zara snapped. "What's the stupid point? I never get what I ask Santa for, anyway." She threw down her pencil and stalked off, flopping herself on a beanbag.

Annalise frowned and glanced toward Zara, then at Maisey. "Sorry."

"Hey, it's all right," Maisey told the teenager. "It's a perfectly reasonable question to ask someone this time of year and it's what the group was talking about."

That seemed to make Annalise feel better and she got back to painting, Tyler filling up the silence by waxing on about how "vital the noise-canceling feature in the new AirPods Pro is."

Since the kids were all talking and working, Maisey nodded to Hannah, one of the sitters, to take over supervision while she walked over to Zara. She slid a nearby beanbag next to the girl's and sat down, hoping she'd actually be able to get up. Maisey might be young, but since she'd had a baby six months ago, her body still wasn't what it used to be.

"Every year, starting from when I was five," Maisey said, "I'd write Santa a letter asking for the same thing. I never got it. Once, I even put my letter in a bottle and threw it in the creek, hoping it would get to the north pole faster."

Zara looked up at Maisey, her eyes red rimmed. "So I'm right. Wishes don't come true. Or my mom and dad would have come back to life."

Oh, no. Maisey felt her eyes well up. "My parents died when I was young, too. I'm so sorry, Zara."

Zara stared at her but didn't say anything, then looked away. Finally, she added, "It's been more than a whole year and I don't know anyone else whose mom and dad died. Except you now. I mean, there are some kids at school whose mom died or their dad died, but not both. Emily and Ethan think it's good for me to go to a talk group of kids who lost parents, but I hate it. At least those kids still have a parent."

Emily and Ethan. Not Mom and Dad. Maisey knew she had to tread carefully with what she said to Zara without speaking to the Harwoods first, but she could certainly be compassionate even though she didn't have even a quarter of the story here. From the little she knew, she figured the Harwoods had adopted Zara and that Zara wasn't yet on board.

"I know what you mean," Maisey said. "When I was in my foster home, there were a couple kids there whose parents were alive but had problems and couldn't take care of them. I used to think, *At least their parents are alive.* But once I got older I realized loss is loss is loss and hurt is hurt. We used to talk about how we felt and it did make me feel better."

"Well, I hate it."

Maisey nodded, wishing she had the right words, magic words.

Zara looked up at her. "You were in a foster home? Were the parents nice to you?"

"I lived in three different group foster homes. And yes, the people who ran them were nice. I was pretty lucky in that regard."

Zara stared at her. "Emily and Ethan were friends with my mom and dad, so they became my parents right after—" She stopped talking, biting her lip and looking away. "I don't think I would have liked to live in a foster home," she added on a whisper. "So did you ever get *anything* you wished for for Christmas?"

Maisey smiled. "Yeah. I guess I did. Not exactly what I asked for, but in its own way, you know?"

Zara shrugged. "I want only what I want."

Maisey gave Zara's hand a squeeze. "I get it."

"Do you think I'm a good painter?" Zara asked.

Phew. This was a much easier topic of conversation. "Very good. I love the color choices for the elf you were working on. Very original and interesting. You put your own stamp on it."

Zara smiled. "I really like painting."

"Wanna go back over and keep working on it? I think you only have the big elf shoes left to do."

Zara brightened and stood, and as expected, it took Maisey a good thirty seconds to lug herself up. "I'm gonna do polka dots on one shoe and stripes on the other. Red and green."

"Love it," Maisey said with a nod.

Zara ran back over to the banner and picked up a paintbrush. Annalise gave her a smile. Then Zara smiled back.

Maisey let out a giant breath, then almost sucked it back in when Rex Dawson walked through the door in his sexy leather jacket, the red plaid scarf around his neck. She tried not to stare as he took off his coat and hung it on a chair, the scarf following. *Keep going*, she wanted to say. *The shirt next...*

This guy might want to give me back Christmas, which I'm not sure is possible, but he's definitely given me back my mojo. She truly hadn't been sure she'd ever see that again.

As he walked over, Tyler got up and grabbed

his basketball and dribbled up to Rex, blocking his path, dribbling the ball on either side of his legs. "Freestyle. Whoever scores a point first is crowned king of the lodge."

"You're on," Rex said.

Tyler dribbled and Rex crouched as if to block his shot, but it was clear he wasn't trying—he also had a good foot on Tyler, who hadn't hit his growth spurt. The ball went in. "Yeah! King of the lodge!"

"Oh, yeah, watch this," Rex said, spinning around and shooting with one hand. The ball went in.

Tyler's mouth dropped open. "Whaaaa?"

Rex laughed. "I got moves for someone over thirty. Barely over, but over."

"Yeah, you do," Tyler said, reverence in his voice.

"Tell you what. I need to start building the set for the holiday show. But how about we play a pickup game in about an hour if you're still here. If not, I'll catch you tomorrow."

Tyler grinned. "Awesome." He dribbled his way back to the painting crew, wedging his way in beside Annalise.

Maisey smiled, her heart annoying her with its pitter-patter. "That was nice of you."

Rex gave half a shrug. "Teenagers are fun. Especially when they're not yours."

She smiled until what he said hit her. Really hit

her. He didn't want to be a parent. Even though he'd be such a great one! *The man does not want to be a dad. Get it through your head.*

And guess what you are and love being: a mom.

You have to stop thinking about Rex Dawson as a possibility. He's not.

The disappointment slugged her hard in the stomach to the point that she winced. She was grateful for the distraction of little Lara O'Leary somehow ending up with her paintbrush full of purple paint getting stuck in her curly blond hair.

"Oopsies!" Lara said, giggling.

The kids' reactions ran the gamut from laughter to dropped-mouth awe.

"Paint crisis," Maisey said to Rex. "Back in a minute." She hurried over to the little girl, catching her breath from the whirlwind that was Rex Dawson. Luckily, the paint was water based and would come out with a little muscle and a paper towel with some soap.

But Hannah already had the paintbrush out of the girl's hair. "I'll take her to the sink station. I got green paint in my own hair yesterday and it came right out."

"I like having purple hair," Lara said, looking at the ends of her long curly hair with a big grin.

The two walked off toward the "cleanup station," which had a sink, soap and hand sanitizer.

"Now, that's my kind of crisis," Rex said. "I could get used to that. A little water-soluble paint in hair." He chuckled.

"If your sister were here, she'd say that life could be yours with a snap of your fingers. Just come work at the ranch."

"Ah, I see you do know Daisy pretty well." He grinned but the big smile didn't last.

He really doesn't want to be here, she thought.

"What would you do if you did come home for good?" she asked out of real curiosity and because she was being Daisy-like in wanting him to think about it. "What job would you take on the ranch?"

He shrugged and shook his head. "No clue. Noah runs the place and quite well. His wife, Sara, is the forewoman. Daisy is in charge of all things guest. Axel's the safety guy and plans and leads wilderness tours, and his wife, Sadie, handles nutrition for the guests and staff. I guess I could be a cowboy. I wanted to be a cowboy when I was a kid."

Maisey smiled. "You're so good with children, maybe you could create some kind of educational program. I've been thinking along those lines of how to incorporate my ideas into the petting zoo and riding and the wilderness tours. We could have an entire program just for kids about ranch life. There's some of that already—Daisy gives great talks about the animals when she ventures into the petting zoo while guests are there."

He laughed. "Sounds like you've got that covered, Maisey. Maybe you could expand your role at the ranch. Director of Children's Programming, including running the Kid Zone and the educational activities."

"Me? Director?" She couldn't help but laugh. "I'm just a babysitter, Rex."

"There's no 'just' anything, Maisey. Caring for children is a huge responsibility. I'm just saying that your ideas are really great. You should work up a plan and talk to Daisy."

Huh. "You think so?"

"I absolutely do."

Maisey could barely contain her smile. "Maybe I'll wait a bit, though. It's my first week!"

"My motto? No time like now."

"Well, I appreciate the vote of confidence. I never would have thought of approaching my boss with ideas for children's programming."

He nodded at her with such reverence that her knees went a little weak. Had anyone ever made her feel like Rex did? Like anything was possible?

Not everything is, she reminded herself.

"Well, I'd better get started working on the

stage. I've got a design plan, and I'll get Axel or Noah to help me with the actual building of it."

Don't go. Stay right beside me and talk to me forever. Looking just the way you do. Looking at me just the way you do.

Boy, was she sunk with this guy.

"Oh—I meant to tell you," he said. "There's a Christmas shop in Prairie City that's open till nine every night till the big day. I thought we could go tonight after you close up and we can get whatever you need for the show, from an artificial tree or the trimmings to candy canes or a Santa suit. They have all kinds of Christmas costumes, too—elves, reindeer with red roses."

"Santa!" Maisey said. "I completely forgot that we'll need a Santa for the show. Can I sign you up?"

His gorgeous blue eyes went wide. "Did I just walk right into that?"

She laughed. "Yup. Sorry."

He shook his head with a smile. "My brothers will never let me live it down."

"I'll take that as a yes."

He grinned. "Ho, ho, ho. How was that?"

"Not bad." *Not bad at all, Rex Dawson. Too good, actually. You are too good. Which does make you too bad for me.*

"You make a list of what you need," he said,

"and we'll get everything tonight—the ranch will take care of the bill via your expense account, so go crazy." He tilted his head and looked at her. "If you're free to go, I mean."

What plans would she have? Singing the show songs to Chloe to get herself more and more used to hearing them. Avoiding the beautifully decorated tree in her living room, the one that Rex was responsible for. She loved the tree and it made her equally unsettled and sad. She kept telling herself that the tree, the holiday music, working on this show was all for Chloe, and it helped keep her thoughts focused on the now—not the past.

"Tonight would be great," she said. Going to the holiday shop—and she knew the one he meant—with a long list and no worries about price felt like a Christmas gift in itself. She'd never had an expense account before; she certainly wasn't used to being able to get the things she wanted so easily. "I'd love to have a bag of gifts for each child, just something small but personalized to hand out after the show. Maybe you can help me choose those, too. Like little plastic snow globes for the Caletti twins. They love the one of Santa's workshop on the front desk."

"I just got good at baby and toddler presents," he said. "I have no idea about big-kid gifts."

"What would you get Tyler the hoop star?" she asked, raising an eyebrow.

"Maybe a pair of neon laces for his sneakers and a Lakers cap."

Maisey grinned. "Exactly. You know more than you think about kids."

He raised an eyebrow. "Huh. I surprise myself sometimes."

Well, that was promising, Maisey thought— until she remembered she didn't put any stock in things turning around or changing. Things were what they were. Especially when the man in question put it right out there.

Leaving the day after Christmas. Not interested in fatherhood...

"Kiss, kiss, kiss, kiss!"

Maisey whirled around to see the kids all grinning and chanting at them.

Annalise stood on a chair behind them, holding up a sprig of mistletoe. Drat.

"Why do we never hear you sneak up on us?" Maisey asked, shaking her head with a smile.

"Stealth," Annalise said. "Kiss, kiss, kiss!"

Maisey rolled her eyes and stuck out her left cheek. Rex gave her a smooch to cheering and clapping.

"I'll, uh, just head over to where I'm gonna build the stage. Cupid, I need your help," he said to Annalise. "And, Tyler, you, too. You can be my construction assistants."

"Awesome," Tyler said, practically floating over beside Annalise.

Rex looked over his shoulder at her. "See you later, Maisey."

She honestly could not wait. But then, one day, she *wouldn't* see him later. She had to remember that.

Rex finally relaxed behind the wheel of his SUV as he turned onto the freeway, cars whizzing by. He'd been hyperaware of Maisey in the passenger seat. She smelled so good, which seemed impossible given that she'd been scrubbing glitter off her arms and one cheek when he'd arrived to pick her up. She'd also been glowing. The woman loved her job—and clearly was enjoying working on the Christmas show. She was definitely getting her Christmas spirit back.

She glanced behind her into the back seat, then bit her lip. "I keep forgetting that Chloe isn't with us. Sure was nice of Daisy to offer to watch her till we're back. First an expense report and now my own babysitter?"

Daisy had happened to pop into the Kid Zone to check on how things were going with the show when Rex had arrived to pick up Maisey, fully expecting to bring baby Chloe along on the trip to Prairie City. But when Daisy heard they were planning to do their shopping tonight, she'd offered to watch Chloe, loving the idea of Tony having a similar-aged little buddy for a few hours. The knowing looks his sister had sent him hadn't escaped his attention, either. She'd been clearly thrilled to give Rex and Maisey a few hours to themselves. Daisy the Matchmaker.

He mentally shook his head. "Well, like you said, Daisy has been trying to get me settled down back on the ranch. Putting us together in Prairie City is right up her alley. I'm surprised *she* didn't rush us with mistletoe."

She laughed. "I was thinking that myself."

Which meant his sister had been chatty with Maisey about how single Rex was.

He could feel her gaze on him. What was she thinking? Probably that they weren't a pair, anyway, even if he *were* the marrying and dad kind who had the type of job that could keep him nearby, home for dinner every night. She was so young, just twenty-three. And he was eight years older and world-weary and jaded.

Even still, Maisey felt like a part of him—she had ever since he'd found that bottle with her letter inside. He had to remember what was really driving him: his protectiveness toward her, the deep need to give her back Christmas. He wanted Maisey to have the world. That meant backing off from even thinking of acting on his attraction to her. Not easy, though. Another peck on the cheek, this one in the Kid Zone earlier today, had sent chills racing up all his nerve endings.

He could just imagine what a long, sexy, hot kiss on the lips, her body pressed against his, would do to him.

Get off the subject, he told himself. *She's not going to be yours. She needs someone who'll actually be around—very literally there for her.*

He cleared his throat. "I'm sure finding a great dad for Chloe is important to you. Daisy really is a serious matchmaker. Talk to her and you'll have five candidates lined up outside the Kid Zone."

He'd said it himself, the words had come out of his own mouth, but he felt a little bit sick because of it. *You're jealous, dope. You want her and can't have her, also at your own doing. So stop mooning over her like Tyler the dribble king does over Annalise.* The poor kid had almost dropped a heavy metal tape measure on his foot while they'd been working on how large to make the stage because he was deeply listening to Annalise talk about her favorite annual Christmas TV special—*Frosty the Snowman*.

This time he didn't feel Maisey looking at him.

He glanced over at her; she was staring out the window, kind of…glumly.

"I don't know," she said. "I do want Chloe to have a father. A great father. But I'm hardly ready to date, let alone to get serious about anyone. I can't even imagine trusting a guy."

"When you find the right person, all that will fall into place. He'll be right, feel right, and you'll find yourself trusting without even realizing it."

"I doubt I could be that carefree again. I got sweet-talked and lied to so many times by my ex. Right now I need to work on being independent. Socking enough savings away so that I have an emergency fund. Starting a college account for Chloe. That would mean the world to me. I'm not sure I'll ever get to college myself, but I'd like her to have the option, you know?"

He nodded. "I went to a state school on minimal loans and working part-time. I wouldn't have minded a big nest egg just for my education, but it just didn't exist. It feels good to make things happen for yourself. Like with what you want to do for yourself. If you want to go to college, you'll get there."

"I've been dreaming of getting a teaching degree forever. Trust me, I'm used to not getting what I want most."

He glanced at her, her cheeks so red that he

quickly turned his attention to the road to give her privacy.

"I hate that I said that. I'm not a whiner."

"What you are is incredible, Maisey. That's all you need to know."

She laughed. "You just feel bad for me." He looked over at her and her smile had faded. "I also hate that. Don't feel bad for me."

"Never said I did. And I don't. I think you've been through some really big stuff, Maisey Clark. And I think you're amazing because of what I've seen in the short time I've known you. That okay with you?"

The smile was back. "Yes. It is."

He laughed. "Good. That's settled, then. And here we are," he added. "Prairie City."

As he pulled into a diagonal spot in front of a coffee shop, she glanced around the bustling downtown. "I love and hate this town. The last foster home I was in was right up there." She pointed to a corner. Leaf Road. "I left the day I turned eighteen with a hug from the foster mom and my social worker, and that was that. Aged out and on my own with nothing."

"Want to show me the house?" he asked.

She bit her lip and shrugged. "I don't know. Maybe seeing it will give me closure on it."

"It might," he ventured.

She wrapped her arm around his, and he was so surprised that his knees kind of shook. Unless he was mistaken, and he didn't think he was, the gesture said *I trust you*. After all, she'd opened up in the car earlier; she did trust him. Certainly enough to show him the home, to have him beside her. To share her history.

He couldn't mess that up. He could not, under any circumstances, do anything to hurt that trust. It was precious and he knew it.

"Let's go, then," she said with something of a smile.

Let's go echoed in his head, all the various contexts and meanings. Every step he took with this woman led somewhere he'd never expected to be.

She looked so nervous about how she might feel about this trip down memory lane that he laid a hand on her arm. "I'm here for you," he said. "Okay?"

"I know you are."

Forget about ending up where he'd never expected. This was territory he'd never been in and had no idea how to navigate.

Chapter Seven

Standing across the street from the house, Maisey pulled her wool hat down low, not wanting the foster home mother to recognize her if she happened to look out the window or come outside. The woman had been nice enough, but first of all, Maisey knew how incredibly busy she was with the kids—seven during Maisey's time—and second, seeing her would just be too much.

Maisey had spent from ages sixteen to eighteen here, earning money by babysitting the younger kids when she was needed, and that was a big help in discovering how much she loved taking care of children. She'd help a couple of the kids with their schoolwork, particularly areas they struggled in, and Maisey found herself as a volunteer tutor, which was how she'd learned she'd wanted to be a teacher.

She stared up at the second-floor window, the farthest one to the left, barely feeling the cold snap of December air on her face. How many times had she sat by that window, just staring out and dreaming of "someday" and that things would be different?

"You okay?" Rex asked. He stood beside her, her arm still firmly wrapped around his.

"Actually, yes. I thought it would hurt seeing this place again since I always avoided this corner, let alone ever ventured down the street to anywhere near the house. But it turns out I discovered my passion here." She told him about babysitting and tutoring the kids. "I'll never forget when one girl I worked with came home from school with her first A ever. I was so proud of both of us." She smiled, remembering Bree's dark braid swishing around as she danced around their bedroom, waving the graded essay.

"Sometimes I think about adopting a child from foster care one day. Does that sound crazy? Too much on my plate as a single mother?"

"I think you could do anything you set your heart to, Maisey."

She felt herself beam. She'd heard people say that kind of thing before, but it had always sounded like a platitude. Coming from Rex, she believed it.

"And we already know you're a great mom," he continued. "I can just imagine what you could bring to a child in a position like you'd been in. You could change a life."

She was so touched she almost gasped. Instead, she wrapped her arms around him and kissed him, full on the lips.

"Oh," she whispered, not stepping back out of the embrace—though she'd meant to. Her brain had planned on it but her feet wouldn't move.

He leaned in and kissed her back. On the lips. Warm and strong and lingering long enough to let her know this was not a mistletoe kiss with kids watching. This was the real thing.

"I'm not supposed to kiss you," he said—and he did step back. "I'm gonna be honest, Maisey. I'm very attracted to you. On so many levels. But I am leaving the day after Christmas. That's set in stone."

"Is it?" she asked before she could stop herself. Maybe if he said yes, it was, she'd stop the back-and-forth on the subject of letting herself explore her feelings for him.

"Yes. Set in stone. I live on the road. My job is

across the entire country. That's who I am, who I've always been."

She raised an eyebrow. "I don't know about that. I've been learning that *I* direct my path, that my past doesn't get to dictate anything. Life changes. Things happen. We both know that. Paths twist and turn. Who says you have to stay on the same one?"

She could forget about giving up the back-and-forth.

He didn't respond for a few seconds. "We'd better get to Christmasland since the list is so long and the store closes at nine."

"It's barely seven," she pointed out. But she got it. He needed to move on. From her. And their conversation.

Not quite yet, sorry.

"So, if I fell in love with you, I'd be an idiot," she said. "That's not a question. Just something you should confirm."

He held her gaze, his blue eyes tender. "You're very smart, Maisey."

Disappointment hit her hard in the stomach, in the chest, in the region of where her heart was. "Got it," she said. "Do not fall in love with this guy. Leaving set in stone. Life on the road."

This time he didn't respond at all. He looked so

uncomfortable that she felt kind of bad for poking at him. But better they got this out in the open.

She knew now, for absolute sure. Because he said so.

Don't listen to Rex, she could hear Daisy Dawson McCord say if she told her about this conversation. *Two of my brothers said the same dumb thing about not being this or being that, and look at them now. Husbands. Fathers. And very happy.*

Luck had never been on Maisey's side, though.

She took one last look at the house where she'd spent two years worrying what life on the outside would be like. Maisey certainly hadn't been expected back for visits once she turned eighteen and had been nicely shown the door. There had been no invitations to Thanksgiving dinner or Christmas. *No wonder I wanted to get married so bad and so fast*, she thought. And then Thanksgiving and Christmas had still been big busts, hardly festive.

"Despite finding my path here, I remember feeling so powerless over my own life at the same time. Does that make sense?"

He nodded. "You weren't in charge of your own life. You were a minor. Back then, as kids, as teenagers, things weren't really in our control. Like my dad's drinking. All I wanted back then was to leave and never come back. Even though I spent half the time at my mom's with my brothers, the hard parts with my dad were the times that were most stamped on me. It's hard to let go of that stuff."

"I know what you mean."

He nodded kind of soberly, but with such emotion in his eyes, in his face, that she wanted to wrap her arms around him again.

"All I know is that, like you said, you're in charge of your own life now, Maisey. Adopting a child from foster care, becoming a teacher, running the children's programming at the ranch—all that you can make happen."

So why can't you give up on your life on the road and come home? she wanted to ask. *You're in charge, right?*

Actually, she knew why. She just didn't like the answer.

Because he doesn't really want to. That had to be why.

Christmasland was a huge party supply store that changed with the seasons or holidays. Over the summer it was a back-to-school center, then Halloween central, now Christmas. Rex had been in Christmasland a few times before, back when he was a kid with his father and stepmother, Leah—Noah and Daisy's mother. Rex, Axel and Zeke had been invited to go, as had Ford. Rex had probably come here with his parents when they were together, but he'd been too young to remember. Noah and Daisy's mother had wanted her stepsons to feel included in their Christmas at the ranch. The last time they'd all trooped over, their dad had taken out his credit card to pay the bill, but the card had been declined and Leah had said she was budgeted to the penny and they'd just have to forgo the tree that year, that Christmas was in their hearts, anyway. When Rex's mother had divorced their dad, she'd packed up all the Christmas stuff and taken it to their new apartment. So there was nothing in boxes in the attic—their dad had long sold off anything of their grandparents' that could bring in money for his gambling habit.

"I have forty-seven dollars from my paper route," Ford had said at the checkout, taking out his wallet and the cash.

Rex would never forget that. Their stepmother had started crying, which Rex hadn't understood at the time, and Bo Dawson had stormed out, embarrassed and angry. Leah had thanked Ford and told him to put the money back in his wallet, that the gesture was loving and generous but it was his money, and she'd repeated that "Christmas was in their hearts" and they didn't need all this stuff, anyway, right?

Rex had blocked out a lot of that time or maybe he'd just been too young to remember, but he'd never forget the little red Hot Wheels car he'd found wrapped with his name on it on the coffee table in the living room when he and his brothers had been dropped off on December 26 for "Christmas with Daddy." He'd overheard Bo and Leah arguing that it was awful that Ford had had to buy his brothers their presents from his father or else they'd have nothing.

Rex still had that Hot Wheels car. In fact, it lived in the front pocket of his carry-on bag, always there. Sometimes he'd dig around for a pack of tissues or gum and his fingers would land on the little car. Always made him smile. Every time that happened, he'd text Ford a hello out of the clear blue sky.

They'd never had a Christmas like that again at their dad's; Leah had apparently discovered that Bo Dawson lied about a lot of things and she budgeted to make sure their Christmas, for all the Dawson kids, was as it should be. When she'd passed away from cancer, Christmas at Dad's on the twenty-sixth had gone back to the old way. For Noah and Daisy, Christmas at Dad's was on the twenty-fifth and they'd learned to make their own holiday from Ford.

Regardless of all that, Christmas was special

but still something Rex had compartmentalized a long time ago as something not to get excited about. He couldn't remember the last time he really cared about Christmas. Because his father had died last December, all the siblings had gathered for the holiday at the then-broken-down ranch since they'd been scattered across Wyoming, Daisy's farmhouse barely standing then. His sister had said that Christmas was so big, so beautiful, that it should loom larger than their complicated grief and their dilapidated surroundings. But it hadn't, for any of them.

Now, as he stood in the brightly lit Christmasland, "White Christmas" playing over the loudspeaker, he wondered just what made him think he could help Maisey Clark get back her Christmas spirit when he had none himself.

"You okay?" she asked, eyeing him.

"Just thinking about Christmas past," he said. "Some whopper memories." He mock-shivered and attempted a smile.

She rubbed his arm. "I appreciate you taking me here, then, Rex. Christmas isn't the easiest for either of us, huh?"

"I always think I should be over childhood stuff, but then a memory floats into my head and pokes at the sore spots when I least expect it."

"Oh, trust me, I know. I just keep thinking

that everything I do, including being here, is for Chloe. New traditions. I think of her beautiful tiny face, her big hazel eyes, with the entire future in them, and everything needs to be about her, not me."

Same for me with you, he wanted to say. *That's what you bring out in me. You take me outside myself.*

Whoa. There it was again, the mystifying deep hold this woman had on him.

He glanced around to shake off his thoughts and get back on track. "Wow. Have you ever seen so many ornaments in your life?" He pointed at the section called Ornament Village off to the left. "Maybe we can find your Siamese cat."

He *had* to find that cat. Had. To. Hanging that replica on her Christmas tree would be the final clincher, the embodiment of Christmas restored.

She glanced over, not looking hopeful at all. "Maybe, but I doubt it. I looked on Christmas-land's website many times, but they never had it. Other cat ornaments, yes, but not the one I'd had in my hand when my dad rescued me from the house."

This time he did shiver. And everything he felt about Maisey Clark was reinforced. She deserved the world.

"Did you have a Siamese cat? Was that the significance of that ornament in the first place?"

Oh, God. Why had he asked that? If she'd lost the cat in the fire, too, his brain would explode.

She shook her head. "My dad was so allergic, but Siamese cats were my mom's favorite. She loved their slinky beauty. My mom told me that when my dad surprised her with the ornament and hung it on the tree, he'd said it was kinda like giving her a Siamese cat for Christmas every year."

He smiled. "That's really nice."

Her smile lit up her face. "Yeah. They really loved each other. I don't remember much about them but I do remember feeling that, knowing that. I guess it's why I'm still something of a romantic."

"You probably like this song, then," he said as Nat King Cole filled their ears.

She grinned and bowed and held out her hand, and he smiled and gave her a twirl, coming to a stop so close against him he could barely handle it.

"Well," she said, stepping away a bit. "We'd better hit the aisles." She pulled out her list from her tote bag. "Let's start with your Santa suit. Gotta have that."

Rex wasn't much of a dancer, but he did like slow dancing. And that one twirl to Nat King Cole had him imagining holding her close, chest to chest, her head on his shoulder, her arms around his neck, his around her waist. Never letting her go...

Two kids in Santa hats with furry white beards Velcroed around their heads went racing past, and he shook off the very pleasant, welcome thoughts about him and Maisey.

"You know, those whirlwinds who just ran past reminded me of something," he said. "I'm ninety-nine percent sure there's a Santa suit in the attic at Daisy's house. I was up there looking for something last time I was at the ranch, and I know I saw the outfit, if not the beard. I can check when we pick up Chloe tonight. If I'm imagining things, I can come back and buy one."

"Okay, annotating my list," she said, grabbing a pen from her bag and jotting that down. "One thing I am—organized. So let's get the kids' costumes. We need ten altogether and I've noted sizes and who's wearing what."

"You mean eleven," he said. "Chloe has to have a costume, too."

She stared at him, a slow, sweet smile on her lips. "You are so right. And thoughtful. You should stop it." She laughed, but he caught something in her expression—wistfulness, maybe? Which reminded him what she'd noted earlier. *If I fell in love with you, I'd be an idiot.*

Was she falling for him? How the hell could he give her a great Christmas if he'd let that happen and then walked away on the twenty-sixth? He'd leave her with a broken heart.

He hadn't figured that in. Rex hadn't allowed himself to get close to a woman since he'd hurt Bethany six months ago. He cared so much about Maisey—no way was he setting her up like this.

Dammit to hell.

"Said too much?" she asked, her lips kind of twisted to one side.

"You said what needed to be said. I should back off, Maisey. We both know I'm leaving for my job."

"For you, you mean."

"No, for my job. For the US Marshals. For Joe, the witness out there somewhere. For all the witnesses, all the victims, their families. What I do is important."

"I know it is, Rex. I didn't mean that it wasn't."

"Let's shop," he said. "That's what we're here for, right?"

She looked down, her expression full-out crestfallen, and he wanted to kick himself in the stomach. "Yeah. Let's shop. Okay," she said, eyes on her list. "Reindeer suit size 3T for Danny Dawson."

He closed his eyes for a second, inwardly sighing as his adorable nephew's face came to mind. Danny would go crazy over his reindeer suit. He would absolutely love it. And Rex would have to say goodbye the day after Christmas when the two of them were getting so close.

"Right. Reindeer suit size 3T. I'm on it."

As they headed to the costume area, Maisey grabbed a bright green elf hat with pointy felt ears sticking out on either side and put it on her head. "How do I look?" she asked with a grin.

"You look really beautiful," he said—too seriously, too reverently. But she did.

Somehow, he'd just have to stop looking at her and thinking about her.

Chapter Eight

Rex stood with Maisey at the checkout, noticing her eyes widen at the grand total of their shopping spree.

"That's more than a month's rent at my old trailer," she said.

He handed over his credit card, that old memory of his father's being declined making him grateful every time he purchased something. "The ranch is doing really well since the grand reopening last summer, and we all want to make the kids' show unforgettable. And trust me, the reason Daisy didn't join you on this mission is because she would have gone way overboard, every bell and whistle."

"I am looking forward to seeing the kids' faces when we hand out costumes for the rehearsals."

"Same here," he said, surprising himself, but it was true. Even just spending a bunch of hours working on the set, he'd gotten to know Tyler and Annalise pretty well just by listening to them talk, how they responded. The Kid Zone bunch were great kids.

"I'm trying to convince my special song apprentice—Zara—to be in the show, but so far she refuses. I think she'll change her mind once she sees her elf costume. I found one with purple felt shoes and purple stripes on the pointy hat, and purple is her favorite color."

"They're really lucky to have you, Maisey. It's obvious how much you care about them and your job."

"Good, because I do care. But I feel like the lucky one. Having the job in the first place, meeting such wonderful people, like this family called the Dawsons." She smiled. "Seriously, all of you are so generous. I know you have issues with your dad, Rex, but in between the hard times, he must have done something right. Then again, maybe your moms were just one thousand percent superstars. Probably, now that I think about it more."

"We did get lucky with great moms. All of us. My dad had great taste in wives." He pictured his mom down in her Florida backyard, cutting into an orange from her own little grove. He'd have to plan a trip down soon. "But you're also right. In between, even far and few, he got things right. He cared about us. We know that. It took me a long time to see it, to believe it, but I understand more about addiction than I once did."

She squeezed his hand and he didn't want her to let go.

"I don't know about you, but I'm starving," he said. "Want to grab some dinner?"

There—nice and casual. Rex could actually go for a filet mignon with peppercorns and roast potatoes, but he wasn't sure he should suggest a real restaurant—à la what would feel like a date.

"Definitely," she said as she took two bags, one dangling from each wrist, and he took the rest. "I need to replenish my energy. Remember, I'm not used to shopping and buying everything my heart desires. Every kid has a holiday costume. The show gets its own Christmas tree. Each song has its own fun prop. I still can't believe it."

"The show would be special with just the kids singing. But Daisy wants to go to town for our guests during Christmas, so might as well go big."

They headed out to his SUV and loaded the cargo space. Then he glanced around at the restaurants lining the main street, looking in the windows for well-lit, no-candles-in-the-center tables.

"You know what I'm so in the mood for right now?" she asked. "A great pizza. With spinach and mushrooms and peppers."

He instantly relaxed. "Can my half have meatball and sausage?"

"Definitely. And garlic knots on the side."

Maisey knew of a small pizzeria that had been in business for decades and had always been her favorite, so they went there. Loud and very brightly lit, the pizza joint was probably the least romantic restaurant in town. But as they sat at their square table and shared their extra-large pie with their favorite toppings and their basket of garlic knots, Rex felt like he was on one of the best dates of his life. Easy, fun, natural. No awkward silences.

Because it's not a date. You and Maisey even covered the two of you earlier. There is no "the two of you." You're leaving and she needs permanence. End of story.

With two slices of veggie wrapped up for Maisey to take home—Rex had demolished his half—they finally got back in the SUV and headed home to the ranch.

Home to the ranch. It was Maisey's home now—not his.

Interesting.

On the way back, they talked about the show and the costumes and whether one day, fifteen years from now, they'd hear that Tyler and Annalise were engaged. Once again, their conversation was so effortless and rich. There was no small talk, nor did they get heavy and deep as they had earlier.

If I fell in love with you, I'd be an idiot...

He'd tried over the past couple of hours to stop thinking about that, but her words had kept popping back into his brain.

As they arrived at Daisy's farmhouse so Maisey could pick up Chloe, he thought about how she'd hugged him in front of the foster home. How she'd held his arm. The way she'd looked at him in Pauletta's Pizza.

The way he'd been unable to take his eyes off her.

They'd already fallen for each other, he knew. And both of them would be smart and not act on it.

"I can't wait to see Chloe," Maisey said, taking off her seat belt. "I miss her so much. I never feel quite right when I'm away from her. Like something is missing."

That's how I've felt since I met you, he almost said, and thank God he didn't. *Whoa.*

How had this woman come to mean so much to him so fast? The combination of the Dear Santa letter, her old dream not coming true, finding out she was a single mother totally on her own again and his wild reaction to her physically, emotionally, mentally. He couldn't spend long with his rogue thoughts because Daisy had clearly heard the car and opened the front door with a grin.

"Chloe is the sweetest, prettiest little thing and so easy," his sister said as she held the door open wide for them. "She and Tony stared at each other and waved their little arms at each other for a while. Then both conked out. They're fast asleep."

"Thanks so much for watching her," Maisey said. "We got everything on the list." She told Daisy about the costumes and the Kid Zone tree and the trimmings they'd gotten. "All that's left are the small gifts for the kids to go under the tree."

"Thanks for doing all that," Daisy said to both of them. "And if you two want to go present shopping after work tomorrow, I'd be thrilled to watch Chloe again."

Another night out with Maisey. Another shouldn't-be-romantic-but-it-will-be-anyway dinner. Another half-hour drive back to the ranch, talking, sharing, being so aware of her in such close proximity.

But they did need to get the kids' gifts. And he couldn't leave that to Maisey on her own since there were quite a few to buy. And he *had* gotten to know some of the children enough to really help out. Rationalizing was a great thing.

"Works for me," Rex said. "Pick you up at six, Maisey?" He only casually glanced at her, no big whoop here, just two…friends doing some Christmas shopping. And really, it was work related.

He felt her gaze on him, lingering before she responded.

"Sounds good," she said. "Six it is."

Daisy beamed. Of course. "Great. I'll swing by a bit earlier to pick up Chloe."

"That sure makes things easier for me," Maisey said. "Thanks. Oh, hey," she added to Rex. "Don't forget the Santa costume. You said there would probably be one up in the attic?"

"Oh, right." He looked at Daisy. "Seemed a waste to buy new at the everything's-marked-up Christmas shop tonight when I'm ninety percent sure there's one in the attic."

Daisy nodded. "There definitely is. In the back by that collection of junk Dad was trying to fix up to sell, I think. Everything up there was stuff he couldn't sell on Craigslist, and good thing— there's a few things I'm glad to have of our grandparents, even if they're very old and if dusty throw pillows live in the attic. I know they're there."

"It's surprising he didn't sell the suit," Rex pointed out. "Very few things had nostalgic value to Bo Dawson, but maybe Santa did."

Daisy nodded and shrugged. "Dad was a mystery."

"Since Chloe's sleeping," Maisey said, "I'd love to take a peek and see what old-timey gems might be hiding in plain sight. I love antiquing."

A kettle started whistling in the kitchen, and Daisy hurried toward it. "I'm about to make a mug of spiced lemon tea, if anyone's interested."

"Thanks, but I'm stuffed with pizza and soda," Rex said with a pat on his stomach.

"Me, too," Maisey added. "But thanks."

"Well, sounds like you two had a *very* productive evening," Daisy said with a grin as she disappeared into the kitchen.

Rex rolled his eyes with a smile. Standard Daisy, all right. "That narrow door in the hallway opens to stairs that go up to the attic." As in the SUV earlier, he was so aware of Maisey beside him as he headed over and opened the door, flicking on the light switch. He hadn't been up here in a long, long time.

"What are those?" Maisey asked when they were at the landing, pointing at the six identical trunks with name labels lined up single file against the back wall.

"My grandparents bought one for each of us when we were born," he said. "There's not much in each. Some baby stuff, kid art, class pictures, the usual."

"Show me something in your trunk," she said.

"You want to see a school picture of my awkward stage at twelve?" he asked. "You'll go running out of the attic."

"No way did you ever have an awkward stage. You're too good-looking. And don't let that go to your head."

"Too late," he said, shooting her a grin. He walked over to the trunk and opened the lid, looking at some old clothes he was surprised his dad hadn't tried to sell, then realized why Bo hadn't. He stood completely still, staring at the brown-and-gold Wyoming Cowboys football T-shirt his brother Ford had given him for his thirteenth birthday. He'd been wearing that T-shirt for good luck under a sweater on his very first date when he was fifteen. The date had been a total disaster. He'd taken the girl to a burger place that now was no longer around, and she'd actually managed to get back together with her ex-boyfriend, a jock whom Rex couldn't stand, right on the date. The reunited couple had actually left together, leaving Rex sitting there with both their untouched plates, which hadn't even been served when his date had abandoned him. Rex had called home for a ride, hoping Ford would be around since it was the weekend, but he wasn't, and his dad had shown up. Bo had come inside the burger joint, and Rex had told him the basic gist, feeling like a total loser.

Bo had sat down, said there was no reason the girl's perfectly good cheeseburger should go to waste and took a big bite, then gobbled up a few fries. Rex had found that both mortifying and hilarious, and his dad told him stories about his own dating days back at Bear Ridge Middle School. They'd talked for a good hour, Rex laughing his head off, and his chest had been bursting with love for his dad. That night, Bo Dawson had gotten drunk and passed out outside, something he often did, and Rex and his brothers, visiting for the weekend, couldn't budge him. They'd had to cover him with a down blanket and leave him on the patio. Half of Rex's goodwill toward his father from earlier that night had been replaced by the usual dread. Complicated.

His lucky T-shirt hadn't seemed so lucky given all that had happened, and Rex had tossed it in the trash in a fit of teenage angst, but apparently his dad had fished it out and washed it and saved it. Because here it was.

"When's the last time you poked around your trunk?" Maisey asked.

He shrugged. "This is the first time. I asked Daisy what was in the trunks and she said old clothes, school photos, nothing of interest. And if Daisy says nothing of interest, there's *really* nothing to see, since she tends to make a big fuss of little stuff."

Maisey smiled. "I'm like that, too."

He glanced around, hoping to find something with a lock that the key his dad left him would look like it fit. There was nothing. What did the key open? Maybe he'd never find out. He'd had an entire year, ever since finding the key in the otherwise empty envelope with his name on it in his dad's scrawled handwriting, to think long and hard about what his dad could have wanted him to find, to open. He still had no idea. At first he'd focused on the personal—what hidden meaning was there? But the less he found a lock the key opened, the more he just looked for any lock to try. He was out of locks.

Frustrated, he opened a box near his dad's collection of broken small electronics and there was the Santa suit—even the beard was there, smushed into the sleeve.

"Success," he said, pulling it out and holding it up. He put on the hat.

Maisey grinned. "Back in Christmasland, I felt like you were my own Santa. Now you truly look the part."

"That's exactly who I'm supposed to be for you." He gave a firm nod, reminded of his purpose in her life. Not to kiss her or fall for her. To be her Santa, to restore her Christmas spirit, to give her the holiday she deserved.

A baby's cry could be heard downstairs.

"That's definitely Chloe," Maisey said. "I can't wait to see her sweet little face. I haven't been away from her this long before."

Rex closed his trunk and tucked the Santa suit firmly under his arm. "I'll get you two home."

But again, he didn't want their night to come to an end.

"I just realized something," Rex said as he carried the last of the bags into Maisey's cabin while she settled Chloe in her high chair in the kitchen.

Maisey poked her head out from the kitchen doorway. "What's that?"

He held out the Santa suit. "I'd better see if this thing fits now before I find out it's three sizes too small on the day of the show."

"Bathroom's right there. It's pretty small, so

don't try to turn around once you get the padded top part of the suit on."

He smiled. "Thanks for the warning."

She sat down beside Chloe's high chair, which she'd just started using a week ago, and dipped the little spoon into her daughter's favorite dinner, butternut squash baby food. Chloe had gotten through half the jar when a "Ho, ho, ho" could be heard in the hallway.

Santa appeared in the doorway of the kitchen, his hands on his hips. "Fits just right. Christmas is saved."

It certainly is, she thought. "All you need is a bag of gifts slung over your shoulder."

"Ah, speaking of that. Maybe we should make a list of what you want to get the kids so that when we hit the stores tomorrow night, we already have the hard part figured out."

"Good idea. By the time you're done changing out of that thing, Chloe will have finished her dinner, so I'll meet you on the sofa. I have half a pie that Cowboy Joe gave me to take home from the cafeteria. Want some and coffee?"

"Definitely," he said before heading toward the bathroom again.

"I like him too much," she whispered to her baby girl.

Chloe's big hazel eyes focused on her, a little smile on her face.

"You like him, too. I can tell. He's pretty wonderful."

"Meow," Snowbell said, slinking between the legs of the chair, and Maisey took that to mean she also liked Rex Dawson. Everyone did, it seemed.

But some people, like herself, had to watch out from liking him too much, even though she was clearly past that point.

She finished feeding Chloe, lifting the baby from the high chair against her chest and giving her some good pats for a burp. Success.

"How about some tummy time?" she asked Chloe. "On your favorite mat." She carried Chloe into the living room and set her on the thick mat with lots to touch and look at. Chloe gurgled and lifted her head, batting at a low-hanging pom-pom from a spiral felt stick.

The bathroom door opened and all six feet two inches of Rex, back in his sexy Henley shirt and jeans, was headed toward her, his hair slightly mussed from the hat.

"I bought my niece and nephews a mat just like that," he said. "Turns out Noah and Daisy both had gotten at least four as gifts. Thanks to having baby relatives, I even know what Chloe is doing is called tummy time."

Maisey laughed. "You're an involved uncle. I love that."

"I surprisingly do, too," he said, sitting down. He glanced at the coffee table. "Hey, where's that pie you promised me? I'm surprised I have room for anything more after all that pizza, but I do," he added, patting his rock-hard stomach. Not that Maisey knew for sure it was, but she could imagine through the thin cotton shirt.

"Oh, right!" she said, popping up.

"Nope, you sit and relax. I'll get it and make the coffee."

Of course he would. He was like that.

"Decaf or regular?" he called from the kitchen.

"Definitely decaf," she said. "With cream and a sugar cube from the yellow bowl on the table."

"Coming right up, madame."

Maisey smiled and leaned close to Chloe's ear. "I could seriously get used to this."

Her ex-husband had never made a pot of coffee or said anything remotely like "Coming right up, madame," let alone told her to sit and relax. She'd thought she'd wanted a traditional guy so that she could be "wifely," but that had gotten old fast. Her ex had just wanted to be waited on, picked up after and catered to, in all departments. If Maisey ever got married again, she'd have a real partner who reciprocated, shared in the household duties, rubbed her feet after she gave an excellent back massage. She might not have had a good marriage, but at least she knew what she didn't want in a husband.

Rex came into the living room with a tray holding two slices of pecan pie and two mugs of coffee, which he set on the coffee table. Maisey scooped up Chloe and gave her a kiss and settled her in her baby swing, her alert eyes following her mother's every move.

Maisey sat on the sofa, Rex just a foot away beside her, and she got out her phone to start the list of gifts in her Notes app. They started in alphabetical order. The As alone took a good fifteen minutes since there were the twins, Amelia and Ava, and Annalise. If Maisey blanked on a good idea for someone, Rex came up with just the right present. They were a solid team.

Solid team. More and more, Maisey couldn't deny just how deep her feelings for him went. Or that if anyone asked her what she wanted for Christmas, it would be for Rex to stay.

Luckily, she couldn't focus on him or wonder what a lasting kiss would feel like because they were moving right along on their mission. By the time their refills of coffee and all the pie was gone, the gift list was practically done and full of everything from art supplies to bug-catching kits to stuffed animals. There was only one name left: Zara.

"Hmm," Maisey said. "I want to get this exactly right. Zara opened up to me earlier today. She's been through a lot."

"Long dark hair? The song apprentice, right? Maybe something related to music or a streaming gift card?"

"Something personal, though." She took a sip of her coffee, hoping the perfect idea would come to her.

"The other day, when I was in the Bear Ridge gift shop, I saw something on a display by the counter that might work. A silver musical note pin, and the store was offering free engraving for Christmas for all the jewelry."

Maisey gasped. "Rex Dawson, how the hell do you do it?"

He tilted his head. "Do what?"

"Come up with the perfect everything?"

That got her a smile. "I just happened to notice the music pins because I was looking for something for my sisters-in-law in that shop."

"What did you get them?" she asked, deeply curious about everything concerning this man and his life.

"Nothing at the gift shop, so I asked for help from my bros. I got Sadie a ten-session class at new-mother yoga since she'll be delivering this spring, and I ended up getting Sara a ton of stuff for her garden bed—seeds Noah said she wanted and a bunch of big planting pots."

"Very thoughtful."

"I still have to get for two brothers—Ford and Zeke—they're the ones that don't live on the ranch, either. And Danny. Then I'm done with family gifts."

"I just have to buy a few. I haven't decided what I'm getting Chloe. I saw some adorable pink-and-purple polka-dot socks. And a couple new books. And I saw a teething toy in the shape of a moose that was so cute."

"I think Chloe will love all that." He finished the rest of his coffee. "Maisey, can I ask you something personal?"

She sat up straighter. "Do we talk about anything else?"

He smiled. "No, I guess not. We go straight for the heart of the matter. I was wondering if you got presents when you were a kid. At the group homes."

"The house parents always bought each kid something small. They tried to make it personal. One year when I really liked drawing, Miss Meredith got me a pack of pastels and a sketch pad. I loved that." She glanced at him. "You were picturing me giftless, weren't you? Not even a lump of coal."

"I hoped not. I just wondered."

"Tell me about a special Christmas gift you received," she said, again way too curious about all things Rex Dawson.

"My favorite Christmas present ever was a mountain bike—I rode that everywhere. And a little Matchbox car my oldest brother gave me one year."

"Hmm, I do think we have a theme—vehicles. Transportation. Movement."

He tilted his head and stared at her. "I never thought about that. But you're probably right. Does kinda represent me."

"You could have one of those buggies I've seen on the ranch. Like Daisy drives around in." Oh, no. Did she just say that? Would he think she was asking him to stay at the ranch? They'd already discussed that and he was leaving. He'd made that very clear.

Chloe let out a giant yawn.

Maisey scooped up her baby girl from the swing and gave her a snuggle. "I'd better get her to bed. Back in a jiff."

He looked at her but didn't say anything. She went into the nursery and changed Chloe, got her into fresh pj's and then settled the baby against her chest in the rocking chair. "How about a story, sweet girl?" Maisey grabbed the book that was on the table beside the chair. "We didn't finish this one about the bunny. But let's start from the beginning." She opened the book with one hand, the other caressing Chloe's back. "'Fluffers the bunny rabbit loves tomatoes. But he's the only rabbit in the whole village who does. All the other bunnies only love carrots.'"

She turned the page but Chloe's eyes were already closed. "Today was a big day. Kid Zone, then a playdate with your new friend Tony. Let's get you in your crib."

She carefully got up and laid Chloe down. Then she watched her baby sleep, her little chest with the penguins across it going up and down. When she turned to leave, Rex was standing in the doorway.

Please don't say you're leaving. I'm not ready for this night to end.

"You're such a good mother," he said. "Devoted, committed."

She smiled. "Go on."

He laughed, then put his hand over his mouth. "I don't want to wake her up," he whispered.

Before she could stop herself, she lifted on her tiptoes and kissed him. A real kiss. *Kiss me back,* she thought. *C'mon.*

He did. He put his hands on either side of her face and looked at her for a moment, then kissed her as if he'd been waiting to all night.

"I'd better go," he said. "Staying here for even one more second is dangerous."

She smiled but she hardly felt it anywhere inside. There was something so tender and beautiful between them, but he wasn't giving it a chance. She shouldn't, either. But just letting him go back to his old world, his old life, when he had this shiny new warm love in his life? Without fighting for what was happening between them?

Was he making love impossible for himself? Or did he just not love her?

Right now, that was the question she had to answer. No—*he* did.

Chapter Nine

The next morning, Noah and Axel stood on ladders on either side of the Dawson Family Guest Ranch Christmas Fair banner, waiting for Rex to determine if it was hanging straight. The fifteen-foot silver poles the banner hung from had been flanking the start of the path to the ranch, just past the gates, for fifty years, and though their dad had crashed into one pole drunk in a buggy one night, it was so sturdy it stayed put. Rex knew Noah had always thought that was a good omen for the ranch itself.

"Noah, up about an eighth of an inch and we're golden," Rex called.

The ranch was now all set for the festivities, a one-day extravaganza for the guests to stop at tables set up along the paths and in the lodge with holiday crafts to make and Christmas cookies to eat and eggnog and spiced cider to drink. Noah and Sara and their crew had decked out the ranch just enough so that it positively twinkled but still felt rustic. There would be stations set up in the Kid Zone to make ornaments and small gifts, free-flowing eggnog and spiced sugar cookies, and candy canes galore. And Rex would be playing Santa for the day in the red-and-green "hut" that he, Noah and Axel had built by the Christmas tree in the hallway of the lodge. He had no idea what that would be like, a lot of kids whispering in his ear about what they wanted for Christmas. What if they didn't get what they asked for? He'd feel terrible. Not that he'd know.

He still felt stung on Maisey's behalf, though. She hadn't gotten her Christmas wish and then had stopped making wishes altogether.

Noah and Axel climbed down, shaking him from his thoughts, and headed to the barn to put away the ladders. A silver pickup came up the asphalt path, which was weird since it was barely seven in the morning and cars weren't allowed on the drives past the gate. Rex squinted to see who it was in the bright morning sunshine.

The driver gave a short honk and stuck his head out the window. "Hey, stranger."

Rex grinned. His brother Ford. And was that Zeke in the passenger seat?

Ford parked by Daisy's house and he hopped out, followed by, yup, Zeke, just as Noah and Axel were coming back from the barn.

"I was talking to Zeke a couple nights ago and we both realized our Christmas vacations were starting this morning," Ford said when they approached, "so we decided to drive up together. We have way too many presents for everyone, especially the kids."

Rex hadn't seen these two brothers in a few months, but not a thing had changed—both still looked exactly like who they were. Ford, a cop, wore aviator sunglasses, had short dark hair and always seemed ready to help in any situation. Zeke, a businessman in mergers and acquisitions, might as well have been wearing a suit for how pristine his button-down shirt and dark jeans were, not a mark on his leather boots. All the Dawsons, particularly the brothers, looked like their father.

"What?" came the happy screech of Daisy Dawson McCord as she ran out the front door of the farmhouse. "It's a Christmas miracle! My five brothers are all home!" She threw her arms around Ford and Zeke, talking a mile a minute about the ranch and the fair. "Staying with us?" she asked them. "We've got room. Rex has been staying at Axel's, but now it's my turn. You guys have to stay at the farmhouse, too. It's my dream come true to have my brothers under one roof."

"Does Tony wake up all night long still?" Zeke asked with a grin. "With this mug, I need my beauty sleep."

"Now that he's five months, he actually sleeps through the night," Daisy said. "Well, till five thirty in the morning, anyway. But that's ranching hours, too, so I'll get your rooms ready with fresh linens." She ran toward the house. "Tony is going to be so happy all his uncles are here. Big dinner at the house tonight—so don't make any other plans!" She headed inside, the storm door closing behind her.

"Guess that's settled," Axel said. "My cabin will feel empty without you and River, Rex."

"River?" Ford asked, getting their bags from the back seat.

"My dog," Rex said. "Shepherd mix. Great guy. Supersmart, knows his commands, no aggression, major snuggler with a certain toddler named Danny Dawson."

"Wait," Ford said. "I'm still on the words *my*

dog coming out your mouth. *You* have a dog? You're here for good?"

Rex felt his smile fade. "No. I'm leaving the day after Christmas." He explained about finding River and taking him to the ranch. "Daisy takes care of River when I'm not around. Which will be a long stretch once I leave. I probably won't be back till…" He tried to think of upcoming holidays or special dates. "Ah—Danny's third birthday in March. I'll try to stay for a couple days."

"You'd better," Axel said. "Danny asks every morning at the crack of dawn when Unck Rex is going to wake up."

"He means that figuratively," Zeke said with a grin.

Rex gave him a playful jab in the side.

"Who's up for breakfast at the Bear Ridge Diner?" Ford asked. "Like old times." Last December, after they'd inherited the ranch, they'd spent a lot of time at that diner, holding family meetings since none of them could bear being on the dilapidated property for long.

"Sounds good. I'll go get Daisy," Rex said.

"I'll let Sara know we're skipping out," Noah said, grabbing his phone from his pocket.

He took the farmhouse porch steps two at a time, waved hello to his brother-in-law, Harrison, told his sister the plan, and of course she was thrilled. Daisy gave Harrison a kiss, handed him Tony and said she'd be back by nine.

Daisy practically skipped down the steps toward the car as the four other Dawsons piled in. "So…"

Rex eyed her. "So what?"

"How are things between you and Maisey?" She all but wiggled her eyebrows.

He mock-grimaced at her. "Things are *not*. Daisy, in all seriousness, don't play matchmaker when I'm leaving town in days."

"The matchmaking part is supposed to make you stay." She smiled but seemed wistful. "You have no idea what it means to me to see you all here at the same time. I'm selfish and want you all on the ranch for good. We're all we have, Rex. Come home."

There was a time when this line of talk from Daisy didn't poke at him—just Daisy being her usual loving, family-oriented self, and he'd always appreciated it since she'd long been the glue for the six of them, asking, bribing, to get them together. But now something was stabbing at him and it wasn't just Maisey and his crazy feelings for her. He'd been restless and stressed for months now, and coming home had calmed him—unexpectedly. But he belonged out on the road, hunting fugitives and helping witnesses. That was his mission in life.

He'd talk to Ford about it. As a cop, Ford would understand the grip the job had on him for many reasons.

Ford drove the half hour to town. The Bear Ridge Diner wasn't crowded, but there were hellos to say to the folks scattered at the counter and tables, including the chief of police at the Bear Ridge PD and one of his officers, both of whom kidded Noah about how they still couldn't believe he'd ever been a wild troublemaker as a teenager and young adult. Rex knew that, once, that kind of talk used to bother Noah, who'd completely changed his life when he'd taken on the rebuilding of the guest ranch. Now even Noah said he couldn't seem to remember himself as that "rowdy kid."

There was a big round table in the back of the diner, their waiter appearing with a coffee urn before he even handed out menus. They all nodded about the coffee, Daisy asking for decaf. Fifteen minutes later, once the plates of omelets and French toast and pancakes were served, the coffee refilled, the orange juice sipped, the siblings dug in, talking and laughing about themselves and the ranch.

"Hey, Ford," the chief of police said, winding his way toward them as he and the officer were leaving. "I know you're on the force out in Casper, but you should know we're going to have two openings after the New Year. One in January, one in March. I have two retiring, like O'Connor here." He clapped an arm on his officer's shoulder. "Think about it."

"I will, thank you," Ford said with a nod.

When the cops left, Daisy pounced. "How many people are offered a job without even asking for one? It's meant to be, Ford. We'll all help build your luxe log cabin on the ranch, and you can start your new job in January or April."

Ford took a sip of his coffee. "Maybe."

Rex almost choked on his bite of western omelet. "Did you just say *maybe*? I thought you said hell would ice over before you ever moved back to the ranch."

Ford took another slug of coffee. "That was last year. When everything the ranch used to be was still very fresh. Now it's hard to even remember those days. Every time I come visit I feel like I'm at the western version of Disney World. Well, not really, but you know what I mean. The place is *happy*."

Huh. Rex had to agree. All the old reasons for avoiding home no longer *were*.

"You'll seriously consider the offer?" Rex

asked his eldest brother as he forked a home fry. Casper was a city with close to 60,000 people. Bear Ridge barely had a population of 2,000.

Ford nodded. "Yeah, I think I will."

There was tension in his expression, despite the poker-face cop neutrality he was known for. Rex could see it. Something was driving him away from Casper. Relationship? Stress of the job? He really did need to talk to Ford in private.

"You could take the other opening," Ford said to Rex, eyeing him with the assessing gaze Rex was used to giving. "You were a cop for a year before you were accepted into the US Marshals' rigorous training program. Given all your experience, you can easily make detective."

"Someone pass the smelling salts," Daisy said. "I might have Ford and Rex moving home? Zeke, I'm still coming for you. But you're safe right now since I'll work on these two."

They all laughed, and the waiter came by to check on them, the question in the air about Rex joining the PD luckily lost in the chatter and then Axel telling a funny story about Danny.

But he could feel Ford's gaze on him, and he knew his brother could tell he was conflicted. Understatement. The call to leave—no commitments, no obligations, no emotional entanglements, no one relying on him except his boss and those he served—was strong, a force deep inside him. But as Maisey and her six-month-old came to mind, he felt the call to stay drumming like a tap in his heart.

At the Kid Zone, Chloe was screaming her head off and none of Maisey's usual tricks worked. Not holding the baby, rocking her, singing to her, burping her, carrying her vertically, horizontally or giving her swing time, which Chloe usually loved. Danny, Axel and Sadie's toddler, had his hands over his ears while sitting at a little table with his superhero coloring book. A few other kids kept looking over with frowns.

I know. Trust me, I know. I don't like the screeching, either. Her ace staffer, Hannah, was in the middle of a game with three kids, and the other sitter had called in sick. And now the Caletti twins were marching over, crying, too, faces furious, and each swiping at the other.

"No, you're the dumb one, dummy!" Ava yelled.

"You are, idiot!" Amelia screamed. "I'm telling Mom the minute she picks us up what you did!"

"Fine! I'm telling Dad!" Ava screeched back.

Maisey rocked and patted Chloe's back, praying the baby would calm down so that she could listen to the Calettis, who were marching closer, about to demand Maisey's attention, and boy, did they need it.

A question Maisey had asked during her job interview came roaring back into her mind. What if her attention was torn between guests' children and her own baby? She'd given an example of Chloe screaming, much like she was doing now, and a kid needing her attention, whether a bullying situation or a badly skinned knee, while the other staffers were busy with others. If she gave her attention to her baby because she'd need to address the crying, would that mean she was putting her own daughter first and not doing her job?

Daisy's answer had made her feel a lot better: *there is no yours or ours or theirs, Maisey.* Her boss had basically said that the kids in her care included guests, staff and Maisey's own, and that no one child deserved more or less attention than another because of who they were. *You have solid experience in knowing what takes priority,* Daisy had said, *and I trust you'll make good decisions.*

That response was soothing right now because quieting Chloe took priority so that everyone else could hear themselves think.

"Ho, ho, ho!" a deep voice called from the front door.

Rex Dawson entered in his sexy leather jacket and a Santa hat, lugging a large piece of wood, part of the backdrop that would appear onstage behind where the children would stand and sit. "Guess what, set apprentices," he called out. "It's backdrop painting time! Tyler, Annalise, that means you," he called out in a funny voice that went up and down and echoed.

Even the Caletti twins giggled.

Oh, Rex, bless you.

"And I need two more painting helpers," Rex said. "Ava, Amelia, how about you guys? You're master painters."

Their faces brightened immediately, but Maisey could see the girls were torn between telling on each other and getting to be on the painting crew with the teenagers, whom they seemed to look up to.

"Only if you're not annoying," Ava said, hands on hips, glaring at her sister.

"Only if you're not," Amelia shot back.

"Hurry, girls," Rex called. "Your paintbrushes— and two specially striped candy canes—await! Okay, fine, every kid gets one! But you can't chomp on them till after lunch."

Both Calettis grinned and ran over, their argument canceled for the time being, anyway.

She definitely owed him one.

Chloe still shrieked her head off, which probably helped the twins want to escape being anywhere near Maisey. She kept one eye on Danny, who was intently coloring, elbow holding down the page, left hand over left ear, little tongue out in concentration, as he colored a dog purple and green. She rocked Chloe this way and that, shushing, there-there-ing.

She glanced at Rex, who was in a huddle with his crew. Then he came over to Maisey and held his arms out.

"Bet Chloe needs a change of hands," Rex said. "My sister-in-law Sara taught me that when I'd be over and the twins would be bawling their eyes out. Usually someone new holding them would quiet them right down, a new face to stare at."

Was he actually asking to take her screaming baby? The man was a saint.

She handed over Chloe, who continued to screech. Rex made a funny face at her, which got him a bigger shriek, but then he held her high up in the air, her legs dangling, swooshing her up and down, up and down, and the crying stopped. Maisey almost fell to her knees in relief. Not only did she have the usual full house, but rehearsals for the holiday show would be starting in a half hour, and four kids needed line refreshers between now and then so they wouldn't get upset during the practice run and torpedo the rehearsal—which had happened twice and wasn't pretty.

"I've got this," Rex said to her, giving Chloe a little bounce against his chest. "I've prepped the crew—Annalise and Tyler will pencil in the design while the Calettis paint the big sections. Then they'll all paint in the scene. So I can hold Chloe and supervise. Take care of whatever you need to."

"I owe you," she said. "Home-cooked dinner after the shopping trip tonight?" Alone with Rex in her cabin? After what had happened last night? Maybe making him dinner wasn't a good idea. She could barely resist him and she had to.

But she really, really, really wanted to be alone with him.

"The last time I was in your cabin, I kissed you. And not some giggling-teen-dangling-mistletoe-above-our-heads kiss."

"I know," she said. "I liked it."

"I did, too. But it's like we're gasoline and the kiss is a match. Kaboom."

Heed the warning, Maisey.

"Yeah, yeah, you're leaving town, life on the road. I know. But you have to eat, right? Oh, wait. No match, no worries. Daisy mentioned she's making a big family dinner tonight, remember?"

"Ah, that's right. Another night, then," he said, holding her gaze.

Except there weren't many left.

Ping. Maisey checked her phone. It was a text from Daisy Dawson.

I'm hosting a dinner party at my house tonight in honor of having all my brothers home at the same time. Love you to join. Don't bring anything, just yourself and Chloe. She can hang with the other littles.

Daisy, your timing is, as usual, impeccable. "Turns out I'm invited to dinner," she said, unable to hide her smile.

But Rex wasn't smiling. At all. In fact, he seemed upset. "I told Daisy not to matchmake when she knows I'm leaving. What is she doing?"

Maisey gnawed her lower lip. *Jeez.* Could he want her there less?

"Crud. I probably shouldn't have said that out loud. I didn't mean—"

"Nothing wrong with truth," she interrupted, though she felt foolish for flirting about the kiss and a home-cooked meal. He *was* leaving, dammit. He was right. She needed to get her head out of the clouds when it came to Rex Dawson.

"Daisy probably just invited me as an experienced set of hands and eyes for all the kiddos," she said. "That's one toddler and three babies. This way, you and your family can focus on the reunion and I can pop up and handle any crying and diaper needs."

He didn't seem to be falling for that. Even she knew Daisy hadn't meant the invitation that way.

"You're not the babysitter at the dinner," he said. "You're part of the clan. I see you that way."

She tilted her head. "What way?"

He stared at her for a second, his complexion paling a bit. "Family," he finally said in almost a whisper.

"You see me as family?" Did he? Goose bumps ran up and down her spine. Being part of a family was all she'd ever wanted.

Chloe let out a gurgle, and he rocked her back and forth. "The letter to Santa," he said, "finding you here, you alone in the world except for a six-month-old, needing so much—"

"So you feel bad for me?" she snapped. "Rex, I can take care of myself. I *am* taking care of myself. And my daughter." She reached for Chloe, but the baby's face crumpled and turned red, and Maisey sighed and held up her hands. "She likes where she is right now and I have to work with the kids on their songs, so I guess I'll see you at six for the gift shopping."

"Maisey," he said, but nothing else came out of his mouth.

I am an idiot, she thought. For one shining moment, she'd thought he'd really meant it, that he felt so close to her that she'd become part of him. Like family. But he was only saying that he felt a sense of obligation to her because she was "poor never-adopted broke-and-alone Maisey," whose old Christmas wish letter he'd found.

He saved dogs. He was trying to save her, including her Christmas.

Well, she would save herself, thank you.

She lifted her chin and was about to turn away to escape Rex and find Zara, her song apprentice, when seven-year-old Lara intercepted Maisey, her head down.

"Maisey, my stomach hurts and I don't want to play anymore."

Maisey gave the little girl a once-over. She didn't look ill, she wasn't clutching her tummy and she was standing just fine. Hmm. Lara was possibly overwhelmed by all the noise and activity. "Want to lie down in the nap cave for a little bit and see if you feel better?"

Lara smiled. "I love the nap cave."

All the kids did. It was a twin futon mattress on a padded section with its own orange canopy

for privacy. The girl raced off, clearly feeling instantly better, and went inside.

She glanced at Rex. "Well, I do have to help a few kiddos with some forgotten lines. You're sure you don't mind holding on to Chloe and keeping an eye on Lara in the nap cave?"

He seemed grateful she wasn't keeping their interrupted conversation going. But she was done with that. For now, anyway. "I'm a pro uncle of babies and have gotten really good with little kids, too," he reminded her. "Look," he added, gesturing his chin at Chloe, who was perfectly content right now, her eyes curious and alert as she surveyed her world from Rex Dawson's arms.

And you'd make a pro daddy, she thought wistfully.

He's not your future. He's your immediate present—in all senses of the word. But you know what you know about him and his plans. And all this attention on you comes from a place of generosity and his need to serve and protect. It's not about love.

She finally understood. Her question had been answered after all. By him.

Chapter Ten

After rehearsal, which went very well except for two missed lines and one small crying jag from a three-year-old, Maisey finally relaxed. Luckily, the tiny stuffed elves that she and Rex had added to the bounty at Christmasland for props had done wonders for little Tommy and Danny, who liked having something to hold. Chloe had stayed silent except for a few happy gurgles. Rex had gotten her teething toy from Maisey's tote, and Chloe had grabbed on to it. The man truly was a baby whisperer.

He was still here, too, using power tools to build the stage with his apprentices' help. Both

Tyler and Annalise wore hard hats and work gloves and seemed thrilled. The stage was now built and ready for the various pieces of the set to be added. Throughout the morning, she'd caught Rex glancing at her more than a few times. Why did she have to feel so connected to him? Luckily, right now, he pulled together a basketball game for whoever wanted to play, and several of the kids did. Zara was practicing "Frosty the Snowman" lyrics with Danny, who was shaking his little elf and singing "Frotty Noman," which made Zara giggle.

The rough morning, made a bit rougher by having Rex in full view, had been much improved, though, because Zara Harwood had agreed to be in the show and had rehearsed with the group. She'd started out silent and sullen when Maisey had first met her just days ago, and now she was front and center, helping others and being a part of things. Of all Maisey had accomplished with the show, that was a highlight. Maybe *the* highlight.

The door opened and in walked Emily Harwood with a bright smile. Her red curly hair spilled from a yellow wool hat. Emily's gaze landed on Zara, now practicing a different song, her solo, with her prop, a big stuffed candy cane.

"Hi, Zara. Ready for the hike up Clover Mountain?" Emily called over. "According to the tour leader, it's a scavenger hunt, too. Sounds like a lot of fun."

Zara frowned, barely giving Emily a glance. "I just want to stay here for the day. I'm working on my songs."

Emily's smile faltered but she plastered it right back on, and Maisey could tell the woman had been doing a lot of that. The stress was etched on her face. "Honey, it's just an hour hike before lunch. Then I can drop you back here to practice. I'd love to spend some time with you, just us two."

"I want to stay here!" Zara shouted and ran into the nap cave, pulling the little curtains shut.

Emily's shoulders sank.

Maisey hurried over to her. "Zara opened up to me a little because I shared with her that I lost my parents when I was very young. I grew up in a few different group foster homes. If I can help in any way, I want to."

Emily looked relieved. "We officially adopted Zara almost a year ago, a couple months after she lost her parents. We finally reached a great place where Zara was asking me a lot of questions about calling me Mom and if she should or if that would make her mother in heaven feel bad." Emily's eyes welled with tears. "Things were good for us as a family. But these last few weeks have been rough and nothing I say or try works."

"Could it be the time of year?" Maisey asked. "My parents died in December and some letters to Santa went unanswered, so it's always been a rough time for me, and I'm twenty-three."

"I've tried a lot of holiday approaches, but she's so resistant. I just want her to be comfortable—and happy."

"Would you like me to try to help her open up a little? Small steps. But just agreeing to be in the show is huge, I now realize."

Emily nodded, her expression so full of hope. "Should I let her stay here instead of insisting on the scavenger hike? Sometimes I'm so unsure how to proceed."

"I know what you mean. I think she'll just close up on the hike. Her head is in the show right now, so why don't we keep that happy vibe going and I'll talk to her."

"Thanks, Maisey. I appreciate your help."

She'd broken through some—maybe between her experience and understanding Zara and a slow approach, she could do some good. She headed over to the nap cave and knelt down to let Zara know her mom said it was okay to stay here and that she'd pick her up for lunch in an hour and a half.

Zara scooted out of the cave on her knees and looked around. "Really? She's letting me stay? She already left?" She sat down in front of the tent.

Maisey nodded and sat beside her. "She'll be back to pick you up for lunch," she repeated since Zara seemed surprised Emily had gone. Ah, Zara was very attached to Emily, she realized; that was clear. And good.

"I know your mom is going to miss you on the hike, but I'm happy you're staying. I could sure use your help with Danny on 'Frosty.' Think you can teach him to say 'Snowman' instead of 'Noman'?"

Zara burst out laughing. "I'll try. He's soooo cute."

"Yup, he is."

"Maisey? Can you call Emily Emily and not my mom?"

Maisey nodded. "Of course."

"I mean, she's technically my mom now because she and Ethan adopted me, but it's not like I don't have a mom and dad—they're just not here anymore." Her expression got very serious, but her eyes were clear.

"I used to think about that for myself," Maisey said. "When I was eight, I wrote a letter to Santa asking for a family to adopt me since I'd been at the group foster home since I was five. I wondered if I'd be able to call my new parents Mom and Dad."

Zara peered up at her. "I thought you said you grew up in different group homes, though."

"Yup, I did. I never was adopted, so I don't know how I would have felt about calling someone else Mom."

"I'm sorry you didn't get adopted," Zara said. "I wouldn't want to live in a foster home."

Maisey gave Zara's hand a squeeze. "The hardest time was Christmas. It's a tough time for you, too, huh?"

Zara looked down and nodded, and Maisey could feel the girl stiffen beside her.

Maisey nodded, too. "I used to avoid the whole season. But now that I have Chloe, having Christmas for her is important. New traditions."

Zara looked at her. "What's a tradition?"

"Well, like having a tree and decorating it is a Christmas tradition. Carving a pumpkin is a Halloween tradition. I used to French braid my hair every Monday when I was a teenager because I wanted to make a tradition of my own. I did that for years."

"Do I have traditions?" Zara asked.

"I'm sure you do. What's something that Emily and Ethan do over and over? Like chocolate chip pancakes for breakfast every Saturday morning."

"Well, Ethan gets bagels and cream cheese every Saturday morning. I go with him and get to pick the kinds. My favorite is cinnamon raisin. But not with cream cheese. Just butter. And every Saturday night after dinner, the three of us and our dog, Poppy, watch a movie together and I get to pick that, too."

"There you go! Two family traditions on the same day every week!"

Zara smiled. "Yeah. I didn't really ever think of it like that. But I guess I have traditions."

"Maywee," Danny called from where he was flying his superhero lion around on a big section of the mat. "Frotty Noman jolly pol."

Zara grinned. "Oh, he needs me."

"Yes, he does," Maisey said, her heart pinging like crazy.

Zara bounced up and went over to him.

"Okay, I'm not crying. You're crying," Rex whispered as he walked over.

Maisey had been aware that Rex was still in the Kid Zone, but he seemed so intent on the work he was doing on the stage. "You heard all that?"

"Well, I was supposedly immersed in my work with this hot-glue gun and plywood, but yes. Every word. You handled that really beautifully. Tough stuff, and you were amazing."

Maisey let out a breath. "It's so important to get it right, so thank you. I feel like I say that a lot to you."

"That mean you're not mad at me anymore?" he asked.

"Just don't ever feel sorry for me, Rex Dawson. I won't allow it."

Did he have to look at her that way? As though she was very special to him?

"Got it," he said. "And I don't. I just—"

She waited, but he didn't finish.

I just care about you. She knew that was what he'd been about to say.

Ditto, she thought, her heart pinging again.

Since dinner at Daisy's was at seven thirty, Rex and Maisey decided to go to Bear Ridge for gift shopping; there was a cute shop open late for the season that carried a lot of baby and kids' toys and interesting little items. When they dropped off Chloe at Daisy's house, his sister cooed baby talk, telling Chloe in a running commentary that she'd be watching her until her mama returned and how much fun dinner would be later, that she'd hang at the baby table with her new besties.

"I don't know what I did to deserve you Dawsons, but thank you," Maisey said, beaming at Daisy.

You deserve everything. You deserve all the happiness in the world. And I can give it to you up to a point, he thought with a frown as they got back in his SUV and headed to town. Luckily, Maisey was chatty on the ride, going over the list they'd made, and he was distracted from his thoughts, which seemed all blurry lately. Yes, his job was important to him, and he used to love being on the road, no real home base. But now everything felt *different* in a way he wasn't... ready to accept.

His feelings for Maisey, for one.

And some other complicated stuff he didn't want to think about. Rex thought he liked change since his entire life was about change. But in reality, he didn't.

At the gift shop, she and Rex split the list, Rex taking the boys and Maisey the girls. There was a basketball alarm clock that played hip-hop music—Tyler, check. A new superhero coloring book and big pack of crayons for Danny—done. Rex was surprisingly good at shopping for various ages, though he had no idea where he'd picked up the skill. Maisey met him at the cashier's counter with a pair of fuzzy purple slippers for Annalise, the music note pin for Zara, and a double check of their list showed they'd gotten all ten regulars gifts.

"I checked their ornaments on the display, but no Siamese cat," she said. "But at least I have this cute thing for Chloe," she added, holding up the cat-shaped teething toy she'd gotten her.

The shop offered to wrap, but that would take forever, so Maisey said she'd do the wrapping herself tonight, adding a few rolls and tape to the counter. Then they headed out and loaded up the car.

"We have a solid half hour left," she said. "You know what I'd like to do? See where you found my bottle with my letter to Santa. If it's close enough."

He nodded. "It's about ten minutes from here. Bear Ridge Nature Preserve."

"I'd just like to see where it ended up. Not that we can know how long it was there. Maybe it got stuck a bunch of times and then moved and then stayed put by the footbridge. But it definitely didn't get far in fifteen years."

Rex rounded the car when he heard someone call his name. He turned around and groaned inwardly. Patrick Mullers. His dad's old drinking and gambling buddy.

"Hey, Rex, right? How ya doin'?" Patrick asked, coming over with a big smile. The few times he'd run into Patrick over the years, the man had called him by one brother's name or another. But this time he'd gotten it right. Patrick looked a lot better these days. Face wasn't so red, belly wasn't so extended. Maybe he'd stopped drinking.

"This is Maisey Clark. Maisey, Patrick Mullers. He was my dad's good friend."

Maisey smiled and shook his hand.

"I miss that crazy lunatic," Patrick said. "Do you know I got cleaned up after we lost him? A few of us did, his old drinking pals. Scared us half to death and we didn't want to get to the other half faster."

"I'm glad to hear it," Rex said. He really was.

"I'll never forget the time your dad and I took you seahorse searching in the river by the cabins at the ranch. Remember that? You were obsessed. Bo insisted there was a family of seahorses that lived in this one spot in the river, a father with six kids—five sons and a daughter."

A vague memory floated into Rex's mind. He had been very into seahorses when he was a little kid, around seven or eight. He forgot all about that. "Hey, wait—yes, he said the seahorses were the Fishly family. I think he even named them all."

"Yup, that's right. The Fishly seahorses. I remember we took you there to look for them and your dad insisted he saw the dad seahorse swimming around but that Pa Seahorse got scared and hid. You were so happy they were real that you said he was the best dad ever. Later Bo told me that was the only time any of his kids ever said that."

Rex could barely find his voice for a second. "I remember that. I didn't know I was the only one to say it. Ever." He glanced at Maisey, glad she was here. Because he felt like absolute hell.

"Well, you were only seven or so, so I'm sure someone else said it in the following years. He loved you kids." He glanced behind him at his truck. Someone was in the passenger seat. "The lady is waiting, so I'd better go. Good to see you, Rex. Nice to meet you, Maisey."

Rex watched him walk away, his stomach churning. "Seahorses. The Fishly family. Hearing you're the best dad ever for the first time. Maybe the only time."

Maisey squeezed his hand. "Well, I'm just glad he heard it. That his child said it to him. And yes, another kid probably did at some point after. Sounds like Bo Dawson was capable of great things as a dad, Rex."

He nodded. "Yeah, I suppose he had his moments. Don't know how I could forget something like that."

"I do. Repression. Memories get socked away when they're too big to deal with, even the good memories. Especially when your memories of someone are complicated."

He reached for her and she opened her arms for a hug. A quick hug over too soon. "I'm glad you're here."

She gave him a gentle smile. "Me, too."

"Let's get over to the nature preserve," he said. "I'll show you where I found the bottle—and my dog."

My dog. My dog. My dog.

He was going to walk away from River? How? And his family? And Maisey?

Maybe having a reason to come back to visit more often was a good thing. The pull to home. Like Maisey said: *complicated.*

He drove to the nature preserve and parked pretty much where he had last month. Once again, not a soul was here, though he'd parked to avoid public view the first time around. "There's a trail that's not tended well but it's there enough to follow. It leads to the footbridge."

They walked over, and every time the cold wind lifted her hair he wanted to wrap her scarf tighter, keep her warm, protect her from any tiny or big harm. After five minutes they arrived at the short bridge over the river. She followed him to the spot where he'd first seen River, sniffing and pawing at the bottle.

"Right there," he said, pointing.

Almost six weeks ago, his entire life had changed when he'd noticed the cute shepherd mix, dirty and hungry and lonely, scratching at the bottle. Of course he was fighting against that change—his life was outside of the Dawson Family Guest Ranch, outside of Maisey Clark and her baby.

She looked down over the wood railing of the bridge to where he indicated. "I can remember writing that letter, tossing the bottle in the creek with my friend, like it was yesterday. Well, maybe not yesterday. More like a few years ago. It feels so recent, so much like a part of me still. How can that be?"

"Probably because of how much you wanted what you asked for." He'd felt that yearning brimming from the paper when he'd held it in his hands, felt it in his cells.

She looked at him and nodded. "I do feel like that eight-year-old girl sometimes. More than sometimes. Even lately."

This was about him, he guessed. And his family. What they were coming to mean to her? What *he* meant to her?

"And you turned out to be my Santa," she said. "In its own way, I feel like that letter got answered. Not with parents. But with…a tribe of my own.

That's how I feel at the Dawson Family Guest Ranch, Rex. Like the place and all of you are my people. Like I belong."

His thoughts had been on the right track. "I wasn't kidding when I said you were family, Maisey. You've become part of the place." *A part of me.*

Tears filled her eyes and he opened his arms. He hugged her for a solid minute, resting his chin on her head, breathing in the scent of her shampoo and the cold snap of air around them.

"Thanks for showing me," she said with a sniffle. "And just thank you."

He gave her an extra squeeze, wishing he could hold her forever. But they had to get back. Family dinner. And she was indeed going.

Yeah, he knew he was leaving on the twenty-sixth. But it was going to be a lot harder than he'd ever thought.

Chapter Eleven

"Would you mind dropping me off at my cabin?" Maisey asked as they pulled up to the gates of the ranch. "I have just enough time for a quick shower and to change out of my work clothes. I think I have an orange handprint on my calf and glitter on my sleeve."

He held out his arm and rolled up his own sleeve. "Purple glitter in this one spot. I scrubbed but it won't come off. I kinda like it. And sure, I'll watch Chloe for you. Then we'll walk over to Daisy's."

Of course he'd watch Chloe and sit around waiting for Maisey—because he was That Guy. The ole prince among men. She'd barely had a boyfriend in high school, and her husband had been her "first" in just about every sense. When she'd stand up for herself, he'd constantly respond that "this is how guys are, Maze." She knew that couldn't be the case. Her dad had also been a prince, so she'd *known*. But she'd chosen wrong out of such a deep yearning to belong, and now she had to choose right to keep her heart from getting so broken that she might not be able to pick herself up again.

No, of course she would get right up again. She'd have to. She was someone's mother and that role came first. As amazing a man as Rex was, his point in her life seemed to be to remind her that her dad wasn't the only one of his kind. There were good, great men out there.

Not that that made her feel better *now*.

She hurried into her bathroom, taking the quickest shower possible, a trick she'd learned as a new mother. She blow-dried her hair and put on a little makeup, then rushed across the hall to her bedroom and put on a long off-white sweater with a beaded V-neckline, skinny black jeans—which she'd just started fitting into again—and boots. Plus a dab of perfume behind her ears.

Rex stood up when she came back into the living room, and she was well aware that he was staring at her. "You look great. And smell great."

She smiled. "Not like paint and glue and baby spit-up and pretzel dust?"

"Like flowers."

She liked that he noticed.

They bundled back up in coats, scarves, hats and gloves, and Maisey grabbed the loaf of Portuguese bread that they'd stopped for at the bakery in town, then headed into the December night air. He held out his arm. She wrapped hers around it and looked up at the stars. If only this was as it looked, she thought, imagining that anyone who saw them together right now would assume they were a couple.

Up ahead she could just make out the Harwood family heading from the cabins on the path to the cafeteria. Zara was actually walking between them instead of lagging behind, head down, as she usually was when Maisey spotted her out with the parents. A good sign.

"I think things are going to be okay there," she said, upping her chin at the family as they went into the cafeteria.

"You did a lot of good. You got involved. You opened up. You bridged a connection. Zara might not have realized that she could be living in foster care if not for the Harwoods. You said it without saying it outright."

She glanced at him, the illumination from the

tall iron streetlamps casting beautiful shadows on his face. He was always her champion. Something she'd never had before. She hadn't even known she'd been missing such a force in her life. Someone she thought was special, someone she respected, respected her right back.

"One thing I've come to understand is that everything's relative to someone else's situation," she said, thinking of a couple of her former foster sisters. "Just because I wanted to be adopted and wasn't doesn't mean Zara should be grateful she was adopted when she's struggling with having new parents. I knew two kids who were adopted and it wasn't all sunshine and roses, so that helped me understand Zara better. Eight-year-old me would have thought she was a brat for not being grateful. But now I get it."

"She's lucky you do. And I'm sure the Harwoods appreciate that she has you to talk to."

Maisey stopped walking as she was thunderstruck by the notion that she loved this man. She knew she'd fallen in love with him, but now that love enveloped her. How was she going to say goodbye in just a few days?

As they neared the farmhouse, Rex sniffed the air. "Hmm, I can smell something delicious cooking from here. Which means Harrison is in the kitchen tonight. I love Daisy, but she usually burns everything."

Maisey laughed. "I'm starving. And I can't wait to see Chloe. It feels so strange to be walking around without her, someone else taking care of her. I feel both carefree and completely anxious."

"I guess that's motherhood for you. I don't even want to think about how overprotective I'd be as a dad. 'Chloe, you're not dating till you're twenty-five and that's final!'" He laughed, then seemed to realize what he'd said and cleared his throat. "Not that I'll *be* Chloe's dad. I mean… Well, you know what I mean. Just an example." He nodded and quickened his pace.

A few days ago all that might have nicked her feelings, reminding her that he *wouldn't* ever be Chloe's dad. But now she found herself smiling to herself because the man was tripping over himself. And something else was coming clear: he didn't know what he wanted anymore.

These thoughts would have to wait till she was alone in bed tonight because they were suddenly up the porch steps, greeted by River and Dude and welcomed inside by Daisy.

Inside were many Dawsons. Ranch manager Noah and his forewoman wife, Sara, and their twin babies, Annabel and Chance. Guest relations manager Daisy and her businessman husband,

Harrison, and their baby, Tony. Safety director and wilderness tour guide Axel and his wife, ranch nutritionist Sadie, and their toddler, Danny. Plus Zeke, also a businessman, and Ford, a cop. Maisey was about to add Rex and herself and Chloe to the count when she realized she was invited because she was an employee who cared for their children and she'd gotten somewhat close with Daisy.

She wasn't "with" Rex here. *And don't you forget it, no matter how much he seems up in the air with what he wants from life.*

Daisy gave her a big hug, gave the loaf of bread to Harrison to slice for the table and brought her into the living room, where Chloe and Tony were in Exersaucers, and Annabel and Chance were sitting close by on a mat, playing with big foam blocks. Eight-month-old Annabel and Chance were two months older than Chloe, who was a month older than Tony. Two-year-old Danny sat with his legs out in front of him, teaching them the words to "Frotty Noman," which had the room in a fit of giggles.

"Baby Central!" Zeke said, scooping up Annabel while Ford picked up Chance. They both snuggled their niece and nephew, then did the same with Tony and Danny. Like all the Dawson brothers, Zeke had dark hair and blue eyes.

"And who's this beautiful little girl?" Ford asked.

"She's mine," Maisey said. "I'm the new head nanny at the Kid Zone. I guess Chloe and I are crashing the family dinner."

"You're such a big part of our kiddos' lives that you felt like family fast," Daisy said, sitting down beside the mat and petting River and ruffling Dude's soft fur. The dogs both sat beside her on the floor, guarding the babies. "That makes you an honorary Dawson."

Maisey smiled but she had to home in on the *felt like* and *honorary*. She wasn't *really* part of this family. She was an employee, and the Dawsons were good and generous people, so she was here.

Suddenly that old yearning was back. To be part of a family. This one.

After dinner, which was a hearty beef stew that Rex had had two helpings of, the group moved into the living room for coffee and dessert, scattering around the big room. During dinner, Maisey had jumped up every time a child fussed, but one of his brothers always beat her to it. Rex loved watching it sink in for her that she'd truly been invited as a guest—not a babysitter.

Now she sat with Sara and Sadie in the group of chairs in the far corner of the room, and he couldn't hear what they were talking about. Hopefully not him. Daisy was on the love seat with Noah, Axel and Zeke. Rex looked around for Ford and found him in the kitchen, loading up the dishwasher.

"Hiding out?" Rex asked with a grin.

"From Daisy. Every time she comes near me I zigzag away so she can't ask me about my love life or the openings at the Bear Ridge PD."

Rex handed him two dirty plates from the counter. "Are you going to join the force here?"

Ford stood still for a second. "I'm ninety percent yes on that. I need to get out of Casper. Something new. Fresh start."

Huh. Ford had always been the most vocal about wanting to get as far from this place as possible, but even his eldest brother had had to admit that nothing about the renovated ranch, now a truly gorgeous piece of property, reminded him of sadder days gone by.

"Law enforcement will be a lot different in a town this small," Rex said.

"That would be a welcome change, too. But the ole serve and protect can be done anywhere there are people. You thinking about coming home, too?"

"Me? Nah. I mean, I've thought about it because the subject has come up. That goes without saying when you're around Daisy." He smiled but felt it fade fast. "Since I was a teenager I wanted to be a cop. Like you." He'd always looked up to

Ford, who was almost five years older. "And then that crazy gambling buddy of Dad's went on that robbery spree and eluded capture. I kept thinking he'd come seek revenge on us in our sleep because Dad swindled him in a poker game. Remember that?"

"Oh, I remember," Ford said, adding a bunch of silverware to the basket in the dishwasher. "Dad was worried sick. The marshals got him a day later." He glanced at Rex. "Is that why you wanted to become a marshal? Track down fugitives? Because of that?"

Rex nodded. "I felt so powerless back then. I couldn't do anything, keep anyone I cared about safe. Now it's my job to do so."

"Yeah, I feel that way, too. But I can do that from here. *Closer* to the people I care about."

There it was again, that *feeling* Rex couldn't quite name. Unsettled. Uncomfortable. Itchy. If he liked the Dawson Family Guest Ranch, liked Bear Ridge, liked being here, and he did, what the hell was the problem? Why was he burning to leave?— and he *was*. That force in him wasn't just about his job; he knew that. So what was this really about?

His father? How rough a lot of his childhood was during his visitation weekends here at the ranch? Maybe all the renovations in the world couldn't fix what lurked underneath: really bad memories. But then a good one would come along, prompted by someone else, like his father's friend had done today, and Rex would be just as uneasy on the subject of his father. He'd loved his father and had hated him. How did you reconcile that? Especially when the person in question was gone.

He could talk to Ford about this. He could talk to any of his siblings, and even the more reticent when it came to deeply personal stuff would let loose about Bo Dawson. But sometimes there was like a cork stuffed somewhere in Rex where he couldn't get anything out.

"Speaking of Dad," Rex said, handing him two bowls. "I still can't figure out what the key he left me opens."

If he could just find the thing already, maybe it would help. Maybe he'd get some closure.

Ford nodded. "I've been trying to follow the map he left me, which indicates where he supposedly buried my mother's old diary that pissed him off for some reason he didn't mention, but I can't find it. Either the map is wrong or I'm just not thinking about it the way Dad would. He wasn't exactly map-oriented or linear. The X and the landmarks he scribbled are probably completely off. He was likely drunk when he drew the map."

No doubt. "I'll help you look if you want," Rex said.

"The ground's too hard to poke or dig in now. Just as well. Who knows what the hell I'll read in that diary—if I find it."

Rex nodded, and for a moment, they just both stood there trying to wrap their minds around it all. "I ran into one of Dad's old poker pals earlier tonight in town. Patrick Mullers. He reminded me of a story about how he and Dad took me seahorse spotting at the river where he said he'd seen a family of them. Across from that big boulder our guests like to sit on to stargaze and make out. Patrick told me I said Dad was the best dad ever while we were there and that Bo was really moved."

"I'm sure he was. Not like Bo Dawson heard that every day. Or ever. Because he wasn't."

Rex nodded again and handed Ford two more plates—and was suddenly struck by a memory. His dad had surprised him with a small fish tank with two seahorses, bright blue gravel, some plants and a treasure chest cave for his eighth birthday, not long after the day at the river. Rex had loved the way the seahorses swam upright and turned into the colors of the plants, green and coral. The seahorses hadn't lived long, though, and Rex had moved on to being obsessed with playing hockey and baseball. He'd all but forgotten about that tank, but he was surprised he had. Maisey was likely right about that little coping mechanism called repression. Made it easier not to be grief-stricken.

He thought about his mom dropping him off at his dad's the evening of his birthday, Diana gently reminding him that his dad was forgetful and if he didn't remember to get Rex a gift that it didn't mean his father didn't love him. Rex had walked in the farmhouse expecting nothing, maybe not even a "happy birthday." But right there on a table in the living room was the tank with a big blue bow on top and a hand-scrawled sign that read Property of Rex Dawson, Age 8.

"Whoa," Rex said, going completely still.

Ford turned to him. "What?"

"There's a small tank in the attic. It must have been the one he bought me for my eighth birthday. It was under an old table and there was stuff in the tank—I don't remember what, a bunch of junk. Maybe the key opens something in it?" Rex shrugged, but suddenly the idea didn't seem nuts or even far-fetched. It seemed like something Bo Dawson would do.

Ford's eyes widened. "Later, dishwasher. Let's go see."

Rex followed him into the living room. "Let me just go tell Maisey I'll be back in a bit."

Ford raised an eyebrow. "Oh, I didn't realize you two were together."

Are we? he wondered. "Well, we came together. So…"

Ford grinned. "Go tell your lady."

She is my lady. For now, Rex thought. He found Maisey standing by the Christmas tree, Chloe in her arms, pointing out the colors of the lights.

"Hey," he said. "Mind if I disappear on you for a few minutes? I want to go check something out in the attic with Ford."

"Sure, go ahead. I'm fine. See you in a few."

He nodded and gave Chloe's back a quick caress, all too aware that he didn't have to check in with Maisey. But he had. Everything meant something these days.

He met Ford at the door to the attic and they headed upstairs.

"Under that?" Ford asked, pointing to the rickety old rectangular table that looked like it could barely hold the boxes of assorted junk on it.

Rex knelt down in front of the table and shoved aside another box, and there it was—the fish tank with more junk inside it. Rex slid out the tank and took the other boxes off the table and put the tank on top to make it easier to go through.

He reached in and removed a half-smashed Sony Walkman that had to be from the '80s. A bunch of batteries, a few rusted metal tape measures, a half bag of blue gravel that must have been from the original tank and a ratty kitchen towel. With something wrapped in it.

Rex glanced at Ford and threw off the towel. Bingo. A small tackle box with a lock.

"How'd he expect you to go digging in here?" Ford asked, shaking his head. "If you hadn't run into his poker buddy, you never would've remembered the seahorses in the first place."

Maybe not. But maybe he would have. He'd been sharing so much with Maisey about his dad that memory after memory had been unearthed. He would have hit on the seahorses and remembered he'd seen the tank up here and that maybe his father put something lockable inside it. He was just relieved he'd found it.

Then again, the key had to work in it.

He fished the key out of his wallet. "Here goes everything," he said and pushed it into the lock. "I don't believe it."

"Classic Dad," Ford said, half smiling, half shaking his head. "If Daisy ever held a yard sale for stuff in here, that's when she would have found the box, not been able to open it and probably tossed it aside until someone tried to jimmy it open. Why would he have been so lax about you finding it?"

"He probably figured I'd spend some time trying to figure out what the key unlocked and go through my old stories until I hit on possibilities. He ended up right. Hey, it only took an entire year."

Ford grinned. "Open it. I'm dying to know."

"Me, too." Rex turned the key and inside the tackle box was what appeared to be a children's pocket watch. It was yellow, made out of plastic and was on a long matching chain. Rex opened it. There was a cartoon illustration of a smiling seahorse and underneath read *It's time for fun!* Around the dial were clock numbers, one through twelve. Rex stared at it and held it up for Ford. Also in the box was a folded-up piece of lined paper.

Rex took in a breath and unfolded it.

Rex,
If you found this, then you remembered your
old seahorse tank. I'll never forget the day
I took you to see the seahorse family in the
river—I can't remember what I named them,
something funny. That day you said I was
the best dad ever even though you didn't see
any seahorses. You believed me that they

were there and I can't even remember the last time anyone believed something I said. That day stayed with me a long time. Till the end, clearly.

Anyway, couple months ago I saw this kiddie pocket watch at a yard sale a girl-friend was having and I bought it for fifty cents. I don't know where you are or what you're doing but I know you've been on the road a long time, chasing old ghosts, most likely. I'm probably right about that even though I get mostly everything wrong these days. Anyway, you'll find this eventually, one day, and when you do, just know your father loved you, Rexy.
Dad

Tears stung the backs of Rex's eyes and he quickly handed the note to Ford, then moved a few feet over to the tiny round window that over-looked the side yard to get ahold of himself.

A half minute later, he felt Ford clap an arm around his shoulders. "When Bo Dawson got it right, he really knocked it out of the park, didn't he." He tucked the folded page into Rex's shirt pocket.

Rex could only nod.

"I'll give you some time," Ford said. "Come on down when you're ready."

He heard his brother's footsteps on the stairs and the door at the bottom close. Rex sucked in another breath.

Was he chasing old ghosts? That was what had gotten him started in the US Marshals, maybe, but his commitment to his job had long been about justice for all. He could feel the letter in his pocket and suddenly it felt heavy. He took it out and put it in his wallet, next to the key.

His father was the old ghost here, haunting him right now. Up and down, good and bad, right and wrong. Bad love and good. *Just know your father loved you, Rexy.*

The attic was making him claustrophobic, so he took the pocket watch out of the box and dropped that in his shirt pocket, then closed the box and put it back in the tank. He left the tank on the table; there was no rhyme or reason to the boxes being here or there, anyway.

He'd come up here looking for what the key unlocked to find some peace about his dad and instead just felt all kinds of conflicted.

Suddenly he just wanted to go home. And that was when it hit him. He had no home.

Chapter Twelve

Maisey had gotten home hours ago from Daisy's dinner party and she still couldn't get the image out of her mind of Rex carrying Chloe the short walk from the farmhouse to the cabin, her baby girl snuggled against his leather jacket. She'd tried to distract herself with tidying up the kitchen, starting a new mystery novel she'd taken out of the library and then flipping channels, but she kept seeing that image. Rex Dawson holding her baby girl so tenderly, so carefully.

And then practically running out the door of her cabin once Chloe was back in Maisey's arms and they were inside.

Something had happened in the attic that Rex didn't want to talk about, and she had the feeling it had something to do with his father. She knew he'd been looking for whatever the key his dad had left him opened. Maybe he'd found it. She had no idea, though, because he hadn't said more than ten words on the way home. That was unusual for him, so she'd given him his space.

Now, in her jammies in bed, she turned on the lamp on her bedside table and grabbed her phone. She couldn't take it anymore; she had to have some communication with him, even a text that he might not respond to till morning. He *would* respond because he was Rex Dawson.

Thanks again for all your help today and shopping tonight. The kids are going to love their gifts. Had a great time at dinner with your family.

She turned off the lamp, put her phone on her chest and hoped for a ping.

Ping.

She smiled and lifted the phone.

Always my pleasure, M. I'll be at the Kid Zone at nine for the dress rehearsal to make sure everything with the set is okay and I can help out as needed.

She waited, hoping those three little dots would appear to indicate he was still typing. She wanted something personal. Something that wasn't about the show or the sets. Something about *them*.

Well, you weren't personal, either, she reminded herself.

She texted: You okay? If you need to talk, I'm here.

A-OK was all he wrote back. Then the three dots appeared, which got her excited. Until she read: See you tomorrow.

Shut out. Or that was how it felt. She pulled the comforter up to her chin and closed her eyes, but she knew she wasn't going to get a great night's sleep.

In the morning, Maisey got herself and Chloe up early to get to the Kid Zone so that she could make sure everything was set for the holiday show before the kids piled in—and so she could be there for a bit before Rex came in all gorgeous and helpful and driving her bonkers.

Tomorrow was the Christmas fair, which would start at nine and would end at four. The children's holiday show would start at five. For the past two days, she'd had rehearsals at that time, too, to make sure the littlest kids could handle that hour, and so far, so good. The kids' gifts were wrapped and tagged with their names and waiting in a locked closet across the hall in the lodge. The sets were done, sturdy and adorable. The props were in baskets on either side of the stage, which had one riser, the taller kids on the second row, the shorter ones in front.

Maisey walked around the room with Chloe still in her chest carrier. "We did it," she said. "We pulled it off in pretty short time. Just think, Chloe, not too long from now, you'll be running around the Kid Zone, building towers out of blocks, hanging out in the nap cave, appearing in the holiday show your own mother started."

She smiled and spun around, taking in the gorgeously decorated room, truly merry and bright. The tree on the side of the stage was twinkling with multicolored lights, a gold star atop. A big wreath hung on the wall behind the colorful stage. And the other walls were bordered by garland.

"All right, I'm ready for the kids, rehearsal and Rex Dawson," she whispered, walking Chloe over to her bassinet since the baby was about ready for her morning nap.

She'd just gotten Chloe settled when the door opened and children and parents poured in, waving hellos, signing in at the front desk, various kids wrapping Maisey in hugs. She loved these hugs so much.

No matter what was going on with her relationship with Rex, she was lucky to have this perfect-for-her job and she'd count her blessings on December 26 when he walked out the door for the last time and wouldn't return. For a few months, anyway, until it was time to visit for a relative's birthday or a special event.

The door opened again and there he was, as usual so handsome and sexy in his black leather jacket and the plaid red scarf, his dark hair a gorgeous contrast with his fair skin and blue eyes.

He waved and she waved back. Then he gave the stage and riser a solid once-over and jumped hard on it a few times, testing for sturdiness. The stage passed his test.

He kept his distance all day, through the dress rehearsal and even through her break, when he was nowhere to be found. So much for having a quick cup of coffee together just so she could try to figure out what was going on. Then again, what was going on was clear. He was avoiding her. Something happened last night that had gotten to him, and he was retreating.

From her, if not from his promise to lend a hand when she and her staffers got very busy during the day. He'd come to the rescue for a couple of meltdowns, including one by his nephew Danny. When she was busy helping a group with their songs, he picked up a fussing Chloe and rocked her for fifteen minutes.

He was his usual helpful self.

His usual there's-nothing-going-on-between-us self. He'd never really veered from that; she'd just suffered from wishful thinking.

By the end of the day, he'd checked in a couple of times by text—did they need anything last-minute? He could run to Prairie City, where the big-box store stayed open late.

He, not we. The man was definitely distancing himself from her, but she had the feeling it had nothing to do with her. Sometimes *It's not you, it's me* really did apply. But in this case, Rex was getting in his own way. Holding on to truths he might have outgrown.

Maybe that was just wishful thinking, too. His job was elsewhere; his life was elsewhere. He'd never said any different, never led her to believe otherwise.

He'd agreed to help out with the show and had. Everything was done; everything was set.

Including the two of them. Done. He was leaving.

Rex felt like hell. He was supposed to be giving Maisey Christmas back, and instead he was acting like a real jerk. Avoiding her. Making himself scarce. She didn't deserve that from him.

With his dog sniffing along the riverbank in front of him, Rex sat on the big boulder in front of the water near the guest cabins, hoping none of them would come along and engage him in small talk. He wasn't in the mood, couldn't put on his cheery face and talk about the history of the ranch back when his grandparents first opened it. The guests loved hearing about the fifty-year run of the place before it had been completely renovated.

He just wanted to sit here, just ten feet from where his father had pointed out the Fishly family of seahorses, trying to make his young son happy. Last night, after he'd walked Maisey home, also barely saying two words to her, he'd gone back to the farmhouse, not wanting to be there, but at least he had a small guest room there with a door he could close so he could just…think. Try to figure out what was eating him.

But Zeke had come knocking. His brothers and sister were having a nightcap of spiked eggnog in the living room and "you'd better come or else."

The spiked eggnog had him unwinding just enough to say too much, which was why he rarely drank at all. He'd told Ford that sometimes he thought his problem was that he was tired of the stress and travel of his job and that it made him feel disloyal—to his personal mission to hunt down fugitives, to his team.

Ford had said that people grow and change and evolve, a necessary part of life, and no one had to work the same job for forty years and get a toaster or a watch like in their grandparents' time. If Ford could change his mind about coming home to the ranch, Rex could, he said. *If* that was what Rex wanted, his brother had been quick to add.

Staying would be about Maisey, though. And he wasn't looking for a commitment. He'd never wanted a commitment. When he'd tried it because he'd fallen for someone, all he'd ended up doing was hurting her because he still couldn't see himself, imagine himself, married to someone. His life, for the longest time, had been about *leaving.* Not staying. Not ties that bound.

"Hey, just the man I needed," came a familiar voice.

Rex turned to find Tyler, the thirteen-year-old star dribbler, carrying his ball and walking toward him. He liked Tyler and was so tired of his own head that he welcomed the distraction right now.

River padded over for a pat on the head and along his side, which he got. Rex tossed a biscuit closer to the water, and the pooch beelined for it, stretching out to enjoy his treat.

"Hey, Tyler. What can I do for you?"

"I need advice about the ladies. One lady. Well, a girl."

Rex tried not to grin too hard. Tyler was a really sweet kid, dramatic but earnest and sensitive, though most people probably didn't realize it.

Tyler pushed up the rim of his ski hat a bit. "So here's the thing. I really like Annalise but I don't think she likes me back. First of all, I'm a whole year younger. And she's two inches taller. And she lives in Utah. So how am I gonna make this happen?"

This time Rex couldn't help his smile. "Well, you could tell her how you feel. And see what happens. Maybe she'll surprise you."

"Right. She just happens to like younger, shorter guys?"

"Maybe she just likes *you*, Tyler. There's plenty to like."

"Yeah?" he asked, tilting his head. "Everyone says I'm funny. And nice. But that usually means friend-zone." He stared at the river for a moment. "Tell me how you got Maisey to like you. I mean, you're taller and maybe older, but she's really pretty. Like Annalise."

"Maisey and I aren't a couple. We're just friends. But she likes me because I'm nice, too. And also funny, if I do say so myself. And because we have things in common. Basic chemistry, really." *A chemistry that's more powerful than I am.* "But if you like Annalise, if you want to stay in touch once you both leave, you need to tell her how you feel. Maybe you'll end up just friends. But that's good, too."

Except when it came to him and Maisey, *just friends* felt so wrong, so inadequate for what was between them. Rex had always been a very controlled person—he was aware of that and it was a good trait for his work. If he let loose, really let himself go with Maisey, he'd lose that control, equilibrium. Like now, the way this unfinished, unsettled business with his dad had him feeling. Off-kilter. Wrong.

"So I just say, 'Annalise, I really like you. Can we try a long-distance romance?'"

Rex smiled. "Sure. She may say no, Tyler. But you've got to be in it to win it."

"First rule of basketball," he said, giving the ball a bounce. He popped up off the rock. "Thanks, bro. I owe you."

"Anytime," Rex said and watched the boy head up the path toward his cabin, tossing the ball in the air every few steps.

He turned back to the river. Both of them—the water and his dog. *His dog.* Those words, together in a sentence, *his* applied to him, always caught him off guard, always stopped him in his tracks.

I can't even think of the best dog in the world as mine without having some kind of panic attack, he realized. He wasn't going anywhere near the words *committed relationship.*

Let alone *wife.*

He'd thought coming down here and checking out where the fictitious Fishly family of seahorses had swum would help him figure things out. But he was just as conflicted. His neglectful, alcoholic, complicated dad had loved him, even if part-time. He knew that. He was old enough to understand the beast of addiction and had long stopped taking personally anything Bo Dawson had done. So maybe this wasn't about his father at all *or* believing he wasn't meant to be part of a committed couple since he'd grown up seeing relationships fall apart for one reason or another.

Then what? What had him thinking life on the road was better than life with Maisey Clark and her baby and his dog and his siblings and their children and this peaceful place full of his family history?

Million-dollar question.

Chapter Thirteen

At 8:45 the next morning, Maisey stepped out of her cabin, Chloe in her chest carrier, to head to the Kid Zone when she stopped and stared all around her. Had a bunch of elves secretly spread their Christmas dust in the night to make the ranch more festive? Even at this hour when the twinkling white and multicolored lights weren't even on, the whole place felt so utterly magical, like a Christmas village. The Dawsons had really gone all out for the fair, decorating the place to the holiday nines. The streetlamps were wrapped with alternating red and green tinsel, and more wreaths had been hung with bright red bows on the barns.

There were white lights lining the outside posts of the pastures, which would be lit up come dusk.

"Merry Christmas," Angie, one of chef Cowboy Joe's assistant cooks, called as she turned up the path toward the cafeteria. The woman waved, a Santa hat on her head, green-and-red-striped tights under her long blue down coat.

"Merry Christmas!" Maisey called back with a smile.

There were a lot of holiday greetings going on, the staffers, also in their Santa hats, heading to their posts and special assignments for the fair, excited for the gates to open and visitors to start pouring in.

"Oh, Chloe, look," Maisey said, pointing across the path at the rescued reindeer pasture. Two of the reindeer were staring right at her and Chloe with their sweet faces, their antlers high and huge. "It's like they're saying 'Merry Christmas' to us, too," she told the baby. "Your grandma and grandpa would have loved those reindeer," she added on a whisper. As soon as those words were out, she realized she wasn't overtaken by the usual fleeting sadness. The thought of her parents felt rich and warm, like a comforting hug. *She* felt...full of anticipation, *happy*.

She stopped walking and gasped. "It's back,"

she whispered to Chloe. "My Christmas spirit! It's back!"

The red and green, the beautifully decorated trees, the wreaths, the signs for Santa's hut in the lodge—nothing she saw right now made her feel sad or reminded her of her losses. Where she once had a hole was now filled in with only the slightest tinge of bittersweet—remembrance versus sadness. Christmas was in her heart, in the air, all around her.

She wasn't even sure if Rex Dawson had given her back the holiday; Maisey had let it in. She'd opened up to it. He'd helped, definitely. He'd been like her own private Santa, bringing his cheer and his goodness. But Maisey hadn't been closed off, just as she hadn't been closed off to Rex. It was how she'd fallen for him. And no matter what happened between them, she was happy she had fallen. Love, for the best reasons, was a good thing, not something to hide from like she'd been doing since her ex had betrayed her.

Inside the lodge, Maisey looked at the Christmas tree at the end of the hall near the grand stairs as she did every morning and every night, and there was no wistfulness, no emptiness—just warmth. Her past was just *part* of her; it no longer consumed her.

You started this, Rex Dawson, so thank you. I

might have finished it, but you set me on the path to Christmas. If I never see you again after the twenty-sixth, I'll never forget what you did for me.

As Maisey headed into the Kid Zone, she knew today would be atypical. The guests and their kids would attend the fair, and if someone needed a breather or wanted to practice a song, they could always come hang out here, where there were a few activity tables set up to make last-minute gifts out of pine cones and Popsicle sticks and pompoms and stickers. She wasn't expecting more than a third of the usual crew, probably mainly the Dawsons' kids since their parents were all working the fair in various ways.

As the clock struck nine, all the Dawson parents had dropped off their little ones. The only Dawson she hadn't seen this morning was Rex, but she was sure he'd be in, at some point, to double-check that everything was ready for tonight's big performance.

Like right now. Her heart gave a little leap as he came through the door. He took off his jacket and scarf on the way over to her, and despite the early hour, she was struck by how sexy he was.

"How is one of my favorite babies?" he asked Chloe in the carrier on her chest. He covered his handsome face and opened up his hands for peekaboo.

Chloe gurgled.

"Rex, just tell me why you've been avoiding me," Maisey blurted out. *Whoa.* She hadn't even planned on confronting him. But she was glad she had. The only way to get answers was to ask questions. "We've gotten too close for this or for you to not be honest. Just say it."

He put his hands down and looked right at Maisey, his expression contrite. "I'm sorry for that. I'm just trying to figure some things out."

She put her hands on her hips. "And so you have to be all distant to do that?"

"Actually, yes. Because you're one of the things I need to figure out, Maisey."

He loves you, too, she knew with sudden clarity. Or her newfound Christmas cheer was upping her confidence. *And it's messing with his plans— and what he thought he wanted for himself.*

"I thought you already knew where we stood," she said. "Nowhere. You're leaving in three days, remember?"

He reached up a hand to briefly touch her face. "If I want to pretend there's nothing between us, sure. But there's a lot between us. More than I ever thought could be."

Finally. At least she knew she was right. He did love her. But he was torn between their very unexpected romance and being a man who never made commitments, never stuck around.

"And that doesn't mesh with your plans," she said.

"It doesn't mesh with my *life*, Maisey. I'm due back to my job on the twenty-sixth. This isn't about me jet-setting around. It's my work. It's everything I am."

He'd said that last part kind of slowly as if maybe he was realizing being a US marshal wasn't everything he was, just a part. Just as his family was a part of him, and this ranch.

And hopefully her.

This conversation had her thinking there was a chance for them. But if she let herself hope, what if she got dashed? She could very easily not come first here. If the fear—if that was what it was—that had him gripped about commitment won out, she'd lose him. She'd been so prepared for him to walk out of her life. But that was before she knew there was a possibility that he'd stay because he *did* have feelings for her.

She wished she knew what to say, the magic words to change his mind, change his cells. She needed that elf dust. She could tell him she'd gotten her Christmas spirit back, but that would be reason for him to leave. Mission accomplished.

Anyway, he'd seen her slowly take the holiday back for herself. Rex didn't miss anything.

"I'm all set for the Santa hut to open at ten. I'll be in there for two-hour intervals till three o'clock. Then I'll be back here to help out with showtime."

"You're going to be a great Santa. I can attest to that."

Even if I'm not going to get what I want from you, Rex Dawson.

Before he could respond, the door opened again, and the eight-year-old Caletti twins came in looking miserable. Their parents stood by the check-in, their expressions worried.

"Uh-oh," Maisey whispered. "I see teary eyes and sad faces. Let me go see what's wrong."

Maisey walked over to them, aware of Rex heading nearby to the chair where he'd put his jacket and tool kit. She could *feel* him ready to pay attention, to listen in. He wanted to see if he could help, she knew. To "serve and protect" was so ingrained in him.

But that didn't mean he had to fight injustice and chase down fugitives across the state, across the country. He could serve and protect right here in Bear Ridge. If he wanted.

"Hey, girls," Maisey said. "Why the sad faces?"

The flame-haired twins were usually so animated, added to by their colorful dresses and striped tights and light-up sneakers. When they were down, everyone always noticed.

"We can't remember any of the words to 'Rudolph the Red-Nosed Reindeer,'" Ava said, panic in her voice.

Amelia nodded, her eyes glistening. "Especially our solo part, when we get to take a step forward and it's just us two singing that one line."

"Well, you definitely know the first line," Maisey pointed out, "because you already said it! It's the name of the song itself!"

The twins brightened a bit. "Oh, yeah!" they said in unison.

Maisey turned to their parents. "Why don't you check in about a half hour. They'll have the song down and you all can enjoy the fair together."

The parents smiled with relief and left.

Chloe let out a wail, and Rex put a hand on Maisey's shoulder. "I've got Chloe. You handle song duty. I don't even know all the words to 'Rudolph' and I've been listening to practice for days."

"Thanks, Rex." *You are the best*, she thought. *So you can't leave in three days and come visit every few months. Stay, stay, stay.*

"Even a grown-up doesn't know the words!" Ava said, a smile finally on her face.

Rex plucked Chloe out of the carrier on Maisey's

chest, standing so tantalizingly close. She liked the scent of his shampoo. The way his dark lashes lay on his cheeks as he looked down at Chloe. His incredible shoulders in that navy Henley. The way his jeans molded to his body. Even his scuffed brown leather cowboy boots were sexy.

As she took the carrier off and set it on a chair, she watched him hold her baby girl against his chest. He headed over to the big window where the reindeer pasture was visible, narrating everything he was going to do: wave hi to the reindeer, tell her why some reindeer had antlers in the winter and some didn't, sing one of the holiday songs that he was sure he'd mess up and show her the tree that would soon have the kids' gifts under it.

Stay, she thought again. *Mischievous elves, get to work on him*. That was the thing about getting back her Christmas spirit. She believed in magic again. And she wasn't above asking for a little holiday help.

"Maisey, Chloe is really cute," Ava Caletti said.

"Supercute," Amelia added. "Does she look like you or Rex more?"

Maisey almost choked. They thought Rex was Chloe's dad? The baby didn't look anything like Rex—she was blond like Maisey with huge hazel eyes that were turning darker and would probably be pale brown like her mom's. Maisey was grateful she did look so much like her and not her biological father.

She froze at the realization that she'd referred to her ex that way. Biological. Because she was ready for a good man to become Maisey's daddy.

And she wished that man could be Rex.

"Rex isn't Chloe's dad," Maisey said, the words like cold water on her head. "He's a very good family friend. And a Dawson. His family own this ranch." She pointed to a sign on the door with the ranch's name and logo.

"Oh, we thought he was Chloe's father," Ava said.

Amelia nodded. "Yeah, he's always taking care of her like dads do. See?" she added, pointing.

Maisey glanced at where Rex was sitting down on an alphabet rug in the baby/toddler section, Chloe sitting beside him and batting at the little dangly bunny he was holding in front of her. A huge laugh came from her, Maisey's favorite sound, rivaled only by the kids singing their holiday songs.

He's good with Chloe because he loves Chloe, too. He loves us. He just either doesn't realize it yet or can't compute. He might need some time. Or he'll just take off on the twenty-sixth as planned and push all the stuff that had been bothering him away. Such as his ambivalence. His unfinished business with his father. Just leave it all behind here.

She hoped he didn't do that.

"Hey, girls," she said, needing to change the subject, "why don't we practice right on the stage? Just the two of you. Let's go!"

The girls grinned and raced over onto the stage. Maisey got out the song sheet and handed each girl a copy, and they sang it while reading. Then she asked them to try it without the sheet. Then one more time.

Perfection. They stepped forward during their solo and got it just right.

Maisey clapped, and Rex stood up and gave his own standing ovation, then scooped up Chloe and walked over. "Girls, you've got this. You know the song inside out."

"Yay, thanks, Maisey," they said in unison with grins, and they ran off to the clubhouse on the far side of the room.

Rex stood beside her, shifting Chloe in his arms. "You're really good at your job. You're good at being a person."

"That's probably my favorite compliment ever." She tried to smile, but she was too touched and didn't want to get all emotional on him. "Turns out the girls did know the song and just got a little stage fright over breakfast when they sang it for their parents."

His phone pinged with a text, and he checked it. "I have to get going. Noah and Axel could use an extra pair of eyes on the various paths and the tables. Daisy's already said that all the families already booked stays for next Christmas. And all the cabins are already booked through next summer and there's a waiting list for cancellations."

"Wow. That's great. I feel like I have serious job security now."

"I know for a fact that Daisy thinks you're doing an amazing job. You'd have security without the ranch being the sudden hot spot of Wyoming. Maybe even the West."

Good. I need this job, this place. With or without you. But the thought of being here without him suddenly seemed unimaginable. He *was* the Dawson Family Guest Ranch. "Thanks for watching Chloe for me. She sure does adore you."

She really hadn't meant to say it. But it was true and just came out.

"It's mutual," he said. He handed her over to Maisey, gave the baby's head a little caress, shot Maisey a brief smile and then headed out.

She watched the door for a few seconds, wishing he'd come back. How could she already miss him?

"What am I gonna do, Chloe?" she whispered.

And then, "Right now, let's go check on Annabel and Chance."

The twins were still sleeping. Danny was playing his favorite superhero game with Hannah by the nap cave, flying his stuffed caped lion overhead while she had an action figure who needed Super Zul's help. Sadie had told her that the lion was named Zul after Axel, who was Danny's hero, but he hadn't been able to pronounce Axel's name when they first met. Axel, then a search-and-rescue worker, had been the one to find missing Danny on a family trip up Clover Mountain—and had fallen in love with Sadie, Danny's mother. If Rex stuck around, she had no doubt he'd be Chloe's hero—after Super Mommy, of course.

The rest of the day passed slowly. Every now and then, she'd be drawn to the window, showing Chloe the smiling guests passing by, marveling at the decorations and the activities and the reindeer. On her lunch break, she'd fortified herself with a delicious chicken burrito and she'd swiped a cup of eggnog to go. A few more kids came in and out of the Kid Zone, wanting to work on their songs, but otherwise she was able to keep a tight rein on the ready-for-showtime stage area, no crumpled hoodies lying around, no smashed pretzels on any of the chairs.

At 4:15, the parents all dropped off their kids

so that they could get into costume, do any last-minute practices, work out any stage fright and get into places. The parents would be back at 4:45 to take their seats and get their programs, which Maisey had created with her boss's laptop and printer. Her two staffers were here to help get the little kids changed. Everything was ready.

Showtime, she said to herself with a little flourish, and it occurred to her that she'd been so busy the past hour that she hadn't even thought about Rex. Maybe that was the ticket—stay superbusy. Of course, the least busy day of the year would be December 26. When he'd be saying goodbye.

Rex had been fully prepared for tears, meltdowns and demands in the Santa hut, but all the kids who'd visited were excited and launched into lists of dream gifts, from Lego sets, to iPhones, to Barbies, to action figures, to a trip to Disneyland. The Caletti twins wanted a reindeer. Zara, whom Rex had expected to talk about her late parents, excitedly asked for voice lessons and had said that Emily and Ethan had already talked to Santa about it but she wanted to remind him. Axel and Sadie had come in with Danny, who didn't quite understand what was going on. All he wanted for Christmas was to fly his superhero lion. That one was easy-peasy. When they'd left, Axel had whispered, "Santa. You never cease to surprise me, Rex," and shot him a thumbs-up, his son in his arms.

Now Rex stood in the curtained "side stage" area from where the kids would make their grand entrance. He was serving as an extra pair of eyes as the two Kid Zone staffers were busy with last-minute buttoning and zipping and soothing worries. He could hear sniffling coming from somewhere and peered around heads.

Uh-oh. Zara, in her really cute elf costume, was suddenly crying.

Maisey was at the door, welcoming parents and handing out programs. He was relieved to see her come "backstage," and he upped his chin at Zara.

Maisey hurried over to Zara and led her away from the group, then knelt in front of her. "Hey, what's wrong, sweetie?"

Tears ran down her face. "My mom and dad aren't here. Emily and Ethan aren't my real mom and dad. I just wish my parents could be here and see me singing onstage."

"I know you're sad about that, Zara. Emily and Ethan love you and care about you and they're here to cheer you on. Ethan even has the video app on his phone ready to record the whole show."

Rex had to hand it to Maisey. She really was spectacular at her job. She gave everyone her full attention no matter what, and right now, with a show about to start, Zara needed her and that was that.

Zara shrugged and wiped her hands under her eyes. "Don't you wish your parents were here?"

"Yes. I do. But you know where they are?"

"Heaven?"

"Heaven and also right here," Maisey said, putting her hand against her chest. "They're always with me."

Zara put her hand to her heart and her chin to her chest to get a look. "They're in here?"

Rex wondered if his dad was in his heart. He didn't feel Bo Dawson there, not that he'd know what that would feel like. But Maisey clearly did, so it had to be real, something you *felt*, were aware of when you really needed to be, something that comforted.

Maisey nodded. "I know it. They're always with you, always watching over you. And something else I'm sure of? They're so glad to know that the Harwoods love you so much and take such good care of you. Because that's what parents do, right?"

Zara sniffled. "Yeah."

"Sometimes something good comes from something bad, Zara. I think Emily and Ethan are something really good."

Aww, Maisey. You knocked it out of the park. She's the best, plain and simple.

"I do like my dog, Poppy," Zara said, her face brightening. "I never had a dog before. And we have a huge fish tank, too, and I got to name all of them except one who Emily named a long time ago. And Emily always brushes my hair every morning and everyone always says they like my hair. And Ethan lets me walk Poppy every night after dinner while he wears this really nerdy hat with a searchlight on it. And I told Emily that I really, really, really want voice lessons for Christmas and she said she'd talk to Santa. I told him about it today in the Santa hut."

Maisey smiled. "Santa's awesome. And Emily and Ethan are sitting in the audience right now, waiting to watch you sing."

"I can't wait for my solo," Zara said.

Maisey gave her a big hug. "It's just about time to go out onstage. Ready?"

Zara nodded firmly, her brown eyes clear. "Ready!"

Rex caught Maisey's eye and flashed her an inadequate thumbs-up for how moving that was to watch and listen to.

She smiled back, and for the millionth time he wondered how he'd deal with not seeing that beautiful face every day.

"Okay, kids," she said to the group. "I'm going to go out there and introduce the show. After you hear me say, 'And now I'm proud to present the children's holiday show,' you'll walk out in the order we practiced and take your places. Hannah will help direct you."

The kids were practically bouncing up and down with excitement.

Rex peered out of the curtain to see all the Dawsons in the first two rows. He took the seat Ford had saved him between him and one of the parents.

"Nice of you and Zeke to come," Rex said.

"Would we miss our nephew's first annual children's holiday show debut? No way." He glanced at Rex and leaned a bit closer.

Rex pulled the yellow pocket watch from inside his jacket and stared down at it. He'd been carrying it around since he'd found it. The letter was inside his wallet, and he hadn't reread that, but every time he flipped open the plastic cover of the watch and looked at that goofy cartoon seahorse—*It's time for fun!*—he smiled.

"Gave you some closure?" Ford asked, his eyes on the watch.

Rex shrugged. "This might be a little heavy for right now," he whispered, "but let me ask you something. You think you're a cop to chase ghosts?"

"I think it gets mixed in there, yeah. I feel like it's time to stop. I want something else, Rex."

"What, though? Besides small-town life and less crime."

Ford glanced at him. "Family. I want to get married."

Rex stared at his eldest brother, truly shocked. "Someone check the sky for flying pigs." He sat back for a moment. "Wow."

"I'm ready. Now I just have to find my wife."

My wife. My wife. My wife. Those were two words that still didn't seem to work together for him. *My* and *wife*.

Maisey came out onstage, and his chest rumbled.

"It can get too late, Rex," Ford whispered. "Everyone knows that. Don't get to that point."

Before Rex could ask what he meant, not that he was sure he wanted to know, Maisey welcomed the crowd and introduced the show, and the kids came out to thunderous applause, including his own. Noah and Zeke both let out a wolf whistle.

The kids were lined up in their places and the music started. Annalise stepped forward and introduced the first song, "Frosty the Snowman."

"I still prefer 'Frotty Noman,'" Axel whispered, turning around from his seat in front of them.

Rex smiled. So did he. He'd miss that. And these kids. This place. He clapped and cheered after each song, from "A Holly Jolly Christmas" to "Rudolph the Red-Nosed Reindeer" to "All I Want for Christmas Is My Two Front Teeth," the audience roaring when seven-year-old Kyra Lopez stepped forward in her reindeer costume and smiled superwide where her two front teeth were missing in a mouth full of baby teeth.

A half hour later, the show was over, and everyone jumped to their feet, giving the kids a standing ovation. Rex glanced over at Maisey, who joined the kids onstage for their final bow. Then she handed each child their wrapped gift to very excited faces and dismissed the group to their families.

Zara ran over to Emily and hugged her, then did the same to Ethan. "I was in my first show! Did you get it on video?"

Ethan nodded, and Rex could see how emotional the man was. "I sure did. You were so awesome, Z."

"Yay, thank you!" she said, hugging him again.

"And guess what's the special for dinner at the caf," Emily added. "Mac and cheese in special honor of the great job you all did. You really were amazing, Zara. You sang your solo so beautifully. We're both so proud of you."

Zara beamed and reached a hand up to her heart, and Rex, who wasn't the biggest softy out there or even among his siblings, almost lost it. He did feel people in that steel-cased chest of his. His mom. His siblings. His niece and nephews. Maisey and Chloe. Even the Dawson Family Guest Ranch was in his heart. But he didn't feel his dad in there. What did that mean? No way could he ask Ford *that*. Daisy, maybe. She could psychoanalyze it for a good hour.

He glanced at Maisey and saw her watching Zara with her parents, her eyes glistening, her hand on her own heart.

She did have *his*, that was for sure.

My wife, my wife, my wife.

Suddenly his head felt stuffed with cotton. His collar was tightening. His skin was itchy. Those words didn't apply to him because his life wasn't set up to accommodate a wife. Or a family. Or a dog, which was why he'd have to leave River with Daisy. He let his head drop back with a hard sigh as he tugged at his collar. Was it hot in here?

"You all right?" Ford asked.

"Just need some air," he said, getting up and heading out.

He had no doubt Maisey watched him leave,

which made him feel worse. He should be congratulating her, high-fiving the brave and talented kids, putting his nephew, who'd made his stage debut tonight, on his shoulders. Instead, he was outside in front of the lodge gulping cold air, and he'd forgotten his jacket, so he was freezing to boot.

"Dude, terrible advice," a voice said.

Rex looked left. Tyler was sulkily walking over to him. Oh, damn. Had he messed that up, too?

"Right after the show ended, I asked Annalise if I could talk to her for a sec. Fine, she says. So I bring her over behind the curtain and tell her I really like her and can we have a long-distance relationship and text and stuff. And you know what she said?"

Rex had a feeling.

Tyler frowned. "She said she liked me like a little brother. Hello? What? I'm not seven! We're just a year apart."

"Sorry, Tyler. I know you liked her a lot and hoped to stay in touch."

"Now I feel stupid. I made a total moron of myself. She'll tell all her friends about the idiot eighth grader who asked her to be his girlfriend— long-distance, too."

"Nope. I think you made her feel good. You gave her a big compliment."

"How?" Tyler asked. "I'm seven, remember? That kid brother."

Rex smiled and shook his head. "You two are friends, right? She does like you. And when someone you like likes you back, even more romantically than you feel, it's a compliment. I'm sure she's very touched, Tyler."

"Maybe we can stay in touch as just friends?" he said.

"I'll bet she'll go for that."

"I take back what I said about the bad advice. In it to win it, right? Even the great Kobe Bryant missed a basket or two. I'm gonna go ask someone to take a pic of us to remember her by. Later, dude. I guess it's better to be friend-zoned than ghosted, right?"

He'd friend-zoned Maisey and now he was going to ghost her. Well, not really. He'd call. He'd text. That meant he wasn't really disappearing from her life.

Tyler ran back inside. Rex was right behind because he was so cold. But Maisey came out with his jacket.

She handed it to him and he gratefully put it on. "I happened to glance out the window and saw you talking to Tyler in just your shirt. I could see you shivering."

"Ah, much better," he said, zipping up to his chin. "Thank you."

Friend-zone. Ghosted. Leaving but texting every week or so: How are you, how's Chloe? That felt so…lacking.

All he knew for sure was that he had to leave, had to get back to his life.

But not before he gave her the Christmas she deserved. He could tell that Maisey had gotten back her Christmas spirit. He saw it in everything she did. The way she gazed with wonder at the reindeer, at the Christmas tree in the Kid Zone, the smile that lit up her face as the kids had sung their holiday songs. He had no idea why that didn't make him feel as good as he'd thought it would, that he could leave easier.

"So, Maisey, I was hoping to come by for a while tomorrow night for Christmas Eve. I have some gifts for you and Chloe and Snowbell."

She grinned. "The three of us never turn down gifts. Well, maybe Snowbell does if it's not catnip related." She smiled and held his gaze for a second. "I have something for you, too."

"You didn't have to get me anything," he said. "But thank you."

Her smile struck him as wistful, conflicted, and he wanted to pull her into a hug and just hold her. But he stayed put.

"Does seven work?" he asked. "I plan to bring dinner, so don't eat."

"Presents and dinner? I could get used to that," she said, then looked away before pasting a bright smile on her beautiful face. "Seven is perfect. Chloe will be up for a good half hour so she can be part of the celebration."

I wish you could get used to it. You should have presents and dinner and everything your heart desires every single day.

He wanted to reach out and hug her so bad. But he stuffed his hands in his pockets. He'd see her tomorrow night, give her the great Christmas he'd planned to, from dinner to gifts, and then he'd feel okay about leaving the day after Christmas. He was sure then he'd get that closure he'd been after when it came to Maisey Clark.

So why did he feel so crummy?

Chapter Fourteen

The next day, Christmas Eve, Maisey's doorbell rang at six thirty, a little too early for Rex, but maybe he'd been so unable to wait another minute to be near her that he was early.

Suuurrre. She smiled at her ridiculousness and pulled open the door. It was Daisy, carrying a bright red bag with green ribbons twirling from the handles.

Her boss, wearing adorable Mrs. Claus dangling earrings, held up the bag. "Just a little something to say not only 'Merry Christmas,' but to thank you for all your incredible work pulling together the kids' show. It was absolutely great.

Even my two-year-old nephew was singing and shaking his little hips."

Maisey grinned and held the door wide for Daisy to come inside. "I loved working with the kids. But I can't take full credit. Your brother was a huge help. Honestly, I couldn't have done it without him. He watched Chloe when she was fussy, he took me shopping, he built the stage and sets, he made me feel like I could do anything— even put together a kids' holiday show in less than five days."

He really did make her feel like she could do anything.

"My brothers and I have all been in total shock this past week, Maisey. Seeing Rex holding a baby he's not related to? Going shopping for kiddie costumes? Painting pieces of wood for a show? Being Santa?"

Maisey smiled. "That all sounds very much like the Rex I know."

"Ha, yeah, because he's *changed*. You've changed him."

She felt tears prick the backs of her eyes and willed herself not to cry. "Nope. I didn't. Or he wouldn't be leaving the day after tomorrow."

Daisy put the bag down and reached out to squeeze Maisey's hand. "Maybe he won't."

"Nah, he will. Is. He told me so just yesterday. He's told me just about every day that I've known him."

"Because he *thinks* he's leaving. Leaving is what he does. But that was before you came into his life."

"I want to believe that. But when someone tells you their plans outright, it's wise to listen. I thought I could save myself the heartache by focusing on the fact that he's in my life temporarily. But nope—heartbreak city."

Daisy gave her a gentle smile. "Yeah, I know how that feels. Look, maybe he will leave like he's been saying. But I wouldn't give up on him just yet. It's not the twenty-sixth. He hasn't tried walking away from the woman he loves—and we all know he loves you. Nothing is more obvious to the five of us. And I'd like to see him try to leave this precious baby," she added, picking up her bag and walking over to Chloe in her baby swing in the small living room.

Rex did seem attached to Chloe. But he also seemed attached to his baby relatives—family—and he easily came and went from their lives.

Just as he would go from Maisey and Chloe's.

Daisy put her shopping bag down again and reached into it. "For you, sweet Chloe." She took out three sets of warm pj's, a board book with chewable edges, three pacifiers, a hair bow, five pairs of adorable socks and one of those little toy license plates with her name on it.

These Dawsons, Maisey thought, so touched she couldn't speak for a second. They were truly the best people she knew.

"Oh, Daisy, this is just too generous. I can't thank you enough. I have something for you, too. Just a little something." She reached into the little door on the console table and pulled out a wrapped gift.

She watched Daisy open it, her blue eyes lighting up at the sight of the mug with World's Best Boss across it, two candy canes below it. "You really are, Daisy." The mug wasn't much or expensive, but she knew Daisy would like it.

"I love this more than you will ever know. Thank you." Her boss gave her a big hug. "And this is for you," she said, reaching into the bag for a big wrapped box. "Kind of a hodgepodge of stuff I thought you'd like. I'm a hodgepodger."

Maisey grinned and opened the box. A gift certificate to the steak house in town. Yum. A beautiful dark red mohair sweater that she absolutely loved. Pink wool socks with sparkly bits. And something that brought tears to her eyes. A framed sign that read Maisey Clark, Dawson Family Guest Ranch Staffer of the Season Award. *You Rock* was written below.

"You're gonna make me cry before Rex comes and then I'll have mascara running down my face. Daisy, thank you so much. For everything."

"You are very welcome. Oh, one more thing." Daisy pulled over a chair, reached into her magic red bag again and pulled out a sprig of mistletoe, then stood on the chair. "Conveniently already has double-sided tape applied." She grinned and pasted it above the door frame.

Maisey hugged her again. As she closed the door behind Daisy, she glanced up at the mistletoe, not sure how much good it would do her. Or them.

Rex might have gone a little overboard with gifts for Maisey and Chloe. He put down the two big shopping bags and rang the bell at Maisey's cabin. When she opened the door, he almost gasped. Maisey wasn't in her usual jeans or leggings or long sweaters. She wore a slinky sleeveless red dress and black high heels. A tantalizing hint of her spicy-flowery perfume got him as he closed the door and set down the bags.

"Christmas Eve," she said. "Had to dress up."

He was glad he had, too—in dark gray wool pants and a black sweater. To stop staring at her, he looked over at Chloe, who was decked out in a red velvet dress and adorable polka-dot stretchy pants, a green headband with a bow in her hair.

"You look very festive, Chloe," he told the baby, kneeling down in front of her and giving her cheek a caress. The doorbell rang and Rex stood up with a sly smile. "You might want to get that, Maisey."

She eyed him with a quizzical smile and opened the door. Two people with Bear Ridge Caterers on their white chef coats wheeled in a cart with several lidded platters and bowls. "What is all this?"

"I said I was bringing dinner. Not that I was making dinner. I left that to the pros. Trust me, you don't want *my* attempt at filet mignon in peppercorn sauce with all the trimmings. Everything would be either burned or half-raw." He signed the receipt from the caterers and they left, his stomach rumbling from how good everything smelled.

"I've never had a catered dinner before," she said. "Not even at my wedding. That was a barbecue with a choice of hot dogs or hamburgers."

Something told him that wasn't the wedding reception she'd dreamed about. Though, knowing Maisey, she probably only cared about the groom, not the trappings. He pictured her sitting at a patio table, eating a hot dog and trying to not drip mustard on her gown. If she'd even worn a gown. "You can never go wrong with a grilled hot dog or hamburger."

"Facts—as Tyler and Annalise would say. I've learned lots of new teen slang and lingo this past week."

He laughed. "Me, too, just from a couple hours the past few days of working on the sets with them. Did you know Tyler has a mad crush on Annalise? I counseled him to tell her how he feels. I hope I got it right."

"Asking is everything. You don't ask, you don't get. I'm all for self-advocating."

"Good. I haven't gotten up to teenagers yet with my niece and nephews, so I had no idea if I was giving him good advice."

"You definitely did," she said, and he forced himself not to let his gaze wander up and down that sexy red dress.

"Shall we?" he asked. "I'll wheel the cart into the kitchen and you can bring in Chloe. I wish she was at the steak stage so she could enjoy this incredible dinner."

Maisey grinned. "She's already had her beloved butternut squash baby food, but she can have her milk while we eat."

In the small kitchen, he put the cart next to the table and transferred the platters, the steaks, drenched in béarnaise sauce and dotted with peppercorns, making his mouth water. There was garlic-tinged asparagus and rosemary roast potatoes, plus French bread and a green salad in a miso-something dressing that managed to smell delicious. He put the tiramisu for dessert in the refrigerator.

Maisey reached into a cabinet and brought out plates and silverware and began setting the table. "I have a bottle of red wine that the Kid Zone staffers gave me for Christmas. Want a glass with dinner?"

"Definitely." He wheeled the cart over by the door. When he came back, Maisey had put the wine and glasses on the table along with a corkscrew and had given Chloe her milk.

"She's started to hold her own bottle," Maisey said, her gaze tender on her daughter. "These little milestones blow me away. Every month, every few weeks, really, it's something new and amazing."

"Her eyes are turning light brown like yours," he said, looking from Chloe to Maisey and back. "She's going to be your mini-me."

"I won't lie. I'm glad she looks like me and not her father."

He opened the bottle of wine and poured. "Think he'll ever come back to see her?" He wanted to know, but did he have to bring that up on Christmas

Eve? He wished he could take it back. Maisey didn't need to be thinking about that right now. He held up a hand. "I shouldn't have asked. Forget I did." He handed her the glass of wine, then held his up.

She clinked. "Merry Christmas, Rex."

"Merry Christmas."

She took a small sip. "I'm glad you asked, actually. About her dad. It's true that I don't love talking about all that, but it's not good to pretend the hard stuff doesn't exist. Plus, if you don't talk about these things, get them out in the open and explored, they fester. That just makes everything worse."

He sipped the wine and realized he was a master at that. Pretending. Sweeping under the ole rug. But he was also a master at not letting the ugliness in his past get to him, let alone fester.

Or was he kidding himself? He'd shut his father out of his heart, hadn't he? Rex mentally shrugged, unsure of any of this. He'd like to think he knew himself pretty well, was self-aware. But when it came to his dad, the memories, the loss—that kiddie pocket watch and letter—and Rex didn't know the first thing about how he really felt. Bo Dawson "stuff" had been long blocked by an impenetrable wall.

This was what he got for asking her a too-personal question. An unexpected perusal of his own head. He reached for the platter of steaks and slid it closer to her.

Her eyes lit up as she took a steak and spooned the incredible sauce over it. He did the same, and as they filled their plates with salad and asparagus and potatoes, he was relieved not to be thinking.

"I don't think we'll be seeing Chloe's father again," she said, about to cut into her steak. "When I told him I was pregnant, he said he doubted the baby was his. He told his family I cheated and that 'the kid' wasn't his. Then when he left me, his family turned on me, too, and said they were done with me. I didn't have much contact with them, anyway, but that was the last I've heard from them." She took a bite of her steak, sitting back for a moment to appreciate it. "This is amazing. To be honest, Rex, I've never had filet mignon."

He reached across the table and covered her hand with his, then lifted his glass again.

She smiled and picked up hers. "To good firsts, then."

"Very good firsts." They clinked and sipped and resumed eating, the steak incredible, the side dishes popping with flavor.

"I didn't ever cheat, by the way," she added, forking a roast potato. "All I wanted back then was a husband, a family. I'd never do anything to jeopardize it, even if the marriage needed a ton of work."

She'd already lived a lifetime in twenty-three years. Loss and hardship and a jerk of an ex-husband. But a beautiful, healthy baby, a great job she loved and true friends who'd do anything for her—his entire family. Plus him.

"Sounds like you really tried," he said, "longer and harder than anyone could deal with."

"I'm ready for cheerier subjects. It's Christmas Eve and a time for festivity and celebrating."

Rex smiled, appreciating her attitude, which was always so positive. He could learn a lot from her. "I'm glad you're enjoying dinner. My brothers and I hired these caterers to whip up a month's worth of meals for Daisy when Tony was born. She raved about the food. So did Harrison when they finally got together as a couple."

"What a great gift. You should know, Daisy put some mistletoe above the door. Your sister is still hoping to get you paired up and staying for good."

"Nah, she'll move on to Ford now he's set on moving back to Bear Ridge and joining the police force here. He told me he's ready to settle down. Wants a wife and kids, the whole thing."

Maisey glanced at him. "Wow. Daisy will be thrilled. That'll be three brothers with only two to go. Or one, since you're—" She stopped talking and cut into her steak.

"I'm what?" he asked. Did he want to know, though?

"I was going to say 'a lost cause' on the subject. But, oh heck, I'm just going to say it. I keep hoping that's not true."

Chloe let out a fussy wail, saving the day. Well, saving him from having to respond when he had no idea what to say. He wanted to stay *and* leave. Something was clearly at war in his head and body. Maybe all that "hard stuff" he had pushed under the rug for years.

"What's the matter, sweetie?" Maisey asked, taking the bottle, but Chloe grabbed it back. She laughed. "Sor-*ry*! Are we leaving you out of the conversation? Is that the issue?" She glanced at Rex, and he knew she was giving him the out. Which he'd take.

They got through the rest of dinner talking about the show and the kids and how she was sure the Harwoods were on their way to good things. He told funny stories about his siblings. She told him what seemed like funny stories about the old trailer she'd lived in, but he hated the idea of her in that run-down place, alone with an infant and worrying how she'd pay her bills.

He forked his last potato, which practically

melted in his mouth with rosemary and chives. He wanted her to eat like this every night. He wanted her not just safe, not just secure, but truly comfortable.

"You know, Maisey, my condo in Cheyenne is really nicely decorated, thanks to the interior designer I hired while I was on the road. I'm never there to enjoy any of it. Why don't I have the furniture shipped here? You could trade that lumpy plaid couch for a plush memory-foam sofa that you'll never want to get up from. Lamps, artwork, tables with great craftsmanship, gorgeous rugs. All yours. Just say the word."

She stared at him for a second. "No, thanks. I'm fine with lumps. That's what I can afford right now. If this cabin hadn't come semifurnished, I'd be sitting on a box with a cushion on it."

"Which is why you should let me ship my furniture." He didn't need any of that stuff. He couldn't even remember the last time he was in that place.

It didn't escape his attention that he didn't think of it as *home*. It wasn't.

She shook her head. "If you want to share your stuff with me, Rex, include yourself. If not, I'll take care of myself."

He felt his face burn. This conversation hadn't gone like he'd hoped. "I just meant—"

"I know what you meant. And I know you mean well. I'm hardly an all-or-nothing person— I *know* I could use help. I *know* I need things for the cabin. But I'll get there. Your fancy, expensive furniture won't fit right in this cozy place, anyway. And I don't mean proportionally. The cabin is about home and comfort and second chances. Not a decorator making choices and spending tens of thousands on furnishings you didn't even select yourself and never use. You know?"

He supposed so. *But I want to give you everything.* If she could read his mind right now, she'd say: *Hardly. You're not including yourself.*

He nodded. "I hear you. I'll get these plates out of the way." He stood up and began piling empty platters on top of one another. "Those guys will be back in about an hour to pick up the cart." He glanced at Chloe, who let out a big yawn. "Oh, I'd better give her her gifts before she has to skedaddle off to bed."

Maisey smiled and stood, too. "It's definitely late for her. But tonight is special. It's Christmas Eve. Before you came into my life, I would be staring out the window, all conflicted. Now I just feel filled up. I've always been a blessings counter, but it's more than that. I'm happy, Rex."

Before he knew what he was doing, he leaned forward and kissed her on the lips, his hands on either side of her face. He pulled away just slightly, looking at her flushed cheeks, her flashing eyes. "I know you are. At least I'll have that."

She stepped back, and he knew he'd said the wrong thing. *Done* the wrong thing.

"I shouldn't have kissed you," he said. "I'm sorry. I—"

She held up a hand. "I'm glad you did. Especially because there was no mistletoe over our heads. It wasn't a *had to* kiss. It was a *want to*."

He smiled and wished he could kiss her again and again and again.

"I'll load up the dishes." She began stacking plates and silverware, very obviously not looking at him.

Maisey Clark, Maisey Clark, Maisey Clark. Her name echoed in his head. Maybe this was what happened when you cared deeply about someone before you'd ever met them, before you even knew how spectacularly beautiful and kind and strong they were.

The cart was ready to go, and grateful for the distraction, he moved it by the front door, and they headed into the living room. Rex pulled all the gifts from the bags and set them under the tree.

"Oh, look, who is this for?" he asked Chloe, holding up a big pink-wrapped box.

Maisey sat down on the rug in front of the tree, Chloe on her lap, and shook her head with a grin. "You do realize she's six months old. How many gifts did you get her?"

He sat down beside Maisey. "One for every month she's been alive."

She laughed and took the pink box. She unwrapped it, holding up the yellow blanket bordered by pastel animals of every kind. She put it against her face. "So soft. And her name is embroidered on it," she added, reaching to touch his arm. "Rex, way too thoughtful."

She unwrapped them all, one by one, emotional as she held out what was inside. There was a year's membership to Totville, which ran baby and toddler classes. Ten children's books. A big stuffed penguin that was actually a baby chair. A fancy dress. A beaded bracelet that spelled out *Chloe*. Three teething toys. A savings bond.

"Um, I think this is way more than six gifts," she said, handing one of the teethers to Chloe, who shook it wildly with a big smile. "Rex, thank you. I love everything. And I know Chloe does, too. Don't you, sweetie?" She bent over to kiss the baby on her head.

Chloe shook the teething toy again, then chewed on it before looking at Rex and letting out a big laugh.

Maisey laughed, too. "That's her way of saying thank you."

"My pleasure, Chloe," Rex said, a little too aware of how special this baby was to him. "Merry Christmas."

This time it was Maisey who leaned forward and kissed him, hot on the lips. And not a fast kiss. Slow and sexy.

"Now we're even," she said.

"So we are," he said, unable to take his eyes off her, his gaze roaming around the curves of her red dress, her long legs, the supersexy black heels.

She popped up as if she needed a little escape from him and both kisses. "Well, time to get Chloe changed and ready for bed. I'll be back down in about fifteen minutes and then we can exchange gifts."

"I'll be here," he said, not wanting either of them to leave the room.

She looked at him, her expression shifting, and he could kick himself. *Here. But not for long.*

While she headed upstairs with Chloe, he picked up all the discarded wrapping paper and stuffed it into the empty bag. The doorbell rang, and the caterers wheeled away the cart.

He stared at the other shopping bag, the one with Maisey's gifts. He hoped he got it right.

Bringing the bag and his wine over to the sofa, which really was lumpy, he sat down and waited.

Finally, she was back, looking even sultrier somehow.

"I'm trying to look sexy, but these shoes are killing me," she said, kicking them off. "I almost tripped coming down the stairs, too."

"All about comfort," he said. "And you look just as sexy without the heels."

She wiggled her toes at him with a smile and sat down on the other end of the sofa. "Let me give you my present first, because if you went overboard for me, I won't feel as bad for only getting you one measly thing."

"What did you get me?" He couldn't even imagine what she'd choose for him.

She opened the drawer of the end table and pulled out a small wrapped box and handed it to him.

He ripped off the paper to find a gold box. Inside was a beautiful old bronze compass.

"It's antique," she said, "but I was assured it's as good as when it was brand-new. And the nice proprietor of the thrift shop engraved it for me. Turn it over and you'll see."

No matter where you are, I'll always be there for you.—Maisey.

Yes, he thought. *You will be. Because you* are *in my heart*.

"Follow your North Star and you'll always be on the right path," his grandfather used to say all the time. The US Marshals Service, finding fugitives, protecting witnesses—his North Star. His mission.

Except he didn't feel that in his heart, either. Which was unsettling. And maybe what had been bothering him lately. His commitment and dedication to his job was as strong as ever, but it was a head thing, not a heart thing. He'd felt the absence of it acutely when he realized his dad wasn't in there, either, after reading that letter. The letter that should have brought him peace and closure.

What the hell was up with him? *Sweep, sweep, sweep*, he told himself. *Stop thinking about it*. It was Christmas. He was here with Maisey.

He turned more fully toward her. "I love this, Maisey. More than I can even say. Thank you." He put it on the coffee table where he could see it instead of back in the box. Then he pulled over the other shopping bag with her gifts. "I did go kind of overboard, but that's just who I am."

He set out the gifts on the coffee table and watched her face light up every time she opened one. A plush white bathrobe and matching slippers. A gift certificate to the day spa in town, where she could get a massage. A red leather journal and a fancy pen to record all her hopes and dreams. A baby book to record milestones and include photos, which she pressed to her heart. Brochures for Western Wyoming University and their bachelor's in education. The last gift was the one he was a little worried about.

She ripped off the silver wrapping paper and opened the box. "Oh, Rex, it's so beautiful." It was an old-fashioned oval gold locket on a filigree chain.

"It opens," he said.

She clicked open the little latch. Inside was a recent picture of Chloe he'd taken the day he'd babysat her at the Kid Zone. He'd resized it to fit in the small locket.

She held it by the chain and examined all the facets. "I love it. I've never had anything like it. Will you do the honors?"

She faced away from him and moved her long blond hair to the side. He wanted to kiss her neck. He fastened the clasp, and she turned back around. "How does it look?" she asked, turning a bit and then right, her smile so beautiful.

"It looks perfect. Like you," he added on a whisper, unable to take his eyes off her face.

The next thing he knew, she was straddling him, her hands on his chest, her mouth fused to his.

He was losing the ability to reason, to even process that this was not only a bad idea but a potentially catastrophic one.

"I want tonight, Rex Dawson. I've taken back Christmas and I want this final night between us to be part of it. Tomorrow I'm sure you'll be with your family, and then the next day you're outta here. Tonight is about us."

Could he have this? He wanted it more than anything right now. But… "You're sure?"

If she even hesitated, he'd get up and take out their tiramisu from the refrigerator and suggest an action movie with lots of car chases.

"One hundred percent," she said and reached behind her to unzip her dress.

Chapter Fifteen

Maisey lay naked under the blanket in her bed, barely able to believe that Rex was equally naked beside her—fast asleep.

Wow. Wow, wow, wow.

She'd only been with one man. Now two. And wow.

He stirred beside her, turning his head slightly toward her, his eyes closed, the long dark eyelashes against his upper cheek. His hair was mussed from her hands inside it. He also might have a few scratches down his back, she thought, wanting to burst out of bed and do a little dance.

I love you, she told him silently.

His eyes opened slowly and lazily, and he pulled her to him, wrapping her in a hug. "Merry Christmas."

"Merry Christmas," she barely managed as warm gooey love spread through every part of her body, stealing her breath. "Last night was something, huh?"

He dropped a kiss on her shoulder. "Exceeded my wildest imaginings."

Her heart leaped. "So you imagined this? Us together in bed?" She'd hoped so and even figured as much, but Rex was a different breed of male and who really knew?

"All the time, Maisey."

She definitely liked knowing that. "I figured you were trying not to. To keep things platonic."

"Well, things should be platonic, but we both got caught up last night. The holiday. The wine…"

Her stomach dropped and her heart felt like a weight was pressing against it. She shifted away from him and lay back, staring at the ceiling. Oh, hell.

"So last night didn't change anything for you?" she asked, sitting up and looking right at him.

"It just made things harder," he said gently. "Harder to leave tomorrow morning." He turned away, clearly uncomfortable, then looked back at her. "Maisey, last night you said sex was about last night—only. Part of Christmas Eve, our last night together before I get wrapped up in family stuff, which of course I'd include you in, anyway."

"I know, but…" she said, the word choking on a sob that threatened to wrench out of her.

Yes, he was right. *You're sure?* he'd asked last night, waiting for her to respond. She'd said, *One hundred percent.* This was her fault. But she'd believed in the Christmas Eve, special gifts and wine haze that the sex, the intimacy, joining the two of them physically, would mean something to him. Something so powerful it would break through whatever was holding him back, keeping him from her, keeping him on the road.

"You're right," she said flatly. "I have no dibs on you."

"Maisey—"

She held up her hand. "Look, it's Christmas. I did want last night for exactly the reasons I said. And yes, I hoped that this morning you would suddenly turn into a different person."

One who loves me more than whatever has you so afraid of us.

"Not that I want you to be different, Rex. You're amazing. I just want you to *stay*." She sucked in a breath. "I think I hear Chloe," she said and ran out of the room.

A little dramatic there, Maisey, she thought as

she rushed into the nursery and closed the door behind her. Chloe was fast asleep, not a peep out of her yet. But she'd needed space between them so she wouldn't burst into tears.

She stood by her daughter's crib, looking down at the baby sleeping in her festive holiday pj's. "Merry Christmas," she whispered.

A tap came at the door. She braced herself, then opened it. Rex was dressed, but barefoot, his hair less mussed.

"I—" he began.

"If you say you care deeply about me, I will throw this stuffed tiger at you," she said, picking it up from the bookcase by the door.

"I won't say it. But I do, Maisey. But I also need to leave tomorrow morning. I have a job and commitments. I've always been up-front about that."

You sure have. She could not be mad at him. She just wanted him to want her more, dammit.

"I used to want a family more than anything in the world, Rex. Now the only Christmas wish I have is for you to stay—with me. But that's not gonna happen. So go. But it's over between us, Rex. Don't text, don't call, don't come see me when you visit your family. It'll hurt too much. I have to accept that you don't love me. Because if you did, you wouldn't pick a lonely life on the road for a job that doesn't seem to suit you anymore. You wouldn't be able to *leave*. It's that simple."

"It's not, Maisey."

"Merry Christmas, Rex." *Let him go, let him go, let him go.*

Her heart clenched as he just stared at her, his blue eyes flashing with so much emotion she couldn't read. Finally, he nodded, then turned and headed toward the living room, where he'd left his socks and shoes. And the compass.

And then he was gone.

A few hours later, Rex sat on a flat rock by the river, way down from the guest cabins by at least five miles. If he walked north—and he had his antique compass to guide him—he'd eventually hit Axel's cabin, where he was expected for Christmas lunch in a little while. It was too cold to walk the half hour up there, so he was glad he'd driven, especially because he had bags of gifts in his SUV.

When he'd left Maisey's cabin earlier, he'd picked up River from Daisy's, thankful she wasn't home to interrogate him on why he looked so miserable, and he had no doubt he had and still did. He *felt* miserable. He and River had gone for a long walk in the woods up near Clover Mountain, the biting cold helping to clear his head. But then he'd think about how his sister had invited Maisey and Chloe to Christmas dinner tonight and how there was no way Maisey would show up after what had happened between them.

Which meant she'd be spending Christmas alone and hurt—and it was all his damned fault.

He shook his head and stared out at the water, watching the current rush over the rocks and big sticks. River was sniffing along the bank, on red alert for any signs of a chipmunk or squirrel. The fast-moving river reminded him how wild it was that Maisey's bottle had stayed put up by the leg of the footbridge in the nature preserve—as if waiting for him to find it.

He had his dog to thank for that. He watched the sweet shepherd mix tilting his head at a squirrel darting up a tree, his ears standing tall, his tail wagging.

Rex had screwed up terribly. His mission was to give Maisey a great Christmas so that he could go back to his life as a marshal, his head and heart settled as far as she was concerned, and he'd almost succeeded until things came to a head this morning.

He glanced at his phone to check the time—he had to head up to Axel's for lunch. "Ready, buddy?" he called to River, who came trotting over like the good boy he was. He knelt down beside the dog and buried his face in his soft fur, getting a lick on the neck. "I'm gonna miss you so hard."

His boss's face pushed into his mind—a good thing. Rex was expected at district headquarters in Cheyenne in the morning, and he'd resume the search for his witness. He'd be consumed by that, his mission, and that would help with the hole in his chest with what he was leaving behind.

As he drove up the gravel road to Axel's, he could see Noah and Sara walking up the porch steps with their twins in their carriers. Axel came out with Dude, Danny on his shoulders to welcome them, his nephew holding his ever-present caped stuffed lion. He pictured Chloe on his own shoulders a year from now, Maisey beside him, walking up these steps to visit, River trailing and sniffing behind them. If he were a different person, that person Maisey had once said she wished he was, he'd be living that life. He'd be a family man. But that wasn't who he was.

As he exited his SUV, he gave his head a little shake to clear it, then got distracted from the image since Dude came flying down the stairs to say hello to his bestie, River. Rex gave Dude a pat and went up the stairs behind the group, swallowed up in family festivities with no time to think—thank God.

They ate buffet-style in the family room and exchanged gifts, the kids scoring a major haul each since all the siblings had gone overboard, their MO. Rex got some great presents himself, from noise-canceling tiny earphones that would come in handy since he'd left his on a plane a few weeks ago, to a very soft cashmere sweater and scarf, to books, including one titled *Don't Let the One You Love Get Away.* Yup, that one was from Daisy, along with two pairs of Smartwool socks and a memory-foam neck pillow for his travels.

His very favorite gift was in his shirt pocket. The antique compass. He had no doubt he'd have it on him wherever he went. Maybe forever.

Daisy sat down beside him with a cup of eggnog. "So, I couldn't help but notice that you never came back last night, Rex. Mistletoe led to good things, I presume?" She stared at him, trying to read him, he knew, and narrowed her eyes, her mouth open. "Aha! You're blushing!"

His phone pinged. Saved by the text—*thank you, universe!*

"Sorry, important text," he told Daisy, holding up his phone sideways and dashing away into the hall, not that he had any idea who had sent it. He hoped it was Maisey, letting him know they could be friends eventually. That of course he could stop by to see her and Chloe when he visited his family at the ranch.

Which was unfair of him. How could they be friends after how they'd left things this morning? After he'd ruined her Christmas.

He eyed the screen and his eyes widened. The witness. Joseph Farmer.

Can you meet me right now? Same spot as last time? I promise to show up this time. I need to talk.

He texted back that he'd be there in twenty minutes, then glanced around the family room. His brothers were all playing with Danny, Tony and the twins watching from their baby swings. He hurried over to Daisy, who was biting into a snowman cookie with one hand and holding crumb-laden plates with the other on her way into the kitchen with Sadie. He called her over. "I have a work emergency," he whispered. "I have to go. Tell everyone I'm sorry. I might not be back to-night. I'm not sure. I'll stop by the farmhouse to quickly pack."

She nodded with a rueful smile. "You'll be back. But go do your thing." She looked at his empty hands. "Wait one tiny second." She flew over to the sofa and grabbed the big red bag with the gifts he'd received. "Just in case you don't get back tonight. But I know you will."

He took the bag and kissed her on the cheek and headed to the door, not realizing River had followed him until he turned to grab his jacket and scarf from the huge wrought-iron coatrack. The sight of the dog sitting in the hallway, staring at Rex with his tilted head, one ear straight up and the other sideways, just about broke him.

He knelt beside River. "I gotta go, buddy. If I can't come back tonight, I'll see you in a couple months. You take care of everyone, okay?" He gave him a hug and flew out the door, setting the bag on the floor of the back seat of his SUV.

Twenty minutes later, his duffel beside the bag of gifts he'd received, Rex reached the preserve and headed to the spot.

Where he'd found River. Where his heart had been stolen by a little girl's letter. Where the witness hadn't shown up. *Chasing ghosts...*

"Hey."

Rex whirled around, this time completely caught off guard, which wouldn't have happened two weeks ago. Or ever. He was distracted, his mind on other things. Home. His family. River.

Maisey. Chloe.

Joseph Farmer, the rogue witness who'd disappeared over two weeks ago, looked pale and worried. "I'm sorry for just disappearing on you. I want to explain. My ex-wife and I were pretty close to getting back together when my life fell completely apart because I saw that drug deal and could ID the kingpin."

"Oh, yeah?" Rex asked. He hadn't known anything about that. His office had been staking out the wife's condo a few towns away and there'd been no contact, as far as they knew. The Farmers had been divorced for almost two years, no kids. Both were in their early fifties.

Farmer nodded. "I've been talking to Val on a burner phone I sent her so that no one could track either side. Finally, today, a Christmas miracle. She said that we could have a second chance if I get all this behind me. That she'd go into witness protection with me. Is that possible?"

Rex nodded. "I'd put you in protective custody and then I'd make arrangements for her to join you." His boss would make it happen. Rex had no doubt.

The man's shoulders sagged with relief. "I thought if I disappeared into some new identity, I'd never get to hear her voice again, you know? We're not even married anymore because I was an idiot, but she never gave up on me. I want this second chance. That's all I care about."

Sometimes love—or the hope for it—really did

conquer all. He was especially grateful it worked for Joseph Farmer. Because it affected a lot of other people who needed him to testify. Including Rex.

"I'm happy for you, Mr. Farmer. Definitely a merry Christmas for you."

"And you, I bet. Sorry for everything I put you through."

"Part of the job," he said. *Chasing ghosts*, he thought again. His father had been right.

Anyway, you'll find this eventually, one day, and when you do, just know your father loved you, Rexy.

He put his hand to the left side of his chest, dimly aware of the faintest glimmer of Bo Dawson elbowing his way into Rex's heart. This past year, his father had forced Rex to take a long, long time to find what the key unlocked—so he'd be ready for it.

But what Maisey had taught him was that being ready was up to him.

"Let's go, then," Rex said. "A new life with your new love awaits."

The man pulled him into a bear hug and burst into tears, swiping under his eyes and sniffling. "I like how you put that. It is new. Well, old and new mixed together. Can't separate them." He glanced at Rex as they walked to his SUV. "You married?"

Rex shook his head. "Nah. Job means I live on the road."

Farmer grimaced. "The road is hell, Marshal. I've been on it for the past two weeks."

The compass Maisey gave him was in the inside pocket of his jacket. *No matter where you are, I'll always be there for you.—Maisey.*

He could definitely feel her in his chest, he thought, reaching up a hand to his heart again. She was there *with* him. She *was* his heart.

"I hear you on that," Rex said, opening the passenger door. Farmer got in and buckled up. By the time they were on the freeway, his witness, rogue no more, was fast asleep. Stress could do that to a person. As they arrived at the US Marshals Service district headquarters in Cheyenne, Joe was awake and less emotional, and even more resolute. He made a call on the burner phone to his ex, and she assured him she'd be right behind him for a *very* fresh start.

Since he was in Cheyenne, he headed to his condo. The place wasn't as sterile as he remembered, but there was nothing personal in it. It could be a hotel suite. He couldn't bear the thought of staying here, certainly not on Christmas, but he'd never make it back to Bear Ridge in time for the family dinner at Daisy's farmhouse. If he hurried, he could probably get there just in time for dessert. He could say a last goodbye to his family, to River.

To Maisey.

He pulled out the compass and turned toward north, thinking about his grandfather's words. *Follow your North Star and you'll always be on the right path.*

Maisey was his North Star. His passion. His reason for everything. There was no denying it anymore, though he'd clearly been trying since he'd met her. She'd eclipsed everything else.

He locked up and headed back to his car, noting he needed gas. A few filling stations were open. He pulled into one with a convenience store so he could grab a Coke and a pack of gum. His shoulder brushed a rack of sunglasses and Christmas paraphernalia, including ornaments, and he gently gripped the top of the rack to make sure it didn't topple over.

And that was when Rex froze, staring in disbelief at what was right in front of him. In this little store at a gas station off the service road was the Siamese cat ornament that Maisey had been holding when her father had rescued her from the house fire. The one that had been missing from her life since some cretin stole her Christmas tree from the trailer. Well, not the original, of course. But a replica.

He was sure it was the one. Siamese cat. Green eyes. Red-and-green bow tie. Long and skinny with an upturned tail. The picture he'd seen of it in her cabin was pressed to memory. This was definitely it.

"Half-off, by the way," the clerk called. "Not the sunglasses. Just the Christmas stuff."

The ornament was priceless.

He held it in his hand, and every moment of his relationship with Maisey Clark came flashing into his head. From the way he'd felt as he'd read her letter to Santa, meeting her for the first time at the Kid Zone, their work on the children's holiday show, Chloe in his arms as he sang her songs and showed her the reindeer out the lodge window. Maisey in her red dress.

Last night. Every beautiful bit of it.

He stared at the Siamese cat, a three-inch-tall painted wood ornament, and had to grip the display rack for a moment as a fierce realization hit him.

He *did* love Maisey. Loved her so much.

And he wasn't leaving until he hung this ornament on the tree in her cabin. It was a way to save her Christmas, maybe, let her know how much he did care.

If she'd even let him in.

Chapter Sixteen

Maisey stared out the window of her cabin at the lightly falling snow. Instead of marveling over the white Christmas, she just wanted to scream *Bah humbug!* at the top of her lungs. But then she'd wake up Chloe, whom she'd put down for the night only a half hour ago.

Maisey had felt even worse about having to miss dinner at Daisy's, but she couldn't exactly have texted Rex not to show up so that she could go. So she'd texted Daisy that she wasn't feeling well, which was true, and Daisy had texted back that she'd send over a plate—of course she would—and that the family would miss her and

Rex. Daisy had clearly thought Maisey knew Rex had left during lunch because she'd added a few details about that and Maisey had pieced together that he'd gotten a call from work to come in.

She squeezed her eyes shut as pain gripped her. Rex was already gone.

You knew what would happen, she told herself. *And you* let *it happen because it had to— speeding train and all that, because who could stop a speeding train?*

She reached for the locket around her neck. What was she supposed to do with this? If she wore it, she'd be reminded of Rex. Like now. The locket symbolized everything between them, but the truth was, there wasn't anything. Not anymore.

He gave you back Christmas. He gave you the knowledge that you can fall in love. That great men are out there. He enriched your life. And now he's gone and you have to accept it.

Tonight, though, because it was Christmas, she'd wallow. She had a pint of Ben & Jerry's Cherry Garcia and she'd watch *When Harry Met Sally* or *Bridget Jones's Diary* and then she'd fall asleep and it wouldn't be Christmas and her new routine would start. Her life without Rex.

The doorbell rang and she dragged herself over, expecting to find Daisy's husband or another Dawson with the plate of traditional Christmas dinner Daisy had said she'd send over.

But it was Rex standing on the doorstep.

"You're far away, though," she said. "Daisy told me you were called in to work."

"I was. I had to take care of something important, but it's done now." Right on the doorstep, the cold night air and snowflakes around them, he told her about the witness and his ex-wife and how they were going to have a second chance in the witness protection program.

"Well, that worked out," she said. "It almost sounds romantic, though I'm sure it'll be a tough adjustment. But they'll do it together."

Why was she standing there talking about another couple?

"I have something for you, Maisey," he said, and she noticed the small white bag in his hand.

He reached inside and held up the ornament she'd been looking for for so many years. She covered her mouth with her hands and burst into tears.

"Can I come in, Maisey?"

She shook her head. "No. No, you can't."

"I was in a gas station convenience store in Cheyenne, and there it was, on a rack of half-price Christmas stuff. It's a Christmas miracle, huh."

He held out the Siamese cat ornament. "You don't have to allow me in. But please accept it, Maisey."

She sniffled and took the ornament and went over to the tree, looking for just the spot for it. She took off a red ball that was front and center and hung the cat ornament on the branch, dimly aware that Rex had come inside and shut the door.

"Thank you for bringing it, Rex. For finding it. You're good at that." She tried for a smile but her tears welled harder. Dammit.

Snowbell brushed along his ankles and he picked up the cat and gave her a nuzzle, getting white hairs on his black leather jacket.

"You'd better go now," she said. "I'm happy to have the ornament, I really am, but my heart is broken, Rex. It's my own stupid fault and—"

He stepped up close and took her hands. "No. It's not your fault. You're optimistic and open and loving, Maisey Clark. It's my fault. But maybe I can fix things."

"Rex, we had this conversation. I can't—"

"Finding that ornament—sheer dumb luck by picking one gas station over another—blew me away, Maisey. And knocked some truths into my head that I can't ignore anymore."

"Like what?" she asked.

"Like that I love you more than anything else in the world. I love Chloe. I thought I didn't want to be a dad until that baby girl grabbed hold of my heart. I love you. And if you'll still have me, I'm not going anywhere. I'm staying."

She wrapped her arms around him. "Oh, I'll have you. I love you, too. Obviously."

He grinned and hugged her tight and kissed her, then stepped back to look at her. "Will you marry me, Maisey?"

She gasped, tears running down her cheeks. She tried to find the word *yes* but couldn't speak.

"The gas station had some gumball machines, and there was one that sold big very faux diamond rings for fifty cents, but I'd rather wait till the jewelry shop in Prairie City opens tomorrow. I want you to have the engagement ring of your dreams. Not that you said yes."

She grinned. "Yes, Rex. A million times yes. And a charm machine ring would have been just fine." She flew into his arms, holding him tight. "Just like you to make every one of my Christmas dreams come true."

"I didn't even know I had Christmas dreams until I met you, Maisey. I—"

The doorbell interrupted him, and she opened the door to find his brother Ford standing there holding a huge plate.

"Merry Christmas," he said. "Daisy sent me with traditional Christmas dinner. We all hope you feel better." He peered around her. "Rex? You're not here. You're off chasing justice."

Rex laughed. "I was but I'm back. In every sense of the word. I'll be talking to the chief about that other opening at the Bear Ridge PD. Looks like we're gonna be colleagues."

Ford extended his hand. "Glad to hear it. I get to make Daisy's night."

"Well, tell her it gets even better. She's about to get a new sister-in-law. Maisey and I are engaged."

Ford's eyes lit up, and he hugged Maisey, then Rex. "Welcome to the family, Maisey."

She grinned. He had no idea what those words meant to her.

After Ford left, Rex took the plate and eyed it. "I missed Christmas dinner and this looks amazing. Turkey, stuffing, ham, mashed potatoes, Daisy's awful green-bean casserole—don't tell her I said that."

Maisey laughed. "I'm starving, too. We get to have Christmas dinner together after all."

"For many decades to come," he said. "I'm going to be a father," he added, his eyes glistening.

"Chloe's very lucky and so am I."

"We'll have a house built here or in town. Whatever you want, Maisey."

"I'd love to live on the ranch. I don't need anything fancy. Just you and Chloe and Snowbell and River. I almost forgot that I get a dog!"

He put down the plate on the kitchen table and pulled her into a hug, the snow swirling around outside the window, the multicolored lights of the evergreen twinkling. "Merry Christmas, Maisey."

"Merry Christmas," she whispered. "I can't wait to be Maisey Clark Dawson."

He smiled. "And how does Chloe Dawson sound? I'd love to adopt her. And if you'd like to look into adopting a child from foster care, I'm with you all the way. We can have five kids if you want. Six, maybe."

She held her fiancé tight, thinking of that little girl who wrote a letter to Santa, stuffed it in a bottle and tossed it in the creek that fed into the Bear Ridge River, hoping it would be found, that her Christmas wish would come true.

Fifteen years later, it did—and then some.

* * * * *

MILLS & BOON

Coming next month

AWAKENING HIS SHY CINDERELLA
Sophie Pembroke

"Trust me," Damon said, with feeling, "it's drawing exactly the right amount of attention to your figure. You look incredible." And he really had to stop looking at his big sister's best friend that way. Not least because she'd never given him even the slightest hint that she wanted him to.

There was that one night, his brain reminded him. That one night when you could have kissed her, if you'd wanted to.

But he hadn't. Because she was Celeste's best friend. Because she wasn't the sort of girl you messed around with, and he hadn't known how to do anything else.

Because she'd seen deeper than he liked, and it had scared him.

Her smile turned shy and she went back to studying the creatures on her dress, thankfully oblivious to his thoughts. "It is like my windows, isn't it?"

Somewhere someone clapped their hands again, and bellowed for them to take their places.

"Come on. We're starting." Damon took her arm and led her towards the bar. He needed another drink, and she hadn't even had one yet. "Let's grab a glass of something bubbly, and you can tell me more about your windows and your work until it's time to shout out the countdown, or whatever we need to do."

"You really want to know more about the windows?" She sounded astonished at the prospect.

"As it happens, I really, really do." And not just because of the way she lit up when she spoke about the things that mattered to her. Or because it would give him a chance to listen to her melodious voice. Those things weren't important to him. Or shouldn't be, anyway.

No, he wanted to know more because he had the inklings of an idea that could help both of them get what they needed in life. If he could persuade her to take a chance on him.

It was just business. That was all.

He just needed to keep reminding himself of that.

Continue reading
AWAKENING HIS SHY CINDERELLA
Sophie Pembroke

Available next month
www.millsandboon.co.uk

COMING SOON!

We really hope you enjoyed reading this book.
If you're looking for more romance, be sure to
head to the shops when new books are
available on

Thursday 26th
November

To see which titles are coming soon, please visit

millsandboon.co.uk/nextmonth

MILLS & BOON

LET'S TALK
Romance

For exclusive extracts, competitions and special offers, find us online:

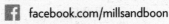 facebook.com/millsandboon

🐦 @MillsandBoon

📷 @MillsandBoonUK

Get in touch on 01413 063232

For all the latest titles coming soon, visit
millsandboon.co.uk/nextmonth

MILLS & BOON

THE HEART OF ROMANCE

A ROMANCE FOR EVERY KIND OF READER

MODERN

Prepare to be swept off your feet by sophisticated, sexy and seductive heroes, in some of the world's most glamourous and romantic locations, where power and passion collide.
8 stories per month.

HISTORICAL

Escape with historical heroes from time gone by. Whether your passion is for wicked Regency Rakes, muscled Vikings or rugged Highlanders, awaken the romance of the past.
6 stories per month.

MEDICAL

Set your pulse racing with dedicated, delectable doctors in the high-pressure world of medicine, where emotions run high and passion, comfort and love are the best medicine.
6 stories per month.

True Love

Celebrate true love with tender stories of heartfelt romance, from the rush of falling in love to the joy a new baby can bring, and a focus on the emotional heart of a relationship.
8 stories per month.

Desire

Indulge in secrets and scandal, intense drama and plenty of sizzling hot action with powerful and passionate heroes who have it all: wealth, status, good looks…everything but the right woman.
6 stories per month.

HEROES

Experience all the excitement of a gripping thriller, with an intense romance at its heart. Resourceful, true-to-life women and strong, fearless men face danger and desire - a killer combination!
8 stories per month.

DARE

Sensual love stories featuring smart, sassy heroines you'd want as a best friend, and compelling intense heroes who are worthy of them.
4 stories per month.

To see which titles are coming soon, please visit

millsandboon.co.uk/nextmonth